DEAD MORN

PIERS ANTHONY
AND
ROBERTO FUENTES

ACE BOOKS, NEW YORK

This Ace Book contains the complete text of the original hardcover edition. It has been completely reset in a typeface designed for easy reading, and was printed from new film.

DEAD MORN

An Ace Book / published by arrangement with the authors

PRINTING HISTORY
Tafford Publishing, Inc., edition published 1990
Ace edition / May 1994

ISBN: 0-441-00052-5

ACE®
Ace Books are published by The Berkley Publishing Group, 200 Madison Avenue, New York, New York 10016.
ACE and the "A" design
are trademarks belonging to Charter Communications, Inc.

PRINTED IN THE UNITED STATES OF AMERICA

10 9 8 7 6 5 4 3 2 1

Mourn not the dead that in the cool earth lie—
Dust unto dust—
The calm, sweet earth that mothers all who die
As all men must;

Mourn not your captive comrades who must dwell—
Too strong to strive—
Within each steel-bound coffin of a cell,
Buried alive;

But rather mourn the apathetic throng—
The cowed and the meek—
Who see the world's great anguish and its wrong
And dare not speak.

Written in prison by Ralph Chaplin, a conscientious objector in World War I.
Printed in *They Refuse to Be Criminals* by Edward C. N. Richards, 1946.

DEAD MORN

PART
ONE

Yellow Six 048197 woke to the timer's gentle chime. He came alert immediately, studying the tiny screen in the ceiling for evidence of intrusion. The warners were clear: no suspicious individuals had loitered in the vicinity during the night, and no official query had been posted on either the apartment or its occupants. He relaxed.

048197, known informally by the latter digits, got up as his wife stirred. "Morning, Three," he murmured, using the address of endearment that she would tolerate from no other man. He leaned across the bed to kiss her.

"Seven," she sighed, responding in kind.

She caught at his ears to hold his lips to hers, running her tongue between them.

197 drew back, feigning shock. "How dare you! That's nonprocreative foreplay—strictly forbidden. I should bite off your tongue!"

She made a moue, as though her tongue hurt. "Remember Capac Raymi—the magnificent festival—three years ago? When you—"

"Huber," he informed her with mock solemnity. "The name of the month is Huber, after Hubert Matos, hero of our—"

"When you caught me in the race, during Capac Raymi,

3

and there in front of everyone—"

"Well, I didn't know you were a Green! To me you were just another naked girl, well shapen and—"

"To be enjoyed on the spot, as part of the fertility ritual," she finished, enjoying the banter. "But when you kissed me that way, I knew you were a Dev—"

"Watch your language, girl!" he said. "I'll have you know I'm an upstanding Yellow. I would never abuse the sacrosanct edicts of Fidelia."

"That's when I began to love you, Seven, even though I knew what it would cost." She pulled him down again. "Let's celebrate it again, just like—"

He put thumb and forefinger to her exposed left breast and flicked the rising nipple sharply. "No time for that, greenie! I have to move out in twelve minutes; you know that. Besides this is Fulgen, not Huber. Wait till next month."

She jackknifed as her grip loosened, her bare knees flipping up to catch his retreating head on either side. The coverlet floated away to show a torso that was serpent-lithe. "Three minutes," she said.

"Ridiculous! I have to dress." But he was teasing her. "Make it one minute. You know the State recommends efficient procreation."

She squeezed his head between her legs, hard. The long muscles of her thighs were quite strong, as they were in all Greens. He knew he would never have caught her that day had she not been willing. "Two minutes, monster!"

"You drive a nasty bargain when you're squashing my ears. We've already wasted thirty seconds. That leaves ninety. Take it or leave it."

Then they were in full embrace. Despite the bargain they had made, it lasted almost two and a half minutes. It was worth it, as it always was, with her.

"She-canine, you have made me late," he said affectionately. "Again."

Green Three 551233 blithely donned a tunic, sidearm, and green sash and pattered barefoot to see to Junior, who had been suspiciously quiet in the adjacent cubby. "Were you peeking again?" she demanded. There was an answering chuckle.

197 cleaned up quickly, put on a white shirt, slacks, and his own green sash and weapon, then stepped to the dinette and punched breakfast for two and a half. By then 233 and their two-year-old son were ready, and they enjoyed a six minute meal together.

Thirteen minutes after the first chime, 197 passed through the portal and stepped into a waiting transport. The car closed about him and accelerated down the commuter tunnel toward Complex Green.

197 let it speed for thirty seconds, watching its screen for convergent traffic. Suddenly he slapped the manual switch, momentarily overriding its preset. In that instant he diverted the vehicle to the adjacent lane and punched an alternate designation. The automatic cut in again, oriented to the new coding. He had accomplished the tricky and dangerous manoeuver neatly. The car had slowed only slightly and made no giveaway hesitation, attracting no attention.

197 removed his green sash, ran his finger along a hidden seam, and opened it into a double-width scarf. The inner lining was yellow. He folded the scarf so that the green was inside, then resealed it. He tied it about his waist again: an authentic yellow sash.

He put the needler into an artfully concealed holster in his clothing. All Greens were armed; no other Caste carried a weapon, so the device now threatened his own life.

Four minutes later the little transport reached its revised destination and stopped. 197 stepped out and stretched as though still not quite awake. He walked up the ramp and entered Complex Yellow.

"Morning, 97," the white-sashed library office girl said. "You're one minute late." She was young and pretty and her smile was special.

"Morning, 64," he replied, chucking her pert chin. "I'll

work a minute into my lunch period to make it up. Don't report me, all right?"

"You know I won't report you!" she snapped. "I'll cover for you. Just stop being so careless about your timing, or one day someone who counts will catch—"

"I'd hitch your skirt right now, 64," he said, pronouncing the first digit so softly that it was almost inaudible. "But I know you have other business."

"It can wait!" she said, flushing at the near use of her endearment number. But he pretended not to hear her as he moved on. He had been bluffing; she hadn't. She was eager to demonstrate her reproductive potential at his expense; and prove herself a good citizen.

He came to his cubby in the Archaic Linguistics section. His treatise notes lay undisturbed: *Speculations on the Influences of Latin American Spanish Dialects on the Mother Tongue*. He sat without preamble and resumed his writing in mid-sentence where he had left off yesterday.

" . . . often originating in the low Caste vernacular. For example—" He paused, and the transcriber halted its script as his voice stopped. "Correction: low class vernacular." The machine eradicated the verbal anachronism and scripted the correction. "For example, the term *bollo*, as used in most Spanish-speaking regions, described a small piece of native bread. *Bollito de maiz*—a fried round piece of corn meal. But in Cuba it became the vernacular identification of the female genitalia, and consequently assumed pejorative connotations. This usage gradually spread until few if any high class persons would use—"

"¡Buenos Dias Cien Novente Siete!"

197 jumped, losing the thread of his narrative. It was his colleague from Archaic Literature: friendly, intelligent, garrulous. "Hola Ochociente Ocho," he responded with a slight stress on the formal triple digit to suggest his annoyance. Then, regretting such curtness, he added: "Don Quixote still charging that windmill?" They were speaking in Castilian Spanish, not Fidelian; it was excellent practice, and there

was a certain pleasure in it. Their own language was largely derived from Spanish, of course, but the intonation differed substantially.

"Do not belittle the sturdy old knight," 808 said gravely. "He had commendable spirit. Many windmills remain today in need of tilting."

197 did not smile. "I know of none."

808 sobered immediately. "A jest señor! I refer only to distaff mills, bless their charming fecundity! When will you marry, 97?"

197 allowed himself to relax visibly, having made his little show of patriotism. "My work is too pressing to permit such distraction, 08. A woman, a family—they would distract my mind from my researches."

808 shook his head in mock dismay. "May I never become so dedicated. Or should I say 'dead-icated.' Cervantes is dead; 464 is alive. Have you not noticed?"

"Now that you call it to my attention—"

808 laughed and slapped him on the shoulder. "She would go trans for you in a moment! Try her señor!"

917 showed his disgust. "Transparent is empty; you know that."

808 sighed. "I do know it. And Yellows grow too academic. Sometimes I almost wish miscegenation were permissible."

197 feigned shock. "Your jests lose their appeal, señor."

808 threw up his hands. "Why must you take what I say so seriously? You know as well as I do that our Caste system is unnecessarily restrictive!"

"I know no such thing." A single careless admission to a colleague could spell disaster.

"And I do not understand how it came about," 808 continued, determined to vindicate his opinion. "After the holocaust we were free. No restrictions at all. We could have set up any system—"

"I would hardly call worldwide radioactivity 'freedom'."

808 shook a warning finger, smiling. "Do not play the

advocate with me, Cuban. The radiation was temporary, and our forefathers knew it. A few centuries at most, together with proper medication—why even now it is possible to walk the surface with minimal shielding in many regions, had we but the courage. But I refer to the social situation."

197 made as if to bite the finger, falling into the spirit of it. "I'm serious, Czech. A restrictive physical environment inevitably leads to social confinement. Why the language itself reflects—"

"Fortunately we don't have to speak Fidelian!" 808 exclaimed. "Our language, and our literature—and even our romantic expressions, unfortunately—reflect the stultification of creativity wrought by the repressive Caste system, not the physical environment. Granted a more liberal social scheme, what a flowering we might have had!"

Did 808 suspect? Was the man trying to lead him into a damaging admission? His words were approaching Deviation.

No—808 was his friend, and hardly the type to be an undercover Green. "The system is necessary to preserve some semblance of civilization," 197 said carefully. What kind of civilization, however, forbade him a woman like 233? "Your argument ignores what a phenomenal effort our ancestors had to make, with a population nadir of mere thousands. Subterranean construction, atmospherics, hydroponics, medicine—in addition to the massive procreative effort required to quadruple their own number every century."

"You exaggerate the problem," 808 said, making half a wink to show his own patriotic readiness to make that procreative effort. "A mere three surviving offspring per generation—"

"Per couple per generation, you mean, assuming that every woman marries and is fertile. But the key word is 'surviving.' The conditions they faced—"

"Must you debate illiterately in the halls?" another voice demanded in Spanish.

Both men stopped. It was Yellow Seven 623500—a grim, capable woman long past procreative age or inclination. It was surreptitiously said of her that she had retired from childbearing with immense relief the moment her minimum quota of five live births had been fulfilled. It was further hinted that her husband had been even more relieved. "Apologies, 500," 808 murmured.

"To comprehend our present society, you must first understand Cuba," she said firmly. "To understand Cuba, you must first understand pre-holocaust Latin America. And to understand Latin America you must first understand historical Spain. Now Spain evolved as an entity only after the collapse of the old Roman Empire some two thousand years ago—"

"Trust the historian to assume command," 197 murmured, smiling to show he didn't mean what he did mean. He would have to find a pretext to break off, as 500 could hold forth on her subject indefinitely. She was a true academic.

"... whereupon the Visigoths were themselves displaced by the Moslems from the south. For some three centuries these western Goths survived only in pockets in the Pyrenees, where they merged with the indigenous Iberians to become the true 'Spaniards.' Their unity was based on Christianity and a common opposition to the Moslems. During the long reconquest of Iberia—"

"But in what way is this relevant to Caste, 00?" 808 broke in gently, affixing a disarming smile. This woman had to be handled with caution.

"I am explaining, 08. The reconquest assumed the aura of a crusade, driving out the urban-oriented Moslem culture and dispensing large tracts of land to favored officers. But these knightly domains began acting as separate nations, creating serious barriers to economic intercourse, and the once-thriving Moslem-sponsored merchant class declined. Only monarchial rule offered the potential to restore unity and avert ruin, and so the Spanish city classes accepted subordination in the hope that—"

"As they did later in Cuba," 197 said. "Havana welcomed the mountain bandit Fidel Castro at first. But—"

"Mountain bandit!" 808 exclaimed, shocked. "The revolutionary hero of our fair enclave—"

"Fidelia," 197 finished for him. "I'm not being derogatory. There was a fine ancient tradition honoring the Latin American bandit heroes—"

"Precisely," 500 continued, undaunted by their diversionary attempts. "Now the Inquisition was the final instrument of kingly consolidation. In the name of the Church, the Jews and the Moslems—one-third of the wealthy trading class—were purged, with ruinous consequence to the economy. Spain seemed doomed to economic chaos. But just then the New World was discovered, and Spain was saved by the enormous external supply of wealth. For a century thereafter Spain was supreme in Europe, possessing the finest military machine ever—"

"But the Caste system—"

"I am telling you, 08, if you will only pay attention." She planted her bulk more firmly in the doorway and took a deep breath. "The Spaniards of the sixteenth century were the world's most efficient conquerers. They knew exactly how to battle Amerind civilizations, for they had five centuries' experience against a similarly organized but technologically more advanced Moslem state. Thus the conquest of America was accomplished in mere decades, and a semi-feudal system could be instituted on a grander scale than ever before, modeled on that of Reconquest Spain, but not subject to its kingly restraints. Thus it endured for four full centuries, right up to the holocaust, and was in fact the social forerunner of our present Caste system. No system, you see, can be effectively imposed on an incompatible base, as numerous examples demonstrate—"

"Oh come now, 00—we are not feudalists!" 197 protested without real hope of silencing her lecture.

But 808 saved the hour. "You are surely correct, 00.

The situation must be compatible. For example, I have heard that the conquering Spaniards readily adapted to the native women, for the maids resembled the Moslem ideal of femininity which the Iberians esteemed. Dusky, with long black hair, splendid secondary characteristics—"

"Breasts," 197 put in helpfully.

"Bathing nymphlike in some clear mountain stream, beautiful—but unlike the Moslem pulchritude, by no means unobtainable! Ah, picture it now: the sex starved conquistador, the nubile Indian damsel—"

500 departed. She possessed the skin and hair of her Inca ancestry, but her secondary characteristics were no longer splendid.

"Magnifico!" 197 exclaimed under his breath.

"I should not have teased her," 808 said with good-natured regret. "But I must return to Cervantes, or the mill will win the bout and poor Sancho will never gain his governorship." He left with a parting gesture.

197 half smiled as he returned to his own papers. 808 was a bumbling innocent but a good scholar who was prone to speak too frankly. He was correct about the decline in radiation. A number of archaeological expeditions had gone outside during the past century, not only exploring the original territory of Bolivia, but making forays to several of the continent's splendid ancient cities: Lima, Santiago, Buenos Aires, Rio de Janeiro, Brasilia, and even north to Mexico—everywhere the radiation was down, green plants were growing, and the atmosphere was almost fit to breathe. Only in the northern climes did the deserts remain. Yet no one was volunteering to colonize the surface; the ingrained fears of centuries were prohibitive.

There were no other interruptions, for few citizens were interested in either Archaic Linguistics or Archaic Literature, Spanish or otherwise. Yet the work went on, a methodical recreation of the past. 197, for all his banter, found it deeply satisfying and knew 808 felt the same. There were indeed windmills in need of tilting: past and present, distaff and other. For any person who dared admit it.

At noon 197 punched a four minute lunch and swallowed the capsules mechanically. His research paper was making tedious progress, despite his fascination with the subject. He might complete another chapter in the remaining six hours of his working day. Meanwhile, he needed a break.

He punched WHITE TWO 400464. "Hi, 64," he said as her face appeared on the screen. "You have an open date?" Again he had made the final digit louder, suggesting intimacy.

She caught the hem of her tunic and brought it into view beside her face, glancing at him questioningly in the course of a slight blush. She had such hopes!

He nodded. "Twentieth Century's getting stuffy. Three minutes now?" He wasn't really interested in her, but 808's unsubtle remarks had given him warning. He couldn't afford too great a show of indifference to the local displays, or there would be a growing question about the outlets for his masculine urges. That could be disastrous.

64 looked genuinely unhappy. "I'm tied up at the desk until next shift. Could we make it eighteen hundred? We could have seven or eight minutes by doing it while eating. . . ."

While eating! She was ambitious indeed. If he gave her any leeway, she'd have him legally enmeshed—and how would 233 react to that? He affected a greater disappointment than he felt. "I hate to wait that long, but very well. I'll take you to a first class booth," meaning that a considerable crowd would see the liaison, and the charge for the food would go on his number. The very publicity of the act would assure that she could claim no commitment he hadn't made. It would be a seven minute stand, no more, and many witnesses would verify it.

"I'm so glad," she said, and waved a handful of material at him as she faded. No doubt she was aware of his reservations, and was making plans to counter them. Probably she had taken a fertility supplement.

197 was tempted to skip it after all, claiming to have confused the appointment in some way, but decided he'd better go through with it. A good show would allay suspicion and so protect 233, who well understood the necessity. Officially 197 was a bachelor, and that meant he needed women like 464 even if he had to take them with his meals. Even the remotest suspicion of Perversion could bring an investigation that would destroy him.

Oops—almost forgot! He punched for water and dissolved an illicit defertility tablet in it. 464 would not snare him that way! The pill, in addition to his own exercise with his illicit wife earlier, should tide him safely through.

His paper languished. *The Influences of Spanish Dialects*—his brain was in harness, but his spirit was with his wife and child. Just one child, that he could cherish, instead of the assembly-line offspring normally required. Yet he had so little time with them, and he had to be so much on guard! All because he was a Yellow and she a Green, and neither was willing to settle for a temporary liaison, and the system decreed that miscegenous marriages were not conducive to a perfect society.

Of course, one of them could go Transparent, adopting the colorless sash, and then their nuptial would be blessed by the state. But that would mean living on a single income, which in turn would require a substantial reduction in life style. And they would have to endure it for the years it took to produce the minimum five live births required, or the six expected, or the seven preferred. 233 might well come out of it looking like 500, and just as bitter about her overworked loins.

197 didn't want 233 living in primitive accommodations, and he didn't want the state to raise his children. So it had to be this way, though his miscegenous secret marriage had made him technically a Deviant. Such an ugly term to cover the necessities of life and love!

808 had hinted that all was not well with this world of the year 2413. 197 had squelched the notion—but this was a

self-defense reflex. His own case illustrated that the system lacked sufficient leeway for human preferences. Because he had loved and wed a Green, and because he preferred some small variety in sex play, he was deemed both Deviant and Pervert. Doubly damned.

Dutifully he reported to 464's desk at eighteen hundred. It was time to make a conformist Caste White clerk believe that a commitment of marriage was incipient provided only that her pudendum carried sufficient voltage. Time to let Fidelia know that loyal scholar 197 was not completely dead between the legs.

She was not there. Instead a representative of Caste Purple stood beside the desk. Rank Eight—an executive of authority.

"Come with me, 048197," the man said, his voice cold.

There could be only one reason for a high rank Purple to approach him like this. Discovery!

197 turned to bolt.

Two Greens appeared. Low-rank police, but not to be treated lightly. 197 started to reach for his hidden weapon, but halted; all Greens were crack shots, and their two needlers would be brought to bear before he could get his own clear. On the other hand, they would probably not draw on him at once, thinking him unarmed, and would rely on a submission hold. . . .

197 stopped at the doorway as though confused, and the Greens came up quickly to take his arms. He slumped despondently, and they marched him down the hall and toward a waiting Greencar.

Now he would discover whether his tediously rehearsed booklore meant anything. He had borrowed a Green training manual from 233 and practiced delightfully with her, so as to be able to imitate her Caste in the face of physical threat. The marksmanship had come naturally, but he had never used the body combat techniques in earnest.

Two Greens, surely competent, but hardly expecting Green technique from a scholarly Yellow. . . .

197 whirled and kicked at the knee of the man bracing his wrist, striking from the side, hard. The knee did not break as it would have if struck by a fully trained Green, but the man did let go of 197's wrist. Immediately he struck the second man on the windpipe with his hand— using the "V" between his thumb and stiffened fingers— and performed a sweeping leg throw. Neither of these were precisely executed, but the combination did bring the Green down.

197 had the initiative, but he would have to make it count or he would soon be finished. He jumped at the staggering first Green and hit him across the throat, knocking him out. But the other, though in severe pain from his own larynx, was ready for him. 197 tried to kick him on the side of the head, but the man caught his foot, holding it up to unbalance him and prevent him from either kicking again or getting away.

Even injured, the Green would be more than a match for him now. 197 clawed out his needler and fired. The gas cartridge exploded, sending a jet of liquid directly into the man's throat. The anesthetic stunned him instantly. Shots from the weapon had to be accurate, for clothing would foil it and a nonvital hit would take too long to slow down the target.

He charged into the transport tube and took the first vehicle, punching a designation at random. The hood slid over him and the transport moved out as other Greens ran into view. They were too late.

197 rode only long enough to catch his breath and convert his sash back to Green. Then he overrode the automatic again and brought the transport to a quick halt. He got out and went to a viz outlet. These, like the transports, were free—so long as the calls were brief. No record was kept, so the authorities would be unable to trace his whereabouts unless they monitored the entire system—an impossible task.

He punched GREEN THREE 551233. He couldn't go

home, for the apartment would surely be watched. He had to warn her before the police came for her too. It would be especially hard on her, because she was a Green herself; the police Caste's internal discipline was savage. She had always feared it would eventually come to this, and had been willing to risk it for the sake of a few wonderful years together. They had a standing plan worked out. 233 could join him in hiding—in Caste Black.

The White operator cut in; the call had not gone through. "That designation is out of service," she said. "If you will leave your identity—"

197 disconnected instantly. They had caught her already! They had cleverly saved him until last, knowing that he would be the elusive one. His wife and child were captive.

Numbed, he found another transport and climbed in. His little paradise had been erased, and he would never see 233 again. The Greens prided themselves on how efficiently they carried out their tasks. In his guise as a Green he had come to appreciate the thoroughness of their operations.

But he could not give up his dream entirely. He would not have challenged the system if he were the kind to capitulate at the first strike. Somehow he would strike back, repaying it at least partially for this wound.

First, he needed to live. He could barely think straight, right now. He couldn't get food, clothing, or shelter without using his number, and they would have him pinpointed the moment he did. Only transport and similar services—air, water, information—were anonymous, but if they wanted him in a hurry even that could change. He had to get away—and in a sealed society such as this, that meant a new identity. Soon. Not the one he had engineered in Caste Black, for the drugs and brainprobe would have that information from 233 before the day was done.

His wife . . .

He sealed that off. Sorrow would incapacitate him now. He had to function without crippling emotion, as a machine, until he avenged her. Or died in the attempt.

He stopped at a mall and began walking, knowing he would be taken for an ambulatory Green on routine duty. Here for the time being he was just one stroller among many appreciating Fidelia's largest open space. It was a good way to relieve repressed claustrophobia. There was more of that than the Purples liked to admit.

The mall was fifty feet high and a hundred wide. It was lined with scenic murals and artificial shrubs and trees so that it looked even larger. The vault above was painted light blue, speckled with white clouds. At the mall's center was a thin beach and a series of twenty-foot wide ponds, with gleaming mechanical fish moving about. Citizens of all ten Castes clustered about these, their children exclaiming over the wonder of all this space and water. Directly above, steam emerged periodically from ceiling vents, spreading and forming into real clouds that rained for a few minutes every hour: the most remarkable exhibit of all.

197 kept a suitably vapid expression on his face and merged with the multicolored throng. "Mourn not the dead," he thought, quoting an obscure poem from somewhere in his memory. He had run across many such figments in the course of his researches, and they tended to recur in times of stress. "But rather mourn the apathetic throng—The cowed and the meek—Who see the world's great anguish and its wrong—And dare not speak."

This was that throng, without doubt. A society whose members never saw the sun, never trod the globe's surface, never sailed an ocean—yet had neither the courage nor the will to protest. Did the dead mourn those who lived? The dead who had died to make a better world despite the holocaust, and only made an animate sepulchre? Would the dead speak, knowing that the living did not?

Such conjectures got him nowhere. What use to suppress his mourning for his wife and child, only to replace it by mourning for his society?

Ten Castes, fifty thousand people in each, five thousand per rank. A little better than half a million cowed and meek! It must be possible to find a secret niche in one of those hundred combinations, no matter how well integrated the society, no matter how tight the seams.

Still, every Purple had his specific political or administrative territory, with no vacancies; every Blue had his lathe, his hammer or his hydroponic valve. There was no way to intrude into these Castes without being quickly discovered. The same was true for Red—it took months to be a nurse, years a doctor, and special training was required even for the lowly hospital aides of the bottom two ranks. Even Orange was difficult, assuming he had any knowledge of sports or entertainment. He could not go Transparent, for he had no one to support him. (464? Her interest in him would terminate the moment she learned he was in trouble. It would be dangerous even to call her.) He could not steal what he needed, for the entire Black Caste would be on guard now.

That left only Brown, the pauper Caste. One more beggar would hardly be noticed in a Caste of beggars. For a while. Very few others ever bothered to verify the credentials of a Brown. Who, after all, would care to cross Caste lines to masquerade as an outcast?

Complex Brown was a region smelling of excrement, infested with vermin, and given to periodic plagues. The housing lacked sanitary outlets, and the only entertainment was personal and physical—for those not averse to unclean women. No ordinary Yellow would tolerate such a life, after the electronically aseptic housing that was his privilege. The very notion revolted 197—but his will to survive was strong.

Browns had special resources. They could use the back alleys, sifting the garbage of richer Castes, traveling along the sewage pipes. They could peer into portals and hang around the Blue kitchen complex for scraps. Browns were everywhere, yet normally unnoticed by others. They were the scavengers, paid only by the worth of what they obtained, like the criminals of Caste Black.

First he had to get a brown sash. He could not apply for one; that would only bring him to the attention of the Greens. But it would be too obvious to steal one from someone on the street, and Deviants of so asocial a nature were lobotomized as soon as they were caught. And they were always caught.

No use delaying. If the authorities reasoned the same way he did, they would watch Caste Brown too. Not that it would be easy to survey; the Brown distrusted other Castes and seldom cooperated effectively. In fact—

Yes, it was worth a try. Do what the Greens would least expect. It might be suicidal, but it might save him.

He took a car directly to Complex Brown, the beggars' headquarters. Even their main office was run down; the walls grimy, the floor mottled and worn. Idle Browns in the vicinity contemplated his green sash suspiciously but did not attempt to interfere with him. In Complex Black it would have been another matter; Blacks and Greens were legal enemies. And Caste Black honored extradition proceedings in cases of Deviation, while Browns often did not.

He went directly to the Records Office, where every legitimate Brown was registered. Here a Brown Ten—almost a contradiction in terms, the highest of the lowest—snoozed, his filthy shoes cluttering the desk. The man cracked his eyes open as 197 entered but made no other motion. What a picture of indolence!

It was an act, of course. Endless jokes were told about laziness being the surest key to Brown advancement, but nobody reached the top rank in any Caste without being thoroughly competent. "I'm in trouble—Deviation," 197 said bluntly.

The Brown yawned and gestured to one side with a thumb. 197 at first thought it was a dismissal, but he looked—and saw an inconspicuous panel sliding aside

to reveal a dark opening. Good—they were offering him
cover until they could verify his situation. The Browns
understood his disaffection with society: the entire Caste
was disaffected.

He passed through and found himself in a dank, unlight-
ed hall. The panel closed silently behind him, and until his
eyes adjusted he had to slide his hand along the greasy wall
to be sure of his way.

The passage continued interminably, winding downward
into the maintenance levels, skirting beaded tanks, hissing
pipes, humming machinery. A typical Brown conduit.
Where did it lead?

Abruptly, he faced a striking, illuminated statue: a
crowned goddess dressed in bright red. She was young,
with flowing brown hair, but of stern mien. With one hand
she held a gold sword on high; with the other, a gold goblet
at breast level. Behind her was a small castle; before her
were assorted and incongruous objects. Machine parts, food
capsules, a tumbler of water, and a tiny gold model of an
eyeball.

197 realized with dismay what he was in for.

This was Santa Barbara in her garb of war: the symbol
of the nefarious Espiritismo cult derived from ancient wor-
ships of voodoo and Catholicism. Espiritismo in its various manifestations—Chango, Babalao, Caridad, and other
fusions from disparate origins—had made some intriguing contributions to late Spanish dialects, and had survived the holocaust with enhanced strength. Both science
and religion had been discredited among many people, so
what remained was mysticism. The Caste establishment
suppressed it—such rites had been surreptitious for centuries though never actually outlawed. Espiritismo remained
popular only among Browns.

Perhaps he should have anticipated this. Next month
would be Huber, the season of feasting, and Santa Barbara's
day. The month of the magnificent festival, Capac Raymi, as
233 put it. December, in the ancient calendar. Browns would

be everywhere in Fidelia, proselytizing, seeking to convert members of other Castes to their "religion." Actually, they were having increasing success in the contemporary decade, perhaps because there was no established religion. 197 knew of Blacks, Blues, and even Whites who openly adhered to Espiritismo, and he was certain that many more adhered secretly to its superstitions. The majority were contemptuous of its barbaric rites—but a smaller majority than there once had been.

He passed the statue and continued down the tunnel. Somewhere along here must be the Brown upper echelon. They would decide whether the fugitive should be hidden or betrayed to the Greens. If the Browns helped, there would be marvelous possibilities, for there was nowhere they could not enter by some back route. He might even— he paused to control his raging fancy—win through to 233, and . . .

The passage opened into a large, dimly-lighted storeroom filled with people. Most were Browns, but a respectable minority were of scattered other Castes. One, astonishingly, was a low-rank Purple! In the center was a thin, ascetic-looking man, very dark in complexion but dressed entirely in white: shirt, trousers, stockings, and shoes— even sash. Only his collar broke the pattern, for it was formed of red and black beads and shells. He held a strange bunch of sticks in each hand: branching affairs with bits of green cloth attached thickly. All around him were dishes containing food capsules: protein, calorie, vitamin, mineral, and moisture. Extravagant waste, indeed!

197 halted, dismayed again. This was no hierarchy— this was a full Espiritismo mass! On no other occasion would such conspicuous waste of precious nourishment be tolerated.

The White priest saw 197. "Come forward, initiate!" he said imperiously.

197 did not move. He was not afraid, but he certainly did not want to be drawn into this squalid ceremony. He

had to find the Browns in charge before the Greens caught up to him.

"You must cleanse yourself before receiving sanctuary!" intoned the priest.

Oh, no! The Browns intended this to be the price of their assistance. He would have to join the Espiritismo cult!

197 sighed. What choice did he have? Every moment he delayed made rescue of his wife even less likely. He walked up to the priest.

"Walk around me, Yellow," the priest directed, flicking 197 with his branches. That was what they were—facsimile branches, made to resemble the limbs of trees or bushes. The green bits were supposed to be leaves. "Take from each dish, pass it over your body, declare the evil will leave you. Cleanse yourself!"

197 obeyed, taking the food from each dish in turn, passing it over his body while repeating fervently that the evil would leave him, and returning it to the dishes except for tiny fragments that he would have to cast away later. The act's foolishness did not disturb him nearly as much as the contamination of edible substance. The priest—197 remembered that the proper term was santero—meanwhile struck him about the shoulders, back, and buttocks, crying out "Go, bad spirits, go!"

The funny thing was that 197 did feel cleaner after this. He could see how easy it was for so many people to cling to this type of ritual, believing that it could free them of their myriad tensions and guilts. Absolution by ritual!

The procession traveled to Santa Barbara. In a strange, resonant voice the priest addressed her: "Who is this man? Is he fit to join our number? Do you take him to your bosom, oh Goddess of the holocaust?"

The statue, of course, did not answer. But 197 was startled to hear a female voice: "Juan Bringas! Juan Bringas!"

He looked about and spied her: one of the women of the mass, a Brown Five, one of the considerable crowd now clustered in the tunnel. She was about forty-five, thin, tall, with unruly hair and wild eyes. She swayed and mumbled, turning her fierce gaze now on Santa Barbara, now on 197. "Juan Bringas!" she cried again, as though addressing him with her meaningless words.

"What do you mean?" the priest demanded, addressing the statue. "Who is this man? What is his—"

"Juan Bringas, you bring death!" the possessed woman screamed. "You kill us all! You abolish our memory! You make us shadows!" She flung herself at him, clawlike fingers clutching at his throat. "DEATH! DEATH! DEATH! DEATH!"

Several men jumped to restrain her, but she was demonically strong, and for a moment 197's breath was cut off. He was frozen and could not protect himself. It was not entirely the force of the attack; he felt that he was in fact damned, he believed it in his heart, though intellectually this was nonsense. It might have been the situation's eeriness, or the naked fear reflected on the faces of those around him, or his suppressed grief for his wife: he felt the aura of destruction.

The men finally tore her off. She fell to the floor in an epileptic fit, writhing in seeming anguish, spittle frothing from her mouth.

The santero stared suspiciously at 197, shivering. "Who are you?" he demanded.

"A fugitive." Complete truth was best right now, for in their present hysteria these people were capable of tearing him apart. "I married a Green in secret, and wear green myself, but I am a Yellow. Now they are after me for—"

"We know that!" the man shouted. "Did you not hear me call you 'Yellow?' We proffered sanctuary for your Deviation, even your Perversion—but who are you spiritually, that you carry death with you?"

"Only if the Greens mean to—"

"They do not know where you are! We diverted them. This is a greater menace you carry; it strikes at all of us, all our world! The Goddess is never mistaken. *Who are you?*"

197 could only stand mute, not comprehending the charge. If they were not afraid of the Greens, he was certainly no threat to them.

The santero brought out a handful of objects and cast them to the floor. "Cachita, help us!" he cried, invoking the alternate name of Santa Barbara. Cachita, or Caridad, had originally been the goddess of the sea, but her attributes had been absorbed by the dominant deity. "Cachita, who is this man, what is his menace?"

The fragments fell in a triangle, their dark sides up. There was a concerted moan. "Death!" the santero said. "The cocos say 'death!' "

Were they planning to kill him? 197 searched the tunnel for an escape route, but saw none. It was packed solid with staring, moaning cultists.

The santero threw his cocos again—and again they landed in a dark triangle. Thin-lipped, he made the cast a third time, exhorting the goddess. Once more the configuration of death appeared. The cultists' low moaning changed, becoming ugly.

"What can we do?" the priest cried despairingly. He understood the crowd's mood even better than 197. There was surely death in the making here, but not a supernatural one.

Abruptly the woman on the floor ceased her struggles and spoke with marvelous clarity. "Let him go—he is only the messenger!" she said. "We cannot stop the dead morn." Then she fainted completely.

Ashen-faced, the Espiritismos parted to let 197 pass. He didn't need to inquire further about his sanctuary; there was none here.

When Yellow Six 048197 regained consciousness he knew he had been drugged with a pacifier. He did not remember the capture; evidently the Greens had needled him the instant he stepped outside Complex Brown. Now his mind was alert to the possibilities of escape, but his body would obey nothing but specific commands from others.

His green sash was gone. He had been cleaned up and regarbed in yellow, to his surprise; he had anticipated the black of the prisoner/convict rank of the criminal Caste.

"Come with us," the Green guard said, not roughly.

197 came, walking as docilely as though he had never dreamed of opposing the system. They were in Complex Purple—Fidelia's capital. They entered a plush office whose floor and walls were carpeted in purple.

Four men were there—a Purple, a Yellow, a Green, and a Red. 197 saw to his amazement that all were Tens. This was a remarkably select panel.

"Sit down, 048197," the Purple said. 197's body obeyed smoothly. Something special must be in the offing to require this extraordinary court. His Deviation could have been established by routine Green investigation, and he could have been lobotomized while unconscious, ordinarily.

"This is the candidate," the Purple said. "Please interview him to your satisfaction, comrades."

The Red addressed 197 first. "Do you hate us, Deviant?" He wore the psychiatric emblem.

"I do not hate you personally," 197 said, conscious of the control the drug exercised on his mind. He spoke the truth as succinctly as accuracy permitted.

"Naturally not," the Red psychiatrist said. "You do not know us personally. But we represent a system that you hate."

"Hate is not the appropriate word," 197 said, searching for the most economical truth. "I feel that the system you represent is flawed."

"In what way?" the Red inquired, seeming intrigued rather than affronted by this heresy. What was he after?

"It is too restricted. People should not be governed by strictly numerical values, when some are functional and others not. They—"

"We are not disturbed," the Red said quickly. "Merely surprised by your attitude. Should the Castes be restructured?"

"Yes. And marriage should be allowed between color-Castes when both parties are useful members of society." That was a bit more than the question required, but it clarified his attitude.

"And this was your sole justification for Deviating? To marry a Green?"

"It was the immediate incentive, because I love her. Perhaps I would have Deviated anyway, later in life, for more subtle dissatisfactions."

"You do not consider yourself morally reprehensible?"

"I feel some stigma. I would have preferred to conform. I was forced by conflicting needs to Deviate. There was no moral solution to my dilemma, since a lone man is unable to alter the system."

"Not necessarily," the Red murmured with an inexplicable satisfaction. "So you elected to betray society?"

"I betrayed the system, not the society, for I feel it first betrayed me."

"Because it is imperfect and not readily subject to correction?"

"Yes." This interrogator had a remarkable ability to summarize what for him must be anathema.

The Red psychiatrist sat back, finished. He seemed oddly pleased, perhaps because 197's crimes were so clear-cut.

The Green took over. He wore the emblem of a combat specialist—a highly dangerous man. "Defend yourself," he said, shoulders falling into a slight hunch, legs bent just a little, arms out from the body.

The directive set 197 physically free, but he did not move. His book-learned hits and throws could scarcely prevail against an experienced fighter who was ready for him, and they both knew it. The Green would strike and it would be over, unless by sheer luck 197 foiled him. The only chance would be to put the Green out of commission unexpectedly, using whatever advantage his comparative youth and speed might provide.

197 moved suddenly, making a feint as though attempting a throw. The man countered so smoothly it seemed he had planned for this exact move. 197 let go with a surprise upper-cut aimed for the Green's solid chin.

It missed, as the head moved aside just that amount necessary. 197 was now open for a deadly counterstroke— but it didn't come. "As you were," the Green said.

197 lost control of his body again. He had also lost the battle, for the Green had anticipated both his feint and his real attack and nullified both without touching him. Experience counted heavily in the mental side of the fight, too—the most important part.

"He is far from expert, but he has good instincts," the Green announced, seeming as mysteriously satisfied as the Red had been. "He would prevail in most ordinary situations."

The Yellow was next. He wore the emblem of his historical research, but 197 had never seem him before. "¿Que tu harias para tener a tu familia legalmente contigo?"

Despite the drug, 197 jumped. The man's Castilian was fluent. Had he crossed Castes to master it, as 197 had done to learn Green techniques? Was he a Deviant too?

No—he was a Ten. Persons of that rank were able to obtain special dispensations. Possibly he had learned the language in order to specialize in Spanish history, much as 197 himself had. And of course he was a Yellow, so such studies did not really represent a Caste violation.

After that initial surprise, he realized the implications of the specific question: what would he do to have his family back legitimately? Did this mean they were ready to sanction his miscegenous marriage? If so, they could ask anything they wanted of him, for there was nothing he would not do for his family's sake.

But why should they bother negotiating with him, when it would be so much easier to lobotomize him and be done with it? Just a little shock through the forebrain, then reclassification as a Blue One menial. . . .

"¿No entiendes la pregunta?"

197 jumped again. He had forgotten to answer! The drug must be wearing off. "Cualquier cosa," he said. "Anything!" he repeated in Fidelian. The contemporary language was actually a blend of Spanish, Czech, and Quechua, with four hundred years of functional modification: not nearly as esthetic as the old pure Spanish.

"¿Te atreverias a matar a un hombre?"

"I am no Black Caste murderer!" he exclaimed. The pacifier was wearing off.

The Purple smiled with that same strange satisfaction. "Your verdict, Tens?"

The others nodded gravely. Whatever the point of all this was, 197 seemed to have conformed to their expectations. But he hardly liked the implications. Asking him if he would even kill a man. . . .

And if he did it—would that stop them from lobotomizing him anyway, together with his family? He had said he would do anything, but he hadn't meant it. He would not let them trick him into becoming a real criminal.

The Purple turned to 197. "We want you to prevent a man from accomplishing a specific act."

So he was not to be coerced into killing! That had been merely another test of his reaction. But the relief was small. Something ugly was developing, something more insidious than Deviation.

"In Cuba," the Green said.

"Cuba is an historical island. It doesn't exist today. None of the ancient nations do."

"Four hundred and fifty years ago," the Yellow said.

Mourn not the dead. . . .

But these men were serious. "Are you suggesting that the—the past can be changed?" 197 asked cautiously. There had been rumors of incipient breakthroughs of colossal significance. Of time travel. Rumors that suddenly took on more authority. Ridiculous, yet—

"We have developed the potential to affect history," the Yellow said. He seemed awed himself, as well he might be. "But the process is fraught with peril."

197's head was whirling. No wonder they were treating him with such ludicrous deference! "So you need a volunteer for a suicide mission, and I'm it. The catch being that I can never come back."

"The catch being that you *must* come back!" the Green snapped.

"On the contrary," the Purple said, overriding his comrade smoothly. "There is no catch. You will return; that is determined. The peril is not to you; it is to those of us who remain in contemporary society."

"I travel to primitive, revolutionary Cuba to stop somebody from doing something dangerous, but you are the ones taking the risk?" 197 hardly cared that his cynicism showed.

The Yellow took over. "It is confusing to you, as it has been to us. Your mission will not change the past significantly—at least, not at the moment you are there. But a small divergence *then* could mean a large one *now*. This is what we contemplate. It has been exceedingly carefully calculated."

The potential significance burst upon him. Go into the past, kill a key figure—the ruling politician of a nation, perhaps—and watch the consequences multiply through the centuries. Suppose a time traveler had shot Napoleon? Ghenghis Khan? Jesus Christ? None of the people alive today would be secure, for they might never be born!

"But there is a danger for me too—or whoever goes," 197 said. "I might be responsible for the death of one of my own ancestors. A number of them were Cuban, you know."

"We do know," the Purple said. "That is one reason we selected you. The laws of temporal paradox, as we understand them, prevent a person from eliminating himself."

197 wanted to ask a question, any question, but the Purple stopped him with a gesture. "Were you to destroy your ancestor, you yourself would lose identity. There would be no such person as Yellow Six 048197—and there would never have been such a person. So your action would be negated, and your ancestor would not die. That is temporal paradox. A self-cancelling equation, meaningless."

"I see," 197 said appreciatively. "But that doesn't explain why you want *me* to go. Why employ a Deviant, when there must be more suitable candidates whom you have more reason to trust?"

"Our agent to the past," the Purple explained, "must speak Castilian Spanish and be familiar with its historical dialects—specifically Cuban."

"There must be several hundred who—"

"He must also have the appropriate physical qualities, so as to pass readily for a native."

"Several dozen who—"

"And be competent to handle himself in personal combat without modern weapons."

"Four or five who—"

"And be suitably motivated to accomplish the mission precisely."

"I'm afraid that excludes me, Tens. You have taken my wife and child from me, and I have no guarantee that you will ever give them back. I do not trust you, and I would happily abolish you all if it meant you would not be able to destroy my marriage." The drug had worn off entirely, but it would not have affected that statement!

"If you succeed," the Purple said evenly, "it has been determined that the nature of our society will change, slightly but significantly. Among the modifications will be a reduction of the stringency of the prohibition against miscegenous marriages."

What promise was veiled in that formal statement! 197 tried to quell the sudden drumming of his pulse. "So I could marry a Green—legitimately?"

"Precisely. You would no longer be a Deviant—not because your attitude or actions changed, but because Fidelia would change. To that extent."

Attractive indeed! The success of his mission would automatically guarantee his restoration of status and permit him his private happiness. If what these men were telling him were true. *If.*

197 thought about it. "But wouldn't it make more sense to train another man appropriately—teach him just enough Spanish, enough self-defense, operate on his bodily features, and so on. One of your own number, perhaps. Or even the whole group of you. I may be convenient, but I'm hardly essential."

"We have no time!" the Green exclaimed. The Purple raised a hand to silence him, but 197 already knew he had a vital bargaining point. He could do the job immediately; a substitute would mean delay—and they were under some kind of time-pressure, despite their perfection of time travel.

"There are other risks," the Yellow admitted. "We feel that a man descended from Cubans should be sent to Cuba, for then the paradox effect, in protecting him, will also protect his family—and those intimate with it. In the process, a substantial segment of our present society should share that protection."

197 was impressed, but increasingly suspicious. The surest way to protect members of this society would be not to tamper with the past at all. "Someone with no Cuban connections—say a Brown of pure Inca Indian descent, or a Blue whose lineage was Czech—could wipe out the entire pre-holocaust Cuba without affecting his own ancestry, and that change could pyramid and destroy you all, for every one of you must have some Cuban blood. But such a change would be impossible for me, for I am almost pure Cuban. There must be many hundreds of my bloodline in twentieth century Cuba, compared to maybe a dozen Czechs and one or two Incas. My leeway to muck around would be

very limited in Cuba. So my ancestry will guarantee the integrity of most of your hides, regardless of my personal preference—if your theory is correct."

"Yes," the Purple said candidly. "The critical nexus for our necessarily restricted purpose is in Cuba. Were it elsewhere, we should certainly employ another man—for that reason."

So they understood each other. It was his ancestry they needed, not his philosophy or skills. 197 might try to make massive changes in the Cuban past, but he would preserve more of Fidelia than he changed, just by being what he was. There was nothing he could do to foil that restriction except refuse to go.

Why not balk? They needed him, and they had little time. They could not execute him or lobotomize him, for then he would be useless to them. He might use this as a lever to save his wife and child in *this* framework. That would be far less risky!

But better to play along for the moment, lest he throw away his advantage by grasping for too much. He knew only what they had told him, and that was not enough.

"Just what is this change that would give me back my family?"

The four Tens exchanged glances. "There is no harm in his knowing," the Purple said at last. "We can prevent him from divulging the information *here*, and it won't matter *there*."

By lobotomizing him—and 233 and his son. Yes, they could silence him, and probably would, if they were sure they could not use him. Careful, careful!

"We mean to eliminate one Caste," the Green said.

"Casticide! Which one?" It couldn't be Purple, Yellow, Green, or Red.

"Brown. The nonproductive ones."

Brown. They could do it, for Brown was mostly Indian, his smallest component. The Constitution declared that the Castes were equivalent, with Purple not inherently superior to Orange, Black or any other. But in practical terms—

*This was the death the Espiritismos had foreseen in him—
the abolition of their entire Caste!*

197 was on the verge of refusing. The cultists had understood his menace to them—yet they had let him go. He
could save them by refusing the mission.

That gesture would cost him his own life, and cost 233
hers—and these determined Tens would find another man,
and get the job done regardless, less neatly.

Still, it was no more than a breath of air that swayed
him. On another day he might have refused.

It made a macabre sense. 197 himself had wondered
why so useless a Caste was tolerated. But he didn't care
to admit that, and didn't have to, now that the drug had
worn off. He would stick to conventional objections. "But
that would make me a murderer many times over—apart
from whatever I do in Cuba!"

"Not so," the Yellow said earnestly, as though convinc-
ing himself. "You cannot kill a person who never existed.
You will merely change our reality a little, a mere trifle, so
that some are not born and others are obliged to seek gainful
employment. Many will remain as they are, except that they
will belong to other Castes. It is largely an administrative
change."

"You don't need to go into the past to make an administrative change!" 197 protested. "Hold a Ten-Caste council,
and let the majority decision abolish—"

"Not feasible," the Purple said quickly. "Tradition—"

"And the other Castes will be proportionately larger,"
the Yellow continued. These Tens were stumbling over
themselves to convince him. "And the production of Fidelia
will be greater, so there is more for everyone. Marriage
between Castes will become tolerable, for there will not
have to be such severe cultural controls. It will be a better
world—painlessly!"

What's in it for you? 197 thought. These men would not
be risking their rather plush existences merely to improve

the system. There had to be a more pressing motive that they declined to divulge—a motive whose revelation would cause them guilt feelings.

Useless to probe that now. Instead he asked: "How will the prevention of one act bring this about—no more and no less?"

"The answer is complicated in detail," the Purple replied, relieved. "We have made a computer-search of history to ascertain what possible foci would have bearing on the particular problem without awkward ramifications, and this was the one given as most suitable. The entire chain of events is far too complex for one mind to grasp, and we ourselves do not know what specific changes in personnel will occur. But we trust the computer model; we are satisfied the analysis is correct."

"And did the computer also pick me out to be your agent?"

"Yes. It knew more than we did of your, ah, marital situation and special capabilities. We thought the description exaggerated, so we did not at first take the precautions recommended when arresting you. That was why you eluded us for a time."

"You are more of an individual than you may realize," the Yellow added.

Subtle flattery. 197 thought it over. He did not like these men. He suspected their hidden motives; but he seemed to have nothing to gain by refusing. And the notion of traveling to one of the actual regions of Spanish dialect intrigued him more than he cared to admit.

"I'll do it," he said abruptly. "Give me the details."

Let them ship him to the past. Then he would decide just how obliging he felt.

PART
TWO

Juan Bringas looked about him, slightly disoriented and more than slightly uncomfortable. He was wet to his chest, with mud caking his legs to the knees, and his skin was itching in several places. He was in a mangrove swamp beside an inlet of the sea. Grossly swollen tree trunks surrounded him, each with its twisted roots clutching the brown, brackish water and its mildewed bark and projecting knees. There were also bushes with interwoven roots; he was standing in some such network, ankle deep under the water.

Why was he here? He could not for the moment remember. All that came to his mind was a bit of information from the concentrated Latin American review he had done in preparation: it had been more economical from the outset of Spanish colonization to specialize in cash crops for export rather than subsistence crops. Cocoa, coffee, rubber, tropical fruit—the proceeds of these commercial estates gave the Latin American provinces the wherewithal to purchase their staples from Spain and sustain a much higher mode of existence than would otherwise have been possible. In Cuba it was sugar.

Something stung his hand. He glanced down to his right to see a small winged creature, an insect, standing on its pointed snout. A mosquito! He reached over with his other hand to pick it up, as it was the first genuine wildlife he had encountered, but it pulled up its head quickly and flew away.

He looked about. The sea was shallow; he suspected he could wade all the way out to the small island he saw. But of course he had been briefed on this: three-fifths of the island of Cuba was basically flat, and such swamps and such islands were all around its coast. He had not realized how phenomenally lonely it would seem in person. It was hard to believe that there had ever been such open, uninhabited landscape—yet now he was physically in it!

Juan Bringas had to fight down a siege of agoraphobia; he had never in his life been isolated in such wilderness.

His hand stung again. The mosquito was back, inserting its proboscis once more into his flesh. Wildlife or not, that was begging for trouble, for he knew such predators harbored many of the loathsome diseases of the past. Had he been immunized against malaria? Bringas brought the other hand across and made a resounding slap.

The insect was dead, its corpse split open. A smear of bright red blood marked the crime scene. Bringas felt nauseous; he hadn't really meant to kill it. He had mistaken its texture, expecting it to be as sturdy as the wire models of insects he had seen in the Natural Life exhibit of the Complex Yellow Museum, back when he had been a definitive number, instead of a clumsy name. But further: he hadn't really believed that the insect was preying on his own precious blood, despite what he knew intellectually. That was disgusting and unsanitary. So perhaps it deserved extinction? Yet it was his fault too, for not warning it away before striking.

He calmed himself by checking himself over. He wore an olive green soldier cap that both weighted and heated his head, making him perspire uncomfortably; a long-sleeved shirt and dark green undershirt; green trousers; heavy knee-length boots laced tightly up the front; and heavy straps passed over his chest and shoulders and around his waist. One belt supported a canteen of water; others had clips of machine gun ammunition, K-rations, and a trench knife. Slung across his shoulder was an M-3 machine gun, and he wore some kind of knapsack. He was equipped to survive—and to kill.

It was appalling. He was certainly no killer! He—

His hand stung again. Another predatory insect! Enraged, he bashed at it—and left another little smear of blood. The dead mosquito dropped into the water.

No killer. Uh-huh.

He knew what was wrong: he was suffering from a temporal disorientation that confused his memory and left him highly irritable. It was one reason they had placed him in a lonely region; he needed a few hours to adjust, to achieve equilibrium. Otherwise he would never accomplish his mission.

But these murder-things that clothed him—gun, bullets, knife—time would never accustom him to them! He tried to suppress his horror, to force the arsenal of death from his thoughts before he became physically ill. All this exotic past-tense landscape, representing the world at the very height of life before the holocaust—and here he was outfitted for slaughter, and already practicing on insects.

Another sting on his hand. Bringas leaped up furiously, stepped off his root-support, and tumbled knee-deep into an unseen hole. He waved his arms desperately, regaining his balance against the ponderous physical and moral weight that clothed him, and staggered onward through the murky liquid. The muddy stench infused his lungs, making him gag.

But the experience sobered him. Here things were combining to bring out the savage in him, and he refused to oblige. He sloshed inland, looking for higher ground. As he walked on more solid territory he discovered that his boots left little marks wherever he trod: there was a configuration on the soles intended to prevent slipping. Who would have thought of that, in fair Fidelia? The footing was treacherous, but caution enabled him to avoid further dunking.

On firm ground at last, he took down the machine gun and studied it. The thing was made of metal with a very thick and long barrel; that was the silencer, he knew, for these weapons made considerable noise when fired. What a malignant instrument. He set it leaning against a mangrove root, and added the large .45 caliber pistol, the ammunition clips, five grenades, and the knife. That was a considerable weight off his body and his conscience!

Then he had a second thought about the knife. He might need that for foraging. He saw that two of the grenades were for making smoke. Smoke was not the same type of mayhem, and he might have occasion to use these peacefully.

The main weight of his pack was built in: the time phaser. Without that he could not return to the year 2413—and that thought chilled him even worse than the notion of murder. Heavy—about fifteen kilograms—but it *had* to stay with him.

He wrapped the guns and ammunition in a poncho and placed the bundle in a fork in the limbs of a mangrove tree, over the high water mark. He covered it with a couple of leafy limbs to conceal it somewhat. It would be pointless to bury the cache here in this waterlogged dirt, and probably no one would come this way in the brief time he required to complete his mission. He could pick it up before he phased back, and the Tens would never realize what he had done. He would have to squeeze off a few shots for verisimilitude, of course—but not at any living thing.

Good. He felt easier already, now that he had asserted himself and affirmed his civilized nature. On with the mission.

He drew a wadded paper from a breast pocket. It opened out into a regional map, and he traced the unfamiliar contours with one forefinger. He was here, assuming he had phased in correctly, in the tract of land west of the small coastal fishing village of La Panchita, in Las Villas Province, on Cuba's northern coast. About a hundred kilometers east of Havana, the capital city. The foreign missile base, according to the "accidental" smear on the map—for a direct notation could mean his death, should a native see it—was between the town of Isabela de Sagua and the fishing village of Caratas. What a novelty, to have so many villages, instead of a single subterranean metropolis. The three-man team would be landing between Caratas and La Panchita, here. . . .

Simple enough. He had merely to prevent their sending a message confirming the presence of the missile base. With that delay of information, the computer affirmed, the order for the U-2 airplane inspection of the region would come one week later, and—well, it was complicated. How he accomplished his mission was his own affair. The Ten hierarchy obviously expected him to resort to violence; surely his aggressive reactions during their pursuit of him had been an important factor in their deliberations. Ship a violent man into a violent situation for a violent mission. . . .

The date was the twentieth day of Camil, 1962. Capac Rami, as 233 insisted: festival of the queen. Except that neither designation was used in this year. He would have to train himself to think in the local calendar, in case he met a native. Not Camil, after Camilo Cienfuegos; September, after the Roman word for seven—though this was not Rome, and it was not the seventh month of the year, but the ninth. No wonder the cumbersome, illogical calendar of the ancients had been superseded!

The team, according to historical information, had landed a few days ago, camouflaged as Rebel Army soldiers exactly as he was now. They had made their way to a montero, a Cuban rancher, or more properly cowboy and woodsman, who was their local contact. Bringas had only to follow this man, Rafa, when he took supplies to the trio. Then—

He started walking. The water came up around his boots at every step, and every so often something stung his flesh again. The unfamiliar clothing and harness chafed. The knapsack grew heavier—first uncomfortable, then painful. It was hot here; his shirt was already sodden with sweat, and his strength seemed to be draining out of his body. His legs wearied quickly because of the clinging muck of this interminable swamp. He wasn't used to long-distance walking even on good ground. Wilderness paradise indeed! This was an aspect of it he hadn't thought about.

Fortunately the mangrove swamp abated a kilometer inland, and he tramped through pastureland. But then he ran afoul of plowed fields, tripping over the deep furrows. Not only was it surprisingly difficult to walk on the freshly turned earth, he was leaving obvious tracks. He had to get away from this and under cover.

But the cover he found was a small forest of marabu thorn bushes. Each bush was two to three meters tall with many leafy limbs and big hard spines. Six to ten feet tall—he'd have to adapt to the local measures, too. He was not able to see through them or to push them without getting stabbed by the huge thorns. He had to crawl along the ground under their main spread—and still thorns from the dead limbs that littered the bottom pierced his hands and knees.

At last he came across a small stream, and slogged through the water. This was far better than fighting the marabu. When the water course emerged into the open he had to climb through a barbed wire fence . . . and couldn't do it. The barbs caught at his pack and ripped at his clothing and skin and threatened to hang him up permanently. Then he got smart and removed his pack and threw it over, then squeezed under himself.

What a journey! He could hardly have gone three kilometers—or should it be leguas, or miles?—and he was hot and tired and hurting already! He gulped down the last of the tepid water in his canteen, climbed back into the pack straps, winced as they chafed familiar bruises, and marched on.

The next fence was alive: Pina de Raton, plants like giant pineapples growing close together, the space between them guarded by spikes. He detoured around it.

Evening came, and he had no place to stay. He had expected in his naivete to complete the mission without having to spend a night in the past—yet he had not even started.

Well, he didn't have to finish everything the first day. Right now his priorities were food, drink and rest. He had food with him, and his briefing had told him how to get the others. There were always clearings in the marabu, and water in the streams.

But the stream he had passed was far behind, and he had no notion where another might be. Now that he thought of it, thirst became a raging fever in him. He had no water discipline; he should have conserved his canteen supply, drunk from the stream. . . .

He found a hollow, and there was a puddle in it. He rushed down—and saw that it had been fouled with cow manure. Good and fresh: the aroma told him that, as did the swarming flies. But this might be the only water he would find.

Bringas lifted out the mass of material and put his mouth to the milky liquid remaining, schooling his body not to gag. He forced it past unwilling throat muscles, wiped off his lips, and went on. Fifteen minutes later he encountered a large, fresh, clear pool, and had no thirst remaining.

He found his marabu clearing: a space around a larger tree that had evidently been there before the flowering weed took over. How ironic that such awful thorns accompanied the vegetation's beautiful white flowers. The marabu had been imported from India for the sake of its beauty; then in the war against Spain a century before, the bushes had gotten out of control and spread across the island. A dry fact of history, now both his torment and his protection.

He removed his pack and scraped out a level space on the ground. He was hardly comfortable, but he could put up with his environment for one night.

The food was another unpleasant surprise. K-rations: small squares of dehydrated black substance, supposedly resembling bread and meat. For all he knew, they had been salvaged from four or five hundred year old supplies. They tasted like sawdust—the tiny fragments of ground wood that fell to the floor when ancient partitions were removed to make way for Fidelian expansion. Most of his equipment had been manufactured by Caste Blue specialists under Yellow and Red supervision, so as to be accurately rendered and functional; they could hardly have made prior excursions into the past just for supplies! But why couldn't they have substituted regular food capsules?

His heavy boots abruptly became unbearable. They constricted his feet, and the more he tried to ignore it the worse the pressure seemed to get.

He growled without employing his vocal cords, jammed the K-ration into the earth, and crawled awkwardly about to remove boots and blood and sweat soaked socks. The relief to his feet was blessed. He leaned back against the tree, shook the dirt off his morsel and took another awful bite.

Something was happening to his feet. They stung, they itched. He squirmed around to shine his miniature flash on them—and found his bare skin covered with the small winged predators he had met before in the swamp: mosquitoes.

Angrily he kicked his feet, but the determined creatures descended in seeming clouds, each one hungrier than the last, avidly sucking the precious blood from his exposed and tender tissue.

Bringas had to disturb his repose yet again to search out the insect repellant in his knapsack. He had thought it was just another prop; now he knew better! He sprayed it liberally over his feet and legs and hands and, for good measure, his face. He closed his eyes but not his mouth:

terrible tasting stuff, almost as bad as the K-rations. But if that was what the mosquitoes tasted when they tried to bite, wonderful!

He returned to his tree trunk, but gave up on the K-ration. He found a sandwich: hard white bread smeared with guava paste, with soft white cheese in the center. After what he had been through, this was delicious. He also had some hard, salty, dried beef strips, the Cuban tasajo—but stopped eating them when he realized what the salt would do to his thirst.

Thirst was not the only problem, however. This crude food did not agree with his pampered twenty-fifth century digestion, and his stomach rumbled resentfully.

Ouch! Needles of fire were drilling into his posterior! He lunged to his feet, slapping at himself. There were red crawling insects on him—stinging ants! He had settled next to an ant hill, and now the things were inside his clothing.

In time he got clear of them and found another spot. Weary, itching, bleeding, and flatulent, he ground down into a kind of sleep. His disgusted subconscious did not even have the grace to send him dreams of lovely 233.

The third time he woke, night was fretting into morning. Juan Bringas stretched, neatly impaling himself on the waiting spokes of the marabu. He broke wind at the obnoxious vegetation and wormed into the open. He shivered; it was not really cold, but he was hardly used to outdoor exposure of any kind. And he was soaking wet from the copious dew. Spider webs stretched across his eyelashes. Multiple insect bites itched, some in embarrassing places.

But he had to get moving before full daylight, lest he be discovered. He picked up his socks, wrung them out, and hauled them on. He sat down to don the clammy boots.

The boots had warped out of fit! No—his feet had swollen, so that no harmonious mating of pedal member and pedal covering was feasible.

What a way to start the day.

But the sooner he accomplished his mission, the sooner he could return to his own framework. 233 would salve his injuries!

That spurred him on. He suffered another lapse of specific memory, mercifully. When he recovered, his boots and knapsack were on and his load was much lighter, and another bit of information from his researches was playing through his brain:

When the Spaniards had conquered the Bolivian highlands, almost the entire Inca aristocracy had been put to death. Since the Inca serfs had never possessed the knowledge of warfare, religion, economic organization, or intensive land and animal cultivation and production, the demise of the aristocracy had destroyed the Indian civilization permanently. In Cuba, the Indian population itself had died out because of exploitation.

Bringas snapped out of it, suspicious. Yes—he had cached the fifteen kilo phaser—the thirty-odd pound phaser—somewhere! A dangerous precedent, but at least there would be no trouble locating it, as the directional indicator set into his left eyelid had been activated. He could orient on the device with the blink of an eye!

He rechecked his map. Rafa's ranch was close, now; he had come farther than he had realized during the night's slog. He could be there by full daylight to catch the man at home. With any luck at all he could spot Rafa as he went to meet the team. Then—

Then what? He had disposed of the weapons, and he did not regret that decision. But these were bound to be tough, hard-driving, practical men. He could not simply go and ask them politely to desist! Had he brought the submachine gun, he might have hijacked them for a few days, so that the message would have been too late. As it was, he was innocently buzzing into the web of spiders that abound so horribly here.

The Tens who had set up this mission had not needed to give him specific directions. They had known he would need the weapons—and would realize it in due course.

But he still refused to be herded into the posture of a killer of men. He would not go back for the guns.

He found Rafa's bohio: a Cuban farm house made of wood with palm leafs on the roof. The planks of the walls were painted white. There was a barn in back for the chickens and goats, a small wooden outdoor privy, and a corral with pigs. The rancher was already busy feeding his stock.

It all seemed so ordinary, in its extraordinary way. In the year 2413 there were no farm animals and few free-growing plants, except for the mutated breeds ranging wild across the surface. Here animals and plants were commonplace. To think that four centuries could change the world so much!

Of course, time hadn't done it. The holocaust had.

Could this farmer really be the team contact man of a mission concerning atomic missiles? He seemed to be in no hurry at all, and he whistled as he worked. Time dragged on, and Bringas dared neither approach the man nor leave.

He reviewed his briefing on Rafa. The montero had been deprived of larger holdings by the revolutionary government, and retained only half a caballeria—fifteen or sixteen acres—of his worst land, the marabu forest, together with his house and livestock. He had worked as a montero in a large cattle farm, but the farm had been nationalized and the cattle killed. The new administration was trying to grow rice on land everyone knew was fit only for cattle; naturally the crop was a failure, and Rafa had become disgusted with the harder work and lower pay of the rice cooperative. So he kept alive by selling his pigs and goats and goat milk on the sly, and he collaborated with the American agents who sought information about local happenings.

At midmorning Rafa took the bucket he had used to slop the pigs, refilled it, and ambled toward the brush. He wore a big cowboy felt hat and boots. Bringas uncramped his legs and followed, staying hidden as well as he could. This must be it!

Rafa continued to whistle as he swung his bucket. Bringas could see the milky fluid splashing out, and for a moment was reminded of the fouled water he had drunk the day before. The man surely wasn't on a spy mission; he advertised his progress every step of the way! But this was lucky for Bringas, for it enabled him to keep track without actually staying in sight. Rafa could easily have eluded him in this wild country, had he made the effort.

About a mile from the ranch Rafa encountered a militia patrol. Three men with submachine guns—there must be a million of those brutal weapons on the island!—stopped Rafa and questioned him. Bringas could not overhear the dialogue, but he saw the rancher gesturing amiably with the soupy bucket. Apparently he passed inspection; the militiamen let him pass unmolested.

Too bad they hadn't caught him, Bringas thought. That would have deprived the team of its local contact, and the militia might then have caught the—

Now he knew how to stop the mission without bloodshed. Let the militia arrest the team!

Bemused by this elementary solution, Bringas almost missed the actual contact. Rafa stopped by a section of marabu forest, changed the tune he whistled—and another militiaman appeared. The stranger's surreptitious attitude betrayed him—and of course a real militiaman would not have been hiding in the thorny bushes. This was a teamsman!

Rafa dipped his hand into the bucket and brought out a sealed package. Food, no doubt. So obvious that neither Bringas nor the militia patrol had suspected it.

Rafa looked up suddenly, hearing something. Both men faded into the marabu, using the little goat paths that penetrated its forbidding fringe. Why hadn't *he* thought of that!

Bringas soon understood their caution. The militia patrol, possibly suspicious, had doubled back. But the fugitives had been alert, and the patrol would never find them now. Unless—

Unless Bringas himself alerted the militia at this moment! Surely the spy team's other members were nearby, possibly in this same marabu. If the militia caught them, the key message would not go through.

Yes! He lifted one of his two smoke grenades. It was a dark gray cylinder with a handle on the side and bright yellow letters: WP-S. He clamped his hand around it, holding down the lever, and pulled out the pin in the end with his other hand. He knew it would not explode so long as he kept the handle down, and of course it was only harmless smoke, but it made him nervous anyway. He threw it quickly toward the militia trio.

He watched the grenade arc over the sugar-cane clump he had used for cover and down the slope of the small rise he stood on. His aim was beautiful; the object fell almost on top of the group. Once they inhaled that smoke they would know something was up!

He had a moment to assess the layout. He was hiding south of the patrol and the marabu was to the left. He had an easy retreat, shielded by the sugar-cane.

The grenade exploded a little to the side of the men, between them and the marabu. It was a firework display: a lovely cone of white sparks, gold streaks, and dark gray smoke. If the militia didn't take note of that, they were blind or bribed!

Then he heard the screams. Two men were writhing on the ground, and the third was shouting. They were burning! The foliage was green, but flames engulfed the men!

Bringas in his amazement exposed himself, and the third man saw him. The gun fired; then the man ran up the trail, fire clinging to his uniform. Bringas dropped to the ground, though he had not been hit, and rolled to better cover under the cane. It hadn't occurred to him that the militia would shoot at *him*. He realized almost too late that a time traveler could be killed right here! There was no paradox; if his own skein terminated here it would hardly affect the basic pattern of the times, for he was not *of* these times. He could die directly, though he could not kill an ancestor; his temporal disorientation must have confused his thinking.

Then he smelled something sweet.

He realized WP-S stood for *White Phosphorus Smoke*. And white phosphorous was a devastating incendiary. Those pretty sparks had been bits of it, inextinguishable fire. Whatever they touched would burn, including marabu, including human flesh. Water would not quench it; the fire would eat right down to the bones and into them. A man with white phosphorus on him could only cut it out with a knife, in a hurry; if he had many particles to deal with, he was doomed.

Bringas had known this, yet he had forgotten. He had lobbed a phosphorus bomb right at living men. That sweet smell was the odor of their roasting flesh.

The dismal contents of his stomach spewed out between his teeth and splashed against the sugar-cane. He heaved again, and again, and yet again.

Finally he sat up. He was weak and shaken. He had claimed to be no murderer! How could he ever justify what he had done? He had not stopped the spy team; he had only killed two innocent men, and done it as cruelly as could be imagined. He didn't even have the nerve to go and look at the corpses. They might not be quite dead yet. . . .

The fire still raged, spreading all across the path. The fugitives should still be in the marabu, for according to his map there was a road along its far side that they could certainly not risk crossing in daylight, and the fire prevented escape this side. There was a militia blockhouse on that road not far away. His mission hadn't failed yet!

He was tempted to run away. How could he cynically analyze the success of his mission when the stench of human flesh attached to him! Was he a monster?

He knew the answer. He had killed by accident—and he had to have his wife back. He couldn't search for the team himself, because he was unarmed and that was an excellent way to get riddled by bullets. His own death would not bring the scorched corpses back to life. He couldn't afford to leave without completing his mission. The complexities of paradox would make it extremely difficult to rectify any mistakes he made this time—any *more* mistakes. Far better to finish the job, whatever the price, than to have to try again on another time-phase. His travel over, he could mourn the dead.

That lone survivor—his wounds would never heal. They would ulcerate and keep spreading. . . .

The Tens must have known it would be like this. That he would react this way. That Juan Bringas/197, having agreed to abolish an entire Caste, was in his soul a Black. A man who could and would kill when the situation demanded, or when it did not demand. A twentieth—perhaps even twenty-fifth century Tamerlane.

Then the militia's reinforcements came. Massively.

Shoulder to shoulder, almost. No more than five feet separating man from man, guns at the ready—not three, not ten, but perhaps five hundred soldiers! And beyond them to the North he heard motors: trucks surrounding the area. A line of hunters coming through the brush, walking through everything. Poking at suspicious objects, kicking stumps, leaving no place for a fugitive to hide, no avenue of escape.

It was a peinazo—the government's system to flush out guerillas. Seal off the entire region, then clean it out absolutely!

The local ruler, the namesake of 197's own nation, had come to power through a guerilla revolution himself. He knew how to deal with those who rebelled against *him*. Fidel Castro—the name sent a shiver through Bringas. In 2413 he had spoken objectively of this man, for centuries separated legend from reality. Now it was 1962, and *Fidel was alive*. Fidel of Fidelia. . : .

Bringas brought his mind back to the immediate point. There was no doubt now: his mission had been accomplished. The authorities had been too smart to send in a minor patrol against men possessing phosphorous grenades, particularly in this region so close to the missile base. They could not know that Bringas had thrown the grenade, not the spy team. History would be changed, the Caste of paupers would be eliminated, 197 would have 233 again.

Except for one detail. Juan Bringas himself was caught in the trap.

The peinazo was sweeping the region, and inevitably it would net him along with the spy team. They would find the other phosphorous grenade and know the truth. What mercy could he anticipate at their hands?

He had blundered again in typically novice fashion. He felt sick again—sick with chagrin and personal fear. It would have been cleaner to have done the job with the guns he had been provided and not to have involved the militia in this highly sensitive area. The carnage would have been no greater, and he would not now be in a remarkably ugly situation.

Perhaps it was the raw experience of the stench of burning flesh; perhaps his realization of his own ineptitude. Probably the horror of his impending fate at the hands of these primitives was the major factor. At any rate, it happened.

Juan Bringas sloughed off his veneer of civilization, his twenty-fifth century values, his human restraint and morality. He reverted to the cunning beast, peering out at the hunters, watching for the opportunity that would preserve his life. He had tried to behave politely when the mission called for ruthlessness, and this was the penalty. He would not be foiled by such scruples again.

The peinazo was moving north to south, skirting the marabu. The line of men would pass the place where the spies were hiding and then approach his own knoll. Probably if the team were not flushed by nightfall, the militia would set fire to the marabu and shoot the fugitives as they emerged. But meanwhile the militia would net Bringas, with his guilty grenade, and his part in the matter would be over. If he fought, they would kill him; if he didn't, they would probably delay long enough to torture him before the execution. Or whatever they did to men who used phosphorous grenades on people.

He had to get rid of the incriminating evidence.

He brought out the grenade and pulled its pin, holding it ready to throw. He waited until the line of men was just past the spot Rafa and the spy should be in. The two could not be far away; the marabu was too difficult to traverse, particularly when they had to guard against pursuit. They would have spent their time digging in, concealing themselves, waiting for the fire to subside.

Bringas hurled the grenade, arcing it as high in the sky as he could. If some sharp-eyed militiaman were watching the sugar-cane at this moment he might spot the motion behind it or see the rising cannister; this was a necessary risk. Most of the men were watching only the ground ahead and to the sides, reasonably enough.

The grenade descended. It would strike behind the— Explosion!

Bringas didn't look. He ran, head down, keeping the scant cover of the sugar-cane clump between him and the ball of smoke. He ran south until he saw the road and the trucks, then fell down and hid his face in the dirt.

No one seemed to follow, but he did not try to reach better cover. He lay there and waited, motionless. He was far enough away from the grenade burst to be disassociated with it—if they flushed the spy team first. From here on it was a matter of luck—but he had improved his own chances considerably. At the expense of many more human beings in the range of the burning white phosphorus.

There was a burst of firing back in the area he had left. His diversion had worked! The militia was invading the marabu, infuriated by the blast.

Bringas craned his neck, but it was hard to see anything without exposing himself. The troops seemed to be trying to storm the marabu, using the goat trails for entry but still getting entangled by the thorns. And there was return fire! They had flushed the spy team, and men were getting killed by machine gun fire from that thick cover.

If they killed the spies in the gun battle, the dead men would never be able to deny their complicity in connection with the phosphorus. Another safeguard for him—at another tax on human life.

The noise abated. The militia was retreating. Were they giving up?

Then a jeep roared over the brush and parked about fifty meters north of him. Soldiers jumped down to unload equipment while Bringas dug himself in deeper. They set up some kind of tripod supporting a squat tube. They angled the tube toward the marabu and shouted a warning. The firing stopped.

One man placed a metal object in the tube's mouth and jumped back. There was a loud bang! followed by a long whistling noise. Smoke gushed out of the end. Bringas' teeth hurt.

It was a mortar! One of the ancient weapons that lobbed a shell high overhead to drop behind defensive fortifications—much as he had lobbed the second grenade.

A section of the marabu burst apart, followed by the sound of the blast. The mortar crew adjusted the tube and dropped in another shell. This time Bringas covered his ears. He saw the shell rise—and explode short of the target.

Now they had the range, and they meant business. The third shot would—

A man burst from the marabu, firing the submachine gun in his hands. He was cut down by rifle fire; they had been ready for this.

A second man came out shouting. His hands were high in the air—the gesture of surrender.

They did not shoot him. Three militiamen came at him with rifles to which small bayonets were affixed, as though to take him prisoner. They did not do so; they rammed those terrible blades into his body, killing him savagely.

Bringas watched with mixed emotions, knowing that each death made his own survival more likely. The acts of the militiamen looked cruel—but they had just been scorched by the near explosion of a white phosphorous grenade, and had seen their comrades die horribly.

Bringas was the real murderer. What a mess!

"Do not move, señor," a man said behind him, speaking with mock formality.

Bringas did not move. During his fascination with the proceedings he had neglected his own concealment, and naturally he had been quickly spotted. It hardly mattered now; he had known he could not avoid the peinazo. His whole effort had been to eliminate his seeming complicity, and to avoid being killed out of hand. Now he should be able to bluff his way back to freedom.

He had balked at killing mosquitoes, yet now he was a murderer many times over. He had killed five or six men directly by throwing the two grenades, and a similar number indirectly through the action he had prompted.

His crime was too big. He could not feel it. All he could do was worry about his own survival.

"Your name?" the interrogating officer demanded sharply. He was a stout bearded man in fatigues, oily, sweating profusely, who gave the impression that words were a waste of time when bullets were available.

"Juan Bringas."

Someone wrote it down, though they had already recorded the information from his papers.

"What is your business here?"

"I came to see someone."

"Who?" The syllable was barked impatiently.

"Rafa." He had to answer without hesitation, or things would become impossible. They were suspicious enough already—and with good reason.

"Why?"

He had his cover story ready. "To buy some goat's milk."

"Where is your permit?"

Bringas put on a guilty expression. This was the first he had heard of permits to buy milk, but better to be found guilty of that minor violation than of spying or killing people with grenades! "I was going to—"

The officer looked disgusted. "You were *going* to! If you got caught. Otherwise a fat black market profit!"

Bringas held the guilty face. What luck! Probably they would let him off with a fine, and he could return to his own time, and to 233.

Never tell her how you won her! he told himself fiercely. A dozen killings . . .

"I do not believe you, prisoner. I think you came for a pig."

"A pig?" Bringas was genuinely perplexed. Was that a more serious offense, or was the officer subtly soliciting a bribe? Pay him the price of a pig—rather than the price of mere goat milk—and go free? But one of Fidel Castro's great accomplishments had been to abolish graft! They had already searched him; they had no need to ask for his money when they could keep it anyway.

"Bring the slaughtered pig," the officer said to one of the guards, then to Bringas: "You are a friend of the montero?"

"I have never met him. Does he also keep pigs?"

The officer studied him thoughtfully. "Of more than one variety."

Two men came, dragging a body. They dumped it before Bringas.

He stiffened. Although he kept chiding himself for the distant horror of being a killer, he had never seen a corpse before. Not up close. The experience was not pleasant. Blood matted the man's clothing, and dirt had mashed into his face as though he was hauled face-down; some of it was sticking to one staring eye. He had died violently and had not been treated kindly since.

It was Rafa.

"Take that pig home with you, eh?" the officer suggested.

Bringas did not need to feign confusion this time. "What?"

"You came for a pig. Here it is. Have you changed your mind?"

"I don't understand—"

The officer stood up. "You were caught in the company of capitalist spies, wearing the uniform of our militia, carrying an unauthorized military map—and you say you don't understand!" He was shouting now, right in Bringas' face. "Do you take us for fools, gringo?"

A studied insult to a man who was obviously *not* white-skinned, delivered in the heat of a sham rage. "Capitalist spies? What do you mean?"

"Your friend here is dead!" the officer screamed. "Another one will live for trial—no longer than that! He has already identified you as one of them!"

Then Bringas knew it was a bluff. The officer had overplayed his hand. No member of the spy team had survived. None of them had known of him.

"I only came for milk," Bringas said. "I know nothing of this man. Did he come for a pig?"

Some genuine anger showed through now, as the officer realized his ploy had failed. "Take him to Havana—there he will get his comeuppance! I have no patience with this trash."

"But I haven't done anything!" Bringas protested, seeing his chances of escape fleeting.

The view of Rafa's corpse had disturbed him as much

as his own killing, and he almost wanted punishment. It appeared he was going to receive it.

The three hour drive did not bring him to famous Havana, a city he had studied raptly in his youth before discovering the joys of pure linguistics. The driver followed a coastal road with low hills inland, beautiful sand beaches on the seaside, and so much open space visible that Bringas felt another touch of agoraphobia. The truck traveled through the city of Casa Blanca and up to an old Spanish fortress overlooking the Bay of Havana. A drawbridge straddled a dry moat, and beyond that was a moss-covered stone wall girt with turrets and huge gates. How quaint! He would certainly like to explore such an historic relic.

Then he remembered: this was La Cabana, at this date a prison for political prisoners and men awaiting trial. He understood that such inmates received better treatment than did common criminals—for what scant comfort that was worth.

He was brought through the outer and inner gates and into a patio. Doors opened to left and right, but he was taken straight ahead to an office at the far end. There he was peremptorily checked in. His clothing was taken away and he was issued khaki trousers and a short-sleeved army shirt with a large "P" dyed on the back.

He was returned to the patio, then marched through the door originally on his left in the barred wall, and into a much larger patio. He saw machine guns mounted on the roof, one at each corner of the courtyard. To the left was a massive stone wall; to the right a series of barred openings. These were the galeras: eleven great cells numbered from 7 to 17 for the mass of prisoners.

Bruised, sleepless, and hungry, Bringas was thrown into "Galera 11," a chamber about forty meters long containing perhaps fifty three-tiered bunks. It was dank, dark, and stifling, crowded with at least one hundred men.

Hands gripped him, helping him orient. "What is your

name?" a huge night-black giant demanded.

"Juan Bringas."

"I am Noah, the galera chief," the man said. "I will assign you to a top bunk, because you are the newest here."

"Thank you," Bringas said, and followed where the man led. The bunk had a thin mattress infested by any number of crawling insects, and no other covering. All the bunks were the same; he was not being discriminated against.

"Batistiano or Fidelista?" someone called at him.

Bringas recalled that Fulgencio Batista, for whom the month of Fulgen—alias the procession of the dead, alias November—had been named, had been Fidel's predecessor. Obviously the word "Batistiano" derived from that, just as "Fidelista" derived from the present ruler. But how should such terms relate to him? "I don't understand," he said. That was an uncomfortable confession, considering his linguistic studies.

The man in the bunk immediately below him explained "Some back Batista. Some back Fidel. They continue to fight each other, even in jail. What are your own politics?"

Local alliances! Of course! This was within five years of the changeover. The transfer of power had not been amicable, and the citizens were divided by their loyalties. Such terminology would not have survived the holocaust, so had not been relevant to his thesis.

"No politics," he said quickly, realizing that some weight attached to his answer. "I don't want trouble with anyone."

"Good," the man said. "Most of us feel the same. What good are politics without guns?" He paused, but Bringas made no comment. "My name is Manuel Jimenez."

"Juan Bringas."

"What is your crime?" a man in the next bunk inquired. No conversation was private here.

"No crime," he replied, and there was a general and bitter laugh.

"Paredon!" Jimenez cried in the tone of a drillmaster. "He has committed no crime! The wall for him!"

There was a louder laugh, shared by many. Bringas recognized this term: paredon, the wall—the wall men about to be executed stood against. There had to be a backstop for the bullets. . . .

These men were grim, they stank of dirt and sweat and many appeared diseased, but there seemed to be no personal animosity toward the new prisoner. That, at least, was a relief; he had problems enough already.

"What was *your* crime?" he asked Jimenez after a bit. There was nothing to do here except sleep and talk, and he remained too tense to sleep.

"I am a cane farmer. I expressed the opinion that next year's sugar harvest would not be as good as the last."

Bringas started to laugh, then realized that it was no joke. "For an *opinion*? You were arrested only for that?"

"It was a counter-revolutionary opinion. Fidel had said next year's crop would be the best yet. Whoever disagrees with Fidel is counter-revolutionary and therefore fit only for prison or the wall. So here I am."

There had to be more to it than that! But Bringas hesitated to push the matter until he knew more. Probably every man here had motives as devious as his own, and as good reason to conceal the truth. An arsonist would claim that he had merely been hiding in the building when the event occured; a spy would represent himself as an innocent tourist. Bringas himself claimed to have committed no crime—as though multiple murder were not worthy of mention.

"I am incarcerated for being against the Revolution," Jimenez murmured. "But I am *for* revolution. The *democratic* revolution!" And there was a muted cheer.

In fifteen minutes Jimenez seemed like an old friend, and the others were warm acquaintances. There was a camaraderie here that Bringas had not experienced before, and despite the extreme discomfort of his surroundings he found he rather liked it. These men were somehow unified, if only by the prison's cruel walls, and they had a common purpose, if only to escape. There was a closeness in this misery, an intimacy, that almost seemed worth the gloom, the heat, and the fecal stench that mired them all.

As the time of retirement approached, there came a kind of muttering that Bringas could not make out. Jimenez whispered to him, "They are chanting the rosary," as though that sufficed.

One of the prison wardens stomped along outside the galeras. "Be quiet!" he shouted angrily. But the chanting swelled in volume, coming from every cell, and it was even echoed by some of the guards. Furious, the warden left.

"Bad business," Jimenez whispered. "They don't have to do it so loudly as to make the wardens angry. There will be trouble."

It seemed it was a kind of religious ritual, one the authorities disliked and tried to suppress. Thus even the nonreligious inmates were inclined to join in, out of spite. But what could the wardens do?

Bringas climbed onto his bunk and tried to sleep, for the day's events had exhausted him. But the mattress was extremely hard, and the crawling vermin appalled him, and whenever he moved the entire tier of bunks groaned and squeaked so that he was afraid the men below would be annoyed. He was shivering, too, for the heat of the day had become the chill of night, and he had no protection.

Noah approached. "You have no blanket?"

Bringas suppressed the urge to make a sarcastic reply. "No."

"Your family will have to send you sheets, blankets, pillows, medicine."

"I have no family." That was true enough, for this situation.

Noah left. In a moment he returned holding a ratty blanket. "Use this until you can find one of your own."

Bringas, weary and despondent, was overcome by gratitude. Now he could at least be warm! He tried to express his thanks, but Noah had already gone.

Only for a few minutes. "Here is a pillow. Its owner was executed; it is now yours."

Bringas did not know how to respond to this quixotic kindness, so he didn't try. "Why are you here, friend?"

Noah laughed. "For giving a militiawoman a big belly! And I would do it again, gladly!"

Bringas laughed too. "Who wouldn't!" This man, so forbidding in appearance, was at heart a nice guy.

With the comfort, he fell asleep.

He was awakened by a loud boom. A mortar shell! He scrambled for cover—and almost fell off the bed.

The other prisoners laughed. "Where do you come from," Jimenez demanded goodnaturedly, "that you do not know about the nine o'clock cannon shot, el canonazo de las nueve?"

Disgruntled, Bringas retired a second time. On this occasion he did manage to dream of 233: her golden body, her lovely smile, her eager thighs. Was she waiting for him now, four hundred years away, his legally wedded wife?

He woke to the sound of rifle barrels striking the bars of the door and a voice over the loudspeaker shouting "Get up! Get out!" The lights came on blindingly.

"Requisa! Requisa!" the guards called, and the cell door opened. Bringas stumbled out with the other prisoners, to the cold of the great open patio.

It was three in the morning. Dazed, he moved with the others, grouped in fours and fives. "Did something happen?" he asked Jimenez.

"The rosary last night—remember?"

"Silence!" a guard shouted, making a threatening motion with his bayonet. "Get in line! Get in line, gusanos!"

Grumbling, the gusanos—worms—obeyed. Jimenez took Bringas' arm so that they would not be separated. "Do as I do," he whispered. "Then you will not be hurt."

"Strip!" the guards cried.

"What *is* this?" an old man down the line demanded.

Immediately a guard was on him, ripping at his clothing. "You deaf, grandpa? You want a bayonet up your *culo*? Get it *off*!"

Another man started to protest. "Leave him alone, butcher! He's an old man! You can't—" His sentence ended in a scream. Another guard had stabbed him in the rear. Blood dripped down his leg as he danced in agony.

"They are new here, like you," Jimenez whispered. "Requisa always means trouble."

No one else objected. In moments Bringas stood naked with the rest. What hell had he fallen into, that such punishment could be levied solely because prisoners had mumbled some religious cant?

The guards moved along in front, checking the clothing. When they found a watch they either pocketed it or smashed it under a rifle butt. Scraps of hoarded food were hurled into the noisome gutter. Paper money that had been overlooked before was passed up to the supervisor of the operation, but coins were ignored.

One prisoner had a walletful of photographs. "Who?" the guard demanded, thumbing through them.

"My wife—my son," the hapless man mumbled. Bringas felt a pang, visualizing his own wife and son.

"They deserve proper respect," the guard said. He dropped the pictures to the ground, opened his trousers, and urinated on them.

No one protested.

At last they were permitted to don their clothes again, shivering, and to return to their cells. The dank chamber seemed almost pleasant after the patio.

The relief was only momentary. The prisoners had built tables, chairs, and lockers for their own use out of the scraps of material available; these had been smashed. The extra clothing, medicine, games, and food brought in by visiting relatives had been taken or broken. Much of it had been piled in the center of the floor, and the bottles of olive oil some prisoners had saved for private cooking had been broken and poured over the clothing to make it unusable.

It would be some time before the chanting of the rosary got out of hand again.

The dreary hours of a new day passed. Breakfast was one cup of watery cafe con leche—coffee-milk, and one piece of hard dry bread that did little to assuage his hunger. Bringas now had little hope of escaping. If men could be incarcerated like this without trial, what was someone like him to expect? By now they would have discovered that his papers had been forged.

In mid-afternoon the guards called out names. "For trial," Jimenez said, "or interrogation."

One by one the men left the cells, to the murmured consolation of their fellows. One was summoned from Bringas' own galera. "I tried to bomb a naval garrison," he said. "It's the wall for sure. Pray for me."

"Paredon," the others agreed mournfully.

Three hours later he was back, jubilant. He was skipping for joy as the guard shoved him into the cell.

"What happened?" the others asked him. "Did they acquit you? Was it a mistake? Are you to go free?"

"No, I got thirty years!" he cried. "The others went to the wall, but I got thirty years!"

Bringas shook his head. Thirty years imprisonment—and the convict was jumping with glee for the reprieve. He would be an old man by the time he got out—provided he survived these conditions. Wouldn't the wall have been more merciful?

"Mourn not your captive comrades who must dwell—Too strong to strive—Within each steel-bound coffin of a cell, Buried alive . . . ?" Bringas murmured, awed.

Bringas was awakened by a hand shaking him. It was a guard, armed. Why couldn't he simply grab that rifle and . . . but no, these machine guns on the wall, and the guards with grenades—there was no escape that way. All he could accomplish by overcoming this guard would be another requisa and more misery for his fellow prisoners.

"Good luck!" Jimenez whispered as Bringas followed the guard out.

"What is it?" he asked the guard as he blinked in the light of the patio.

The man frowned. "You have been tried by the Revolutionary Tribunal and found guilty of counter-revolutionary activity. La paredon for you!" the man exclaimed with relish.

Already, the dread wall of Death. And he had never been given the chance to speak for himself!

Again he was tempted to use his combat skill to overcome this guard and make a break for it. But where could he run to, in this massive fortress? Better to die with dignity.

He was taken through the patio, past the office, and on through the other door he had seen on entering the prison. This was Galera 22, for rebel military prisoners. At the far end of this chamber was another door: the entrance to the nefarious capillas, punishment cells, without illumination, stinking of human ordure. If there were people in those awful cells, they were very quiet, for he heard nothing as he passed. And finally out into what seemed to be a dry moat, where they turned left.

He realized that he was actually outside the prison—but there was still no escape. He was manacled with iron handcuffs and brought to stand against the fortress wall. The huge old gray stone blocks must have dated from the original Spanish construction, but here they were pockmarked with bullet holes and stained with dried blood. This was the paredon, without doubt.

Six men appeared with what he now knew were FAL Belgian automatic rifles, and the officer in charge carried a .45 pistol. "Any last words?" the officer inquired grimly.

Bringas tried to quell the tumultuous beating of his heart, to make some reasoned protest, but his mouth was too dry.

How could it end so suddenly?

The officer shrugged indifferently. "Preparen!" he said, and the six rifles came up.

Bringas' courage collapsed. They were doing it! and yet—he *was* a murderer; he had no right to protest.

"Apunten!" Aim. His life was nothing to these men— nothing but an inconvenience. The local government could know nothing about his real mission, or comprehend that he had actually helped Fidel by preserving the emplaced missiles from premature discovery. His sentence was based on suspicion and ignorance—but he was about to be executed offhand. Not even a blindfold—

"Fuego!" His racing thoughts made the series of commands seem slow, and the firing of the guns seemed to take forever, yet there was no actual delay.

"233!" he cried as the rifles flashed in the dark and the blast of sound struck him, seeing her face in that last moment. His whole body seemed to let go at once.

He swayed there, feeling numb but without pain. Was he dead already?

There was a raucous burst of laughter.

Bringas opened his eyes, only now discovering that he had shut them tightly at the gunflash. The firing squad was chuckling as it filed away.

They had used blanks: powder without lead.

"Next time real bullets," the officer said jovially. "Vamos que te orinaste!"

Now Bringas felt the wetness of his prison trousers. Blood? No; he had lost control of his bladder when the blanks exploded, but had not felt it until the officer's ridicule brought it to his attention. Dying with dignity? What a sorry coward he had proved to be!

Gradually, as he walked back to the cell beside the chuckling guard, his fear and shame turned to anger. They had played with him, making him ludicrous in his own eyes. But in some manner they had also absolved him of his guilt, for he had stood ready to die for the murders he had committed and had not shrunk from that reckoning.

Now, emotionally, he was a free agent.

Not that it made any practical difference.

Jimenez understood. "I should have warned you," he said. "They say they do not torture prisoners, but—"

"I've got to get out of here," Bringas muttered. "Somehow."

"Maybe your sentence will be light," Jimenez said without conviction. "Five years—maybe even three, if you promise to betray all your friends."

"I can't stand even five *days*!"

Jimenez shook his head. "Where would you hide, if you escaped? The militia are everywhere."

"Not where I'm going!" But he feared he had said too much. He might indeed get a light sentence—provided they never realized his origin.

Fortunately Jimenez did not push the matter. "Cheer up! While you were gone they took a group to the Isle of Pinos. Our bottom bunk is vacant, so I'll take that and you can take mine."

Apparently that was a kind of privilege. The two of them shifted down, and later in the day Noah assigned a new prisoner to the top deck. It was Bringas' turn to educate the confused stranger.

At least there was no requisa next morning. Breakfast was at eight, and when the cell gates were opened by the guards Bringas guided the new man to the patio.

"But when do we eat?" the man whispered, looking at the meager fare. Bringas just shrugged like an old timer; the lessons of prison existence were harsh. This was all the food they would receive.

Then they returned to Galera 11 where they were locked in. The guards came to make their daily headcount as each prisoner stood in front of his bunk.

The conteo was correct; nobody was missing. After that they were permitted to return to the patio or to visit the other galeras.

The new man's family brought him blankets and extra food. Grateful for Bringas' help, he shared the latter. Bringas felt guilty, but hunger compelled him to accept. It had taken him only a day to get set in the routine, but it might be years before he was released from it.

There was a Coca-Cola vending machine in the patio. Bringas did not at first know what it was, but Jimenez soon showed him how to insert the medio, the five-peso piece, into the slot to conjure forth a cold bottle of the sweet liquid. The prisoners were allowed to keep small change, and the machine had a steady clientele.

Bringas did not like the drink, for it fizzled unpleasantly against his teeth and he suspected it of having narcotic properties. Jimenez prodded him to take bottle after bottle. "Believe me, Juan—you will acquire the taste!" he said. There was meaning of some kind there, so Bringas went along.

Two days after the joke execution, a truck came to service the machine. The driver opened the front of the gaudy device to reveal the innards and loaded the huge bee-hive mechanism with full bottles.

There was a distraction farther down the patio. A fight had broken out between the political factions: Batistianos against Fidelistas. There had been skirmishes and bad feeling before, for the factions never forgot their basic loyalties; but this one was almost a pitched battle.

The guards did not interfere at once; they were of course all Fidelistas themselves and were rooting for their side. They had no real sympathy for the inmate Fidelistas, since the prisoners had been stupid or unlucky enough to run afoul of the administration, but they certainly weren't sympathetic to the more numerous Batistianos.

Bringas was ready to watch the action. Prison life was, more than anything else, tedious, and this broke the monotony. But Jimenez pulled him aside. "I bribed the leaders to stage it now," he whispered. "Here." He gestured quickly to the truck. "Slowly."

Bewildered, Bringas followed. They came to the machine, reaching into their pockets for coins. The driver was bending over to pick up a crate of empty bottles.

Suddenly Jimenez threw himself down beside the truck and rolled under it. Bringas thought the man had stumbled—then realized the truth. He dove after his friend.

Jimenez had already hauled himself up under the vehicle, jamming his feet over the rear axle housing and hugging his shoulders against the chassis. Bringas scrambled to the other side and imitated the position as well as he could.

The underside of the truck was filthy. Layers of dust and grit coated layers of old grease and oil. Bringas had to grab three times before he found a hold that sufficed, and then it hurt his hands. He rammed his legs as far over the axle as he could, trying to make a counterweight for his sagging middle. How long could he hold this position?

The answer was elementary. He could hold it just as long as his life and freedom were worth more than his comfort.

The truck started. Exhaust fumes washed by. "Dìs mì!" he swore under his breath in the fashion of the locals. The exhaust pipe passed along his side, and it had corroded. Small fierce jets of hot vapor struck his body, and the smell was awful. But it was the odorless part he feared: the carbon monoxide pollution that these quaint internal-combustion motors discharged. Would he have any oxygen left to breathe?

The truck moved, and a blessed draught of fresh air bathed him. What a relief!

But the motion made his handgrip even more treacherous. His body seemed to weigh three hundred pounds, and then as many kilos; his hands skidded along the slimy metal. Yet if he let go—

The truck bumped to a stop. The driver spoke to someone, but Bringas couldn't concentrate on that when his body seemed to be falling apart. There must be an easier way to break out of jail!

Then another grueling drive, this time over bricks. It was as though the small bones of his hands were being pried from their sockets one by one, and the tendons of his arms pulled from their moorings. Another stop. Another exchange of words.

Get on with it! he wanted to scream, feeling his body sagging, his muscles giving way to fatigue.

The truck accelerated once more, then ground around a corner. Bringas' torso swung heavily, almost ripping loose from its numb connections.

"Now!" Jimenez cried, as from a distance. "Watch the wheels!"

Bringas saw the body drop. Without thinking he let go— or tried to. His torso sagged, his feet dropped—but his hands refused to unwind. He bumped against the moving road—and finally dragged loose, the agony stretching from sore shoulders to rigid fingers. The truck passed over, the rear wheel mashing the pavement inches from his face and momentarily blinding him with its spray of sand.

Bruised and half-conscious, he lay in the bright street, lacking the ambition to move. But Jimenez wouldn't let him be. "We're not safe yet!" the man cried. "Get up! Get up!" He hauled Bringas up.

"You're worse than the requisa!" But he knew Jimenez was right. Bringas staggered to his feet, leaning heavily on the smaller man. Dizzily, he let Jimenez take him into an alley, wipe his face and hands, and check his torn clothing.

"We must change out of these prison uniforms," Jimenez said. "I know a man who will dye them another color—but it is risky for him. Can your friends help now?"

The man thought Bringas had local connections! No wonder he had been so helpful! "No—I know no one in Havana—"

Jimenez's eyes lighted. "But elsewhere—perhaps a way to escape Cuba?"

How could he explain. "Yes. But it is difficult."

"All life is difficult, amigo. We have to get away from here." Jimenez led the way down a small country road, keeping alert to avoid both cars and pedestrians.

Before long they came to Guanabacoa, opposite Havana. "You wait here," Jimenez said. "Hide behind a tree if anyone comes. I think I can reach a telephone."

Bringas waited, glad of the chance to recover from his exertions. He was not even worried about Jimenez; the man would not betray him so long as he thought Bringas had a way to get out of Cuba.

Jimenez came back smiling. "You told me you knew no one in Havana! You forgot to count the women, eh?"

Bringas kept his expression neutral. He had never been here before, and had not even existed in this world. His name had been adopted from the ravings of an epileptic cultist four to five centuries in this world's future. If Jimenez were trying to bluff information out of him—well, let the man hope! "She must have confused the name."

"She did not sound confused to me, Juan. She described you very well. Adelita is eager to help."

"Manuel, I tell you I don't know anyone here. Could she be a— a government agent? Sent to track us down?"

Jimenez was thoughtful. "Possibly. G-2 has agents everywhere, and they are clever. But my friend Luisa speaks for her, and Luisa would never knowingly betray me." He shrugged. "But we'll soon know. She is bringing new clothes here for us within the hour."

"This girl is? She's risking her life for two convicts because of a phone call!"

Jimenez laughed briefly. "I did not talk to the girl. I talked to Luisa, who checked with the others to verify your identity, in case you were a known spy. And this Adelita told Luisa she knew you, and Luisa told me, and we compared notes, and if that girl does *not* know you, amigo, she has a remarkably accurate imagination! Unless she's an Espiritismo adept and can see—" He paused as

Bringas choked, taking the reaction as a kind of admission. "Then Luisa told me to go shoot myself, I sounded counter-revolutionary, and she was calling the police."

Bringas stiffened. "The police are coming?"

"No. That is merely Luisa's way to discourage the G-2. They suspect her, and sometimes try to trap her. She will send the girl who knows you here with the merchandise—if the way is clear." He leaned toward Bringas seriously. "I hope you are not G-2 yourself, for then I should have to kill you. Good people could die for what I have told you. . . ."

"I'm not G-2!" He wasn't certain what G-2 was, but the sudden glimpse of Jimenez's capabilities was alarming. The man meant what he said: he was prepared to kill to protect his friends. "But I'm not whoever this girl thinks I am, either! I don't like this."

And particularly he did not trust his new friend's evident familiarity with anti-government interests. Jimenez had claimed to be a farmer who had merely criticized a potential sugar crop! He acted more like a professional saboteur.

"You can tell me now, Juan. Are you CIA?"

More mysterious letters! Bringas merely looked at him as if Jimenez were stupid. Let him make of that what he would!

They waited silently. Bringas had no choice for the moment; he would only get into trouble trying to strike out on his own now. Obviously the girl was lying—but that did not necessarily make her an enemy. If she were willing to help, whatever her motives—well, give him a day to reach the time phaser, and her motives would become irrelevant.

But he was unprepared for the reality. Adelita was a Latin beauty! She was of medium height with very white, creamy skin and sensuous red lips and dark black eyes. Her chest was deep, her bosom large, her waist so small he wanted to measure it with his two hands, and her thighs heavy. Her blue-black hair traveled down to the small of her back.

She gave a little cry of recognition, shoved the package at Jimenez, came to Bringas and embraced him with a warmth that was little short of obscene. 233 herself could hardly have been more exciting! "Juan, Juan, you came back!" she murmured, catching his head and drawing it down for a thorough kiss. His hands fell of their own volition to her rear, and he felt her large soft buttocks. "They told me you had drowned a year ago, but I never believed it!" Her hair smelled of camelias.

"Yes. . . ." he murmured as her breast flexed against him. What could he do but play the game this intense and beautiful stranger demanded? It was certainly better than prison!

Jimenez nodded knowingly as he tore open the package. "You were smart to keep your secret! I only wish my acquaintances were as rare as yours!"

Adelita disengaged reluctantly and began organizing. "Change into these shirts quickly. We'll take a taxi to Luisa's—she can hide you for a day, no more. It's bad right now; the militia are savage, and the G-2—" She rolled her eyes expressively.

Bringas cooperated, bemused by her certainty. Her show of recognition had no flaw; he almost believed in it himself.

The taxi came. He didn't trust himself to look too much at the woman, so he concentrated on the scenery. He had perused maps of ancient Havana many times, even after specializing in linguistic studies, for it was Cuba's most important city and the heart of the island's living culture. It was a wonderful experience to see it come to life like this!

From Guanabacoa they went south and west, circling the Bay. As the water came into sight on the right he saw on the shore big oil tanks with a tanker moored nearby. This was the oil refinery, and the ship would be Russian; part of what his mission was about was the presence of Russian equipment and arms here in the political sphere of hostile America.

The taxi took a small jog, detouring to avoid congested traffic ahead. They passed a park with a large statue of a woman dominating it. "La Virgen del Camino," Adelita murmured, as though remembering something intimate. The Virgin of the Highway.

Then back to the Via Blanca, the main highway, and on up around the curve of the Bay of Havana on the Malecon. There were ships in harbors to the right, and the great city of Havana on the left. As they circled north he saw the narrow inlet of the Bay, and across it La Cabana; the prison-fortress he had so recently escaped. It was a handsome structure: this vantage offered no hint of the horrors within.

On the left the buildings grew tall and handsome, the parks more frequent. This was classic twentieth century pre-holocaust architecture. He knew that the Latin American nations had prided themselves on elaborate capital cities, but hadn't realized how impressive such design was in its realization. There was probably more construction and a larger population here in this one city than in all of his twenty-fifth century world!

There was Castillo de la Fuerza, a naval fortress; there was the statue of Maximo Gomez on his horse—Maximo had become a month in Fidelia, February, the great ripening!—in a circular area where the tunnel under the Bay started, with the many elegant buildings rising beyond. Then on westward, with the beautiful clean blue waters of the Atlantic Ocean to the right, more and more buildings to the left. There were so many he knew he could recognize, if only he had a good map with him and time to orient himself; but the taxi moved on through the thick traffic heedless of his sensitivities. What a tour!

They slowed as they rounded the tall monument of General Maceo, a black man who was one of Cuba's liberators, another month on the later calendar. They passed a tower and cut away from the sea at last, into one of the city's teeming streets. Bringas hardly paid attention; he was dazed by the beauty and power of this open metropolis, that existed before radiation had made the surface of most of the world untenable for human life.

The taxi stopped. They were beside a three-story yellow building: Luisa's? Adelita paid the taxi driver and guided Bringas into the house.

Inside the front door was a parlor with two sofas, deep chairs, and dark red curtains. This seemed elaborate for a private residence; who was this Luisa? Then through a small patio and up a flight of stairs to a large room. Inside was a huge double bed, a chair, several mirrors on the wall and ceiling, a small blue light, a washbasin . . . and several religious works of art. There was a portrait of Jesus Christ with a red heart in his hands, and on another wall a big crucifix which the mirrors multiplied endlessly. Luisa must be connected with the Catholic Church.

"Luisa is busy now," Adelita said. "Tomorrow—"

The men needed no urging. It had been a bruising, busy day. They fell upon the lush bed and slept.

In the morning Bringas learned the nature of this fine residence. It was a casa de putas, a bayu—a house of prostitution. "The girls are all against Fidel," Jimenez confided with a knowing wink. "He has been very bad for business."

Bringas was incredulous. He had understood that the Christian religion of the past had never favored nonprocreative sexuality. "But the religious pictures—"

"Of course they are deeply religious!" Jimenez said, as though that were the natural order—which apparently it was. "They—"

Adelita Suarez entered with a private breakfast of cafe con leche, white Cuban bread with butter, a glass of orange juice, and some yellow cheese. All of this reminded Bringas unpleasantly of his recent prison fare and prior traveling staples—but this food was of much finer quality, more plentiful, and served by extremely attractive hands. "We would serve you better," she said apologetically, "but times have changed, as you know."

"Oh no, it's very nice," Bringas protested, looking at her figure rather than the food. She smiled.

Jimenez finished his meal quickly, expressed due appreciation, and absented himself. "Little girl I know here . . ." he explained. What else—in a place like this?

Bringas caught a glimpse of the "little girl" before the door closed. She was short, with a good figure though a little bit fat, long dyed blonde hair, big eyes, slight buck teeth, but an expressive picaresque face suggesting good breeding. She was also nearing forty years of age. "That's his dream girl?" Bringas inquired, surprised.

Adelita looked at him quizzically. "Don't you remember Luisa?"

Luisa! He had almost insulted his hostess! "I just didn't know he was that intimate with her," he said lamely.

Immediately Adelita leaned over to speak confidentially. "Your friend—G-2?"

G-2 again! Bringas shrugged, not knowing how to answer. Apparently G-2 was bad and CIA good—if only he knew what they were!

"Luisa says he had come here for two years, before he was arrested. She likes him, but she is not *sure*. He could have turned us in long ago, but the G-2 doesn't work that way. These days—"

"Oh, I don't think he's a government spy," Bringas said, despite his private doubts. "He helped me escape from La Cabana."

"Yes—you are a marked man. Could he have been planted there to befriend you, to learn your secrets?"

Bringas was shaken. What kind of labyrinth was he navigating? Who was really his friend, who his enemy—and why should he rate either friends or enemies here?

"I don't see why," he said, regretting the lie. "I'm just a man who came to buy some milk at the wrong time."

"You were out of prison, then? You look so much better—"

"I only went to prison a few days ago," he said. Then, seeing that this dismayed her for some reason, he hedged. "What happened before was—complicated."

She spoke with surprising intensity. "Juan—Juan—why do you still pretend not to know me?"

She was not being bluffed—not at all. Bringas looked at her carefully. This morning she wore a low-cut dress exposing the upper surfaces of her generous breasts, the material square cut into the shoulders, leaving half her arms covered. The outfit was tightly cinched at the waist, exaggerating her remarkable proportions, and went on down in ruffles to the middle of her calf. The dark blue velvet served as the foundation for the black of her hair, that flowed from a center part to the sides of her head and across her shoulders in waves. Hardly the type of costume he was accustomed to, but it would be easy enough to acquire a taste for it!

Around her neck hung a heavy gold chain with a large medal—a gold disk imprinted with the portrait of a woman and a boat. In fact, he realized with excitement, this was una medalla de la Caridad—a representation of three fishermen of different races in a rowboat, caught in a storm. They prayed to Caridad, the patron saint of Cuba before the holocaust, and were saved by her. He had seen such medals in the museum, relics of the time when the saints had been separate from Espiritismo, but never like this! So women actually wore these precious artifacts as decoration.

But she wore much more than that. Heavy gold bracelets embraced her arms, and one had gold coins all around it— 20-peso pieces with Jose Marti—Marti of the month of January—on one side. On one finger was a ring with a small diamond; on both ears were earrings set with red rubies. This woman was worth a small fortune as she stood, exclusive of her figure!

She had asked him a direct question, and there was only so much time he could legitimately expend contemplating her wealths of jewelry and anatomy. She seemed to be sincere—and though he could hardly claim to know her, he strongly suspected that it would be dangerous to deny her acquaintance too abruptly.

Hell had no fury . . .

"I'm in a difficult situation. I'm not permitted to explain—to anyone. Any possible friend of mine—you know, the G-2. I tried to tell Jimenez that I knew no one in Havana—"

"But you know you can trust *me*!" she exclaimed fervently. Her eyes were wet.

"Of course. But I can't speak for the consequences of my actions. Those closest to me will be hurt most if I am caught, especially if they have any information at all, and I can't allow—surely you understand."

She sighed beautifully. God, that cleavage! He loved his wife, but—!

"Juan, it must be true, for I have never seen you like this. It is as though you have never seen me before, as though I never touched your manhood. You are tight, guarded, strange. You look younger, you seem older. . . ." She studied him a moment more, then straightened her shoulders. "Very well, I must help you all I can, even though being a stranger to you is like having a knife stuck in my heart."

"Thank you," he said, immensely relieved. The last thing he wanted to do was quarrel with such a beautiful woman, apart from the myriad other awkwardnesses of his situation.

She stood up and took his hands in hers. "But promise me this: when this thing is done, come back for me! Let it be as it was before, but without the MRR."

"I will," he said, feeling even more guilty for the lie. MRR?

"I love you. I shall not say it again."

He nodded.

"You must leave here this afternoon," she said, suddenly businesslike. "I will have a trusted taxi come when Superman is here—that way no one will suspect. Will Jimenez go with you?"

How far could he trust her? Could Jimenez be an agent of some sort? Possibly even another time traveler, sent to alter the mission in some devious way? "He wants to—and I do owe him a favor for helping me escape prison—but it would be better for me to go alone."

She smiled understandingly. "We will distract him when you go. We know how."

I'll bet! he thought, almost jealous. "Thanks."

She remained with him a while longer, obviously wanting to be kissed—or more—but he knew better than to wander that route. He was, after all, a married man. And he would soon be returning to 233.

Superman was a coffee-colored mulatto about forty years old, of slim build, and barely over five feet tall. There was a crowd of spectators to see him, many of them paying twenty pesos—or the same in American dollars—admittance to his show. Neither Bringas nor Jimenez had to pay, however, being guests of the house, and native Cubans were charged only half the tourist rate.

Bringas looked about the room. He saw European Czechs and Russians standing beside Latin Americans from Chile, Uruguay, and Mexico, who were in turn beside Canadians from North America. Some of these visitors could speak no Spanish, but all were eager for a glimpse of the showman. What was Superman's secret?

There was a hush as the stage lighted. A lovely, slim, fair-skinned childlike girl came out, swirling her short red hair about. She wore an elegant gauzelike gown that hardly concealed her more intimate femininity.

Bringas smiled. Now he understood: this was to be a public sexual demonstration, similar to those of his own time!

A testimonial to the joys of procreation. But why should people actually pay to witness such an ordinary act?

Then a black-haired mulatto appeared, throwing off her clothing to reveal a statuesque torso with extremely heavy buttocks. This was more like it!

Now he remembered: at this point in history, people tended to be secretive about the natural functions. Thus procreation possessed the petty allure of the forbidden, and there were even laws in many regions restricting it to hidden locales. Apparently men were obliged to pay far more to *watch* than to *do*, ludicrous as that was.

Bringas stiffened. *The girls were—to each other—*

Perversion! It was like a rifle barrel smashed across the face—this abrupt obscenity inserted into the fertility ritual! An abomination, to pretend that one woman could impregnate another, or even stimulate her to—

He had to look away, lest he betray his horror. Then he noted the reactions of the other spectators. The watching men were avid. Their mouths were open and some were making sucking motions similar to those of the redhead on the stage. Even the females in the audience were staring, their hips making motions similar to those of the nude mulatto.

But of course this was an act! It was intended to shock, to prepare people for the genuine procreation to come. With that realization Bringas was able to relax somewhat.

Then Superman entered in style, resplendent in a gaudy, gold lamé bathrobe. The two girls came to attention as if he were a deity, rapt awe on their pretty faces. He flung open the robe and stood there in his astonishing frontal nudity.

Magnificent he was! His masculine member was already erect: about nine inches long and thick in proportion. It seemed even larger because of the diminutive stature of the rest of him.

The mulatto went to him, obviously much more interested in a real man than in a pretend-man. That had been a very neat introduction; it had certainly brought a response from Bringas! He was quite ready to witness the procreative effort of the supermember.

"Very soon now."

Bringas jumped. Adelita had glided up beside him, to inform him that the taxi was almost ready.

Superman was fondling the mulatto. But now the other girl, making a show of jealousy, kneeled down and applied her mouth to his—

Perversion!

But this time Bringas controlled his reaction. "How long does this go on?" he asked Adelita with affected nonchalance.

"It's his regular show—half an hour, two ejaculations," she replied dryly. "He's put it on several hundred times already, and he still seems to be in good form."

Superman made a short exclamation of urgency. The redhead jerked her head back. Bringas himself grunted as he saw what followed. The sheer waste of potency—

Once more he covered by studying the audience. This was scarcely reassuring. Many of those present were obviously men of position in the world, yet they were entirely committed to the atrocity on stage. They were sweating, their eyes gleamed lustfully, their hands rubbed their fronts, they grimaced. Some were wet already.

Adelita followed his gaze and chuckled. "Disgusting, isn't it?" she murmured tolerantly.

"Yes. . . ."

Incredibly, Superman's gross member had not subsided. Now the man decided he wanted the redhead more directly. But she was afraid of him, of the awesome size of him, and retreated. The mulatto, seeing her chance for revenge, took hold of the other girl and wrestled her down for Superman's access.

"He must sleep twenty-three hours at a stretch, recovering!" Bringas muttered.

"Hardly," Adelita said. "After the show he will go home with some lucky couple for a mere fifty pesos. He gives good value for the money, too, I understand."

Bringas shook his head, bemused. The shocks were losing their impact from repetition, as the killing had a few days ago. "Is he married?"

She laughed. "Him? He hates women! He only uses them in the show to work up the spectators; he never really enjoys the act with them. He goes home to his boyfriend, the only one who can give him real pleasure."

Numb, Bringas could not do anything but look back at the stage. But that was no help. The mulatto was sitting on the other girl's head, holding her down, while Superman drove his monster into—

Perversion!

"You mean Superman is—?" he heard himself ask.

"As a two-peso bill." Mercifully, then, she tugged at his arm to lead him out. It was time for the taxi.

If sex was like this in Cuba, no wonder its public performance was restricted! He had never imagined anything so completely grotesque. No effort at all to impregnate—

"This man will take you anywhere you wish, no questions," she said, indicating the waiting car. "And he will never tell a thing to any other person, not even me. Only—"

Bringas jerked himself out of his morbid reflections. Adelita had been talking matter-of-factly, as though this were a routine transaction, but when she paused he saw the tears beading her eyes, and he became aware of the tremendous tension within her. She was an armed grenade, a tightly restricted package of phosphorous, and he feared the explosion that was coming. Surely she did love him, nonsensical as it seemed—and he would find it difficult to get away if he did not make the break promptly.

"Hasta el proximo"—until next time—he whispered, and climbed into the vehicle. "East," he told the driver, avoiding the girl's strained, almost haggard gaze.

The taxi moved out.

He could not explain why, but Juan Bringas felt like a colossal heel.

PART
THREE

P AL'IMP-SEST, n. 1. A parchment or other writing material written upon twice, the original writing having been erased, wholly or in part, to make room for the second.

AD'UM-BRA'TION, n. 1. A slight sketch or outline. 2. A foreshadowing; obscuration; shadow.

(FUNK & WAGNALLS *New Standard Dictionary of the English Language*, 1913 edition.)

Call it a palimpsest: the seeming parchment on which reality is recorded and re-recorded.

Call it an adumbration: all history from the middle of the twentieth century through the following millennium. Real though it may have seemed to the participants, it is only the initial sketch for the complete rendering.

For convenience in identifying a situation that cannot be accurately rendered in language, the initial reality shall be addressed as "Text A" and the revised reality as "Text B." Certain significant samplings:

TEXT A, 1962—The Union of Soviet Socialist Republics emplaces offensive missiles in Cuba. Number and range are sufficient to cover all potential targets within the United States of America and Central America. Shortly before these become operational the United States confirms their presence, blockades the island, and prepares to invade. The Soviet Union withdraws the missiles and the crisis eases.

TEXT B, 1962—The Union of Soviet Socialist Republics emplaces offensive missiles in Cuba. Number and range are sufficient to cover all potential targets within the United States of America and Central America. Although there is suspicion in September, the missiles are operational by October before the United States confirms their presence. The matter is suppressed in the news media of both political spheres. The Soviet Union declares the city of Berlin, Germany to be an integral part of East Germany, and advances troops into the former American, British, and French sectors. The United States issues a strong protest, but takes no other action.

TEXT A, 1963—United States President John F. Kennedy is assassinated while touring the country. He is succeeded by Lyndon B. Johnson.

TEXT B, 1963—Under pressure from Moscow, Finland agrees to join the Soviet Union.

TEXT A, 1965—President Johnson sends 50,000 American troops into the southeast Asian nation of Vietnam to defend it from Russian and Chinese sponsored insurgents.

TEXT B, 1965—The former French colony, Vietnam, becomes a repressive Communist state. President Kennedy is severely criticized by conservatives for his inaction in the face of Communist colonization.

TEXT A, 1967—Israel, in Asia Minor, devastates its aggressive Arab neighbors in six days and occupies the territory extending to the Jordan River and the Gulf of Suez.

TEXT B, 1967—Israel, in Asia Minor, is initially victorious over Arab forces, but after two days the Soviet Union intervenes with troops, tanks, and planes, effecting a temporary stalemate. The United States is instrumental in establishing the "July compromise." Soviet presence is limited to existing degree, Israel to withdraw to its original borders and pay reparations to Egypt and Jordan.

TEXT A, 1967—Che Guevara, Argentine revolutionary of Cuba, is killed in Bolivia.

TEXT B, 1967—Che Guevara, Argentine revolutionary of Cuba, makes his triumphal entry into La Paz, Bolivia, and proclaims the first Andean Liberated Republic.

TEXT A, 1968—Richard M. Nixon is elected President of the United States over Hubert H. Humphrey. Lyndon Johnson's policies are continued.

TEXT B, 1968—Nelson Rockefeller is elected President of the United States over Robert Kennedy. John F. Kennedy's policies are continued.

TEXT A, 1970—Salvador Allende, an avowed Marxist, is elected President of Chile.

TEXT B, 1970—Soviet spy satellites discover an extensive battery of nuclear warheads placed throughout Turkey by the United States, capable of first strike capability over two-thirds of the eastern Soviet republics.

TEXT A, 1975—A massive communist offensive overthrows the Saigon regime in South Vietnam, following the withdrawal of American troops.

TEXT B, 1975—American and Soviet negotiators trade information about weaponry as an assurance against either of them launching a pre-emptive nuclear strike.

TEXT A, 1980—Ronald Reagan is elected president of the United States as a response to what many voters see as appeasement of communist interests. Chinese and Russian troops fire at each other across the Mongolian border; the incident is denied by both governments.

TEXT B, 1980—Great Britain, France, India, South Africa, and Israel agree to scale back their nuclear arsenals. China refuses.

TEXT A, 1985—Little-known party boss Mikhail Gorbachev is elected Secretary General of the Soviet Union's communist party. He begins a reorganization of domestic and international policies.

TEXT B, 1985—The Chinese "gang of four" is reinstalled as the supreme revolutionary council. Their "cleansing" of society—Cultural Revolution Redux—leads to violent anarchy in the streets.

TEXT A, 1989—Chinese students protesting in the capital city of Beijing are massacred by government troops. Crackdowns on internal dissidence begin throughout the country. East Germany announces the demolition of the wall separating East and West Berlin. Communist governments in Hungary, Romania, and Czechoslovakia are replaced by governments espousing "free market" economies and greater civil liberties for the populace.

TEXT B, 1989—Large scale fighting in Jordan breaks out following an attempt to dethrone the ruling family. Egypt, Israel, Saudi Arabia, and Palestine side with the ruling family. Iraq, Iran, Syria, and Libya side with insurrectionists.

TEXT A, 2004—China, not party to Soviet/American understandings and trying to refocus internal dissent, supports Pakistan's ballistic missile strike against nuclear warhead silos in India, and begins mass troop movements throughout Southeast Asia. The United States and Great Britain, unprepared for conventional action here but desperate to halt the threatened Chinese encroachment on

Australia and New Zealand, resort to tactical atomic weaponry. The Chinese respond. The Soviet Union is unable
to remain aloof. World War III.

TEXT B, 2004—China, not party to Soviet/American
understandings, ignores requests by Pakistan for support
in first-strike against growing Indian nuclear missile capacity. Instead, China masses troops as a defensive measure
against the Soviet buildup in Siberia, feeling it threatens
her flank. China uses a converted Soviet submarine to
launch a sea-to-ground nuclear missile—captured from a
Soviet surrogate country—to counterfeit a Soviet attack
on defense installations around Seattle, Washington. The
United States, which does not break the code confirming
the attack plan until two hours before the launch, notifies the
Soviet Union; the latter launches an immediate pre-emptive
strike against China. Fighting spreads throughout the world,
and the United States is unable to remain aloof. World
War III.

TEXT A, 2008—The first post-war survey indicates
that the entire northern hemisphere has been devastated,
with two important exceptions: East-Central Europe and
the Caribbean islands. Because of ocean radioactivity, the
coastlines of all southern hemisphere continents are uninhabitable, but the interiors and highlands remain habitable,
despite low levels of radiation. Internecine national and
tribal warfare following the holocaust decimates much of
the remaining sick and dying populations. The randomness
of nature and political chance leave Czechoslovakia and
Cuba as the only effective governments: the former is
better equipped technologically, the latter more powerful
militarily.

TEXT B, 2008—The first post-war survey indicates that
the northern hemisphere, with the exception of two-thirds
of the state of Florida and most of Poland, Hungary, and
Czechoslovakia, has been devastated. There are two important exceptions: East-Central Europe and the Caribbean

islands. Because of ocean radioactivity, the coastlines of all southern hemisphere continents are uninhabitable, but the interiors and highlands remain habitable, despite low levels of radiation. Internecine national and tribal warfare following the holocaust decimates much of the remaining sick and dying populations. The randomness of nature and political chance leaves the governments in Prague and Havana as the only effective ones on the planet: the former is better equipped technologically, the latter more powerful militarily.

TEXT A, 2014—Czechoslovakia, beset by continuing incursions of local radioactivity and savage nomads from what was once the Soviet Republic of Lithuania, initiates a migration to the Uganda region of Africa at the headwaters of the Nile river bed. It is hoped that this isolated highland will be free from radioactive fallout and easier to defend. A short-wave broadcast of the news is picked up in Havana which, trying to avoid the drift of a radioactive airmass from the north, and hard-pressed by tribes coalescing in the jungle, begins a similar migration to the highlands at the Amazon's source in what was once Bolivia. Hubert Matos negotiates an agreement via short wave radio to share, to the fullest extent possible, resources and knowledge between the two groups.

TEXT B, 2014—Prague, beset by continuing incursions of local radioactivity and savage nomads from what was once the Soviet Republic of Lithuania, initiates a migration to the Uganda region of Africa at the headwaters of the Nile river bed. It is hoped that this isolated highland will be free from radioactive fallout and easier to defend. A short-wave broadcast of the news is picked up in Havana which, trying to avoid the drift of a radioactive airmass from the north, and hard-pressed by tribes coalescing in the jungle, begins a similar migration to the highlands at the Amazon's source in what was once Bolivia. Hubert Matos negotiates an agreement via short wave radio to share, to the fullest extent possible, resources and knowledge between the two groups.

TEXT A, 2035—No human has been born since the holocaust. Desperation construction of subterranean facilities commences, utilizing all resources.

TEXT B, 2035—No human has been born since the holocaust. Desperation construction of subterranean facilities commences, utilizing all resources.

TEXT A, 2043—The Czech/Uganda enclave fails as a severe six-year drought reduces food supplies until workers are unable to continue construction. A sizable contingent of the group's remainder sets out on boats to transfer to a Cuban enclave. 56% survive the journey, soon assimilate, and are instrumental in helping finish the subterranean facilities three years ahead of schedule.

TEXT B, 2043—The Czech/Uganda enclave fails as a severe six-year drought reduces food supplies until workers are unable to continue construction. A sizable contingent of the group's remainder sets out on boats to transfer to a Cuban enclave. 32% survive the journey, soon assimilate, and are instrumental in helping finish the subterranean facilities two and one-half years ahead of schedule.

TEXT A, 2058—The first baby is born in Fidelia due to laboratory intervention in the natural fertility process and to a couple residing four years continuously underground, but it is deformed. The parents are among the youngest in the enclave, having both been born in 2002.

TEXT B, 2058—The fifteenth baby is born naturally in Guevaria, to a couple residing three years continuously underground. It is healthy.

TEXT A, 2095—A tight society is formed about the precious nucleus of two thousand post-holocaust babies. A Caste system is established to ensure the continuation of high-level civilization, with all essential occupations filled competently. But strife between newly integrated linquistic and ethnic factions causes debilitating compromises, such as the formation of Brown and Black Castes and prohibition of inter-Caste marriage.

TEXT B, 2095—The first generation of approximately five thousand babies forms an elite society, all completely protected from environmental contamination. A Caste system is established to ensure the continuation of high-level civilization, with all essential occupations filled competently, but provision is made for a gradual phaseout of its regulations as the enclave becomes better established.

TEXT A, 2200—Phenomenal but disciplined breeding overcomes the liability of deformed births and increases the healthy population to over 8,000.

TEXT B, 2200—Breeding strictures are curtailed when the population reaches 17,000. The mandate on the size of individual Castes is relaxed, and inter-Caste marriage is permitted.

TEXT A, 2400—The population is just over 500,000. Tight controls are maintained in face of rising unrest, notably in connection with the Espiritismo cult. Discussions are begun of exiling criminals following their lobotomy to above-ground labor colonies.

TEXT B, 2400—The homogenous population is just under 800,000. Discussions are begun of the potential for aggressive above-ground development.

"Yes, she went Transparent yesterday," 197 said. "We celebrated the occasion with more of the same." He chuckled, remembering how delightfully his wife had performed.

808 did not react conventionally. He stared. "What is it you are wearing, 97?"

He put a hand to the strap. "This is a knapsack, of course. I used it in Cuba."

"Cuba?"

"It contains the time phaser, so—" 197 paused. What was he doing discussing this with 808 of Spanish Lit?

808 stood up. "I confess to mystification. One moment we are discussing your charming wife's pregnancy, then this—this knapsack appears on your back. It is a clever performance, though its significance escapes me at the moment; now will you tell me how you managed it?"

197 forced a laugh. "I wore it when I entered, 08. I merely concealed it. This is, as I said, an archaic item of costume used in pre-holocaust Cuba and elsewhere. I thought it would interest you, as it does me." *Talk fast, 197!*

"It does, certainly," 808 said politely. "But what is this 'time phaser' you mention?"

"Well, I put on this knapsack and I pretend I can travel back into the period and place of its origin. As though I could merely phase in to a past time, and see what reality lies beyond my linguistic researches. I have succeeded very well with Cuba, for example; I feel that I know it as well as a native might. From its handsome mangrove coastal swamps to its abysmal prisons to its ravishingly lovely women."

"I envy you your morbid imagination," 808 said, smiling. "Perhaps I will fashion myself a knapsack and pay a call on Enrique Jandid Pancila. 'How did you come to write *La Tournce de Dios*?' I shall ask him. And he will say—"

"You have the idea," 197 said. "But I must return to my work. I wouldn't want my son to think of me as a loafer."

808 chuckled at this allusion to the four kilogram baby due to be born eight months hence, and did not take offense at 197's abrupt departure.

Alone in his office—a larger one than he had had in Fidelia—197 sat down heavily. He had phased in to his own time, all right—the calendar showed Huber, 2414, or just after the new year. In Cuba, he reflected, the new year would not come for another month, as it occurred only with the onset of Marti, or the month they called January.

But something was wrong.

He had obviously been here in Guevaria all along, for this was the new reality and his family line was inviolate. In fact he had been talking with 808—he remembered the conversation, beginning with his friend's inquiry about 464's recent Caste change. In Text B "Transparent" meant simply that a woman was pregnant and did not have to work during gestation.

Yet he had been in Cuba, too, until the moment he phased in here, complete with the pack on his back, but retaining modern dress. He was, literally, an amalgam of two selves, with even his clothing merging!

What had happened to the original 197B—himself before his return from the past? Had that man been phased out of existence? No, for he had complete memory of 197B's life experience, superimposed on his own in the palimpsest manner. There was no break in the continuity; nothing had been lost.

But *he* was from Text A; that was the identity he felt, and his memories of it and of Cuba proved that. So did the presence of the knapsack with the phaser. Obviously the phaser was not of this text; its development must have been a fluke in the other reality. But he could not have returned from the past without it; that would have been more than mere paradox! Everything else could phase in neatly, but not these extra memories and the time traveling device.

He had to work this out, for there were nebulous aspects that continued to bother him. He removed the knapsack, wondering what agency had brought it here while leaving behind his Cuban clothing. Natural affinity? The clothing gravitated toward its own framework, while the phaser . . .

He shrugged and locked it in his private closet—he had no such closet in Fidelia—and stepped into the hall. He was skimping on his working day, but he could get away with it in this more liberal world.

He walked along the concourse, finding it newly unfamiliar, for he saw the original text of the palimpsest along with the current one. An adumbration . . . the old city mall had been a hundred feet wide, and now it was larger. There had been scenic murals and artificial vegetation; now there were genuine shrubs and trees. The high vault had been painted sky-blue; now it was transparent, and the real Earth's welkin showed through. Guevaria was beginning to recolonize the surface, for the radiation was down considerably; but no one of procreative age was permitted there yet.

He knew the way, despite the changes, for he had lived in this text too and it was as real as the other. But it remained a unique experience, shifting like this from one reality to another. No other citizen could know this feeling, for only his own identity was inviolate, by the natural laws of paradox.

He perceived the social palimpsest, too, for both systems were engraved in his memory. He visualized the joint organization charts, pinpointing their differences.

1. PURPLE: Executive (administrative, finance, legal) A&B
2. YELLOW: Intellectual (academic, scientific) A&B
3. GREEN: Militia (disciplinary forces, special projects) A&B
4. WHITE: Clerical (office, communications) A&B
5. BLUE: Productive (construction, transport) A&B
6. RED: Health (medical, dietary, psychological) A&B
7. ORANGE: Entertainment (all aspects) A&B
8. BROWN: Pauper (unemployed, incapacitated) A
9. BLACK: Criminal (asocial elements) A&B
10. TRANSPARENT: Casteless (maternity, juvenile) A&B

Actually, Caste Brown had not been eliminated in Text B; it had been shifted from pauper to some of the functions of the overloaded White and Blue Castes. The unemployed had been moved into Black, on the theory that any person who would not or could not work was asocial, a parasito. The legitimately incapacitated, whether by age or injury, had gone to Transparent. Despite this, Black was by far the smallest Caste in Guevaria, for there was no fixed size for any Caste, and so more people were able to obtain amenable employment in the others. White and Blue were larger here, despite their loss of communications and transport, and their services were superior. Materially, Text B was certainly a better world.

It was socially superior, too. Guevaria was a freer society than Fidelia. Miscegenous marriage was permitted, though not encouraged, and religion of any form was accepted without overt or covert suppression. That, as much as the change in Caste Brown, accounted for the greatly diminished potency of Espiritismo here. He had, indeed, wiped out that cult by his mission to Cuba.

Caste itself was almost completely optional. Any number of citizens could select to be of any given Caste, with the job pool and pay of each rank diluted to accommodate them. In fact—and here he paused in amazement, realizing how fundamental this difference was—any person could change Caste at any time merely by putting on a new sash!

197's A-self wrestled with this concept, marveling that civilization did not collapse, while his B-self had never thought to question the system. Didn't it render Caste itself immaterial? Yet the system *did* function, and in practice it was very like the other.

Gradually he comprehended what he had known in discrete portions. First, no substantial imbalance of Castes developed despite the freedom of choice from "dilution." When four people did the job that three could have done, four drew the pay of three. When two did the work of three, they split the pay of three. Thus the understaffed employments became more desirable, and a reasonable balance was achieved as people constantly shifted from oversubscribed to undersubscribed Castes and ranks. This was very like the economic theory of the "invisible hand" regulating markets of pre-holocaust times, and he was surprised how well it worked in practice.

Second, Caste ethics differed. In Fidelia no person could change Caste once he had been settled—not without complex effort. To wear the sash of another Caste, other than Transparent, was Deviation, and unthinkable. In Guevaria, with completely free change, Deviatism did not lie in change of sash, but in failure to conform to the precepts of the selected Caste and rank. A Blue machinist who assumed the position of a Yellow literary researcher, and proved unqualified, was ostracized and usually disciplined.

Here he could don the Green sash, for he could handle many Green jobs. He could not don the Red sash, for he had no medical or hospital training—unless he wished to become a Rank One food processor. Most important, he could marry anyone of any Caste without altering his own status. There had been no such thing as miscegenous marriage for over two centuries—though only very recently had any widespread crossing occurred. His own family line had been unaffected, obviously.

This was essentially the society he had been promised, and he could find no fault in it. It was far more open than the original, and its creature comforts were superior. He had been right when he told 808, back in Text A, that a restrictive physical environment had to lead to a repressive social climate.

So what was disturbing him? 233 was his!

He paused again, feeling an ugly chill. Here was the wrongness that the complexity of the doubled texts had concealed. He brought them together again in his mind, working it out step-by-step, looking for a loophole, for some way to avoid the disaster that menaced.

He had married later in B. The pretty White Two librarian 400464 had joined him only three months ago, and was just now leaving her Caste in favor of maternity. She was a good, loving wife, still with the aura of honeymoon about her, but of course not in the same class with 233.

464 . . . 233.

Here he had married the wrong person!

No. Worse. *The woman he loved did not exist here.*

He had changed the stream of reality, knowing it could not affect him—and had erased the family line of the woman for whom he had done it. No paradox was involved; 233's ancestry was Czech, not Cuban. She had had no protection from *his* changes.

He leaned against the trunk of one of the genuine trees, feeling numb and nauseous. What a price he paid for his folly!

Yet he could not feel the complete loss, ironically, for his Text B-self had not experienced it. 197B had never known Green Three 551233. He had never had a son. He had run down another girl during the magnificent festival, one who had hoped for a different captor, and there had been no follow-up. He had drifted along with occasional liaisons—and some of them had been beautiful!—until social pressure had forced him to marry and start his quota of live births. Population growth was a serious business in both texts.

It was like half a headache. Part of his mind was untroubled; part was mortally wounded. What was he to do now? Go home and sink his listless member into eager 464?

"Mourn not the dead," he thought. He had gotten what he wanted, but had lost his will to endure it. "Mourn not the dead that in the cool earth lie—/Dust unto dust—/The calm, sweet earth that mothers all who die/As all men must. . . ."

No—why mourn her, who had never lived? Mourn himself for being a fool! And if he could not now live with the consequence of his naivete, there was the calm, sweet earth!

Except that 197 was not the mourning type. He hardly

intended to settle for the situation he had discovered. Not when it meant that he couldn't have 233.

The Tens of Fidelia must have known or suspected that something like this would happen—that they had made him an empty promise. But he still had the phaser! He could go back, change it again, stop just prior to the time of his arrest, take his wife and child—

Or could he? They must have thought of that too. They would hardly trust him to settle down quietly. They would have made quite sure he couldn't hurt them.

Why hadn't they made the phaser a one-shot item, so as to leave him stranded in the past? But the answer to that was quickly apparent: stranded, he might have wreaked vengeance on every ancestral line except his own, deliberately restricting the protections of paradox. That would have been a severe threat to them all. So they had let him return to the present. Perhaps, even, paradox had required that return.

Paradox, paradox! What paradox would result if he went back and met himself and told himself not to block that message? If he *didn't* block it, then this entire alternate text would vanish, together with his place in it, so he could not have returned to—

It seemed to be a variant of the self-protecting paradox, but this time it would prevent him from interfering with what he had done in Cuba before. Or would it? He had eliminated Text A; why not Text B? If he had abolished the society that had invented the time phaser by which he—no. The self-protecting paradox would apply doubly to the phaser! It must have been developed here too.

The Tens of Text A had surely anticipated all this, and covered every contingency. Undoubtedly they sent him back to the earliest possible crisis point—the earliest time where his action would not inevitably affect his own line, and therefore be prevented entirely by paradox. Had he gone to a later nexus—say, the period of actual Caste formation—he might have been able to change it all back by making the Cuba trip. As it was, he was prevented by paradox from meeting himself, and he was helpless. They had placed paradox between him and any possible revenge!

He walked on down the mall, torn by impotent fury. The Tens had used him—used his foolish idealism and his love for 233. They had gotten their improved society— or whatever it was they had wanted. He had been only a Deviant in their eyes—a man fit for rehabilitation, the euphemism for lobotomy. A man to dupe into taking the risk and discomfort of historical revolutionary Cuba; a man whose life was a matter of no consequence once his service had been rendered.

Was there any way to strike back at them from Text B? Unlikely, for the Guevarian Tens would know nothing of the matter. It was the Fidelian Tens who were guilty—and they were completely beyond reach.

Yet somehow he *would* reach them! He promised himself that. If it took the rest of his loveless life, he would make them pay.

Meanwhile, he would have to go underground. Or at least conform to the life laid out for him in this text, and give no overt sign of his true intent. The Tens of this world would be as ruthless as those of the other, if they ever suspected what he was.

And they might suspect. Their minds would work in similar fashion, and they probably knew of time travel. They might even be the same people he had met, for they would not voluntarily have eliminated themselves! That meant they could have analyzed history and pinpointed the crucial change; perhaps they recognized his intrusion as that of an outsider. But they wouldn't be certain who was the agent of change, for the two texts surely differed enough to make others besides himself eligible here. Unless he gave himself away.

His Cuban experience had taught him caution and cynicism. He knew what sort of mistakes not to make. He knew what would happen if he were to march up to Complex Purple and ask for advice!

464 would be waiting for him at home. She, at least, was blameless. She had wanted him in the other world, and had obtained him in this one. He had promised her a liaison; now he would have to honor it.

While the loss of 233 tore at his spirit.

The hell with rationalization. He was going back to Cuba now! If the paradox effect existed, let it probe itself. He would be even more of a fool to let himself be bluffed out of the obvious action!

197 returned to his office in Complex Yellow, noting that in this favored world it was not even locked in his absence. He donned the time phaser and reset it for Cuba, Camil/September 1962. He activated it, bracing himself for an awakening in ancient wilderness, for another bout of temporal disorientation while the mosquitoes hovered greedily.

Nothing happened.

He checked the setting and the meters on the instrument. They were in order; it was functioning and retained a full battery of phasing power, having recharged itself in the return trip.

He set it for a century earlier and tried again. Nothing, unsurprisingly; normal paradox would account for that. He set it for a century later. Failure again. Apparently it simply balked at taking him back, now that he had interfered with the past. Paradox had indeed exerted its muscle.

But one thing more. He set it for a similar distance in the future, this location, and activated it again. This time it functioned; he felt the dazzling wrench, the massive disorientation.

He willed himself into some semblance of equilibrium and opened his eyes.

And looked out on chaos.

* * *

There was no office. There was no Complex Yellow. There was no landscape. The text was without form, and it was void.

He felt vertigo—not the dizziness of phasing, but of nullity. He tried to orient himself, but there was no gravity, no substance, no here or there. No air, no light, no vacuum, no dark, no space—*or any absence of these.* Just a melange of suggestion that might conceivably be ordered into the flux of existence. Nothing, until something, suddenly!

A woman, her eyes staring, hair standing out, screaming "DEATH DEATH DEATH DEATH!"

He knocked her down, bent over her as she writhed in a seizure, tore away her tunic to expose her writhing posterior. "I am Superman!" he said calmly, and slid his juggernaut into her tight perversion.

"Being a stranger to you is like having a knife stuck in my heart," she whispered, twisting her back to face him. It was the Saint Caridad, and he was on the medal with her, imprinted in gold, and his elephantine perversion was thrusting toward her heart.

He made a grunt of urgency, there on the stage, and the slack-jawed spectators rubbed their perversion.

It shot out with a shower of bright sparks. She opened her mouth and the sweet smell of burning flesh wafted out. "Seven! Seven! Seven!" she cried and died.

"But I did not mean to kill *you*, Three!" he protested as the phosphorus puddled her beloved gut into amorphous silt. He reversed the phaser and stood gasping, reeling, crying in his office.

He was back in Text B, but the nightmare was back with him. Murder, Perversion—how could he go on as though he were fit for existence?

First—three men with a phosphorus grenade. An accident—readily avoidable, but for his stupidity.

Second—several more men with the second grenade—and *that* had been deliberate.

Third—several more militiamen shot down charging the marabu, exactly as he had premeditated.

Fourth—the American spy team and Rafa, by mortar and bayonet—as he had premeditated.

Fifth—his own wife, 233, for surely one of the men killed in that Cuban slaughter had been her ancestor.

And what had he done in penance for this needless havoc? *He had gone to see Superman and watch Perversion*!

But he had to be *sure*. All the other deaths were less than that of his wife. He could check the ancestral records, trace down exactly which of her—

He clapped his hand to his forehead, feeling a shooting pain. *He was still a fool!* There would *be* no record— *because records were not kept on people who had never existed.*

197/Juan Bringas had no recourse but nightmare.

Four days later 197 paused at the portal of the Complex Yellow main library. He was on his way to do some special research, theoretically in linguistics, actually in symbolic logic. His days had been sufferable; his nights torment. Sometimes the massive guilt of his Cuban mission lifted, a cloud whose precipitation had passed; sometimes it centered on the present, the extinction of the Espiritismos, who had known he was their executioner yet had let him go. Sometimes his chest burned with an emotional phosphorus, until it seemed there must be nothing but an ash where his heart once beat. But guilt was the new reality for him, whether lonely or afire, and he dreaded the empty days as much as the savage nights.

He had come to the library to find some tool with which to analyze his temporal situation, for his only hope was that there was some way to circumvent his prison and undo the mischief he had wrought. He hardly believed the possibility, yet he *had* to believe it. He had to try, and try again, and keep on trying until, somehow . . .

He felt something: an eerie oneness, an intensity of self, a familiarity, a deja-vu. But there was nothing to account for it, unless this were yet another aspect of his guilt.

Nothing in Text B. Suddenly he realized that the contact stemmed from Text A, whose outlines were still apparent whenever he chose to search them out. The streets and structures were plain; the people were mere blurs, in that other reality.

He had thought that Text A existed only theoretically, in his memory and aspiration. That would account for the sharper image of the more stable features, while the people, who never stayed long, blurred much as they would in a time-exposure photograph. But now he realized that those blur-people were actually moving. He was seeing them *now*, not remembering them. And one of them had affected him as it passed through the spot he occupied. A and B coinciding momentarily.

Text A and its people still existed.

233 existed. . . .

His heart was no ash; it was beating so wildly that he feared for its integrity. If Fidelia somehow remained real, why couldn't he return to it?

A new concept of reality burst on his mind: time itself was a stream. Dam it near the source or anywhere along its length, divert its course, and it could find an entirely different channel to the sea—but it was the same river. Remove a cupful from the first flow, pour it into the second, and the river hardly changed.

197 was such a cupful. Poured four hundred and fifty one years upriver, it had dislodged a critical pebble and acted to divert the river slightly, into Channel B. Much of B overlapped A, but it was still a separate course. Then that same cupful had been withdrawn and poured downstream roughly opposite its origin, leaving only the moved pebble behind.

This river's water was not static. It was constantly renewed, and it constantly flowed toward its termination. But a cup dipped out became an entity in itself, independent of the channels or the flow. To a certain extent. The parallel could not be exact, for time was far more than a river; the interactions of reality had to be complex, as consideration of paradox demonstrated. But it explained several things.

The water of Text B only started with his Cuba change. The river could not fill hundreds of years of a virgin channel instantaneously. It had had "time" to flow 450 years while he languished in Cuba's prisons—but had not yet reached the following centuries. Perhaps the rate of recovery was fifty years timeline for every day realtime, so that it had barely caught up to the present in the nine or ten days he had stayed in Cuba. So he had phased into a primeval chaos—before the water of reality had filled that portion of the channel of probability. There was no "future" for him yet, though there would be in a few more days.

Text A, in contrast, had had plenty of time to fill its complete conduit, for it had been flowing for all time, however time was defined. But now its source of water had been largely diverted. Fidelia would lose reality as the remaining water seeped out; the reality level of Text A history was already dwindling. Soon the world of that channel would evaporate, and after it its future, until nothing but empty potential—chaos—remained.

If he intended to cross over, he would have to do it while Fidelia still existed. Even then, he would suffer along with his world. His cup of water would perish with the rest, unless the entire river were diverted *back*.

197 shook his head, dismayed on several levels. Was there no way to recover 233 and *live*?

He put that problem aside as too complex for the moment. He was good at putting problems aside, he thought bitterly; otherwise he should already have turned himself in as a multiple murderer and paid the penalty.

What had called his attention to Text A at this moment? He must have passed through many other-reality figures before; this was the first time he had felt it.

He had no answer for that either. He seemed to be trapped here, experiencing mysteries without finding the solutions. He could only go so far into the future, until it formed; he could not return to the critical nexus of the past because of the paradox barrier. He seemed free, yet he was confined in a more formidable penitentiary than La Cabana!

A few days later it happened again. He entered Complex Red for a routine health check, and in the hall suddenly felt that deja vu, that compelling familiarity, that certainty he had done this before, but not routinely.

This time he looked immediately into Text A. The walls of the Complex were almost identical to those of the other reality in this particular spot, making it easy to concentrate on the blur people.

The presence faded.

But he saw something else. A glow, a man-sized nimbus, as though a weakly illuminated ghost glided along Fidelia's halls. Something he was almost certain was not natural, even allowing for the peculiarities of adumbration.

He dived for it. He passed through the glow without effect, to his surprise and disappointment, and came up to the retreating figure beyond.

197 felt the presence, more strongly than before. He caught his balance and paced the evocative shape. This was the source of that feeling, not the glow—but who was it? 197 picked up no trace of personality; instead his own perception seemed strengthened. He was depressed, for he had no way to know whether 233 was alive or lobotomized; wouldn't it be better after all to accede to the—

He collided with a solid figure in Guevaria.

"Pardon," the man said, though obviously not at fault. He adjusted his Brown sash and went on. 197 did not reply; it took him a moment to remember that Caste Brown was respectable in this text. He, 197, should have apologized.

The familiar Text A figure was gone. Who had it been?

Then he realized. These thoughts—they had not been his own. Not in this text. He had been intent on the figure, searching for its identity—and had found himself mulling over 233's fate. Not whether she existed, but whether she was whole or rehabilitated.

That had been the mind of the other person—*and that person was his Text A self*. No wonder it had been familiar.

He went through the medical ritual without attention, struggling with the sense of wrongness he had about that. Certainly it made sense for him to react to his own presence; he was the only unchanged person. Unchanged in original memory and experience as well as body. Yet—

What was he doing in contemporary Fidelia?

He should not be there, for he had gone into the past and not returned. Not to Text A. He was here in B, obviously. Yet he was there in A, too.

What revisions were needed to his cup-of-water theory?

He searched his dual memory, hoping that it contained some hint of the solution. If he had departed Fidelia, as indeed he had, when could he have reappeared there? Did this vision mean that he would somehow succeed in going back and rerouting the river again, sometime in his personal future? If so, it would be this vision of his successful self in Text A that showed it was possible, prompting him to find the way to accomplish it. Wasn't that another paradox? And why should that successful self be so morose?

The Fidelian memories were vivid—until the moment he had phased away to Cuba. Then the Text A impressions diminished into ghosts, hardly even adumbrations— *but they did exist*, in addition to his strong clear Cuban experience. It was like reading the colorless indentations left on the paper below the one written on, complicated by the overlay of sharp Guevarian memory for the same time. An impossible task, to read those buried thoughts.

No—there was a gap. He had phased into Text B later than the time he had left Text A. By several days. The span he had spent in Cuba. He had apparently phased in at the same age—which made sense when he thought about it. An older 197 was not the same as a younger 197, obviously, and no doubt minor biological paradoxes shaped the merging. At any rate, this left a brief span in Text B in which memories were almost as faint as those of Text A, and did not obscure them so commandingly. Right in the critical period!

What had happened then? Text B was routine—office, 464, office, 464's assumption of the Transparent sash, office, then the merging. He quickly closed that off into a background image. Text A—he was there, a seeming shadow of himself *but there*, not routine, not office research, alone, confined—

He was a prisoner! Food was provided, and the conditions were excellent compared to those of the Cuban prison—but there was no doubt about his status. He was free to visit Complex Yellow for references or Complex Red for physical attention, but he wore the Caste Black sash with a prisoner identification signal attached.

That hardly bespoke success! It was as though he had never—

He traced it back until the Cuba departure—and he was there all along in Fidelia. He saw himself leave—yet his shadow-self remained. What could it mean?

He pored over the evanescent images in his mind. How could he have left yet *not* left? In A1 he had gone to Cuba, and that reality vanished from his second sight. In A2 he had refused to go—so he was a prisoner for his supposed crime of miscegenation and his actual crime of asserting his independence of choice. That was the reality that continued—or at least the one that contained the figure (himself) he could spot from Text B. There might be a million alternates, or there might not; evidently his cross-text vision was a personal thing, and he could see no reality where 197 did not exist. Regardless, both A1 and A2 had to exist, in the same fashion as A and B—divisions of the flow of water, one exhausting the old current, the other swelling with the new.

. . . until the larger change wrought by his Cuban venture deleted the water from both A's. The A1/A2 split was a transient phenomenon, of no lasting moment. Except that it provided him with a temporary connection to the main text, for what that was worth.

His presence *there*, in whatever capacity, helped him not at all *here*—for there he had neither 233 nor freedom of action, unless he agreed to undertake the mission the A Tens wanted—which would merely bring him back to B. Pointless exercise, paradox aside.

Yet it renewed his determination. Already he knew far more than he had before, and perhaps the next revelation. . . .

More days passed, uneventfully. His life with 464 was nothing; he lived through the Guevarian routine with his mind and passion phased out, motions only. He located the place of his Fidelian confinement and made plans to visit the Guevarian equivalent, so that he could merge with himself at greater leisure and see what could be learned. The Tens were not holding him at a normal Caste Black or Caste Green center; this was a private suite. In Guevaria it was occupied by a Blue Ten: a construction foreman, who didn't exist in Fidelia.

How was 197, a mere Yellow Six, to gain access without arousing dangerous suspicion? Simple enough in this free-Caste society. He donned an Orange sash and drove over.

He arrived at the apartment during the normal duty-period for Blues, whose shift differed from those of other Castes in order to avoid clustering of vehicles or peak drain of power. The Ten should be on the job, but in case he was home, he would be treated to a private entertainment: "Just a survey, sir, a trial audience response before we put it on the air. Keep it private for the present, please. I'm going to tell you about Superman. . . ."

Blues were notorious for their fundamental taste in humor. Superman would go over big, particularly here where Perversion was taken less seriously. 197 was almost disappointed to discover the suite empty. It would have been entertaining to be an entertainer!

The presence was there. The rest was serious.

But it was not in himself—his A self—that he found his answer. It was in the afterglow.

He had forgotten the glow, supposing it to be merely an effect of the palimpsest, a function of his doubled presence there, or possibly representing yet another presence in some other alternate text that was too distant or devious to register properly. But this was not the case.

For one thing, it was not visible to his A-self—deliberately. 197A never looked at it or through it, as he would have were it only an optical ghost B observed. It maneuvered to stay behind A's head. And it faded before other Text A people—which implied that it would be visible to them, too. Some independent mind must control it.

It was for 197B's eyes alone. No one else could see from one text into the other; no one else could orient on the presence of 197A this way. Why?

He studied it avidly, anticipating his most important breakthrough. As he concentrated, it came clearer. The shape was spherical, not manlike . . . and within it was a picture.

A woman's face. Blonde, fair complexion, some tint to the cheeks, hazel eyes . . .

233! He hadn't recognized her immediately, because she was strange. This version of her was tired, pale, almost gaunt, when normally she was ruddy and quite pleasantly plump. She had Czech ancestry; he had teased her about that, and about the Indian tilt to her cheekbones. But this picture—it was as though she had been confined in isolation and hopelessness a long time. She was older—by years, perhaps. But indisputably her, and lovely yet.

His pulse raced. This was the object of his drive: his wife, alive and free. Some outside agency knew it; knew he was looking now; had in fact set the image near his A-self where he would be sure to find it. Not the Text A Tens, certainly; they lacked both the technology and the desire to communicate this way. Who, then?

The picture had to be genuine. He knew his wife too well to be fooled by an imitation. He knew how she would age under stress, for he had seen the little signs during tense moments when they feared discovery. An aura verified the legitimacy of this portrait. He knew it was subjective, yet it could not be a present photograph; too little time had passed.

A *future* likeness?

What did that mean?

Was it a promise? That she would be there for him if he returned? Not for imprisoned 197A, but for dynamic 197B?

But he had *not* stopped himself from killing her ancestor with a phosphorus grenade, and paradox prevented—

Unless that conjecture were mistaken. Perhaps her demise had stemmed from more devious aspects. In Text A the missile sites had been disbanded. In Text B they had remained and probably Russian and Czech technicians had serviced them, and one of those might have married a Cuban girl instead of a Czech girl who was 233's great-great-great . . . grandmother. Something like that. And if it were not directly tied in with the *way* he had preserved the missiles, and if paradox did not prevent some other termination of those missiles . . .

He concentrated on the picture, trying to fathom its meaning. He stared at her sensuous lips, her cheekbones, the waves of her hair, the sparkle in her right eye.

That sparkle seemed to brighten as he bore down on it. The light expanded, filling his perception. The rest of the picture faded, dulled by the bright contrast. The eye was everything.

In fact, it was a picture by itself! A golden coin on which was a scroll, an illuminated manuscript, an unwinding text, written in elegant archaic Spanish script. *He could read it!*

It appeared to be a selection from a history text. Fascinated, he read:

"Juan Bringas appeared in Cuba on the twenty-eighth day of January, the holiday of the birth of Jose Marti in the year of Our Lord 1958. He landed at La Esperanza in Pinar del Rio, buried his time phaser near the beach, and spent some weeks in hiding before taking a bus to the city of Havana where he entered the Babba Ran Bar and ordered a Cuba Libre. . . ."

PART
FOUR

PART
FOUR

C uba Libre," Juan Bringas said.

The bartender obliged without a word, mixing native rum with American Coca-Cola. Bringas placed an American dollar bill on the counter, Washington's portrait up. "*There* was a revolutionary. . . ." he murmured as if to himself. Then he looked up. "Give me Cuban change."

The man brought Cuban coins.

Bringas counted these carefully: two quarters, a medio, two two-cent pieces and a penny. Sixty cents change. He frowned. "Ramon told me to pick up some of the twenty-cent pieces. He says they don't have them in the U.S. of A."

The man exchanged the quarters for two pesetas and a real. The pesetas had a five pointed star on one side and the Cuban shield on the other, and were silver. "Ramon the atheist?" the bartender inquired as though the matter were unimportant.

"Does an atheist pray to the shrine of Santa Barbara?"

The bartender glanced toward the statue of the saint above the bar and shook his head before turning away. Had he responded to the key message, the bonafides described by the illuminated Spanish manuscript?

Bringas finished his drink, feeling disoriented already though he knew the alcoholic content could not have affected him yet, and walked slowly to the shrine of the Virgin. So far he had had to take the instructions of the mysterious scroll on faith, phasing in when and where directed, biding a month incognito in far western Cuba, then abruptly coming to Havana without even pausing to admire the sights. That the particular setting used had allowed him to return to the past was immensely encouraging; apparently at least one chink lay in the shields of paradox. But after a month, he was well ready for more positive evidence that the scroll knew whereof it spoke!

It had told him to become a double agent, first joining the 26th of July movement, then the MMR, the *Movement for Recuperating the Revolution*. Only in this complex and dangerous manner could he achieve the contacts he needed . . . to win back his wife.

The scroll hadn't revealed his chances for survival, let alone success. Perhaps that was just as well.

Santa Barbara was about half life-size and wore a red dress. Chango in the Espiritismo pantheon—as he remembered with a shudder. She had flowing long hair and a sword in her hand, and before her were assorted offerings of the faithful: money, a plantain, a fat cigar, a glass of rum, candies. The saint must lead the good life!

Nothing happened, and he felt conspicuous standing near her, so he set one of his pesetas down before the statue and turned to glance around the bar. His time in Cuba had conditioned him to the relative plenitude of food, but still it made him nervous to see so much wasting before a statue.

There were religious paintings all along the walls. He smiled momentarily, remembering the similar icons in Luisa's house of fornication, and the confusion he experienced. He knew Cuba better, now! He saw a saloon with pullmans, their deeply padded seats, high backs, and shaded recesses creating deep intrigue where he was sure little existed. Just people drinking and conversing, some couples caressing, a girl fondling the crotch of her escort . . . ah, Superman!

Superman—that still reminded him of his awful guilt. He had been numb while still in Cuba 1962, then crushed in the Text B twenty-fifth century. In this past month in Cuba 1958 it had begun to fade, and some nights he did not dream. . . .

"The green Ford," a man said in his ear. Bringas managed not to jump. This was his contact!

He did not know a Ford automobile by sight, since cars had been the least of his recent concerns. But fortunately there was only one green car in sight, a taxi with a sleeping driver. How could the man make a living, with industry of that kind? Bringas walked up and climbed in, finding the vehicle surprisingly comfortable inside.

"To the dime store," he said.

"Ten Cent?" the driver inquired. "Which one?" Evidently he hadn't been as sound asleep as he looked.

"Woolworth's, of course." This was the final key— for Ramon, a terrorist, had just bombed the Galiano Woolworth's and the news was not out yet. Only those party to the act could know the significance of this address at this moment.

The taxi wheeled north on Avenue 26, passed the Parque Zoologico on the right, and picked up speed, paying no more attention to traffic regulations than any other vehicle did. Bringas shuddered; he hadn't expected to risk his life like this!

A few blocks along he spied the Chinese cemetery, with offerings of flowers and food on top of the tombs. Then the main Havana Cemetery, with caballerias of marble monuments and statues, shining white for the most part, but some of them red and others of black marble. This was a stone display that surpassed anything he had imagined. In his own world rock was almost exclusively functional, seldom decorative. He had read that this Havana burial place was among the finest of the pre-holocaust world. . . .

Caballerias? No, he exaggerated a bit. Historically, the Spanish conquerors had dispensed two types of land grants in Latin America: peonias of about a hundred acres for the foot soldiers, supposedly enough to support a single family; and caballerias for the cavalrymen, at least five times as large. But in Cuba of the twentieth century a caballeria was thirty-three acres.

"Mmph!" he exclaimed as the car accelerated through a red light at Calle 23 and swerved around vehicles that had the temerity to claim the right-of-way. But now the scene was a block-long section of open-air food vendors, Mercado del Vedado. The sights and smells distracted him. Then they came to the bank of the Rio Almendares, and went through the tunnel under the river, past a big fountain with colored lights and mermaids, delightful fantasies of the past—what a continuous splendor of surface artifacts, treated so casually by the populace! They must have thought it would be here forever!

Well, perhaps it would. In both texts he knew that Cuba had been spared the direct ravages of the holocaust. In Text A the island had not been important enough to bother with; in Text B the missiles, largely obsolete, had been held in abeyance pending a local strike that never came. Their purpose had been served; the missiles were no longer a significant factor in the balance of terror. Russia had controlled them and had used that leverage to gain considerably in other parts of the world. And when the enemy became China . . .

They were now cruising west along Avenida 5, with stately houses on either side and red poinsettias in the center mall. A clocktower . . . parks . . . statues . . . palm trees . . . churches . . . marvelous! He read the name of the second church he saw: Jesus de Miramar. Treasure these, he thought. There would be no genuine religion a century hence.

On past El Barrilito, a bar built in the shape of a monstrous beer keg—and next time he had better stick to beer, for his head was dizzy from the Cuba Libre!

Around another traffic circle and past the stately old Havana Yacht Club. Bringas shut his eyes, overwhelmed by the intoxication of wealth and pleasure and freedom—and alcohol.

He looked again and spied the Vilanova University, its wedge-shaped cluster of buildings, courts, and trees. A right turn into a new development along the sea, just a few houses. Finally the taxi stopped before a large, modern edifice.

Bringas paid the driver and got out, moving a little unsteadily. An austere woman emerged, heavily outfitted with bracelets and a medal, as all women here seemed to be. This medal was on a gold chain around her neck and bore an imprint of an old man on crutches with a dog licking at his sores. San Lazaro—what a concept to find displayed on the bosom of a mature woman!

"Ramon sent me," he said. This had to work, or he was in trouble, for the mysterious manuscript terminated at this point. The next four years, he was on his own. If this was the proper connection, they would hold him here for a day or so while they checked with Ramon to verify that Ramon had indeed sent him. But Ramon was dead, killed this same afternoon, so his bluff could never be called.

She brought him inside, then questioned him cautiously. "I am ready to fight the dictator," he said simply. "I can fight, I can shoot, I have five hundred pesos."

She fed him and gave him a room for the night. There were religious pictures on the walls here, reminding him again of Perversion, death, and guilt, the phosphorous. How could he ever free himself from that legacy?

In the morning, a servant brought him breakfast. Then he waited, knowing why. He drank five or six cups of coffee. Cubans were the world's greatest coffee drinkers, and the addiction must have been genetic, because he had acquired it after a lifetime without it.

Finally the woman talked to him again. He saw that she had been crying and realized that in a way, he was a murderer again, for he had known Ramon was going to die, and he could have come to Havana a day early and prevented it.

"Ramon," she said. "Only nineteen, such a good Catholic—"

"Did something happen to my friend?" Bringas asked with feigned alarm. Hypocrite—he had never met the man!

"So violent—a man of violence—but good at heart," she said, the tears flowing again. "His vow of chastity—"

"Of course," Bringas agreed quickly, to cover his surprise at this revelation. After what he had seen before, he had thought no Cuban was chaste.

"Yesterday—he went to see his family in Vedado—near the church there—he was walking—the police stopped—"

"The police!" Bringas was beginning to feel sick. He was making such selfish personal use of a tragedy!

"They tried to arrest—he is so strong—a judo black belt—"

Bringas tried to look crestfallen, and it wasn't hard to do. Ramon sounded very much like 197—or what 197 might have been. It would have been good to know the man. "He killed a policeman!"

"No, no. He threw them down, but one of them shot at him. In the back—and they put him in the car, bleeding, and the police captain came and shot him through the head."

So Bringas was home free. Still, he felt remorse at the preventable loss of life.

She looked at him, in control of herself for the moment. "I see it hurts you as it hurts me. I believe you were his friend—but I must consult. You understand."

"I understand." *I would have been his friend*, he thought fiercely. Juan Bringas would not betray another Cuban, whatever the cost! Not like that.

She made a phone call in his presence. "A man," she said. "Ramon sent him. . . ." She listened for a moment. "Dark hair, medium dark complexion, about five-ten, twenty-five, fairly powerful. Yes, Cuban. He has suffered—a woman, I think."

Bringas stiffened. He had been more closely observed than he had supposed!

She listened a moment longer, then hung up. "We will send you."

That night she put him in a car with two other men. The driver was another silent type, but the passengers talked freely. One was American—a nationality Bringas had not observed closely before. Tall, white-skinned, straw-colored hair, loud in the presumed fashion of Americans. He delivered a monologue in a condescending tone, rapidly, in English, a language that neither Bringas nor the third man, a Cuban, spoke. But Bringas' intensive studies of the variants of Spanish enabled him to pick up a number of similar words in the foreign speech, so that he got the gist. "Newspaper reporter," he concluded. "Visiting Fidel for a few days. A dangerous mission. For an article that he can't say much about."

"Ah, yes," the Cuban agreed with a wide smile. He was stocky, perhaps five feet four inches tall, with wide shoulders and wide hips, but not fat. His skin was deeply tanned and his hair was dark and wavy. "American newspapers can tell the truth. Our own cannot—not while Batista rules. I cannot read, myself. I was too busy to go to school. But freedom of the press is very important, and we shall have it again when we conquer. Fidel has promised."

Bringas could not recollect whether that promise had been honored, historically. Meanwhile he seemed to have been elected permanent translator. He cast about for words that the American would understand. *Libertad*, of course—

"Forget it," the American said, dismissing Bringas' stilted attempts at English. "I should have known the natives wouldn't be able to communicate. Just so long as Castro can!" And he pointedly tilted back his head and closed his eyes.

"He says he understands, but he is very tired now and must rest," Bringas said diplomatically in Spanish. He wasn't sure whether to laugh or be angry at the American's snobbery. He made a mental note: it would be wise to learn English, just in case, when he had the opportunity.

The Cuban was undaunted. "I am Nilo Perera, from Encrucijada. I am a guajiro, but too lazy to farm. That's why I came to join Fidel."

A guajiro—one of the peasant farmers, and illiterate. Too lazy to work? Bringas studied the squat musculature of the man and doubted it. No one would become a revolutionary merely to avoid rough living. "Encrucijada?"

"Just north of Santa Clara," the man explained happily. "Between Santa Clara, Remedios, and Sagua la Grando. Great country!"

"Ah, yes," Bringas said, recognizing the region with a shock. Sagua la Grande was the largest town in the immediate vicinity of the missile base he had skirted on his first trip to Cuba. Odd that this farmer should hail from there—but coincidental, certainly, since it was now four years earlier, and there was nothing but wilderness at the critical site. Then, responding to the other's expectant silence: "I am Juan Bringas, a Cuban born in Uruguay."

"A Cuban from Uruguay?" Nilo repeated, surprised.

"My parents went there when Machado fell. For a peaceful life. This is the first time I have been to Cuba myself. But I am Cuban, and I want to liberate my country. I know how to fight and shoot."

That should be sufficient to explain why he was unfamiliar with many local affairs. There would be very few genuine Uruguayans in Cuba to challenge him.

"Ah, you have come to the right place! Fidel needs good shooters. If he had had more of them on July 26, he would be in power now!"

"In less than a year?" Bringas inquired, surprised. "That would be a swift revolution."

"July 26, 1953—five years ago," Nilo explained. "Fidel

led a hundred and fifty men—two of them girls—against the Moncada Army Post and its thousand soldiers. And he would have won, but he did not have the weapons."

"Against a thousand trained soldiers?" Bringas inquired with polite skepticism. He remembered now—there *had* been an historical note about some such episode, from which the revolutionary movement took its name. He probably would have made the connection sooner, except for his preoccupation with more immediate matters. The scroll had told him to join the July 26 Movement, after all.

"They were very brave, and they fought for freedom," Nilo said. "But the soldiers were too stupid to join them, so they lost. Only ten of Fidel's force were killed in the fighting; but a hundred were slaughtered in cold blood after surrendering, some of them after being tortured. Fidel was to be killed on sight, but the lieutenant who found him was a friend, and brought him in alive."

Bringas wondered what the other side's version of the incident was. "If he was captured, how is he free now?"

"Batista was stupid; he made an amnesty for political prisoners. He thought it would make him more popular with the people."

It was normally a fifteen hour trip to the town of Bayamo, in Oriente Province, and the driver stopped to take two six-hour naps along the way. In that time Bringas received a good peasant's eye grounding in the local politics, the impossibilities of women, and the fine points of cock-fighting. Nilo Parera might be illiterate, but he evidently possessed a healthy peasant cunning, and he knew the local scene.

Fidel would see that free elections were held, Nilo asserted, and that every man received a fair share of land to own. Fidel was good.

Ah yes, Bringas thought. Historically the cry of revolt in Latin America was almost always prefixed by "Land!" Only in his own society had that changed, for there was no land left. Had the cry "Rank!" supplanted it? Not entirely, he decided.

And, between the lines, it seemed that Nilo had an agenda other than more laziness for his departure from home. He was cagy about the details, but Bringas got a picture of an unfaithful woman, savage jealousy, a fight with machetes . . . and manslaughter. Wanted by the local authorities, Nilo had suddenly elected to work for "the people's revolution." He might talk of naivete and indolence—but Bringas knew now that the Cuban would be a very dangerous man when enraged.

At Bayamo, in the wee hours, they changed cars and drivers. Out of town they turned onto a dirt road. Clouds of dust marked their passage as they rode inland to the foothills of the Sierra Maestra range in southeast Cuba. This was the island's highest mountain chain. They approached at dawn, from the palm-dotted plains to the north. By the time the vehicle had traversed the thickening wilderness of trees and tropical bushes and underbrush, the damp heat of the day was stifling. Bringas saw the great range rising through a bluish morning mist, the peaks shimmering as "the covers" lifted.

The foothills were a jungle with patches of pine. Travel had to be by foot, following a taciturn guide. Bringas was fascinated by the abundance of wildlife: brightly colored parrots flew out of their way and big spiders lurked in the hot shade. The plants, too, were exotic. He recognized the huge purple fruits called caimitos and mangos. Parasitic plants clung to the foliage and the ropelike limbs of lianas dropped down to seek the soil. In the jungle's depths, Bringas became eerily self-conscious of any noise he made.

All this—so soon to wither under radioactive fall-out! Had no one stopped to consider the cost of the coming war? If they could only look ahead and see how dead the morn was going to be. . . .

The thought fled as soon as Bringas had to put his whole energy into forcing his tiring body forward. He had the wide hips and good musculature of his own Cuban ancestry, but his environment had not prepared him for this. Nilo did not complain; for all his small size and expressed laziness, he climbed indefatigably. The anonymous American reporter cursed monotonously in his own vernacular for no discernable reason. Had he expected to be chauffeured all the way into Castro's camp?

As they mounted higher it turned blessedly cooler. Some sections were covered with ferns and pockets of mist. They stopped at a mountain stream to drink, and the water was clear and so cold that Bringas' throat stiffened. Higher stood an almost prehistoric landscape with large ferns. But their party kept to the lower passes, scrambling over the rocks following a dry stream bed.

At last they reached the territory controlled by Fidel Castro. They were, as the cliche went, so tired they could not lift their souls.

There was no respite here. The guerillas were tough and had little sympathy for ignorance or physical weakness. Lice infested them; scratching was constant and largely unconscious. Both men and equipment were dirty, and at first the smell was oppressive. (Later the nostrils would simply tune the steady body odors out.) The recruits slept in a different place each night, sometimes in a bohio—a palm-front lean-to—and sometimes outside in hammocks. They often went hungry. It was plain that outsiders were neither respected nor trusted.

One "veteran" of perhaps two months became too overbearing with Bringas and got chopped across the larynx in response. The action increased Bringas' stature among the rebels, for they liked a man who could take care of himself. Nilo had a rougher time of it—until the day someone accused him of being ignorant about cock-fighting. Bringas, honestly afraid the maddened guajiro would kill the man, stepped in quickly and patched up a truce. Nilo had a temper, all right!

The American reporter, on the other hand, was treated deferentially. He ate well, slept well, and had no onerous duties. He did not even carry a canteen. After a couple of days, he was escorted to another camp to interview Fidel himself.

Camilo Cienfuegos headed this band of about fifty men. Camil—September—had been named after this man, so for 197 it was like history coming to life. Camilo in the flesh struck Bringas as capable, honest, dedicated, and quite sociable. His black beard hung down to his chest, his black hair fell to his shoulders, and he was tall and thin. In fact, he looked Christlike at first glance. He had been a tailor in Havana, and very poor; yet here he had charisma and was a leader of men. He hated dictatorships and accepted neither Batista defectors nor professed Communists into his ranks. Bringas found it easy to respect him.

In two weeks they had settled in, and the load lightened. New recruits arrived, and Bringas felt like an old hand. He suspected that Nilo had been on the verge of deserting, but hadn't wanted to go alone. There were ugly stories about the fate of deserters.

There was a profusion of religious medals and necklaces, even here in the mountains. The barbudos wore strings of carnocoles, seashells, and colored red and white beads, and especially powerful voodoo amulets. Espiritismo was here. . . .

Bringas was now allowed to carry one of the precious Springfield rifles—precious because although they were of little use during a fire fight, being seven-shot bolt-action, they had been fitted with telescopic sights and were extremely accurate at long range. Precious, too, because the rebels had very few decent weapons. Most of the men were poor shots, having had very little training and no chance to practice firing. But Bringas had demonstrated his superior aim at the outset. He had expected the rifle to kick him with its recoil, for it was a solid projectile weapon, but still had had no practical experience with it. His shoulder had been sore for days, and he had not dared to show it—but he had hit the target every time. When did they master the recoilless venting?

Cienfuegos himself led a band of ten, including Bringas and Nilo, down into the lowlands for a raid. The rebels never ravaged the homesteads of the local campesinos, for the farmers were "friends" by definition, little as they cared to advertise this classification to the government authorities. All food and equipment were scrupulously paid for, sometimes with receipts to be made good after the revolution had been won, but paid for. The rich owners forwarded blackmail money so they would not be molested either. Thus neither the wealthy ranchers nor the poverty-stricken squatter-farmers were raided. Only those who directly supported the dictator—sometimes by declining to contribute voluntarily to the revolution—were attacked. It was a point of honor with the rebels to ravage one of the giant holdings every so often, as notice of the movement's growing strength. It may not always have been true, but it kept the natives honest.

This mission was not routine. They were ambushed by an army platoon. Bringas dropped and scrambled under the bushes at the first shot, but he could tell by the screams that others had been hit. He had a mental picture of marabu, of men running out with their hands up, of bayonets . . . but there was no proper cover here. They were near a village. The recruits froze with fear, standing straight, and were much easier targets than they needed to be. The murderous fire raked them from two sides, and men died.

Bringas found himself back to back with Camilo, sowing bullets wherever the muzzle flashes of the ambushers showed, while a third man lobbed grenades. Grenades! Bringas winced, even though he knew they were not phosphorus. It was dark, of course, and he could not see the enemy directly; otherwise he might not have been able to bring himself to shoot. His experience in this land before, in 1962, had made him less reticent about the taking of life, but he was not a hardened killer. Not yet.

There was another gunflash, on his side, and he swung to cover it. But his finger jammed on the trigger, inexplicably stiffening, and by the time he squeezed the shot off his aim was bad.

"Let's get out of here," Camilo said. "Before their reinforcements come. Check for their rifles; we need the weapons."

Bringas started to warn him that at least one government soldier remained alive. But the words would not come.

Then they heard a crashing. The man was running away. Cienfuegos fired, but to no effect.

They checked. Bringas' marksmanship had been good: three dead men lay where he had aimed. Possibly they had been killed by grenades . . . but there was new blood on his hands. Except for his inexplicable balk, there would have been a fourth. He might rationalize, but he remained a killer.

He found the Batistiano rifles and carried them to Camilo.

Four of their own men were dead, and two more were wounded. Nilo had been hit; he had a bleeding leg he could not walk on. "De cara el sol," Nilo whispered, grimacing with the pain. "I want to die with my face to the sun!"

"Then you'll have to wait until dawn," Bringas said with rough camaraderie. He hauled his friend over his shoulder while the three unhurt men took care of the other wounded one and the captured weapons.

"Ambush—very clever," Nilo gasped. "I will remember that. . . ."

But Bringas had no breath to respond to Nilo's delirium, for Camilo was leading them back at a grueling pace.

Bringas remained upset about his performance, however, despite the climb's formidable distractions. He had been fighting in self-defense, really, so he didn't have to call himself a murderer. Just a killer. Those soldiers had been trying to kill him, and would have succeeded if he had not picked them off. All but that last one. . . .

But did that justify his action? He was back at the same question. Was it conscience that had stopped him from firing at the last? Because the man was ready to break and run, and did not need killing?

Then Bringas felt a special chill. There was another explanation. The paradox shield he had been warned about. The last soldier might have been one of his own ancestors, or in a position to affect the actions of his ancestors. So he could not be killed by Bringas.

His mind became marginally easier as he mulled it over. More likely it was a *secondary* paradox effect: the man was in a position to affect Bringas' own actions of 1962. If he were killed now, it would change what had already happened in Bringas' scheme. A minor matter, but still enough to account for the lapse. He hoped.

"You did well," Camilo told him the next morning. "You did not panic, you fought bravely, and you made every shot but one count." Sharp observer there! "You brought back your comrade and saved his life, for though the wound was not mortal, the Batistianos would have executed him as a known rebel after torturing him for information."

"I did what I had to do," Bringas said. "I did not enjoy it."

Camilo smiled grimly. "We all do—but some of us have to do more than others. Nobody enjoys it, except maybe Raul, the maricon, the queer. Some have to lose their nerve under fire; others have to die. It is time for you to meet Fidel."

Fidel! That meant his probation was over, and he was to be accepted as one of the trusted regulars! That was what he had wanted, for his mission required that he remain solidly in the rebel leader's good graces, as well as establish his anti-rebel bonafides . . . another difficult task.

Fidel arrived that afternoon. There was no mistaking

this bold figure of a man: six feet tall, olive skin, dark hair, shaggy beard, and a magnetic personality that was almost hypnotic. He was not aloof, despite his stature— Fidel's uniform was as dirty as the rest, and he had been as long without a bath.

Bringas was impressed. Here was real charisma! A warrior to command warriors! The man for whom Fidelia had been named. Here stood the raw stuff of history!

With him were Hubert Matos, one of his top lieutenants; a regular troop of guerrilla-guards; and a woman. Matos of course he recognized, for he was on the coming calendar and was famous for his Amazonian navigation after the holocaust. As much as Fidel, Hubert was history, and it was phenomenal fortune to encounter both of them and Camilo so soon. The woman was Celia Sanchez, Fidel's secretary. His mistress too, undoubtedly, although she seemed also to serve him intellectually. She was a woman of breeding, out of place in this rough camp, yet seemingly quite at home. She was perhaps forty years old, tall, thin, majestic now, probably beautiful in her heyday.

Fidel talked privately with Camilo, pausing to urinate at the camp's edge. Then he reviewed the recruits, walking among them informally. "I will take the wounded," he said. "My camp has better facilities and more guards." Nilo Parera was removed, and Bringas was glad for him, and further impressed by the leader. Yet how could it be otherwise, with Fidel of Fidelia?

"You!" Fidel barked suddenly at Bringas. "I tell you that man's hat is a Batistiano!" He pointed to a guerrilla standing guard a hundred feet away.

Bringas smiled. With a single motion he brought his rifle up and fired.

"Hey!" the man cried as his fatigue cap flew off his head. The others, seeing that he was unhurt, laughed.

Fidel put his arm around Bringas' shoulders. "You are mine!" he said. And that act of impulsive warmth and camaraderie by the great man moved Bringas powerfully.

He had come to this time and world on a unique mission, but he could not remain aloof from its motives and passions.

That was how Juan Bringas, to his own amazement, became the personal bodyguard of *the* Fidel Castro.

In March, about the time Bringas was joining La Revolucion, Fidel's brother Raul of the future month of Raul (August) was taking a hundred men north to open a second front. Reports suggested that this endeavor was doing very well, though Bringas knew that allowance had to be made for exaggeration. Raul established a large rebel territory in eastern Oriente Province, setting up indoctrination schools, bulldozing new roads, and executing suspected informers. The government's motorized columns entered the region, but were harried by snipers, ambushes, and land mines; and could make no headway.

Batista mounted a major offensive in May. Well-armed troops commanded by Major General Cantillo forged out from Bayamo and laid siege to the entire Sierra Maestra range. Fidel seemed pleased. "This is the decisive battle!" he proclaimed. "We know this territory best. We shall smash them!"

Nilo was not so sure. "I am no general," he said. "I only know what I hear. And I hear that General Cantillo has twenty thousand men, and we have hardly five hundred, and half do not have guns. Cantillo is not like most government officers—he made his rank on merit, not patronage, and he is a good tactician. I tell you, I would much rather be chasing my yegua blanca, than standing up to the rifles and tanks of the General."

Bringas laughed at the incongruity of the comparison. Yegua blanca—a white woman—or a white mare. Applied to a woman, it could mean either that she was very female or that she was a prostitute. What man *wouldn't* prefer to chase such a woman, rather than to face the weapons of the enemy? "You mean to say you fornicate with horses?"

"Oh, not just any old mare," Nilo replied, taking the pun in stride. "My Natacha is very special. She is better than a woman, and I am true to her." He paused, becoming serious. "A horse is not fickle. You don't have to watch her all the time to see what man is—"

Fidel Castro appeared, cutting short what might have been a more personal confession. "Come—we shall talk to the men," he said.

Nilo and Bringas exchanged smiles. Fidel's talks were strictly one-man affairs: just him and his audience.

Fidel's magic never seemed to wear off. To listen to him was to be convinced, even when what he said was preposterous. Those he commanded believed that a single rebel with a defective carbine could demolish a battalion of Batistianos supported by artillery and aircraft.

With high morale the revolutionaries went forth to battle, sniping at Cantillo's advancing columns. They inflicted high casualties on the government troops, but were steadily forced back by the sheer mass of disciplined soldiers. The intermittent battles continued for days and weeks, and the outlook grew more pessimistic. Slowly but inexorably Cantillo was cleaning out the Sierra Maestra.

Privately, Fidel was worried. He paced the length of his temporary headquarters, talking, talking, talking, though there was no one but Bringas and a score of other trusted rebels to listen.

"What Cuban does not cherish glory?" he demanded rhetorically. "What heart is not set aflame by the dawn of freedom? There has been an attempt to establish the myth that modern arms render the people helpless to overthrow tyrants. Military parades and the pompous display of the machines of war are utilized to perpetuate this myth and create in the people a complex of absolute impotence. But no weapon, no violence can vanquish the people once they have decided to win back their rights. Both past and present are full of examples. . . ."

And Fidel gave the examples, one after another, drawn

from an astonishing array of sources. The man looked like an illiterate fugitive, but he sounded like a history professor. Bringas had long since grown accustomed to the incongruity. Vintage Fidel!

"But more importantly we base our chances for success on the existing social order, because we are assured of the people's support. When we speak of the people we do not mean the comfortable ones, the nation's conservative elements, who welcome any oppressive regime, any dictatorship, any despotism, prostrating themselves before the master of the moment until they grind their foreheads into the ground. When we speak of struggle, the *people* means the vast unredeemed masses, to whom all make promises and whom all deceive. We mean the people who yearn for a better, more dignified and more just nation; who are moved by ancestral aspirations of justice, for they have suffered injustice and mockery, generation after generation; who long for great and wise changes in all aspects of their life. People who, to attain these changes, are ready to give even the very last breath of their lives—when they believe in something or in someone, especially when they believe in themselves. The demagogues and professional politicians who manage to perform the miracle of being right in everything and in pleasing everyone are, of necessity, deceiving everyone about everything. A revolutionary must proclaim his ideas courageously, define his principles and express his intentions so that no one is deceived, neither friend nor foe."

"That's *us*," Nilo whispered. "Courageous revolutionaries—"

"Seven hundred thousand Cubans are without work," Fidel continued, paying no attention to Nilo, "who desire to earn their daily bread honestly without having to emigrate in search of livelihood. Five hundred thousand farm laborers are inhabiting miserable shacks, who work four months of the year and starve for the rest of the year, sharing their misery with their children, who have not an inch of land to cultivate, and whose existence inspires compassion in any heart not made of stone."

"Yes yes!" Nilo breathed raptly.

"Four hundred thousand industrial laborers and stevedores whose retirement funds have been embezzled, whose benefits are being taken away, whose homes are wretched quarters, whose salaries pass from the hands of the boss to those of the usurer, whose future is a pay reduction and dismissal, whose life is eternal work, and whose only rest is in the tomb.

"One hundred thousand small farmers who live and die working on land that is not theirs, looking at it with sadness as Moses did the promised land, to die without possessing it; who, like feudal serfs, have to pay for the use of their parcel of land by giving up a portion of their products; who cannot love it, improve it, beautify it, or plant a lemon or orange tree on it, because they never know when a sheriff will come with the rural guard to evict them from it."

"Yes!" Nilo cried, loud enough to make Fidel pause. "If they came to evict me from *my* land, I would shoot them!"

Fidel smiled. "Thirty thousand teachers and professors who are so devoted, dedicated, and necessary to the better destiny of future generations and who are so badly treated and paid. Twenty thousand small businessmen weighted down by debts, ruined by the crisis, and harangued by a plague of filibusters and venal officials. Ten thousand young professionals: doctors, engineers, lawyers, veterinarians, school teachers, dentists, pharmacists, newspapermen, painters, sculptors, etc., who come forth from school with their degrees, anxious to work and full of hope, only to find themselves at a dead end with all doors closed, and where no ear hears their clamor or supplication.

"These are the people, the ones who know misfortune and, therefore, are capable of fighting with limitless courage!

"To the people whose desperate roads through life have been paved with bricks of betrayal and false promises, we are not going to say: 'We will eventually give you what you need,' but rather 'Here you have it, fight for it with all your might so that liberty and happiness may be yours!' "

"Yes!" This time it was Bringas who had exclaimed, thinking of his own arduous quest.

"Yes, you, Juan!" Fidel cried abruptly, wheeling on him. Bringas jumped. "My dream is your dream too, isn't it?"

"Yes," Bringas said again. Fidel was almost desperate in his need for encouragement, and this was a side of the leader he had not seen before. But it was true. It was impossible to listen to these spellbinding words and not be caught up in the man's ebullient sincerity. Beside Fulgencio Batista, Fidel Castro was an intellectual and moral giant. The people loved the charismatic rebel, and so did Juan Bringas, and hardly without reason. The world needed the example this great leader would make!

General Cantillo was not there to listen. The officer's determined campaign thrust methodically into the very heart of the rebel sanctuary; even Fidel's rhetoric could not halt the encroachment. His men were dying as they retreated, however bravely, and the supply of recruits had been cut off. The rebels might kill five or six men for every one they lost, but Cantillo had forty for every one remaining, and he was tough. The end would be long in coming, for there were many devious retreats in the mountain fastness, but unless some miracle happened . . .

Fidel talked on, a firebrand holding the wolves at bay—so long as it burned. Celia Sanchez was there, seated on the ground near to Fidel. Her eyes never left his face, though she must have heard this monologue many times before. Bringas was suddenly struck with envy and longing—not for Fidel's woman, but for his own. It was so important to have a woman, and not only for the sexual availability; what counted most was the constant emotional support, the steady faith her man was right and strong *no matter what*. That was what Celia gave Fidel; that was what Juan

Bringas needed more than food or bullets in this time of increasing stress.

It was late afternoon. Soon they would have to go see about eating—if there were enough food to go around. And about tending to the newly wounded—if enough medicine and bandages remained. Fidel was even running short of cigars.

"Fidel! Fidel!" someone cried, and the rebel chief broke off his solitary harangue as though relieved to have a distraction. He did not need to acknowledge; every guajiro in the Sierra Maestra knew him by sight.

It was an old woman, dirty and gasping from the climb. "The soldiers—my husband . . . my daughter . . . they kill, they rape, they burn—"

Fidel needed to hear no more. "Juan! Take four men, help this loyal campesina! We cannot let them harm our friends."

Bringas was on his way with Nilo and three others, following the woman. He feared she would collapse at any moment, but somehow she kept on, scrambling down the steep wooded slopes at a respectable pace.

Her bohio was two miles distant. They saw the smoke rising long before they got there. There had been a raid, all right.

The old peasant-man lay on the ground not far from his smoldering hut. He had been severely beaten, but he lived. Bringas administered hasty first-aid, but there was little encouragement he could give. The man would recover, with proper medical care—but the rebel supplies were exhausted, and a trek into government territory was out of the question for the man in this condition. If the siege lifted, he had a chance.

Nilo was searching the terrain, quite canny about potential hiding places for the enemy. He was no slouch at survival, and Bringas always paid attention to his friend's advice in peasant matters. The soldiers seemed to have departed—but had they gone back to their camp, or on to ravage another farm?

"My daughter! My daughter!" the old woman wailed.

There was no daughter. "Spread out," Bringas snapped to his men. "Watch for troops. See if the girl is here. She may be unconscious." *Or dead*, he thought. He wanted to find her before the woman did, in case it was ugly.

The recruits obeyed nervously, combing through the coffee trees. These ranged from two to five meters in height, with red berries. These plants had not been burned, though evidently the soldiers had tried to fire them. That was not idle destruction; the purpose was to eliminate any possible source of supply for the rebels.

Nilo shook his head. "If she is young, she is with the troops," he said meaningfully.

They did not find the girl. They found an ambush.

The farm was in the foothills on a small level piece of land, but there were many boulders suitable for hiding places. The hut was gone, and the cornfield that surrounded it was still smoking, but away from that immediate region there were far too many places where soldiers might lay in wait. Even the small creek that wound through the farm was suspect. But a well-set ambush was almost impossible to defuse—without springing it.

A machine gun opened fire from beyond a rock outcrop dominating the field. Despite Bringas' awareness of the danger, the surprise was like a physical shock, and he thought he would fall dead from alarm. The shots were very loud in his ears, and every one seemed as though it would strike him. Every fourth bullet was a tracer, leaving a red streak in the air.

One of the men fell at once with a cry of agony. Bringas and Nilo dropped into a ditch, rolling quickly out of the line of fire. They crawled on their stomachs toward the gun emplacement, hugging the ground like serpents.

Bringas made a signal and Nilo nodded. Both knew better than to depend on recruits under fire; this had to be a two man operation. Nilo crawled on a distance; then Bringas opened fire to draw attention to himself. The machine gun quickly oriented on him, spraying bullets into the far slope of the ditch. But the same terrain that made the ambush easy made the defense against it easy too: the bullets could not quite reach him.

Meanwhile Nilo left the ditch unobserved, and began circling around behind the gun. By and by there was a larger blast, and fire erupted from the vicinity of the machine gun nest. Nilo had gotten behind and dropped a grenade on it.

But that hardly meant the battle was over. Bringas launched himself forward, out of the ditch, trying to get to the gun before any surviving crew got it functional again. Nilo was there before him. "All clear!" Nilo called.

Three men were sprawled beside the mounted weapon, an old .30 caliber machine gun with a big jacket around the barrel for water cooling. They were all uniformed government soldiers—no doubt a rearguard left by the patrol. That meant there were more troops in the vicinity.

"A smart ambush would have had *two* nests," Nilo said, "so that there would have been no place to hide." He had become something of an expert while his wound was healing—he wanted to be sure he never got wounded that way again.

One soldier lay dead, his face obliterated by the force of the explosion. Another was critically wounded; shrapnel had ripped an ugly hole in his chest. The third seemed only to have been knocked out by the concussion.

"I did it," Nilo murmured, looking at the casualties, and Bringas had some idea of his friend's emotion. To kill in the heat of outrage with a machete, man to man, was not the same as blowing apart strangers from a distance. Yet this war . . .

Behind Nilo, the third soldier moved, struggling to bring a pistol to bear. Bringas kicked it away, disgusted. There had already been too much killing, and he still was not inured to the blood on his hands. Grenades . . . phosphorus . . .

More shots sounded, and he dropped again. Soldiers were charging from the forest of palm trees above the farm, firing as they advanced. This was no isolated platoon of ten to fifteen men; this was a Batista company of a hundred! They had the way to the rebel retreat cut off already; there was nowhere to go but on down the mountain.

Nilo was more practical. He hauled the machine gun around to cover the enemy. It was mounted on a tripod and was highly maneuverable. But Nilo had never had access to such a weapon before, and did not know how to fire it.

Bringas dived over and took control. He had been briefed for this sort of thing before making the first phase into the past of 1962. Now he welcomed the information he had rejected before.

The gun fired a burst into the ground in front of the troops. Then he got the range, and—it jammed.

He cursed as he fumbled with it, trying to make it operative again. The enemy quickly grasped the situation and resumed the attack. Bullets started hitting all around them. "There isn't time!" Nilo cried.

So they fled. Had this been a deliberate trap, set in the hope of capturing Fidel himself? Was the old woman a traitor? Or hadn't she known the strength of the attacking forces? And the jamming of the gun—had it been an accident, or another manifestation of the paradox shield?

It hardly mattered now! He would be lucky to come out of this alive. If the Batistianos really thought they were netting the big fish—

The two surviving recruits had the same notion. They came charging down the hill, dodging to avoid being easy targets. It worked; there were a few shots from behind, but no one was hit. Marksmanship was always poor at dusk.

Nilo and Bringas joined them. Right now the most important thing was to *get out of range*!

They made it. Probably the government troops were afraid of a countertrap in the dark, so pursued cautiously. But they did not give up the chase.

If paradox struck again, Bringas thought as he ran, it might mean that another of these men had some connection to his own ancestral line. He couldn't shoot—but *could* be shot! It was a most unfortunate aspect about participating in the past.

Bringas led the way down, avoiding the scattered bohíos. The troops would check every dwelling and farm, and probably beat or kill any campesinos who tried to hide a rebel. The farmers were friendly, but they were not suicidal.

"Spread out again," Bringas said. "They may think they've caught a larger force. Individually we might slip through, some of us, in the dark. Together we have no chance."

"May we meet again," Nilo said. Bringas felt a pang, realizing that there was no assurance that they *would*. They were in bad trouble.

The others ran nervously off to the left and right, and he was alone in a slanted pasture. For the moment he did not hear the pursuit, but he knew it was there—and that there would be trucks and ambushes below. The troops under General Cantillo did not let up, once they had a party of rebels trapped. That was what made this whole mountain situation so desperate, and what probably spelled the end of Fidel Castro and his 26th of July Movement.

No—for Castro had been in power in 1962. He must have escaped somehow, and used the experience to perfect his own peinazo technique. But how many of his men had done the same?

Bringas suspected he had a respite of perhaps ten minutes. Then it would be kill or be killed. Most likely both!

He cast about for suitable camouflage. The troops had not seen his face. If there was some way to alter his rebel appearance—

Something moved in the deepening gloom. He whipped

his rifle about. Was it one of his own men—or a soldier?

No, neither one, for it did not move furtively. A stray horse? No, smaller.

He remembered Nilo's remark about the sexual aptitudes of mares, and stifled a bark of laughter.

Then he saw the outline against a white rock fence. A woman!

Bringas had seen few women since his arrival at the mountains. Only Celia, whom no man touched but Fidel. Suddenly a strange chemistry worked in Bringas, composed in part of Fidel's majestic visions, the ferocity of recent combat, the fear of death, and the twist of history that had rendered 233 nonexistent.

It was a young woman before him, a girl of about twenty, small and white and hippy. Or so she seemed, in this treacherous light. His glands didn't care. He might have no more than minutes to live. By daylight she might have the face of a warthog and the posterior of a baboon; but this was dusk and she was female. Before he died, he had to have this satisfaction—one last good sexual fling!

He came up behind her. "Who are you?" he called, keeping his voice low.

She gave a startled cry. "Leave me alone!"

He dived for her, catching her around the waist. She was small and white and healthy. "I am with Fidel," he said, invoking whatever magic the name might have for her. "The Batistianos are coming. If you scream—"

"Fidel!" she exclaimed, twisting in his grasp. "Why didn't you help an hour ago?"

Then he realized. "The campesina's daughter! We thought the soldiers had—"

"They did," she said, sobbing now. "Seven, eight—but there were too many, and they fought over me, about whose turn was next, and I ran away." She paused. "My mother! My father—"

"Your mother found our camp. We came immediately. Your father is alive." He didn't tell the rest. "But now one of our men is dead, and the troops are closing in. Neither one of us is safe here."

"I am more than a puta, I am a yegua, a prostitute," she said bitterly. "Eight men in nine minutes. Or nine in eight, I don't know. What is my life worth now? What do you want with me?"

Then he was ashamed, but his passion fed on this too. Eight men—and he was to be denied? He wrestled her around and kissed her savagely. It was like the naked race during Capac Raymi, the magnificent festival, and he had caught his woman.

She did not resist, to his surprise and vague disappointment. He backed her against the stone wall, pushing against her hot and heaving bosom with one hand while his other got his trousers open. He felt the metal of the medallion she wore at the same time as he felt the metal of his buttons, and it was as though he touched two terminals of an electric generator, and the current magnetized him and drew him to her body inexorably. Her fleshy thighs spread as he drove mindlessly at her. Her dress was torn and she wore no underclothing. The soldiers had seen to that, of course. . . .

"Don't hurt me," she whispered. "I'll do it, but I'm so sore—"

But he was huge and hard, feeling like a superman, certain that he could never be sated, that he could pump an endless essence into her moistly yielding female genitals. Her bollo—once an academic example for his language thesis, now a compelling reality. He *would* hurt her! He knew it, though a part of him regretted it—but there was no abating this monstrous urgency.

Then—shots! A volley.

Involuntarily he jerked back, afraid not so much of death as of discovery with a woman not his own. "Chinga!" he cried, cursing. He could almost feel the bullets in his back.

Then she tore away and was running down along the

fence, and he was charging the other way, his frustrated member pointing the direction. Damn! Damn! Thirty seconds more, and he would have—

He hurled himself into a clump of yucca, knowing it was hopeless. The troops would rout them both out, killing him and finishing their business with the buxom girl. Those shots must have gotten one of the recruits. And he hadn't even gotten the pleasure of his final orgasm!

A star shell went off high in the night sky, illuminating the area. "El coño tu madre!" he swore. Were they using air support in the mountains? Ridiculous; they never did that at night.

No! That was thunder! And stiff winds were rising. A storm was forming directly overhead.

Almost immediately the rain came across, pelting down in sheets so heavy that he doubted any individual droplets had formed. Bless it! Bless it! The Batistianos would never run him down in this waterfall! Nature had saved him.

The deluge plastered his hair to his head and soaked his clothing and cooled his projecting penis. Yet that sharp regret remained, as he put his open trousers back together: he *could* have completed his liaison with the yegua, had he known. . . .

How Nilo would laugh, he thought ruefully.

But Nilo did not laugh, for Nilo was gone. Whether the soldiers had killed or captured him no one knew; his body was never found. It was possible that he had deserted, not realizing the significance of the rain. Bringas refused to mourn for him, in the hope that they would, as agreed, someday meet again.

The rain was more than a personal miracle. It was the revolution's salvation. Every day the waters descended torrentially. Every day the mountain roads grew worse for vehicles of any type. This did not matter much to the guerrillas, who seldom used highways; but the government vehicles bogged down in the deepening mud, their wheels sinking into the twin ruts to the axles until mired. Equipment failed, and the troops lost morale. The rebels were highly mobile, striking repeatedly at the Batistiano troops and their extended supply lines.

Cantillo's strategy was sound, but the weather and terrain had stalled his offensive. The tide of battle was turning.

Fidel Castro had known it from the start. The gods of the skies and earth were with him; he could not be vanquished.

The government battalions thrust almost to the rebel headquarters—and were surrounded, the rains and the snipers cutting off their supplies and decimating their manpower. A third battalion surrendered after a ten-day encirclement. These were concrete victories—the first major ones of the 26 July Movement. Bringas was amazed how readily the Batistianos crumbled, after coming so close to victory in a grueling campaign; with just a trifle more backbone in his officers, Cantillo would have won regardless of the rains.

The propaganda value was fantastic—and Fidel knew that too. Indeed, he fought more effectively through propaganda than on the field, and newspapers all over the world lauded his efforts, from the redoubtable *New York Times* on down. All the world took notice except Cuba: Batista had tightly censored the media. But the campesinos received the message well enough!

The army slowly withdrew to the lowlands, leaving the territory and the victory to the rebels. Now there was no challenge to Fidel's authority in the entire Sierra Maestra range!

Bringas celebrated with the rest, drinking Johnny Walker whiskey that Fidel's pilot Diaz Lanz flew in from Fort Lauderdale, Florida, U.S.A. Fidel himself drank Spanish cognac laced with benzedrine—a potent mixture!

Bringas remained obsessed by thoughts of the peasant's daughter. The beautiful yegua, as she had so bitterly styled herself after the mass rape—what had become of her? He had returned to the farm to bury the bodies and look for Nilo, but it was that sexual vision that drew him there most insistently. He found the peasant family gone and the coffee trees heavy with unharvested berries. The neighbors purported not to know where the family had moved. Maybe they thought he was investigating a suspected traitor, or maybe they knew the truth; at any rate, he was effectively balked. The guajiros never openly refused to answer, but it was impossible to pin them down.

Oh, he had not forgotten lovely 233 and his son; never that! But his wife did not exist in this world, and would never exist anywhere unless he completed his devious mission and changed history back to its original state. And he had four more years to endure alone before that could happen. Meanwhile, he craved a woman. *This* woman, for she tied in with his frustration and the turning of the tide of battle. She might have meant nothing to him in other circumstances, or if he had only completed the act with her, there in the night field. But as it was, he had an unsatisfied erection. He could not get her out of his mind.

In August Fidel initiated his first formal island-wide offensive. His ranks had been swelled enormously by the recent successes, and there was now an atmosphere of victory about the entire movement. Fidel's underground exploded bombs daily in Havana and other major cities, and Batistiano canefields were burned. The Argentine doctor Che Guevara marched west from the mountains with almost two hundred men, demonstrating that the revolution could exist in lowlands as well as highlands. The treks were not easy—Cienfuegos especially was hard-pressed—but they *were* accomplished, despite the enormous numerical and supply superiority of the government forces. The tide of revolution was accelerating.

In November Fidel's popular guerrilla chief, Hubert Matos, laid siege to Santiago, a city second only to Havana in strategic value. Bringas became a liaison man, carrying private messages between the top officers and offering Fidel private assessments of what he had observed. Bringas could shoot well and take care of himself in close combat; that was what had recommended him for this solitary employment. Perhaps Fidel was aware of his passion for the anonymous yegua, and wanted to give him room to roam?

Thus he was present for part of the action at Santiago. He found Matos to be sincere and competent, as befitted the hero he was later to become. He was a dedicated revolutionary who put the welfare of his officers and men foremost. His forces were not strong enough to stage a frontal attack on the city—none of Fidel's forces were!—but they had effectively cut off almost all land communications, and Santiago's sea and air supplies were insufficient for its needs. Time and attrition would overcome the defenses; no one could doubt that.

By what prescience 'he could never after be certain, Bringas joined a publicity raid on the city golf course. This was not a dangerous mission, as such things went, though there was always some risk. He had not participated in urban guerrilla action before, and was intrigued by the differences. Here there was no wilderness to retreat into—only houses and streets. Yet it might well be easier to fade into the teeming population of the metropolis, than into the sparsely settled wilderness, for in company there was anonymity—for those who had the nerve to employ it.

Still Bringas was distinctly nervous as they passed the scattered houses of Santiago's outskirts. Any citizen could have sniped at the bedraggled party from any window with virtual impunity.

Yet none did.

"The people are with us," the team leader said, observing Bringas' worried glances. "They know we molest only the Batistianos—the military. We never pillage wantonly. We carry freedom in our guns—all the freedom and justice of the marvelous 1940 Constitution the corrupt politicians set aside. Just think of these houses as bohios, inhabited by urban campesinos: we are their friends. And besides," he said, smiling grimly, "one shot from one house, and we pay it a friendly little visit. To explain. To remonstrate."

Bringas had some notion of how effective such visits might be. The remonstration of rifle-butts! The motives might be exemplary, but war was war.

Nearer the city proper they were far more cautious. Partisans had a delivery truck ready on Carretera Central, one of the main streets leading into Santiago de Cuba. The truck took them south, directly into the city, just as though it were on routine business.

A man nudged Bringas. "There to the left—Moncada Barracks!"

Bringas looked, not certain of the significance. The buildings were surrounded by a high yellow wall, a little like the defense of a medieval castle, and all the structures were painted a dull army yellow.

He was saved by another man's exclamation. "Where Fidel started it, July 26th! Glorious!"

Of course—this was the site of that fateful attack, for which Fidel had been jailed in 1953 and thereby become famous as a revolutionary. How could he have forgotten!

The truck bore left on Avenida de Victoriano and headed east. Finally it brought them into Vista Alegre, the city's newest and most expensive section, and a hotbed of anti-Batista sentiment. They got out quickly when the truck halted, and crowded into an elegant private house. Bringas was relieved; there were entirely too many troops about!

Here they were to spend the night. A local hideout like this was essential for urban guerrilla activity, for there were no mountains to flee to if things got rough. They shaved and adopted civilian clothing, so as to blend into the population. Bringas luxuriated in his first bath in months. There might be less security in the city, but there certainly was more comfort!

In the morning, well clothed, well fed, and well rested, they proceeded to the mission. Two cars came to the house to pick them up.

They went south to the park of Loma de San Juan where there was a big bronze statue of an American soldier and an old Spanish fortress. There was also a car filled with weapons. The men picked up M-2 carbines, sawed-off shotguns, grenades, and pistols—the larger weapons were put into sacks on the floor, the smaller ones in their shirts for emergency use. It was important that none of this hardware show during the drive.

Then back along the highway, past the Santiago zoo, right onto Avenida Central Cebreco, and on out of the city to the east toward the Caney Country Club. This area was famous for its orchard fruits, said to be the finest in all Cuba. The guns were in the bottom of the sacks, with the rest filled with exotic fruits: anones that resembled green hand grenades, brown delicious zapotes, spiny guanabanas and more—spiny chirimoyas, pink guayabas, yellow-orange canistels, mameyes looking like pear-shaped brown grapefruit, mamoncillos, mangos filipinos y puercos . . . Bringas could not resist eating a big purple juicy caimito. If anyone challenged the party, they would protest they were merely out buying fruit.

If only they could take a carload of this fruit back to the mountains! It seemed a shame to waste it as camouflage.

Their precautions were superfluous; the trip was without event, and they reached the country club safely. The closest they came to action was seeing the old battlefield of San Juan Field, with its trenches and its statue of a Roosevelt Rough Rider. Warfare had changed!

"Here," the leader said, and they pulled up beside the shiny cars of several wealthy golfers. "Remember—our purpose is to make a demonstration, a show of force that will be the gossip of the city tomorrow. Don't hurt anyone unless you have to; just make enough of a scene to impress them. And be ready to move out rapidly!"

Bringas, a novice at this type of action though he approved of it, stayed to guard their vehicles while the others went out to impress the golfers. And in the solitary wait he discovered that he didn't like this as well as he had supposed; there was too little protection, too much dependence on the dubious motives of a besieged city populace. He understood the theory of psychological warfare, but in practice it was too easy to get killed—in which case some of the propaganda value would be reversed. Well, that was Fidel's genius: publicity. Fidel had won more territory through that medium than through physical conquest. His courtesy to amenable reporters—such as the snob who had ridden in with Bringas and Nilo—had won him a phenomenally favorable press in America.

A car pulled in and parked down the lot. Evidently the driver was not yet aware of the local commotion.

Then the man saw Bringas, standing there with his neat city suit and his sawed-off shotgun at the ready. The visitor looked startled, then dismayed. He revved the motor and sideswiped a parked car in his impatience to get away.

Let him go! Bringas thought. Let him spread the word, telling the world he had single-handedly fought off a squad of rampaging guerrillas! By the time anyone checked, the Fidelistas would be long gone.

Then Bringas saw the girl in the car.

He brought his weapon to bear and blasted away at the tires. The pellets sprayed out in a circular cloud, the sound was deafening, and the recoil rocked him back painfully. He had fired from the waist, but aim was hardly essential with a monster like this, the most murderous available at short range. A tire exploded and the car careened to the side and slewed to a stop.

Bringas ran up. "Yegua!" he cried.

The man was dressed in a white linen shirt and was fat, gross, and dark—the typical local politician. He was obviously terrified, but like a cornered rat he put up a show of opposition. "What is the meaning of this?" he demanded, flashing a hand bearing two large diamond rings and a third ring of ruby.

Bringas hardly looked at him. "Filthy capitalist swine,

get out of here before I stuff your rectum with lead!" he shouted.

The man almost swallowed his cigar as he tumbled out of the car and lumbered down the parking lot without further protest. He had evidently come to play cards and was entirely unprepared for this reception.

The girl held her position in the other seat, her legs crossed, her countenance cool. She wore very tight white slacks, pretty sandals, and a light jacket. She was beautiful.

"Yegua," Bringas repeated, gazing at her avidly over the hot barrel of his shotgun. "I have found you at last."

She returned his gaze haughtily. "If you mean to shoot me, get on with it," she said.

Bringas was taken aback. "Don't you remember—that night on the mountain, when the storm came, my little yegua? Where did you—"

But he did not finish, for she reached across the driver's seat and slapped him smartly on the mouth. "Kill me if you will, barbarian; do not attempt to insult me again."

Then he recognized her definitively. Not as the yegua, for this high-class property was no campesino's child—but as Adelita Suarez, the woman who would help him four years from now. No wonder she had seemed to know him then!

But what a coincidence that he should find her like this! In a car at a golf course he happened to be raiding!

Coincidence? Never! She had known him in 1962 because he had met her here in 1958! If he had not met her now, she would have been a stranger then. This was the true onset of that acquaintance—only she was as baffled now as he had been then. She was not the yegua—his yearning had never been for the yegua, but for Adelita—the woman vaguely suggested by the yegua, that night! He had been unaware of the impression this woman had made on him during that brief encounter in Havana, and had mistaken his emotion on the mountain, incredibly, imagining that mere superficial sex-appeal—

Or had it been another aspect of temporal disorientation?

And what about the secondary paradox shield? Why hadn't this acquaintance been blocked? Was it because *he* had met her first in 1962, and now that shield was working in reverse, guaranteeing their acquaintance?

And 233, his wife of his own framework—what about her? What was he doing chasing after *any* woman of the past?

"*Must* you stare so?" she demanded, as though that were on the same level as kidnapping her or calling her a prostitute. She could not know that he had not intended it as an insult.

Bringas hauled open the door on the driver's side and slung his shotgun into her lap. "Hold this, Adelita," he said, getting into the seat.

Startled, she accepted the weapon, not seeming to realize that it gave her power over him. "How do you know my name?" she demanded as he started the motor.

He ignored her, concentrating on the driving. Cars were plentiful in this world, but not in his own, and he had had very little opportunity to drive one himself. This one didn't respond properly, though the engine was straining. He checked the brake and the gearshift, but couldn't locate the problem. "Something's blocking the wheels," he muttered.

"Your bullets," she said.

He had forgotten! He had shot out a tire! That rubber was just an inert drag on the mechanism.

And of course he couldn't desert his guerrilla patrol, whose cars he was supposed to be guarding. What had been on his mind?

A woman. What else?

"You'll have to ride with us, then," he snapped. "Come on!"

He got out and ran back toward the cars. She followed more slowly, carrying the heavy weapon.

"Wait in here," he told her, opening the door to the car he had come in. "If anyone challenges you, tell him you're mine. Here—I'll take the gun."

"What is your name?" she asked with a hint of a smile as she yielded the weapon.

"Juan Bringas."

And that was the way he took his Cuban mistress.

The raid was a success. The rebels frightened several golfers by threatening to burn their cars, but departed as instructed without actually hurting anyone. The soldiers summoned by the country club management arrived too late. Frustrated by what they deemed a malicious false alarm—nothing seemed to be damaged—they sacked the place themselves, beating up club employees and looting freely. The result was that the club closed and five ex-employees defected to the rebels.

Meanwhile the rebel party departed Caney in good order, avoiding Santiago and taking a route that led to Puerto Boniato, the highest hill in the area. They took the "scenic" road, driving right past the circular Boniato jail where Fidel had once been imprisoned. They paid their respects by pelting it with ripe fruit from the sacks. Yes, it had been a good mission!

Hubert Matos was jubilant. "More raids like that, and we won't have to capture the city at all!" he said. "They will all be Fidelistas!"

Bringas had his own satisfactions. But the mountain life did not agree with Adelita. "I am no guerrilla," she protested one night in their tent. "I am a college girl, and one day I will be a teacher. I stay with you because you are more of a man than any I have known, and I'm not referring to that organ you're so busy with. But I belong in the city."

He tried to silence her with a kiss, but though she returned it she would not be distracted. "All this killing—it sickens me," she said. "The brutality, the lying—"

He ran his hands over her beautifully formed torso. Four

years of youth had taken nothing from the splendor of her body, yet she had a mind too. She could discourse on art and politics and history with excellent discretion, and her attitudes were civilized in the highest sense. She was probably as intelligent as he, once allowance was made for the backwardness of her times.

"The brutality is Batista's," he pointed out. "We only fight to liberate the island from poverty and tyranny."

"You and the communistas," she whispered tersely.

The communists were one of the contemporary political/social phenomena, more popular in Asia than in America. The local party owed allegiance to the nation of Soviet Russia, but was a small minority in Cuba. So he laughed. "Is Hubert a communist? Camilo? Fidel himself?"

"No," she admitted as she writhed under his touch. "Not Matos, maybe not Castro. Cienfuegos, though—"

For a moment he was angry. "I fought in Camilo's group! I will not listen to—"

"No, of course not," she said quickly but without conviction. "It was probably a lying rumor the Batistianos spread. But Che Guevara and Raul Castro—"

Bringas dismissed the matter "Fidel is our leader, not Che or Raul. He knows what he is doing. After we win Cuba, I will give you a beautiful apartment in Havana, rent-free. And you can be a teacher—we will need many of them, for we shall bring good education to every campesino. What will you teach?" He was willing to inquire about her future, but not about her past, for he did not want to know what she had done or whom she had traveled with before he found her. For all he knew, now, he might find himself in her past, and he didn't want to foul it up.

"English," she murmured, rolling lithely on top of him. "French."

He wrapped his arms around her sleek back and crushed her to him, front to front. "Some day I must learn English. Then I will be able to make love to you in two languages!"

"Hey, slow down!" she cried. "Why do you always try to do it all in two minutes? This isn't a motor race! We have all night."

He paused, embarrassed. It was true: time was far more leisurely in this world, and there were few deadlines to meet. But his conditioning to the minute-and-second precision of 2413 prevented him from obliging her. His act of love had to occur rapidly, and this particular performance was no exception.

"I'm no yegua, despite what you think," she said afterwards. "But I am going to teach you something tonight. One hour—and let's see how good a revolutionary you really are!"

"But I'm finished," he protested regretfully.

"Well, *I'm* not!" And she caught hold of him where it hurt, particularly at this moment, though not unpleasantly. "I am going to teach you amor a la Cubana—love Cuban style," she said, lowering her head to his body.

"Hey!" he cried, surprised. But her head bobbed up and down and her medal swung from side to side, brushing her breasts and his torso, and he lacked the words to make his protest. He had a vision of Superman, girl kneeling at his crotch . . . Perversion, then, but less so now. In fact not objectionable at all; would Adelita do it if it were?

In his own society procreation was essentially a function of the state, with the individual granted only technical right to the act. The form was explicitly prescribed, and insemination was an open and often public matter. Here in Cuba, in contrast, the intimacy was almost invariably secret, often with the lights extinguished so that even the participants could not observe the forbidden organs operating. But that same privacy permitted considerable deviation from the norm, since the variation was limited only by the desires of the participants. The state need never know that portions of the amorous urge were savagery, that there could be infertile intercourse. This world was already overpopulated; maximum live births were *not* its primary concern. In fact, the state did not even *care* whether issue resulted from any given intercourse, and contraceptive devices were openly marketed!

Adelita's hand slid down along his thigh, around— "Hey!" he said again, jumping. Even Superman had not— but it did feel good. He knew, anatomically, what pressure on the prostate could do, but this—

She lifted her head. "You talk of horses," she said with mock grimness. "Well now you're ready to ride!" And it was so, for her remarkable stimulations had brought him to renewed readiness.

He started to turn over, to get on top of her, but she held him down. Instead, she mounted *him*, knees flexed by his sides, body leaning forward impressively. "*Ride! Ride!*" she exclaimed, and galloped like a horseman, but with her bottom anchored by his saddle-horn. Her heavy breasts flopped up and down, her hair flung about every which way, and the medal yanked at its chain as though possessed of demonic animation.

Bringas was so amazed by her performance that he was hardly aware of his own, but it was a phenomenal experience. She had taught him something, all right!

Now he was really ready to rest. But she wouldn't let him be. "My turn," she said firmly. "I have shown you how. . . ."

At the end of that intensive hour he lay beside her exhausted—but he had learned enough to last him a fertile lifetime.

"Yegua. . . ." he muttered as he cooled into sleep, and jumped as she slapped him resoundingly on the buttocks. Jesus, but they had known how to live and love in the past!

Her arguments also lingered with him. There *was* brutality in the revolution—and was it all necessary? Communists were among Fidel's top lieutenants; their idea of freedom differed substantially from that of the majority of revolutionaries. He knew that brutality was commonly an attribute of oppressive regimes, such as the present one in Cuba and a number of others of this world.

It seemed important to Adelita that the new regime be gentle and democratic. Bringas wanted her to be happy, for he had several years to go in Cuba and she was a fine woman. So such matters became his concern too, apart from his long-term mission. What was Cuba like in 1962? The prisons had been bad, of course—but he did not delude himself that they would be typical of the nation. He had not had a chance to study it objectively, and he had not been concerned with that aspect of history. Thus he really did not know the future, despite his origin and his mission.

As a result, the episode of the campesino occurred at an impressionable time for him, as a portent of the possible nature of the Castro regime.

Raul Castro, Fidel's younger brother, was a slight, beardless man whose longish hair tied back in a bun made him seem effeminate beside the roughly bearded rebels. From behind it was possible to mistake him for a woman, and there were snide jokes about this even within the rebel camps.

The Castros, like many Cubans, were of mixed descent. Angel Castro, Fidel's father, had come directly from Spain, a shrewd—some said unscrupulous—farmer and businessman. Lina Ruz, Angel's common-law wife, had Chinese blood dating from the importation of coolies for field labor some generations before. The mongolic strain seemed to account for Raul's oriental aspect, and his embarrassing inability to raise a beard. It was odd, however, that he differed so much from his brothers.

Whatever the reason, Raul carried a considerable if undefined grudge against the world. The men loved Fidel; they learned to fear the hawklike Raul. Common gossip held that Raul was a secret communist.

Bringas, continuing his travels, was a member of a scouting party led by Raul in the Sierra del Cristal mountains, in the eastern section of Oriente Province. It was the last leg of his liaison route before he returned to Fidel with his reports. He had been met by Captain Sotu and Commandante Nino Diaz, who naturally wanted him to take a good impression back to headquarters. They all knew Fidel was planning a major offensive; that was why he had to have accurate and recent information on both his own and the enemy dispositions.

This mission was routine, probing the defense of the city of Sagua de Tanamo. Raul was skilled as any man except Guevara in the daily necessities of revolution. But the men were tired and grouchy. Bringas himself was eager to return to his woman's arms.

Shots sounded. All the men dropped flat. Then they spread out, taking advantage of the available cover to close in on the sniper unobserved.

Raul reached him first. "Pig!" he cried, standing up suddenly with his rifle ready. "You dared fire on the Revolution?"

The farmer whirled around, startled. "No! No! I was only—"

"Death!" Raul cried, licking his lips. The rifle jumped in his hands.

The others rushed up as the victim clutched his chest and fell. "A campesino!" someone exclaimed. "Why did he do it?"

Bringas picked up a dead guineo, a wild hen. This was a small gamebird of the region, gray, and a swift runner. "He didn't. He was only hunting his dinner."

They looked at the bird silently. Raul had gunned down an innocent man.

"He shot at *us*!" Raul screamed. "Give him a rebel trial! We shall establish his guilt. You are witness! He deserved to die!"

Bringas just hefted the dead fowl sadly. "We should have let him explain."

Raul's weapon swung around, but Bringas did not flinch.

Raul was no fool, and he knew the mission Bringas was on, and also that there would never be an opportunity for a second bullet if the first were not mortal.

Seeing that the majority was not with him, Raul changed his tack so smoothly that it seemed he had never considered any other course. "It was an accident. He is dead and no man can change that. But we can make him useful, so that his death is not in vain. Make a sign to hang on him, saying that the Batistianos did it. Because he helped the Revolution, bringing fresh fowl to the guerrillas. All the campesinos in the area will turn against the dictator!"

To this the men agreed, not wanting trouble with Raul, who was the very devil about holding a grudge. They rationalized it until it made sense. Raul mutilated the body so that the farmers would think that the soldiers had tortured the man to get information before shooting him. Bringas had to admit it was an excellent ploy, and perhaps a necessary one. But he felt unclean, being involved in it.

Raul was a bitter, twisted killer. He was Fidel's brother so he had to be tolerated, but he demeaned the spirit of the Revolution. Fidel himself was clean. The Revolution itself was noble and necessary.

A seed of doubt sprouted in Bringas' mind. God help the Revolution if Raul Castro should ever have complete power!

PART FIVE

The climax came with breathtaking suddenness. In November they were waging determined war against the entrenched regime, knowing that years would be required to beat back the government forces extant. In December Christmas season, 1958—Fulgencio Batista presented the rebels his biggest conceivable gift.

He abdicated.

As the bells tolled for the midnight conversion to the new year, 1959, Batista closed up shop and packed his airplane. Within two hours he was out of the country with his fortune, never to return. His most intimate henchmen departed with him, fearing for their welfare under rebel jurisdiction.

General Cantillo set up a provisional government, but no one paid attention to it. Fidel Castro was the heir apparent.

Fidel himself was astonished. "It is a trick, a trap!" he swore, and neither Bringas nor anyone else cared to debate the matter at the time. "We will not have the strength to drive him out for another six months!"

Certainly the rebels were unready to assume control of the island. But something positive had to be done, or the immensely promising situation would deteriorate—if it were *not* a government ruse.

They discussed it tersely. All agreed that Fidel would be foolish to put his head into the noose that Havana just might be. But he couldn't hold back, either, for there were other guerrilla groups, and they would be quick to fill the power vacuum if he did not.

In the end, they decided to stage a maximum-publicity victory parade the length of the island, taking a week to make the trek to Havana. This would give tremendous publicity to the rebel cause while protecting Fidel from treachery. By the time he arrived at the capital city, his vanguard would have seen to his security there.

Fidel came through with one of the greatest spectacles the island had ever witnessed. Beginning at his home base in Oriente Province, the Castro motorcade traveled along the Central Highway traversing the length of Cuba. Fidel's troops traveled in cars, jeeps, trucks, and tanks, grinning and waving at the citizens who lined the road to cheer them on. No rebel could stop without having flowers placed in his hat, his beard, the barrel of his rifle. The barbudos were the exciting symbol of Cuba's new freedom. Nothing was too good for them.

Three cars made up Fidel's personal entourage. Fidel occupied the first; Bringas and other select bodyguards had the second; American reporters and photographers were in the last. Fidel made a big show of embracing Bringas and the others, of having them at his side in this hour of triumph; but that was about the last such attention they were to receive. Fidel was going to meet his destiny.

The sheer adulation of the people was amazing. Fidel became Christlike in their eyes. Women broke through the guards to kiss any part of him they could attain. Children, teenagers, adults, oldsters—all were there to grin and wave and cheer, and when Fidel stopped at a town to make an impromptu speech—as he did with increasing frequency and enthusiasm—the crowds acclaimed him wildly.

"Our revolutionary government, with the people's backing and the nation's respect—" he said, and was interrupted by applause, for he *had* the backing of these people and the respect of this nation. "After we cleanse the various institutions of all venal and corrupt officials—" More interruption, for corruption was a way of life to much of Cuba's government. "We shall proceed immediately to industrialize the country, mobilizing all inactive capital—some billion and a half dollars—"

But such a vast figure was meaningless to much of his small-town audience, and he quickly went on to matters closer to their own awareness. "We shall settle the small farmers on the land they now rent—*as owners*!" It took minutes for the delirium to subside. "We shall distribute good land among the peasant families who have none—" It seemed as though he would not be able to say more, so great was the response. "We'll establish cooperatives for efficient farming and cattle raising; we'll provide resources, equipment, protection, and useful guidance to the campesinos—" Finally, he gave up trying to finish the speech, the people would not stop cheering.

At the next stop he hit them even harder. "We shall solve the housing problem by cutting all rents in half, by providing tax exemptions on all homes inhabited by the owners, by tripling taxes on rented homes, by tearing down hovels and replacing them with modern multiple-dwelling buildings, and by financing housing all over the island on a scale unheard of before! Just as each rural family shall possess its own tract of land, each city family shall own its home or apartment. There is plenty of building material and more than enough manpower to make a decent home for every Cuban!"

And later yet: "With our reforms, the problem of unemployment will disappear! And we shall reform the educational system. Do not forget the words of the Apostal, Jose Marti: 'A well-educated people will always be strong and free!' "

"But where will the money come from?" someone demanded. There was an immediate motion in the crowd to close in on that man, for it sounded as though he were criticizing Cuba's savior, but Fidel pounced on the question.

"Where will the money be found for all this? An excellent question, brother! When there is an end to rife embezzlement of government funds; when public officials stop taking graft from the large companies who owe taxes to the state; when the country's enormous resources are brought into full use, meaning we no longer buy tanks, bombers, and guns for a country which has no frontiers to defend and where such instruments of war are used against the people; when there is more interest in educating the people than in killing them—then there will be more than enough money. Cuba could easily provide for a population three times as great as it now has, so there is no excuse for the abject poverty of a single one of its present inhabitants. The markets should overflow with produce, pantries should be full, all hands should be working. This is not an inconceivable thought. What is inconceivable is that anyone should go to bed hungry, that children should die for lack of medical attention. What is inconceivable is that thirty percent of our farm people cannot write their names and that ninety-nine percent of them know nothing of Cuba's history. What is inconceivable is that the majority of our rural people are now living in worse circumstances than were the people Columbus discovered living in the fairest land that human eyes had ever seen.

"To those who would call me a dreamer, I quote the words of Marti: 'A true man does not seek the path where advantage lies, but rather, the path where duty lies, and this is the only practical man, whose dreams of today will be the law of tomorrow, because he who has looked back on the upheavals of history and has seen civilizations going up in flames, crying out in bloody struggle, throughout the centuries, knows that the future well-being of man, without exception, lies on the side of duty.' "

• • •

What a smashing climax it was, the day Fidel rode into fair Havana! As the calvacade neared the city it became larger and larger. People joined it in increasing numbers, bringing their spanking new uniforms and weapons—and many men their newly begun beards—into this parade of the victorious. If there had been a tenth of this number in the Sierra Maestra, Bringas thought wryly, the revolution would have been won a year ago! But of course Cubans always flocked to the winner—it was a national trait. Even the hated Batista policemen had jumped on the bandwagon, wearing their old uniforms with the red and black armbands of July 26.

The police were necessary, however expedient their conversion! The crush was tremendous. The people thronged so thickly that there was nothing but faces, faces, faces— a million of them crushing up against the walking line of police and militia, peering from the windows of every building, waving from the rooftops. Women mad with passion for the savior of their nation, men eager to emulate the famed barbudos, children screaming with delight for the parade. The cheering was incessant, a constant noise like the roaring of the ocean waves against a jagged cliff. Fidel rode part of the way through the city in a tank—and perhaps it was just as well! Police were injured trying to hold back the surging masses determined to have the hero lay his hands upon them, even for an instant.

Bringas looked out the window of his crowded car and saw a row of yellow buildings. Suddenly he was struck by the feeling of déjà vu—he had been through this before!

Then he realized: the buildings were the Talleres del Ministerio de Obras Publicas—public workshops. Opposite them were the Havana oil refineries, and just ahead was the Rio Luyano, the river into the bay. He *had* been here before, and in a car with Adelita beside him, in late 1962, almost four years from now chronologically. Adelita would know him well then, and must have remembered this trip affectionately—while he just stared out the windows, thinking her a stranger!

Bringas put his arm around her and squeezed. If only he could have known!

When he looked out again they were passing Castillo de Atares, the old Spanish fortress on top of its hill, with the police car pool below. Then up around the curve of the bay again—this time not as a fugitive from the law but in the entourage of a conquering hero!

Still, the sight of La Cabana chilled him, for he knew how cruel it was, or would be, inside. He never wanted to repeat *that* experience!

He listened to the continual applause of the masses and allowed himself to be cheered. This was a time of joy; prison had no relevance. There were so many marvels to appreciate, and such a good life ahead!

The cavalcade went on by the house where Bringas and Jimenez had spent the night in 1962. What had happened to Jimenez, and where was he now, in this earlier time? It had been too bad to leave him stranded in Cuba, after his invaluable help! The cars turned down Calle 23, and still the people crowded the streets, craning for a view of Fidel and his entourage. The entire city must have stopped every other activity for this occasion!

Bringas suffered another shock of recognition as they skirted the huge, beautiful Havana cemetery. He had been there more recently; in fact he had passed it on his way to join Fidel himself! Then on across the Rio Almendares and down Avenida 41 and on, until at last the car pulled up at Camp Colombia where Fidel was to make his big speech.

Fidel's speech was a masterpiece, even for him. At one point, as he spoke on the great outdoor stage, a cloud of pigeons was released. Hundreds of birds spread out over the audience—and one of them flew to Fidel's shoulder and perched there. "The dove of peace!" he exclaimed, pleased, and the effect was electric. What better sign of divine approval could be given?

Bringas was on duty, moving through the crowd to spot any adverse element. Fidel was enormously popular, and no one in his right mind would wish the hero harm—but there was always the tiny sick minority, the fanatic or the otherwise insane, who would shoot God Himself if given the opportunity. Particularly if it would make a headline for the killer. Consider Kennedy of the U.S.A., he thought—and suddenly realized that if this second mission of his were successful, Kennedy would be killed again. Reality would revert to Text A.

No time for such morbid reflections now! If he saw a gun in civilian hands, he would have to act quickly.

Meanwhile, Fidel was performing splendidly. He projected a tremendous personal magnetism. He knew what the crowd wanted, and he gave it to them in full measure—yet he seemed to be speaking to every man directly, even Bringas, who had heard most of the speech before along the route to Havana.

"The right of rebellion against tyranny has been recognized from the most ancient times to the present by men of all creeds, ideas, and doctrines Consider Article 40 of the Constitution. . . ."

Amen! Bringas thought. There should be the right of rebellion against even so sophisticated a tyranny as Fidelia, centuries hence, that would not let a man marry outside his Caste or indulge in non-reproductive sex-play. . . .

Fidel gesticulated frequently, dramatizing his points, at times his body oddly contorted. He was angry, sad, contrite, humorous, sarcastic, and always surprising. No one could anticipate what he would say next. He knew exactly how to keep the attention of the people, and he deftly combined his lawyer's eloquence with stories about his recent life in the Sierra, all of it pitched at the level of the common citizen.

"Armas para que!" Fidel cried. "Weapons why?" Many factions retained their weapons, such as the underground anti-Batista DRE, which had seized a government arsenal in Atares Castle. But there was no need of weapons now, no need whatsoever, for Batista was out and democracy was in. Only the forces of the 26th of July should retain weapons, to keep order; only gangsters would seek to arm themselves privately, now that the revolution had been won. Thus those factions would be forced by public pressure to yield their hoards, disarm themselves and the country, so that the barbudos could go home. Fidel had acted to prevent a disastrous internal conflict from developing, and at one stroke was promoting a lasting peace and harmony.

"Schools and not fortresses!" And right here at Camp Colombia, Fidel promised, he would build a school.

He also announced what was to be an extremely popular measure: Cubans should not pay their debts to garroteros, the grasping moneylenders, but should denounce these culprits so that they could be prosecuted. The common man would not be at the mercy of such vultures henceforth!

Abruptly Fidel turned to Camilo Cienfuegos, who was at his side with a strong protective force. "Voy bien, Camilo?" he demanded. "Am I going right, Camilo?"

Cienfuegos, caught offguard, broke out laughing. "Yes!" he replied, and the people applauded wildly. What a masterstroke! Bringas could see that even those few who were still suspicious of Fidel in the audience had been disarmed by this aside, for it showed that Fidel was human and humble, not above consulting the opinion of his barbudos. New interest focused on Camilo, the head of Fidel's troops. Surely this was another great man, people were thinking, to give Fidel advice in public!

And yet Adelita thought Camilo was a communist?

After that dialogue with Cienfuegos, the mood of the crowd became more relaxed, and Bringas no longer had to search for fanatics. Nobody was going to shoot now!

At last it was over. "Patria o muerte, venceremos!" Fidel finished. "Fatherland or death, we shall win!"

And it was a storybook denouement, as Fidel's marvelous new government unfolded.

President: Manuel Urritia Ileo, the judge who had boldly supported the rebel movement in Santiago when a group of captive Fidelistas had been brought to trial before him in 1957. Urritia had acquitted them—and fled the country. Now he returned in glory.

Premier: Jose Miro Cardona, once Fidel's law professor, and head of the Havana Bar Association. He had once escaped from the Batista police by garbing himself in priest's robes. No longer!

Minister of State: Roberto Agramonte, the reformist Ortodoxo Party presidential candidate in 1952—the year Batista had usurped power.

Minister of the Treasury: Rufo Lopez Fresquet, one of the chief moneyraisers for the rebels, married to an American.

Minister of Public Works: Manuel Ray, a leading figure in the underground and an excellent engineer.

Chief of the Army: Camilo Cienfuegos.

Fidel himself was not a member of the Council of Ministers.

What better interim government could be imagined? Surely these same officers would be returned overwhelmingly at the first elections! The bad times were finished; the new millenium had begun and Cuba had taken its place in the sun!

Every man was equal in the new order, but the favored members of the July 26th Movement were naturally provided with the finest facilities by the grateful populace. Juan Bringas had acquitted himself admirably in the Sierra Maestra and was favored with the rank of Captain.

The homes and possessions of the fleeing Batistianos were available as legitimate spoils of war, and quickly appropriated by the barbudos. Camilo Cienfuegos became extremely popular with Havana's upper social register, attending many parties and being seen with prominent debutantes; he seemed to be as well regarded as Fidel himself. The Havana Hilton Hotel was taken over too, providing excellent rooms at free rent, and the best restaurants were free. Nothing was too good for the nation's liberators!

Bringas got a beautiful luxury apartment at Calle 1 and A and installed Adelita there in splendor. It took up the entire floor of the building, with a marvelous view of Havana on one side and the sea on the other, from their fifteen story elevation. There was wall-to-wall deep carpeting, very expensive velvet drapes, four bedrooms, two baths (one with a sunken tub), dining room, kitchen, library, parlor—what a life the fat cats of Batista's time had had! Even a black mahogany bar stocked with several hundred dollars worth of liquor.

In the capacious closets there was clothing for male, female, and child. Adelita exclaimed over some hundred bottles of expensive French perfumes. She also discovered jewelry, including a fine gold bracelet with American twenty-dollar coins suspended from it and lovely pearl filigree pendants.

"But I can't wear this!" she protested.

"I promised you the good city life," he said, checking over the masculine wardrobe. "You're no slouch at wearing jewelry!"

"My own, yes. But this must be returned to its owner. It isn't right just to take—"

"You *are* the owner, now," he assured her. "The Batistianos are gone with their ill-gotten foreign bank accounts; what they could not carry with them reverts to the Revolution."

"Then these things should be turned in to the Revolution. We can't just—"

"Look at this!" he exclaimed. It was a .45 Colt pistol inlaid with gold and mother-of-pearl. "What a beauty! I'll wear this myself!"

Later that day Bringas spotted a lieutenant taking two girls for a ride in a bright red 1958 American Cadillac convertible, so he pulled rank and, when it became necessary, his ornate pistol, and acquired the vehicle for Adelita. She had always wanted such a car, he knew, and red was a favorite color.

Yet possession of all she had desired had a strange effect on Adelita. She became pensive, even cold. She would not wear the new jewelry or drive the car, or use any of the elegant appurtenances of the apartment except the smaller bathroom. "It isn't right," was all she said. "We can't begin this way." He thought at first she was joking; then he thought she would get over it. But she only became more inhibited, and he did not know what to make of it. This was a side of her he had not appreciated before—this withdrawal. What was wrong with her?

Frustrated, but not wanting to have trouble with her, Bringas left her alone. He arranged to spend the night with a fellow officer, Pepln Naranjo, who had another fine apartment in the Focsa, a tremendous building in the Vedado section of Havana formed in the shape of an obtuse angle. It was only a mile's drive from Bringas' location, but it seemed farther—because Adelita had become more important to him than he had supposed until now.

Pepin was surprisingly glad to have company, though he was not a close friend of Bringas'. They sat up talking until late, about inconsequential matters. It was as though Pepin did not really want to sleep. When he finally did retire, he took a potent sedative. Bringas observed but did not comment.

Bringas woke, startled, in darkness. A man was screaming about murder and death, and for a moment in the fog of sleep Bringas thought it was himself. The white phosphorus grenade killing still haunted him upon occasion, though he had lived a year since that episode. Of course the men he had killed were alive now, and would remain alive for three more years, which mitigated the nightmare somewhat.

But it was Pepin who screamed now. Bringas shook him awake, cautiously, for the Sierra veterans often awoke fighting. But the man was shaking with terror or horror; there was no fight in him.

In the following half hour Bringas learned the truth: just a few days before, Pepin had been present when Raul Castro—there was that malign presence again!—rounded up a group of suspected traitors near Santiago de Cuba, herded them into the country, stood them before an open ditch, and massacred them all.

"There must have been eighty people," Pepin groaned. "Twenty civilians, a couple of newspapermen—even a child of eleven! We machinegunned them all without trial—"

Yes, that was Raul's way. Bringas understood the man's terrible anguish. What could he say that would relieve Pepin's agony? What possible way was there for *anyone* to excuse a crime of this magnitude? That it should happen in the name of the Revolution—

There was nothing he could do. The deed was done. Pepin would simply have to work it out in his own fashion. It would be useless even to complain to Fidel, for Fidel was blind about his brother. Raul was just the cross the Revolution had to bear. But such rationalization could not help, and Bringas didn't attempt to present it to Pepin.

To be party to a massacre. . . .

Bringas did not stay. Instead he drove home, back to Adelita.

She met him at the door with tousled hair and red-rimmed eyes, but she was still beautiful to him. "Throw it away," he told her, not needing to specify what. "All I want is you."

That was a lie, for it was really 233, his wife of this world's future, that he wanted most. But it was enough for Adelita. She made him savagely welcome.

It was awkward to cope with the adulation that over-lapped the Fidel/Camilo charisma and enriched Bringas' personal life, but he became accustomed to it fairly rapidly. Adelita remained pensive, but her distress was not directed at him. She even gave him a gold identity bracelet, with Chinese-style lettering: Juan. And she announced her intention to help the Revolution by becoming a teacher in one of the new schools that would soon be built. The outlook was good.

The only cloud on Bringas' horizon was the nature of his mission. Somehow in the next two years he had to obtain his bonafides as an anti-Castro underground agent—an appalling prospect.

Then the executions began.

"I thought there was to be an end to the death penalty," Adelita exclaimed, distracted. "The war is over. Why does the killing go on?"

Bringas tried to sooth her. "The fighting is over, but not the war. Not until after the last war criminal has been tried. It would not be right for the Batista butchers to exploit the populace for years, then escape rightful punishment when the revolution fostered by their misdeeds finally comes to power."

"The worst ones went into exile with Batista," she said. "There are only minor ones left. Why not just give them jail sentences?"

He shook his head. "The mood of the people will not tolerate wrist-slapping measures. An example must be made. If these criminals are not executed promptly, the people will take the law into their own hands,, and there will be a monstrous bloodbath. Then it won't just be the guilty that die; many innocent people will be drawn in too. Orderly government could break down while mobs range the streets. Fidel is too kind to let that happen. He is giving the people swift, definite justice, that will satisfy them in this time of passion. In a week or two it will be over, and then there will be no more executions. It may not be pleasant at the moment, but considered long-range this is by far the best and *least* bloody course."

He had spoken of the people taking the law into their own hands, but it was Raul Castro he was thinking of. Raul would have no pretext for further murders!

Adelita shook her head dubiously. "Never in all the history of Cuba have the victors turned on the vanquished like this. Traditionally there is a policy of national reconciliation and forgiveness. Even after Machado's fall—"

"Never in the history of Cuba has there been a revolution like this one. This is no palace coup!"

"In the past twenty years the death penalty has only been invoked once," she said sadly. "Now . . ."

He let it lie. He knew she would understand when she saw the long-range benefits of the brave new programs. Her own dreams of teaching would come true, once the schools had been constructed and the initial problems solved. A nation was being remade, for the first time along truly revolutionary lines. Cuba's entire way of life would be transformed. Fidel would set a shining example for all the hemisphere!

Bringas knew this, for Cuba alone had survived the final holocaust as an entity. Fidel alone was responsible. It was impossible to explain his certainty to Adelita, because of the paradox shield.

He also could not explain his facts to the American press. Loud newspaper headlines condemned the executions, and there seemed to be no comprehension of their real significance. A reporter mentioned this criticism to Fidel a week after the triumphant Havana arrival, and of course Fidel himself had no patience with such obtuseness. "If the Americans don't like what is happening in Cuba," he cried, furious, "they can land the Marines and then there will be 200,000 dead gringos!"

Bringas laughed when he heard about that, and gleefully repeated it to Adelita. "The Colossus of the North will not be allowed to meddle in *this* government!" he added. "The Americans don't like anything in the hemisphere they can't control or exploit."

But she remained pensive. "The Americans never threatened to land Marines. They only criticized the needless killing. And when did Cubans ever talk of 'gringos'? That's Mexican slang. We have no racism here; Batista himself was of mixed blood."

She was right, he realized, to that extent. She knew her language and politics, as he should have remembered, and she had beaten him at his own specialty. "Gringo" was out of context in Cuba, and it was odd that Fidel had used that particular term. Perhaps his prior sojourn in Mexico . . .

"He was only making a point," he said. "Fidel has nothing against America. He only wants their politicians to keep their nefarious noses out of our internal affairs, as we keep out of theirs. No more interference; no more Platt Amendments." The Platt Amendment to the Cuban constitution had given the United States the right to intervene militarily to protect its interests, and it had been invoked several times historically.

"But that was finished thirty years ago!" she said. "What are you, a parrot that only repeats what Fidel says and cannot think for himself?"

"I hope not! I just happen to believe that Fidel means well. Why not give him the benefit of the doubt?"

"Sure," she agreed, and he thought she was content. She made love with a kind of desperation and imagination that tantalized him as much as it gratified him.

Bringas had argued in favor of the executions, but he had not realized how relevant they were to be to his own concerns. For suddenly he was assigned to be a member of the Revolutionary Courts, passing judgement on the accused. There was of course no moral question involved, as there was only one feasible verdict, but the experience disturbed him deeply. He was disgusted by the apparent bloodlust of many of the spectators who were regular attendees. The prosecutor was one Major Humberto Sori Marin, and he was savagely eloquent. "Paredon! Paredon!" he cried, calling for execution while Bringas winced at the memory of his one-time experience with that concept and almost felt the urine soaking his trousers again. The defense witnesses were insulted and threatened, and sometimes the death sentences were tacked up even before the trial ended—*and the spectators applauded the sentence.*

Bringas had not suspected that such ruthlessness and disregard for human rights and dignity could be invoked among civilian Cubans, ordinarily the fairest and friendliest of people. Surely Fidel was not aware of the details of these trials; he would never sanction them otherwise! Yet perhaps it was a necessary catharsis for the nation, this ugly elimination of the final vestiges of the old order. What might these savages applauding have done if there had been no trials? Would each have blossomed into another Raul. . . ?

Yet the savage in Bringas wished the *spectators* could be put on trial with similar dispatch.

Weeks passed, but the trials and executions did not stop. Bringas understood their basic rationale, of course—he had explained it often enough to Adelita—but he was also aware of how many people inside and outside Cuba did *not* understand. Not all of these were Batistianos or traitors. The excesses of the extemporaneous courts were increasingly hard to justify, even for *members* of the courts like himself.

"One word from Fidel," Adelita murmured, "and it would stop. The people would understand." He could not debate that point—but he hesitated to approach Fidel himself. There was no telling how Fidel would react to implied criticism from an officer of the Revolution; it could make the trials twice as bad. Certainly it could cast suspicion on Bringas himself—a suspicion he could by no means afford, if he were to proceed with his own mission.

The trials dragged on into February, casting a pall over the once-bright vision of freedom and justice. Bringas was on the panel that conducted the trial of Captain Sosa Blanco in that month. This was the first of the "circus trials": it was held in the huge Havana Sport Palace and was televised to all the island. It was immediately apparent that Sosa was a very brave officer of the Batista forces, and had fought hard against Fidel in the Sierra. Had that been the extent of his indictment, he would surely have been pardoned. But he stood accused of crimes that could not be pardoned, and Bringas found it curious that a man of such courage and ability should have such an ugly side to his character.

Did he really have such a side? Witnesses were brought in to identify the accused, who was manacled and in prison uniform, and were unable to do so until he was specifically pointed out. Obviously Sosa was a stranger to the majority of his accusers—which didn't make sense.

There was an increasing protest from the spectators about the proceedings, for Sosa was anything but a skulking criminal. Finally, the trial had to be suspended and finished in private lest it become a complete mockery.

Bringas eventually pieced together the truth: the crimes of which Sosa Blanco stood accused were actually those of another officer who fled to Miami, Mero Sosa. No wonder there had been confusion about identification and reputation!

But the other members of the court would not pay attention. "This man is innocent!" Bringas cried. "How can we convict him in secret of another man's crimes? We are treating him as Batista treated Fidel in 1953!" That shook them, but in the end they could not admit the mistake, and they outvoted him 4 to 1. Sosa was executed.

Adelita raged at such atrocity. "I heard they killed a young blond boy," she said one evening. "The priest moved away, and then this prisoner told the firing squad that they were shooting an innocent man. 'When you go home,' he said, 'you may find that one dear to you has died in an accident.' And when they fired, only one bullet hit him, and that not mortally."

"This is ridiculous," Bringas snapped. "They *all* claim to be innocent. We do study the evidence, and—"

"What finally happened to that boy?" she demanded sullenly.

He sighed. "Captain Marks, the American supervisor, stepped up and shot him twice through the head with his pistol. Then he arrested the entire firing squad."

"And we fought this civil war to abolish the death penalty, for the return of justice!" she said witheringly.

"It was necessary," Bringas said, though he did not like defending Marks. The American was nicknamed "The Butcher" and was the type to pull the kind of joke execution Bringas himself had experienced in Cabana prison three years hence. "Discipline must be enforced, or law means nothing."

"*Justice* means nothing, when Major Marin prosecutes," she said, turning away.

Actually, Marin was more complex than that. He was sincere in his prosecutions, and believed he was ridding the new nation of old criminals. But Bringas could hardly blame Adelita for her opinion; more and more, he shared it.

Then came the trial of Captain Jose Castaño. Castaño had served for a decade in the bureau for anti-communist repression, and was said to be one of Cuba's most intelligent and dedicated officers. He spoke several languages, and probably knew more about communism on the island than any other noncommunist. The trial was a farce; protests were raised by the United States, Spain, Britain, France, the Vatican, and even prominent Cubans. This time Fidel was swayed, and promised to suspend Castaño's sentence and give him thirty years in prison instead.

Relieved, Bringas suppressed his qualms about La Cabana and visited the prison not long before midnight, intending to talk to Captain Castaño about communism—if the man were awake. This was mainly because Adelita felt so strongly about the subject, and Bringas had never really understood why so many people should be so strongly affected by a simple difference of governmental philosophy. Surely Castaño was the man to clarify the matter!

Actually, Bringas would have made the excursion another day, but Adelita had a premonition of danger and insisted that he go tonight. Probably she knew how he hated the Cabana, and suspected he would never go if he didn't do it while the trial was fresh in his experience. She could be right. . . .

He did not get to see the prisoner. Che Guevara met him in the office. The man had cut the shoulder-length hair he had worn in the Sierra, and now the black curls were largely covered by a black beret, but the fringe beard and major's star and fatigue uniform identified him absolutely. "Juan Bringas!" he cried with affected fraternity, for he was not socially inclined. "How fortunate to see you again! I have been meaning to talk with you."

Bringas had had few direct dealings with Guevara, and would have been happy to discuss matters with him at any other time, but the moment was awkward. Guevara was surely a communist, and so would be a prime topic for Bringas' discussion with Castaño—and here he was at the prison! Certainly one of the most intelligent members of the Revolutionary high command, he could easily become suspicious of Bringas' reason for visiting La Cabana at this time. That would be disastrous.

"You are an extremely interesting fellow," Guevara remarked, guiding Bringas toward the exit. "I was impressed with your abilities from the start, and I know Raul hates you, so naturally I investigated." He shook his finger in friendly warning. "It is best not to balk Raul; he is a very determined, dangerous man."

Not half so dangerous as Che Guevara, though! If he had already investigated—

"But Fidel likes you," Guevara continued after a pause. He was breathing quickly, for he was asthmatic. Suddenly Bringas understood what fate he might have had, granted

Raul's enmity, had Fidel *not* been favorably disposed. A man like Camilo Cienfuegos could afford such conflict—it was well known that Camilo and Raul hated each other—but Juan Bringas was a sparrow among hawks, in this context.

"I like Fidel," Bringas said honestly. And realized with a start that he was discussing the leading figure of the Text A future—with the leading figure of the Text B future! What a significant nexus of history he stood at now! "Che, I—"

"*Doctor Guevara*, not Che!"

It was like a backhand slap across the cheek, that instant reprimand! Guevara was vain, and he had a violent temper. It was rumored that he often clashed with Fidel himself—with apparent impunity. Better to forget pride and apologize in a hurry; even in a good mood this man was trouble!

"*Doctor* Guevara, of course. I just wanted to say how much I admire you, too. I—"

"It seems you have no past," Guevara said, mollified. "You did not come from Uruguay, and Ramon Rodruigez was not responsible for your referral to our underground. Yet you are not a Batistiano or an American agent. Strangest of all—" He broke off, his alert brown eyes glancing sidelong at Bringas.

Was Guevara going to turn him in? No—they had merely come to the main gate, and the guards were in earshot. But that would be a very brief halt. Well, he would have to let the man have his say; obviously Guevara was working up to something.

"That is what I mean," Guevara said outside. "I cannot talk about you to others. I cannot reveal what I know to anyone—except to you directly. It amazes me, and it alarms me."

"What do you mean, Doctor?" Bringas asked, fearing what the man did mean.

"There is something about you—a force, a block, a curse—that makes me helpless to affect you. And the records—do you know that your name appears in no records—even the ones we ourselves have made? It is as though you do not exist—yet here you are."

Then Bringas understood. The secondary paradox shield! His name in history would represent a change in that history. And until he acted at the crucial point to divert the stream without eliminating himself, he could not affect it in very many other ways. So all records of him disappeared, even during his stay here. Only the memories of his acquaintances remained—and they could not change things either. When he passed from the scene, they would forget him entirely, and it would be as though he had never existed—except that his highly selective changes would have been accomplished.

Guevara had fought the paradox effect and lost—and knew it!

"Who are you?" Guevara demanded. It was the same question and the same tone the Espiritismo priest had put to him in his own time.

Why not tell him? If the shield was functioning this consistently, it would make no difference. Perhaps he had been grotesquely over-cautious. If he could tell Guevara, he could also tell Adelita!

"I am sure you are not a traitor—not yet," Guevara said. "The Castro regime and Yankee imperialism are engaged in a death struggle, and we both know that one of the two must die in this fight. But you have served loyally, and you have not been ambitious for power. In fact you have shown consistently humanitarian instincts that will soon cost you your position on the revolutionary courts. Once the paperwork sticks! That is not my doing, for I have been unable to affect you and I do not really care. How do you explain yourself?"

Why not tell him?

"You do not answer me," Guevara observed wisely. "Is it because your master has stricter discipline than mine?"

Guevara's master: world communism? Why not—

Then Bringas realized. Guevara could speak, but *he* could not. Not about this. Information of this nature in the mind of a key figure like Che Guevara would surely affect the future, and evidently in a way as to invoke the defensive shield. Thoughts could be more potent than actions! Guevara could conjecture, but could not spread his notions to others; Bringas could know, but could not confirm for Guevara. The paradox protected level upon level of actions! He would never understand its ultimate sophistication. Yet as water invariably sought its natural level no matter how intricate the terrain, so did the ramifications of this paradox. He had tried to tell Guevara three times, and had simply rebounded in silence. That was the way it acted: silently.

"Are you from another world?" Guevara asked. "I am too busy to read science fiction, but—"

"Not exactly," Bringas replied, surprising himself. He *could* say some things!

"Are you here to observe—or to affect?"

Bringas was silent.

"You have given me an answer," Guevara said.

Bringas felt a strange, ugly pain, as though part of his individuality had been wrenched from him. Guevara was too intelligent; he was forcing Bringas to give him information: *and it was doing something indefinite but appalling to the structure of the time-stream.*

He had to get away from this man! Guevara certainly *could* affect him—and knew it.

"You are afraid now—and that is another answer," Guevara said relentlessly. "You die a little when I question you. So I *can* touch you—"

The pain came again, an immaterial knife cutting into his immaterial being. In a moment the shield would perforate; he might cease to exist. Or worse.

Bringas ran.

But Guevara followed. "One more question, little fish, then I will let you go," he cried.

Could Guevara be his ancestor? Was that why mere

knowledge, that the man could neither act on nor impart to others, was so sensitive here? For knowledge had to affect the knower, in some fashion, however subtly. . . .

"What is my fate?" Guevara shouted.

"Bolivia!" Bringas gasped—and abruptly the pain ceased.

Che Guevara, astonishingly, was satisfied with that answer. Perhaps even now, eight years before his death—or success—in Bolivia, he had the notion. He did not need to ask whether he would succeed, for he had no concept of failure. The word "Bolivia" meant he would achieve his destiny. But because it was in fact no answer, Bringas was off the hook.

Guevara stopped, turned about, and went back toward the prison. Bringas went on, nervously following the same route he would use to escape in 1962. He would stay well away from Che Guevara from now on!

Next morning Bringas learned why Guevara had been at the prison. He had come with the assassin Herman Marks, taken Captain Castaño out of his cell, told him his sentence had been commuted—as indeed it had—and shot him in the back. Castaño was dead; he had known too much about communism to be permitted to live.

The murder had occurred after midnight. Bringas had arrived almost at the critical moment—and Guevara had skillfully diverted him. What a diabolic display of control! What would have happened had he made it all the way to Castaño's cell? Could he have saved the man's life?

Would the paradox shield have *permitted* him to save Castaño? Or was *that* what had relieved the pain of Guevara's questioning: the fact that Bringas had been driven off, and so could not interfere? All he knew about the shield was conjecture and experience, and he had little faith in the former.

That effectively finished Bringas' part on the court, as Guevara had suggested. He had discredited himself with the authorities by being too consistently lenient, and the court had discredited itself with him by murdering a man Fidel himself had pardoned. He was glad to be off the court, and glad it was because of his affinity for human rights, rather than from overzealousness. Bringas had been sick when he realized, during his first foray into Cuba, that he had killed men, and the memory still weighed disquietingly on his conscience. Pepin had reacted similarly, but men like Raul and Che murdered deliberately, taking a personal interest in the details of bloodletting. Bringas thought of himself as a victim of circumstance who had made serious mistakes; but these hardened revolutionaries reveled in their viciousness. These would be the glowing heroes of future myth, honored in the texts of coming centuries!

Fidel himself seemed to be clean, however. He *had* commuted the sentence.

Figuratively clean; physically was another matter, unfortunately. Bringas had had occasion to visit Fidel's office a few times, and had been appalled at the man's continuing messiness. Food soiled his uniform, his hair and beard were unkempt, and there was the odor of months about him, as though he were still fugitive in the Sierra Maestra. Other officers had cleaned up, once the war-pressure was off, maintaining only their shaggy beards as a mark of honor. Not Fidel. It was as though he liked to be dirty, or at least had absolutely no concern about his appearance and hygiene. It was a strange attitude in a leader of his stature.

A week after the Castaño assassination came the trial of forty-three Batista airmen and mechanics, before a tribunal in Santiago. Bringas was not associated with the trial, but he kept abreast of it with interest. He had a certain fond memory of Santiago de Cuba, for that was where he had discovered Adelita. If there was one thing that made this cruel, barbaric life bearable, it was Adelita!

There was no arbitrary condemnation in this case. The president of the tribunal was an honest rebel officer, and the lawyers fought hard and well. Charged with genocide, murder, and homicide in the bombing and strafing of villages during the war, the airmen were nevertheless acquitted.

Bringas noted the verdict with satisfaction. This went far to show Adelita that Revolutionary justice was not the mockery she had imagined. He reminded her of Fidel's own remark some weeks before, concerning the airmen then awaiting trial. "They had a right to bomb," Fidel had said benevolently. "Could we ask them not to fire on us? Let's be fair about this."

"Yes," Adelita agreed. "Yes, the decision was fair."

Then came a rude shock. Fidel Castro denounced the three judges as traitors in a televised broadcast and called the airmen the worst criminals of the Batista regime. He invoked the Nuremburg trials as a precedent, and pointed out that when legal grounds could not be found it was entirely proper to sentence such war criminals on the basis of moral conviction.

"And Fidel is a lawyer himself!" Adelita exclaimed, as though Bringas were at fault. How could he answer her?

At the retrial, twenty-three of the airmen were given terms ranging from twenty to thirty years at hard labor. Twelve received lesser sentences, and two mechanics were released. One of the more impassioned defense lawyers was himself imprisoned. Later, the presiding judge of the first trial, who had acquitted the defendants, was found dead. Suicide.

Adelita withdrew into an almost mindless state, and Bringas became quite concerned about her health. She was a creature of moods, and he understood that now, but such an extreme reaction to something that did not directly concern her could not be normal. 233 had always been resilient and hardy, even under the increasing tension of their illicit relationship; but Adelita seemed to be made of softer stuff.

Yet he was disturbed himself. He saw in her attitude an exaggeration of his own tendencies. Realizing that, he put on a positive front, and in a few days Adelita was back to normal. She was a woman who needed a man—and that meant he had to *be* a man. . . .

In April Fidel visited America, and Bringas knew that the dark tide was turning at last. There had been problems in organizing the new government, and some unfortunate mistakes, but now it would be smoother. Fidel was coming to terms with America, and he was well received on the continent. An excellent sign. Headlines favored him again.

That month Bringas received an invitation to attend a party given by Efigenio Almejeiras, Chief of Police. Bringas remembered his host from the Sierra: one of the original eighty-two immortals, the men who had made the initial assault with Fidel, landing from the *Granma* boat in December, 1956. Most had proved altogether too mortal; all but twelve had been captured or killed by the Batista forces. Those few survivors were now high in the councils of government. Fidel, Raul, Che, Camilo and Almejeiras, of course, and Agusto Martinez Sanchez, who was Minister of Labor, Armando Hart, Minister of Education—if by chance that last attended, he might wrangle an introduction for Adelita!

At any rate, Bringas was flattered by the invitation, now that his position on the courts had lapsed and he had time for social life. Naturally he took Adelita along.

Almejeiras greeted them at the entrance. He was a small man, a mulatto with an uninspiring face and straggly goatee, but an engaging personality when he turned it on. He had been a rugged fighter in the mountains, and not the kind of person Bringas cared to associate with socially—but now, of course, he *was* Chief of Police. Position did make a difference.

"So glad to see you again, Juan!" he cried with more gusto than was necessary. "And your beautiful yegua!"

Bringas winced. That had been a private joke, and he didn't like it being blared out in public. Adelita acted as though she hadn't heard.

Almejeiras was well stocked. Liquor, tobacco, luxury

delicacies, and expensive furnishings—life had never been like this in the mountains! "You'll have a good time here!" the host exclaimed. He had obviously commenced his drinking—or more likely, his drugs—long before the party got under way. Marijuana, cocaine . . . "And you'd better! I tell you, friend—I am no communist, but I am with Fidel wherever he goes. Things are changing; we all have to get our pleasures while we can, before the communists finish all fun. Live as though there is no tomorrow—for tomorrow may not be worth living."

Drunk or drugged he might be, but the prophecy was obviously sincere, and it gave Bringas a chill. What did Almejeiras know?

From this inauspicious beginning, the party degenerated steadily. There were many government officials present, including Camilo Cienfuegos himself. Most were drinking themselves into stupor. There were even more young, pretty girls, obviously sexual professionals, and they were taking good care of the men. Bringas became increasingly embarrassed to have Adelita witness this, for it was evident that Almejeiras had been speaking literally when he called her a yegua. The sex was neither monogamous nor private; they had to step over pairs and trios fondling each other in the halls. Bringas had shed much of his personal objection to "perversion"—and had acquired some of the contemporary notions about the importance of sexual privacy—but this disgusted him. While the new government was preaching morality and an end to corruption, the Chief of Police was sponsoring open debauchery. . . . It had a bad smell.

The serious gossip was no more pleasant. "Say, didn't Fidel take care of that Costa Rican idiot!"

"You mean Jose Figures, who was president of Costa Rica? I thought he supported the Revolution with weapons."

"He supported *Hubert Matos* with weapons. Now he thinks he can come to Havana and tell us how to run

Cuba. He thinks we should—get this—turn out the communists!"

There was a burst of laughter. Bringas didn't understand the precise source of the humor, but he had a notion he'd rather be on the side of Hubert Matos, evidently no friend of these. He respected Matos.

There followed several harsh jibes at Romulo Betancourt, President of Venezuela, and Munoz Marin of Puerto Rico—both of whom were leftist figures who had also supported Fidel with weapons and money, but who were by no means communists. Why were they being held in such contempt now?

Camilo greeted Bringas in friendly fashion. But his words were low and specific: "Juan, get her out of here. This isn't your type of thing."

Obviously it wasn't.

In May the Cuban Telephone Company was intervened and taken over by the government. In that month also, Sori Marin and four other ministers resigned their positions after a stormy cabinet meeting in opposition to the stringent Agrarian Reform Law then being drawn up. Bringas took note of that. Marin, the devastating prosecutor, had not been Minister of Agriculture long, and if *he* were repelled by the proposed law, how bad was it to be?

On June third he found out—and wondered why the reaction had been so strong. The published Agrarian Reform Law had provisions to expropriate farmland, reduce the size of farms and ranches, and eliminate foreign ownership. To Bringas these were good, logical steps in the reform of past excesses and in the redistribution of national resources, and in line with what Fidel had been saying all along.

Yet Adelita had little enthusiasm. "This is communism," she said, and he was reminded once more how seriously she took these political labels. If only he could have talked to Castaño and learned what it was all about! "The Americans won't like losing their investments."

"The bully never likes being put in his place," Bringas said.

"Sori Marin is no American! He is an intelligent lawyer, and he knows what this law means."

"I thought you said justice meant nothing to him."

She left the room, frustrated.

On June 30 the Chief of the Air Force, Major Pedro Diaz Lanz, wrote a letter to President Urritia charging communist intrusion in the Rebel Army. He resigned his position and fled into exile in America. Bringas was cynical, knowing that internal military politics had as much to do with Major Lanz's action as communism. Urritia condemned him as a deserter. Even the Americans gave Lanz little credence.

But on July 17 Urritia himself was forced to resign and seek asylum in the Argentine embassy before fleeing to America. A communist replaced him: Osvaldo Dorticos Torrado. Premier Cardona also resigned, and Fidel himself assumed that office.

On July 26, a highly significant date, Fidel made another speech: "Elecciones para que"—"Elections—for what?"

Bringas no longer had any doubt: Fidel's government was sliding left. Those people who best understood and supported the Revolution were naturally finding increased influence within it. Fidel was doing the best he could to make *all* his visions come true, and those whose vision fell short, however sincere they might be personally, had to give way. Urritia had been too stodgily conservative; by the logic of the Revolution he was unfit for the office he had held. And elections—Fidel was right. Why put on such a charade, when the people would brook no alternative to the present government?

"Don't you care at all that he is breaking his solemn promises, one after another?" Adelita demanded. She still refused to understand.

Somehow, despite these measures, the economy was declining. Income taxes were raised considerably, and a sales tax of twenty percent was imposed on radios and refrigerators, and thirty percent on new cars. What was wrong?

In August they both had occasion to find out. Adelita's assignment as a teacher came through, and Bringas was appointed an Inspector of Agrarian Reform. It would mean considerable travel, taking him away from Adelita, but he was glad for the opportunity. It had seemed as though he were slowly falling out of favor with the administration. He suspected that Raul Castro had something to do with that, holding a long grudge about the episode of the guajiro. Or perhaps Bringas had never been as important in this framework as he had fancied himself, and only now the truth was leaking through to him. Regardless, he chafed occasionally at the neglect he felt; he didn't *like* being relegated to the same sort of anonymity he had experienced all his life in the twenty-fifth century. He had had a taste of importance in the Sierra Maestra, and he found he liked it well.

Now he was important again. The job meant extra money, too. He was getting along well enough on his Captain's salary—obviously *that* paperwork had not been fouled up, despite what Guevara had claimed—but the days of free food had passed. Adelita would not allow him to make extra money in the little illicit ways available to a man in his position—such as getting someone a fast permit to leave the country, or confiscating illegal material like Yankee dollars. Bless her stern moral fiber!

Bringas traveled all over Cuba in August, visiting farms, attending meetings, making notes. He learned.

Things were changing, certainly—but the implementation of the Agrarian Reform was fraught with unforeseen peril. Had Sori Marin foreseen it, and protested in vain . . . ?

The latifundia was being broken up—the tremendous plantations and ranches, much of which land had been kept deliberately idle by the wealthy landowners. Small farms had been portioned out to the campesinos, and livestock provided from the formerly private herds. But the campesinos had promptly slaughtered the animals for meat, and then had nothing with which to farm. At the old King Ranch, in Camaguey Province, a breeding bull worth perhaps fifty thousand pesos had been roasted for a feast.

Meanwhile, the government had been negotiating with other nations in order to obtain superior breeding stock to upgrade the new Cuban herds. What savage irony!

The campesinos were hungry, and they had never been trained to manage complete farms on their own. They could not be blamed. But obviously an immediate redistribution of land and livestock was impractical, and the government was wisely desisting until such problems could be solved.

Yet they could not wait long. "We are not getting title to the land!" the campesinos protested more and more persistently, refusing to understand. "Fidel promised. . . ."

The little farms were inefficient, for a thousand little reasons apart from the hunger that forced the slaughter of livestock and the consumption of seed-grains. For example, tractors had obvious advantages: they were inedible, they could work indefinitely, they had no special winter upkeep. But it would be ludicrous to issue a monster diesel tractor to the owner of a one-caballeria farm. Such mechanization had been suitable for the pre-Revolutionary giant holdings, and would still be excellent—for giant Revolutionary holdings. How could this conflict between efficiency and humanity be resolved?

The answer seemed to lie in cooperatives, as Fidel had suggested from the outset. These could be of suitable size, yet would be owned and operated for the benefit of the people. With enough heavy equipment and personnel, and with larger, protected herds and plantations, the greatest good for the greatest number could be achieved. But the guajiros felt that they had been promised individual holdings, regardless of the good of the nation; to them, a cooperative or "People's Farm" was merely a different master. They felt they had been betrayed, and they would not work. Perhaps their children could be educated.

Education and distribution, those were the goals of Fidel's revolution Adelita and Bringas were working for. Adelita educating the children, Bringas overseeing the distribution—or should he say the redistribution—of wealth.

Bringas thought of it as an irony of change: sometimes wealth means as little as fertilizer. He arrived at the island's main port for the northeastern section. The campesinos there were mixing both animal and human droppings into the soil they tilled, claiming the industrial fertilizer they had been promised had never arrived—two months after Fidel promised it would!

"Why hasn't the fertilizer our Russian friends sent us last month been forwarded to the distribution center?" Bringas demanded of the harbormaster.

"Fertilizer? May I see the papers so I can take this up with the person who signed it in?"

"One hundred tons of fertilizer arrived on the *Leningrad* approximately two months ago."

"I am not supposed to do anything without the papers, Captain, but perhaps they have been mislaid here, or maybe they are being checked in Havana. Nevertheless, I will be happy to let you move the fertilizer if you will tell me exactly where it is."

Bringas sighed. "It is on the docks somewhere. Take it away."

"A hundred tons of it? Where are the trucks you will move it with? Parked in their depots, no doubt—those that remain operative. There seems to be a shortage of decent mechanics—"

"Well get them in motion!" Bringas cried, forgetting for the moment that he was merely an observer. But the farmers' problems had become *his* problems, after what he had seen. "Crops will fail if that fertilizer isn't delivered immediately, and then the country will *really* be in trouble!"

"Get me the drivers," the man said tiredly. "Get me

authorizations. Get me the bills of lading. Then we shall see whether we can locate your fertilizer, if it hasn't been spoiled already by exposure to the salt air."

"Bills of lading! That's *your* department! What happened to them?"

"They are normally mailed to this office. But the mails, too, are under new management. Sometimes the documents arrive late; sometimes never."

"Well, we can't wait on that, then," Bringas said, exasperated. "Cut that red tape; get the stuff loaded *without* bills of lading. It isn't as though anybody would steal a hundred tons of fertilizer!"

"Excellent," the man replied wryly. "I am happy to cooperate. We need the dock space. Pick out your crates and load them."

"I can't pick them out without identification! I know nothing about fertilizer except that it stinks when it's fresh—just like bureaucracies."

"Then you know more than I do, Captain, and more than the truckers."

"Well, *who*—?"

"Who knows about fertilizer, stinking or sweet?" The man smiled malignantly. "The management of the proper ties we expropriated under the reform law. The latifundia owners. They certainly know their business. Why don't you ask *them*—those who remain in Cuba. They should be deliriously happy to donate their expertise along with their property, don't you agree?"

Only then did Bringas begin to appreciate the full magnitude of the morass Cuba had entered.

It was an immense relief to return to Havana and Adelita. But he discovered her wound up in her teaching assignment, and she was a different person.

"There is a tremendous job to do!" she told him. "I think nine out of ten of the most skilled teachers and administrators have gone—but the children remain, and they need help! Something has to be done!"

"The teachers wouldn't have left if they had been decent-
ly treated," he said, half in jest. There had been a great
exodus of professional people, who thought they could do
better in America now that things were being equalized
in Cuba.

"The irony is that there's a great future for teachers in
Cuba," she said. "We mean to abolish illiteracy, to see that
every child no matter how poor gets the best education.
We'll need three times as many schools and teachers as
there were before."

"More schools and teachers don't necessarily mean better education," he chided her. "Not if they use the same
dull methods."

"But we're working on it," she said avidly, not realizing
that he was baiting her. "There are ways to bring good
instruction into every classroom. Television, for example—
it has never really been exploited for this purpose. Once the
programs are organized—"

"That will reduce illiteracy? *Watching television?*"

"With the right programs, yes," she said. "We're going
to see if we can get volunteers to go into the back country
and teach at least the rudiments. We—"

"*We?* I thought you were against Fidel?"

She paused, nettled. "I'm not against Fidel. I just dis-
trust communism. But I can't let ideology interfere when
there's a real job to be done. Those children—they are
hungry, ignorant, hopeless, Juan, and they'll never have
a better life without education. If Fidel makes that possible—"

"Fidel will make it possible," he said reassuringly. But
privately he wondered. Good intentions were not enough—
not nearly enough. If the educational bureaucracy were as
fouled up as the economic one, there were rough times
ahead for the children.

But he was glad she was coming around. Naturally there
were problems at first, in every aspect of revolutionary

existence. But now the nadir was passing, and the positive side was developing.

Adelita plumped herself into his lap and kissed him. "How is it you weren't shaved with the rest of the barbudos?" she demanded with womanly consistency of subject.

"Shaved? Why should I shave?"

"You *have* been out in the hinterlands! Didn't you know that they hauled the barbudos into the barbershops and stripped them of their whiskers? What a scene!"

"My beard is a mark of honor!" he said. "It shows I was with Fidel in the Sierra. Anybody who takes a notion to shave *me* had better come with his pistol drawn!" He was exaggerating, but not greatly. He did like his beard.

"That's what the others said. And there *was* shooting. But there are no more genuine barbudos."

"Well, I'm not shaving," he said. The prospect disturbed him oddly. Why should the government suddenly abolish the mark of distinction of Fidel's most loyal followers?

But it was a false alarm, for him. Barbudos of the officerial ranks were exempt, and he was still a Captain.

In September—Camil in the Fidelian calendar—customs duties were raised to one hundred percent.

"We have to encourage Cuban industry," Bringas explained to a doubting Adelita. "And to discourage wasteful luxury. These are all necessary measures for the good of our nation. The common citizen is not hurt by things like taxes on cars; he has no car."

"I will not debate the point," she said with deceptive submission. "But will you do one thing for me?"

"Anything for you," he replied lightly. He hoped she wasn't back on the anti-Castro side of the pendulum.

"Will you read one book?"

He began to laugh, but saw that she was serious. So he nodded.

She gave him a small volume. "*Animal Farm*, by George Orwell," she said.

"But this is in English! I can't read it!"

"I'll read it to you," she said grimly. "Right now."

He was trapped. He would have preferred to be making love, but he had promised her. No doubt this was a heavy treatise on the sanctity of life or agricultural morality, and he would insult her by falling asleep, but what could he do?

He had an inspiration. "I'll listen to it all. Just let me get comfortable."

"Juan!" she screeched as he reached under her skirt and took down her panties.

But he got comfortable, lying on the bed while she sat on his hips, book in hand. "Now you take four hours, if you wish," he said. "I'll stay right where I am."

"I should never have taught you how to extend it," she grumbled. "Next thing you'll be trying for twenty-four hour intercourse."

"Uh-huh. Read."

She read it, translating the text word by word and phrase by phrase, making sure he paid attention by twitching her buttocks every so often.

It was a children's fantasy, with talking animals and a simplistic plot. Apparently Adelita only wanted him to relax a while, to get his mind off contemporary problems. . . .

But it didn't take too long for him to see that her intention was the opposite. He even became so interested, at times, that he forgot their physical contact.

It seemed that these animals of the novel belonged to an English farm and did not like the oppression of the human supervisors. They staged a revolution, drove out the humans, and set up a new regime run entirely by the animals. The pigs assumed the administrative tasks, while the other animals did the other chores with great zeal. Especially the great horse. Where was Nilo Parera now, with his love of horses, he wondered idly.

It was a wonderful experiment in freedom—but gradually it soured. Somehow the enormous and unified efforts of the animals did not bring increased rewards. Somehow the profits gravitated to the new leaders, the pigs, and the swine became more and more like the hated men. The old slogans changed, the original projects were modified, and fear in the form of vicious hounds governed the community. Yet the shift was gradual and subtle, and no animal could draw a line and say "Here our revolution was betrayed." Yet it *was* betrayed.

It was late at night by the time Adelita finished, but Bringas made no effort to cut short the narration. "This is Communism as you see it," he said at the end, finally grasping the nature of her concern. "The name of freedom, graven on a heavier chain."

She only shrugged.

"But you are suggesting parallels that do not exist," he continued, annoyed for no specific reason. Was it that he saw himself as a hound, in the animal farm framework, or worse, a pig? "We are not animals; we are not likely to be so simply deceived. So long as men like Camilo Cienfuegos and Hubert Matos hold positions of power, Cuba cannot be like that. I know these men well, I fought with them in the mountains. They are incorruptible. Che Guevara cannot subvert the Revolution by himself!"

"Of course not," she agreed, and still he was disgruntled. They finally completed their act of love, but it was not very satisfactory.

On the morning of October 19, 1959—the month of Caxixto in the Fidelian calendar—Adelita answered the door. "Oh!" she exclaimed, surprised. "Come in, Camilo."

Who? Perplexed, Bringas went to see, tucking in his shirt. It was too early in the day for social calls!

But it *was* Camilo Cienfuegos. "Will you turn your man over to me for a few days?" he asked her gently.

Camilo, of course, was Chief of the Army. If he required

the services of Captain Juan Bringas, nothing short of a direct countermand from Fidel would deny him his man. Yet he seemed to be asking it as a personal favor from Adelita.

"Will you answer me one question, Camilo?" she asked bravely.

"Of course I'm available," Bringas said quickly. He knew what she intended to ask, and though Camilo was friendly this was pushing it.

Camilo smiled, also understanding. "I cannot deny a pretty woman, and you are more than pretty," he said. "Yes, I am a communist, the same as Raul."

The same as Raul. Yet the two were enemies. This was a bad portent.

Then Camilo spoke to Bringas, before Adelita could organize another query. "We will be traveling two or three days—perhaps more. There may be unpleasantness. That's why I need a good man."

"Juan is no communist!" Adelita cried, immediately responsive to the threat in this situation.

"But he *is* a good man," Camilo said, chucking her under the chin. "I fought with him in the Sierra, so I know." This, by coincidence or design, was so similar to Bringas' own remarks about Camilo that they all had to laugh, and her arguments were stifled. If Camilo were not Chief of the Army it would still be impossible to deny him! He was one of the most popular figures in Cuba, and this was why.

In the car Camilo was more frank. "We are assured of privacy here," he said. "My chauffeur is Captain Cristino Naranjo, and you will see that I trust him absolutely. Juan, we have very bad trouble in Camaguey. Hubert has written a letter to Fidel."

"A letter?" Bringas almost laughed at the letdown. Major Hubert Matos was now Military Commander of Camaguey Province. This meant that he had the final say in all matters in Camaguey, for there were no civilian authorities now. He supervised expropriations, land reform and executions. All appeals of the Revolutionary Courts in the province were decided by him. He was quite competent in the office, and answered only to Fidel. He must have written scores of notes!

"Of resignation."

Oh-oh. Officers did not simply resign from the government, as the Diaz Lanz case had demonstrated. "Ill health? I had no idea—"

"Protesting the infiltration of the government by communists."

Real trouble! That was the worst thing a man could do, these days, for Fidel was sensitive to such accusations. "Has he defected, then? It is hard to imagine him—"

"No. He has merely written the letter. He wants to retire to civilian life. Or, as he puts it: 'I do not want to become an obstacle to the revolution, and believing that I must choose between adapting myself or going into a corner in order not to do damage, the honest and revolutionary thing to do is to go.' Of course I shall have to arrest him."

Bringas was no longer so naive as to have to inquire why With Fidel's present mood, Matos' act was tantamount to treason. Of course it would blow over in time, but the next few days would certainly be awkward.

"I admire and respect Hubert," Bringas said, "and I know the communists *are* infiltrating the government. Why should you, a communist yourself, want *me* along for this ridiculous arrest?"

Camilo glanced out the window as though thinking his own thoughts. "Perhaps because you are his friend. You could persuade him to retract his statement, to apologize to Fidel. It would be better for him."

"Nonsense! Hubert is a man of honor. No one can change his mind that way—and I wouldn't try."

Camilo was silent for a while. "What do you think of Fidel?" he asked at last, and there was a measured quality to his speech that suggested that this was no idle question.

"He is a good man who has assumed a difficult responsibility." True and safe.

"Of course. And his policies?"

Did he dare answer frankly? He was talking to a confessed communist about communism. Would that be like telling a pig to stay clear of the swill? When that pig was one of the leading figures of the farm, and his swill caviar? Though Camilo certainly had not *acted* like a communist in the time Bringas had known him. Still, this man, barring the intervention of the paradox shield, could have him instantly removed from the scene. He liked Camilo personally, but had no illusions about the man's capabilities. They *had* fought—and survived—together in the Sierra; Camilo could and would kill when the need arose. Was this a trap of some sort?

Camilo turned to him, meeting his gaze. "Juan, if I wished to be rid of you, I would not invent a pretext." True enough: Raul and Che were devious; Camilo was forthright. He probably had never checked Bringas' record, or he would have realized, as Guevara had, that something was funny. "Tell me your truth, and I will tell you my truth, and it shall be between us only. Cristino will not talk, I assure you."

Major Naranjo, the chauffeur! Bringas had almost forgotten the man's presence. But this was a commitment he was inclined to trust. "Fidel himself is good, and I think he means well, and his name will be famous in history—but there are some unfortunate ramifications of the Revolution. The country is becoming a shambles economically, the people are becoming dissatisfied, and the executions—well, consider what Raul did in January, or Che at La Cabana more than once."

"Raul. . . ." Camilo said ironically, and Bringas knew he had scored. Perhaps that was one of the things that inclined him to Camilo: the man's bad relations with Raul Castro. Of course the enemy of an enemy was not necessarily a friend, but it created a compatible climate.

"Certainly the problems are not easy to solve," Bringas continued, trying to be fair. "Nothing short of a complete revolution could have dislodged the prior corruption. But so many promises are not being kept, and the people are really no better off than before. If only Fidel would reconsider—"

"You know Fidel! He does not consider or reconsider, he just bulls ahead. Criticism only makes him angry; it does not change what he does."

"True." Let the Americans criticize and Fidel talked of gringos dying. But in fact Cubans were criticizing, and Cubans were dying. "But you say you are communist, Camilo. Surely you do not object to the influence of the communists!" Let him chew on *that* leading question!

Camilo smiled, still partially distracted by his private thoughts. "There are communists and communists, Juan. They are as different from each other as are Raul and I." Then he faced Bringas again and spoke with force. "I believe in the principles set forth by Marx and Lenin. My father was a founder of the party in Cuba, and I have been dedicated to it since childhood. But I am not a fool. Here in Cuba we have a tremendous opportunity—but Fidel is destroying it. He means well, as you say, but he is making calamitous mistakes. He is proceeding far too boldly, he is alienating essential elements, forfeiting the support of the people, squandering resources he should be adapting to our purposes. He is baiting the United States and making it a premature enemy, and that is the sheerest folly, for Cuba's entire economy and cultural sphere is bound to that nation."

"But how can Cuba be communist," Bringas asked, intrigued by this viewpoint, "and *not* antagonize—"

"By being discreet! As I was in the Sierra, as all disciplined communists were. Not believers-of-convenience like Raul! We had only to maintain the pretense a while longer, cementing the Revolution's friendship with the Colossus of the North, selling it sugar and tobacco at a good price,

obtaining loans from it—the kind that are never repaid—
and supplies, machinery, technical know-how, rich tour-
ists, even arms. Then, even after the true nature of the
Revolution could no longer be concealed, we could maintain good relations—just as Yugoslavia does, as Poland
will. America does not really hate communism, whatever
its politicians claim; America hates *affront*. By subduing
our pride, by biding our time, we could have had it all.
Good government, good living *and* hemispheric good-will.
Certainly for a number of years. If America finally turned
against us, we should have had time to become economically and militarily sound. But Fidel—surely he will pro-
voke an economic boycott against us, alienate us from
our friends in Latin America, and perhaps even bring an
American invasion of our territory—*and for what*? For
the privilege of calling Americans 'gringos'? For superfluous executions? For latifundia and industry we can't
even manage properly? For stupid interventions in Latin
American affairs, futile military expeditions and the like?
What a waste of men and resources, when we are not even
consolidated yet and facing internal opposition like that of
the Catholics and the unions. We will have opportunity to
deal with America later, when we are strong; the only
thing Fidel has gained is to put the Colossus on guard. I
tell you, he gave the wrong speech in July. It should have
been 'Enemies—For What?' and then four hours of false
flattery for President Eisenhower, Dulles, Nixon, American
apple pie—everything, no matter how sickening. Such a
little gesture; such a vast amount to gain from the clumsy
giant!"

Bringas nodded agreeably. It did make sense, considering the anarchy that was international ethics of this violent
pre-holocaust period. But why was Camilo telling him all
this?

"I am about to speak treason to you," Camilo said seriously, and Bringas gave a bark of laughter. The man had
already earned execution, if Fidel learned of this speech.

But Camilo was serious. "I am trusting you not to betray me."

"Camilo, I'm not a communist. I'm not on your side in that respect, even if I'm not exactly against you. I do respect you personally. I'd rather not know anything that would make me dangerous to you."

"You are honest. That's why I trust you. And that is why Hubert Matos trusts you, even in this time of his turmoil. I think you can help me save his life—if you choose."

"Save his life!"

"My friend, you were not with Fidel aboard the *Granma*, as I was. You cannot appreciate how seriously he reacts when stymied by one of his own, particularly one as personally popular as Hubert. It isn't just show; when Fidel throws a tantrum, he means it. Hubert is not merely resigning; thirty-four of his officers are resigning with him. Fidel will crucify them all!"

"I can't believe that. Certainly there will be a great noise, and Hubert will lose his good-standing. But after a few days—"

Camilo shook his head. "Paredon." The word was spoken with such sincerity that Bringas was shaken. Matos was no traitor, and everyone knew that, but after the way Fidel had acted in the trial of the airmen, and when the President had tried to go his own way—well, it just might be.

"What do you want with me?" he asked reluctantly.

"I want you to talk to Hubert before I arrest him. Convince him that I am sincere. He won't believe me directly, because he knows me as a communist."

"Sincere about *arresting* him? That hardly needs—"

"No. I mean to stage a coup d'etat, march on Havana, and oust Fidel. But I must have Hubert's support. Only the two of us together can hope to rally sufficient support against Fidel's popularity."

Bringas sat stunned. Treason indeed!

"I will give him my present post—Chief of the Army. I will exclude communists from the government. I will stop the executions, revoke the Agrarian Reform, revise the 1940 Constitution, permit elections—"

"But if you are communist yourself—"

"You keep coming back to that! I tell you I am Cuban first, communist second. There are virtues in the capitalist scheme—" He paused, and Bringas suspected he was thinking of the fabulous upper-class parties he had attended in Havana, the society girls he had bedded. Camilo professed communism intellectually, but his heart seemed that of a capitalist. "American support is essential. The Americans may not trust me, but they know that Hubert is honorable. He may be the only man in Cuba that both the people and the Americans will support. Of course I will dispose of Raul and purge Che, and the Americans will like that, but it is not enough. And I *will* help the common people— *help* them, not make perpetual promises while things grow worse. Will you assist me now?"

"I—" But it was too sudden, too massive. Bringas had to think through the ramifications. His own experience as Inspector made him question whether Camilo could do much to reverse the economic trend, unless he were actually successful in obtaining massive American aid. Meanwhile, how would such a coup affect his own mission? Camilo had carefully avoided naming the fate of Fidel, but obviously no counter-revolution could be secure while Fidel lived. What was right?

"Without Hubert, I dare not try it. I can bring the communists in line, even for non-communist programs, for I understand their motives. Hubert can enlist capitalist support, and that is crucial now. Together we can do it, and the people will follow us. But if Hubert refuses, the present order will continue. Then I will have to arrest him, and what follows will follow. This is not a threat; it is a statement of the inevitable."

"I—can't answer you," Bringas said.

Camilo smiled again, somewhat nervously. "No honest man could, immediately. But come with me, consider the alternatives, and when you see Hubert—talk to him. Say what you will. I will give you time. I am not confident that he will join me—but I know he will not betray me if he declines. It will just be the three of us. And Cristino, of course."

Just four, Bringas thought. Already three too many for such a secret.

They arrived at the city of Camaguey, in Camaguey Province, the following day. Bringas wrestled with the problems of ethics and paradox, his fear for Matos if the arrest proceeded, and for the Text A future if the coup went through. He could come to no decision. His sleep had been fitful and consumed by forebodings. If he collaborated with Camilo he might undermine his own mission, but Cuba might benefit enormously. Was the good of the country worth the risk of 233's very existence several centuries hence? And what of Adelita, right now? Would she suffer a reprisal for Bringas' own part in it? Yet again, could this be a better way to avert the missile crisis? Could he thus avert the emotional stigma of his own phosphorus murders? Camilo was a communist, but he promised not to antagonize the United States, and he *was* good at not antagonizing people, and the missiles of 1962 were surely antagonistic! But to betray Fidel, the hero of the entire Text A future—

Unable to make up his mind, he decided to let the paradox shield make the determination for him. He would back Camilo—*if he could*.

And he could! He presented the case to Hubert Matos without interference from either external or internal sources.

Matos took it calmly enough. "I am no traitor," he said. "Do you think I would resign in protest to communist infiltration, only to support a communist coup? I want only to retire in peace and not interfere with the good Fidel is doing despite the communists."

"But Camilo will have to arrest you! He says you will get paredon!"

Matos laughed. "Do you believe that, Juan?"

"No, of course not. But—"

"A communist will say anything to accomplish his purpose. He sets no value on his given word, and has not the slightest respect for those who are foolish enough to believe what he says. You can trust a communist only to act in his own best interest, however narrow that may be and however many others are hurt. That's why I oppose this looming communist influence on Fidel so strongly. Fidel is not communist; he is merely being deceived by those about him. By Raul, by Che—those two are extraordinarily clever and unscrupulous, and the web they spin is monstrous, but they are innocents next to the true communists. Don't let Camilo lead you astray. He is a likable fellow, and I like him myself, but I know better than to trust him in a matter like this! Fidel is not my enemy. Perhaps my action will remove the scales from his eyes, and he will comprehend the menace Cuba faces. That alone will make it worthwhile, no matter what my personal fate."

"But Camilo will eliminate the communists from the government! He will purge both Raul and Che—"

"By executing them? While he promises an end to executions? I think you have seen what such compromise leads to."

He had indeed! "He didn't say he would execute them. Just—well, eliminate them from the government."

"He tells you this now, when he needs your help and mine. Perhaps he believes it now. But does he really have the strength or inclination to root out his own kind? Communist discipline is more savage than anything we know. No—Fidel is our only chance."

Hubert would not be moved. It was Bringas who was being moved. Fidel was tempestuous, but he *was* basically sincere. He merely had placed his trust in the wrong people. And Hubert himself was incorruptible. That explained why there was no paradox effect: Bringas could not affect this scheme.

But Camilo was not ready to give up so easily. "I will talk to him myself. Of course he doesn't trust me! He is right not to trust me! But I must have him with me! I will give him anything. Even the premiership—let him root out the communists himself, if he doubts my capacity! With his integrity and my popularity—"

And Camilo tried, listing for Matos the people that could be relied upon to join such a venture: the anti-communist guerrillas even now operating in the Escambray Mountains (Bringas hadn't known about that!); the increasing number of disaffected urbanites who were losing their style of living; Camilo's own troops and those following Matos here in Camaguey; the majority of the university students; men like Morgan, Menayo, Almeida, Almejeiras—"Almejeiras is thoroughly corrupt, but he knows the present regime is destroying the kind of life he craves"—Aldo Vara who was once head of the July 26th underground against Batista, but bitter now because of insufficient reward; former Cuban president Carlos Prio—

Bringas could not keep up with the impressive stream of names, though Matos was obviously familiar with them. The electrical workers, almost the whole of the labor movement—Matos cut it short. "These same people followed Fidel, and now they are dissatisfied. They would soon be dissatisfied again, and then what would you do?"

Camilo had answers for every question, but somehow the answers were less impressive than the questions. There was no decision that day. Camilo finally asked Matos to remain in his quarters but not under technical arrest; obviously he still hoped to sway the man with a little more time.

The issue hung fire, one hour after another, all that night and into the morning of October 21st. Bringas tensed with apprehension, knowing that Camilo could not stall the arrest much longer without arousing suspicion.

He was talking once more with Matos when the tableau shattered. Raul Castro burst in surrounded by his bodyguards.

"Arrest these men!" Raul cried, and abruptly, without resistance, Hubert Matos and Juan Bringas were prisoners, handcuffed like convicts on the way to the execution wall. "Arrest them all!" Raul said. "Every officer who supports this traitor! I want them in Havana by nightfall."

The majority of Raul's men departed, but Raul stayed to have a few words with the captives. "Fidel was worried—a whole day and no news from Camaguey! With you planning a little private coup, perhaps?"

"No," Matos said, accurately enough.

Raul pretended not to hear him. "So you are in on this too, Bringas! This will certainly be a pleasure!"

"I came with Major Cienfuegos."

Raul was about to speak again, but at the moment Camilo himself stormed in with members of his bodyguard. "What is the meaning of this! I am in charge here! I give the orders!"

Raul turned to him with as malicious a smile as Bringas had ever seen. "Not anymore, party boy! You proved incompetent to perform a simple errand, so Fidel asked me to take care of this."

"*Incompetent!*" Camilo cried, enraged. None of his winning personality showed now. "You pervert murderer! *I* am Chief of the Army. You can't come in here and interfere! Leave at once!"

"No pseudo-communist can give *me* orders!" Raul said, his face reddening. "Shut up, you high-living traitor!"

"You damned double-bastard! I'll—"

Bringas did not comprehend the significance of this epithet, but Raul bared his teeth in sheer fury. He grabbed for his pistol, and there was murder in his face.

Camilo knocked the weapon out of his hand. "Maricon! You dare to draw on me? I'll put you in hell!" And Camilo's own pistol was in his hand as he stood over his enemy.

But Camilo's own men intervened, pushing aside his arm, cautioning him against murder, and in a moment he recovered control. "Get out of my sight, lover of bugarrones!"

Raul stood up again, beaten but by no means cowed. "Get back to Havana in a hurry, traitor! Fidel wants to see you today. I'll finish up here."

Camilo stalked out to verify the order by phone, leaving Raul the seeming victor after all. Bringas had never witnessed such naked hate as these two men had for each other—yet once the crisis passed, each proceeded competently to his business. Hate was a reality of their existence; they knew how to live with it.

Raul gave efficient orders for the dispatch of Matos and his officers to Havana, then took Bringas with him to a private office and dismissed his guards.

Bringas feared Raul was going to torture him for information, or possibly execute him on the spot as he had done with others before. But he had underestimated the man. "Watch how we deal with traitors," Raul said, and picked up the telephone.

Bringas, still manacled, made himself comfortable in an easy chair and listened, perplexed. Raul was not even questioning him!

"Give me the tower commander, Camaguey airport," Raul said into the phone, his voice calm. Then: "This is Raul Castro. My associate Camilo Cienfuegos will be boarding a plane for Havana in about an hour. Set up a flight chart that routes it over the sea."

There was a pause. "Of course I know the shortest route is over land! But this is Fidel's order. Tell the pilot there is bad weather over Santa Clara and he'd better fly around it. Major Cienfuegos is far too valuable to risk." His smooth tone gave no hint of the malice in his face. Evidently the tower commander assented, for Raul thanked him briefly and hung up.

Raul dialed another number. "Osvaldito? An airplane is being readied for takeoff in an hour. A small Cessna with a flight plan to Havana over the sea. Install your merchandise on it. . . ." A pause. "About thirty minutes, I think. It must happen over the water, comprendes?"

What was the man setting up? Obviously this boded ill for Camilo.

Raul made one more call. "Mori? The tower commander at the airport—make it a suicide. Yes, leave a note: 'It is my fault Camilo died.' Time it properly . . . yes."

"A bomb!" Bringas exclaimed, finally making the connection. "You're putting a bomb on Camilo's plane!"

Raul shrugged, a smug expression on his face.

They waited silently in the office for an hour and a half. Bringas was manacled, and he knew Raul would kill him gladly if he gave the slightest pretext, so he affected unconcern about Camilo's fate. Surely Camilo could take care of himself! Yet he would be in a hurry, and preoccupied, formulating his explanations for Fidel . . . would he check the plane?

The phone rang, making him jump. Raul answered immediately. "Oh, hell Che. So you have a spy in my guard. . . . No, my quarrel is with Camilo, not with you. . . . Yes, I very much fear something dreadful has happened. . . . Who? . . . No, I trust your judgment. . . . Very well. For you. This time."

He put down the phone and stared at Bringas. "Che— one of these days he will tread over the line. But until I run down his man in my group, I must humor him. I don't know why he chooses to intercede for you, but there it is. I was going to let you go anyway, and now Che is in my debt."

Che Guevara had interceded to save him from Raul! What possible reason could the man have? Was he afraid that Bringas's prediction of his Bolivian destiny would be negated if Bringas died? Or was it a trap of some sort?

Perhaps it was the paradox shield? Che had said he could not affect Bringas, which meant he had tried. Maybe he was still trying, just to ascertain the limits—he was that sort of man—and paradox required that Bringas live beyond this point. It was the shield that had saved him, acting subtly through Guevara's devious motivations!

The phone rang again. "So Camilo left on schedule? On that fight plan? Very good," Raul said, and hung up.

He came over to Bringas and unlocked the handcuffs. "You can go now, Juan. Remember this day, and be guided by it." He made no overt threat. He didn't need to. He had indeed shown Bringas where the power lay in Cuba, and the consequence of opposing it. If Bringas valued his life, he would toe the line and keep his mouth shut.

But Raul Castro had almost demonstrated unequivocally that the Revolution had to be overthrown. Bringas no longer felt guilty about the latter portion of his mission.

Camilo Cienfuegos disappeared, of course. There was a tremendous search, with even the United States assisting in the massive sea and air canvass. The whole island mourned the terrible accident, Fidel most of all.

Behind the scenes it was quite another story. Camilo's trusted chauffeur and bodyguard, Captain Naranjo, was shot and killed "by mistake" when he entered Camp Columbia. Another surviving supporter, Captain Beaton, a Sierra veteran, made it to the foothills of the Oriente Province range. He succeeded in escaping in a military jeep and drove to Estrada Palma, in the heart of the area once controlled by Fidel's guerrillas. With five other officers he started on foot up the mountains. Fidel himself gathered a force of some twenty thousand men and surrounded the area, using the peinazo technique. Captain Beaton was captured, his five men killed; then he was shot before Fidel's eyes. The tower controller at the Camaguey airport committed "suicide" because of his grief at his responsibility in Camilo's death.

Bringas knew better than anyone else that Camilo Cienfuegos had conspired against Fidel. This was the natural consequence of failure. Had Camilo taken power, Fidel himself would have fared no better. This was the way revolutionary politics were conducted; nobody followed the Marquis of Queensbury rules. Fidel had done only what he had to to preserve his power. Fidel himself was not really culpable.

So Bringas told himself, temporizing. He knew he had to begin acting against the Revolution, establishing his credentials with the anti-Castro underground, yet he could not quite bring himself to oppose Fidel himself. What should he do?

Absent a decision, he did nothing.

In November both Manolo Ray and Lopez Fresquet resigned from the Cabinet. Raul Castro was appointed a Cabinet member as Armed Forces Minister, and Che Guevara became president of the National Bank—one of the most influential positions in Cuba.

Yes, it was obvious where the power lay. . . .

The National Catholic Congress convened in Havana. Fidel himself attended the mass that followed the immense torchlight parade. It was a concentration of people even larger than that of Fidel's January arrival. Two hundred thousand souls were at the congress, and Bringas and Adelita were there when the crowd chanted massively "Cuba sí, Rusia no! Cuba sí, Rusia no!" Fidel departed at that point, but the people remained despite the cold rain. They knew, they knew!

That night Adelita made love with special fervor, and he realized how deeply she had been moved by the demonstration. She was Catholic, of course; he had always known that, but hadn't realized the significance of communism. Catholicism and communism—they were fundamental enemies. He had no emotional commitment to either, but if he had to choose to be one or the other, he would be Catholic.

Adelita seemed to have been flirting with the Revolution's expressed ideals, but after this she reverted to her original attitude. She continued to teach, but she no longer talked much about it.

In December Major Hubert Matos and his officers were brought to trial. Bringas anticipated clemency, for surely

Fidel knew now that Matos had steadfastly refused to join the conspiracy. Had Matos' attitude been otherwise, Fidel might not be in power now, for Camilo had been right about that: both Camilo and Hubert had been extremely popular, and Camaguey would have been a bastion straddling Cuba's midsection, dividing Fidel's resources at the outset. At the minimum, Matos' defection would have led to civil war—but he had been loyal to Fidel, despite his serious opposition to the communist intrusion in Fidel's government.

Bringas was not called to testify, to his mixed relief and regret. He wanted to speak on behalf of Matos, but knew he would have to implicate himself to do so. Had Che Guevara kept him clear of it, again? Or was it the paradox effect once more, preventing him from being widely publicized?

His hopes for Matos were not to be realized. Fidel Castro was the principle witness against the defendant. He spoke for seven hours, calling Hubert a conspirator and coward.

Bringas watched the entire circus on television, a bottle of fine Spanish cognac in his clenching hand. How could this be happening to Hubert Matos, as fine a man as the Revolution had produced? Matos was certainly no traitor! Even if he had joined the conspiracy he would have done it only to save Cuba from communism, not for personal aggrandizement. His only fault was that he was too staunchly anti-communistic. That he should be crucified like this, this supremely honorable man, when in fact it was Fidel's own brother Raul who was the traitor to the cardinal principles of human decency. . . .

Adelita left him strictly alone. She served him good meals, for she was home; she kept the apartment beautiful; she acquiesced readily to his extemporaneous sexual demands; but she did not bother him otherwise. She knew how he felt about Matos.

Bringas tried to leave the television set, to get away from this horror, but he was unable to concentrate on anything else and was drawn back, again and again. He had to watch

Fidel shouting accusations that Fidel himself had to know were false, destroying a man who had been more loyal to the principles of the Revolution than any other. If there were a traitor to the Revolution, it certainly was not Hubert Matos. It was Fidel. He refused to curb the evil men of his government, he refused to stand up for men of the people like Matos.

At last Bringas smashed the bottle against the television screen, shattering Fidel's ranting face in splashing cognac. "Put me in touch," he said, not looking at Adelita.

She did not seem to hear him. But two nights later as they made hour-long love she whispered a number. This time *he* pretended not to hear . . . but he filed the digits in his memory even as he penetrated her. By the numbers they climaxed—those secret numbers that marked the irrevocable turning point of his career in Cuba.

When she slept, he got up and went to the phone. He dialed for the operator, as he had to make a long distance call to Santiago de Cuba.

"Matos is *not* a traitor," the operator said. "May I help you?"

Startled, Bringas almost forgot his number. He had had no idea that support of Matos went so deep! He had somehow supposed that it was his personal problem, unrelated to the common pulse. This voice on the phone was like the prompting of his conscience. How many citizens had been similarly alienated by this one issue?

"May I help you?" the operator repeated, sounding doubtful. She was risking her job by such a political statement about the trial, and she could even be arrested herself. Anyone could turn her in. That nothing had happened to her yet implied either she was very lucky—or that support for Matos was phenomenal. If Matos *had* supported Cienfuegos—

"May I—" she faltered.

"MATOS IS NOT A TRAITOR!" he shouted, feeling an almost sexual exhilaration and release. It was good to speak the truth aloud! Then he gave the number.

Adelita seemed to be asleep, though his shout should have disturbed her. But as he got into bed beside her she rolled over and hugged him fiercely.

"I'm afraid!" Adelita said. "How far have you gone, Juan? What are you planning now?"

He kissed her. "I am a man of action. You know that. Stick to your schoolteaching; don't make me lie to you."

"I should never have given you that contact," she muttered. "These past few months—I thought it was just a propaganda outfit. Leaflets, speeches, maybe even an underground newspaper—"

"It *was*," he said. He had phoned a representative of the new MRR—Movement for Recuperating the Revolution— headed by two men he had met during his guerrilla days: Captain Sotu and Major Nino Diaz. They agreed with him: they were not traitors to the Revolution. They had remained true to the principles for which they had fought in the hills. It was Fidel and his cronies who had changed.

Actually, none of this had been said on the phone, but he had gotten his message through. A few days later a brother officer had contacted him. Because actual officers in Fidel's army were at once the most valuable and most suspect members of the counterrevolutionary movement, his enlistment had been a delicate matter. As it was, he knew it would be a long time before he was trusted with any important function within the MRR, and he would have to prove himself many times over.

Bringas had become a double agent: one for his future, one for his conscience. The tiny anti-Castro cell he carried had been converted from a benign growth to a malignant one. He could not just coast along, a passive member; he had to accomplish feats that would make him widely respected in underground circles. Even the Americans must trust him, when that time came. He liked to believe that this was the ethically necessary course; that he was not doing it solely because the mysterious palimpsest document required it. . . .

"I am afraid," she said. "I look at you, and I see the pocked wall behind you."

Paredon. An apt premonition.

He took her by the arm and sat her down. "Would you have me stand idle while the animal farm goes communist?"

"You're trying to push my buttons!" she accused him. "Communism means nothing to you."

"A button here, a button there," he said, pinching her two nipples through her blouse between his thumb and forefinger.

"Stop that!" she exclaimed, laughing through her anger. "Every time I try to get serious, you get sexual."

"And who taught me perpetual sex?"

"That's not the point. Ouch!"

For as she spoke, he pushed the third button—in the middle of her soft stomach, squeezing her waist hard.

"What is so bad about communism?" he asked as she recovered. "From each according to his need; to each according to his ability."

"Oh, you've got it backwards!" she cried in frustration. "*To* each according to his need, *from* each ac—oooop!"

He had finally scored on her nether button, through her panties, and her scream was part shock, part excitement.

"Hasn't Fidel instituted agrarian reform?" he asked her rhetorically, hand poised near her derriere. "What's wrong with that?"

"Juan Bringas—if you pinch me again—!"

He pinched her again.

She grabbed at his beard with one hand and kissed him furiously while her other hand tore at his trousers. He tickled her inside the thighs, one-fingered. He could smell her eagerness. Anger aroused her as readily as love!

When the ensuing melee subsided, they were sprawled sidewise on the couch. She had a scissor-hold around his waist, but he had impaled her through torn panties. Her resiliant bosom was open to his face, and he had a breathtaking mouthful of button #1 along with part of her blouse.

"Now stop it or I'll smother you!" she said, taking a handful of his hair with her unpinned arm and pressing his head in.

In response he used his own unpinned hand to pinch her yet again, from behind. Her buttocks tensed violently under his palm, and the reflex of her body enclosed his deep member so that they climaxed together.

"To answer your implied question," he said formally as their flesh melted jointly, "there are two fundamental flaws in true communism. First, there is no provision to ensure that the totalitarian governmental structure 'withers away' when the appropriate time comes—"

"You're incorrigible!" she said. "Every time I get sexual, you get serious." She shifted to a more comfortable position. "You know, *your* totalitarian structure is withering away!"

He sighed and withdrew it. He was not, after all, a superman. "So it becomes in fact a dictatorship, subject to the myriad ailments of the species. Second, there is no inherent personal incentive for the individual to excel, for everything goes to the state and returns from it impartially. And when the masses don't have reason to produce, the economy as a whole deteriorates, until—"

"Tyrants at the top, lazy peasants at the bottom," she said. "Why don't you come teach school, if you know so much about it! Shut up and kiss your yegua, professor!"

"Why?" he asked, still teasing her though he knew the time for it had passed. "You're better at communism."

Then she was angry again, but she showed it subtly. She stood up and walked across the room, pulling her clothing into some kind of order. "Very well, tyrant—shall I take my peasant offering to the G-2?"

"They wouldn't have you in that condition." Why did this banter have to take a cruel turn? Was it guilt for what he could not give to 233? Was he reminding himself not to get too intimately involved with Adelita? Or could it be concern about his coming mission for the militant underground? He just might get himself killed, and in that case it would be better for Adelita if she didn't love him too much.

"You have no interest in this?" She brought out her hand, and now she was fighting back the tears.

It was a metal tube about the size of a short pencil.

Bringas felt an ugly chill. "What are you doing with that?" he asked tensely. "Where did you get it?"

"One of your anonymous friends delivered it this afternoon while you were out. A package of them. All neatly wrapped. He said there had been a problem somewhere, and that you would have to keep them. He said not to drop the package, or set it on the stove—"

Now Bringas began to sweat. If she had inadvertently crushed or heated any of those items—

"It must be a mistake," he said. "A—a confusion of names."

"Don't fence with me!" she cried. "I was in the mountains too, remember? Do you think I was asleep all the time I wasn't spreading my legs for you? Do you think I don't know a blasting cap when I have one shoved in my face? Do you think I can't guess the game you are playing? This really is paredon, Juan!"

"Don't wave it about like that!" he whispered, appalled. "Those things are touchy!"

"What is it," she said evenly. "Sabotage? Arson? Murder? Didn't you have enough of that, putting Fidel into power? Do you have to start it all over again? Those senseless crimes against mankind in the name of the 1940 Constitution?"

Strange—she had been cool toward his efforts when he supported Fidel; now she was more than cool when he opposed Fidel. Could he be certain of her personal loyalty? He was converting the original propaganda group into an effective action group, and this entailed a complex and careful building effect. They needed reliable contacts for supplies, for temporary hideouts, for information; and every contact was a security liability. Someone had bungled already, putting those blasting caps into Adelita's hands!

"Only a building," he said, his eyes fixed on the explosive device she held. "A warehouse. Nobody there. No killing. Motor parts. Without those replacements, half the trucks in Havana will grind to a halt in months."

"And who will suffer?" she demanded. "Not Fidel! The campesinos, who have to haul their produce into town to sell, the utilities needing repair from trucks—the little people. Those are the ones you are hurting! Why not just another mass execution while you're at it? Shoot the peasants! They're always the real target."

"You're overwrought." But there was enough truth in her words to make him feel guilty and uneasy.

She set the blasting cap down carefully and came to him again. "Juan, Juan—they will kill you! The G-2—"

He looked at her sadly. "As you say, I helped put Fidel in power. Now he has betrayed the revolution and put the communists in control. What can I do, in conscience, except help put him *out* of power? And it has to be this way. I can't go back to a mountain guerrilla existence; the peinazo is death to guerrillas. We have to organize the lines of supply in the cities, establish support to maintain our urban guerrilla offensive. We have to hit Fidel where he least expects it, keeping him offbalance, with special attention to his transportation so that he cannot attack *us* successfully. It is the same thing he did to Batista. We can't hope to overthrow him right now; all we can do is sabotage him, assassinate his communist hierarchy, stir up the people against him. Perhaps the little man *will* suffer, as he did before; that is the price we have to pay to right the colossal wrong we have wrought. To end Fidel's betrayal of our prior efforts."

"You said that lack of incentive under the communist system would destroy the economy anyway; why must you stain your own hands with blood?"

"I also said the totalitarian hierarchy would *not* wither away of its own accord. Cuba may grind down until it is the poorest country in the world, but Fidel will still have his cognac. My way, Cuba may suffer for months—but then it will be over. The operation is painful, as any surgery is, but the disease must be cured."

She dropped her eyes. "Why don't you marry me? Then when you go to the wall I'll be a real widow."

"You will see me again," he said seriously, thinking of their contact in 1962. "Even if something happens, and word reaches you that I am dead, I will come to you. Perhaps not to stay, at first—"

She was staring at him, horrified. "Are you leaving, Juan?"

He realized how carelessly and cruelly he had spoken, trying to comfort her. What could she know of time travel or of the life that waited for him in his own culture, once he had completed the larger mission? How could he explain that it was essential that he establish his bonafides as an anti-Castro partisan, for the sake of the message he would send at the time of the missile crisis?

It was time to mend his home fences. He put his arms around her reassuringly. "I was speaking metaphorically. I was trying to say I love you."

She made an effort to resist him, but those words destroyed her willpower. She collapsed against him and sobbed.

What use was it trying to prevent her from becoming too deeply involved with him? He could no more say no to her emotion than she could to his actions. She loved him, and it gave him a responsibility he could not avoid. How could he preach to her about his moral commitment— which was for him only a half truth, since he was serving his own purposes more than those of Cuba—while reneging on his moral commitment to *her*? He loved 233, but that did not justify destroying Adelita. The two women were in separate spheres; time itself prevented any conflict between their interests.

Bringas did not go on the planned mission that night. He made hasty excuses to the group and passed along the blasting caps. Then he took Adelita to the Jesus de Miramer Church, where all the priests opposed the government. He talked with Father Villalonga and arranged to dispense with the usual vows and ceremony, for he feared the paradox shield if the matter were not kept secret.

There, in a private courtyard, with date palms and royal palms the only witnesses, Juan Bringas married Adelita Suarez.

That same night, as they made the wildest love yet, a carful of dynamite went off prematurely, killing two members of Bringas' action group. Either the touchy explosive or the touchy blasting caps had been jolted too hard when the car struck a pothole.

It was the mission Bringas had deserted at the last moment. But for his decision to marry Adelita, he would have been in that car.

The realization reminded him how narrowly he was skirting death these days, and jogged something else in his mind. "Adelita—did you see the woman in the church?"

"There were several people there," she said. "They go at any hour to pray."

"The short blonde woman in good clothing?"

She considered. "Yes, I did see her. In her late thirties, but well proportioned. Do you know her? I think she looked at you—"

"That's Luisa. She's a—well, she really *is* a yegua. But a good woman. If you are ever in trouble and you need help, go to her."

Adelita looked at him oddly, but nodded.

That was all there was to that, but he was to wonder about it many times thereafter. Had the paradox shield saved his life only so that he could tell Adelita how to locate him when he came, unknowing, in 1962? And if so, had he now satisfied the conditions of the temporal inversion, so that it had no further need to protect him?

Suddenly he felt distressingly mortal.

The group was in a sorry state. It had not occurred to most of the men that the merchandise could be as deadly to the handler as to the target. They were novices at this type of warfare, where the sides were not clear-cut and the weapons were not mere bullets. The various underground factions were dependent on the United States' CIA and similar sources for their weapons, and the CIA for reasons of its own acted to prevent these factions from ever unifying into a single, centralized, effective group. The Cuban G-2 searched out conspirators ruthlessly, making anti-Castro activity of any kind extremely hazardous. Disaffected Cubans who might have helped the underground were leaving the country steadily, siphoning off the raw material of the underground. This left an at-times motley crew. Members knew each other only by first names, and suspicion was constant.

Having seen two of their members perish violently, they were even less inclined to become active terrorists, and but for Bringas' expertise and drive the group would have dissolved. They were hoping that the United States would act to overthrow Fidel Castro, so that the underground could merely play at revolution while assuming good credits to cash in when the new order occurred. Bringas knew better. Fidel would remain in power many years to come, and the communists longer yet, in the two futures he knew personally! All of this was futile—but he had to participate for the sake of 233.

Bringas decided to dispense with dynamite. What they had been using was old, beginning to extrude oily droplets of nitro, and if he trusted it much further he would be begging for another accident like the last. So he located a source of plastic explosives, and studied the manual carefully so that he could instruct his group in its use.

A month after the explosion they received their first shipment of Composition C3 in M5 demolition blocks. The wooden box weighed about forty pounds and was delivered directly to Bringas. Adelita knew what he was up to, but kept her peace. There was a tacit understanding between them: he had married her, even if no one knew it; she covered for him during his underground missions, though she hated them.

Bringas brought the box to the group's meeting-place. They were all there, nervous but intensely interested: Melchor, Luis, Macho and Baro. Five men, including him—were going to rock Havana, literally!

"I am going to introduce you to a potent lady," Bringas informed them. He opened the box carefully, though he knew there was no danger from its contents. He lifted out one of the two packages inside. "This is a haversack, so you can carry her around handily." He swung the bag in a circle once while the men winced, knowing the deadly properties of that bag.

He set down the haversack and opened it, removing a cardboard container colored olive-drab. It was about eleven inches long and two inches square in cross section. "She is a nice package, as you see. But let's remove her dress. . . ."

He pried open the cardboard and revealed another wrapping of glazed paper. "And her underclothing. . . ." He stripped away the paper. Within it was a bar of yellow material. "And here she is, the star of our show: Miss Plastic Explosive!"

"Smells like shoe polish," Baro said.

"Perfume," Bringas explained lightly. He set the bar down on the table and drew on a pair of doctor's rubber gloves. He didn't want that smell adhering to his hands. Then he picked up the bar again, grasped it by each end, and snapped it in half at its middle perforation. The men winced again.

"Now Miss Explosive is quite amenable to handling," he continued. "She won't lose her temper no matter how you

mistreat her. Not like most women. Watch." He dropped
the bar on the floor.

This time all four spectators scrambled for cover. But
there was only a dull thud. "Are you nervous about something?" he teased them, though his own pulse had jumped.
This stuff really was inert!

Bringas picked up the battered chunk and twisted off a
piece the size of his thumb. The waxy coating on it covered
his gloves and the shoe polish aroma became stronger.
"Give her a hotfoot and she won't scream," he said, striking
a match. The men again dove for cover as he applied the
flame to the fragment.

The plastic burned—rapidly but hardly explosively. The
men looked sheepish.

"You can shape her to any cavity," Bringas said, forming
his one-pound mass into a crude figuring of a nude woman
with huge breasts and hips. "No fuss, no muss, no bother.
No one will know she is there—until she goes off."

"But *will* she go off?" Baro asked dubiously. He touched
the figurine in an intimate region. "How do we know she
isn't just colored clay?"

"Wait until we use her," Bringas assured him grimly.
"She packs a stiffer punch than dynamite or TNT, weight
for weight."

"How *do* we set her off?" Melchor asked. "If ignition
and concussion don't do it—"

The men were becoming almost contemptuous of this
doughy mass. Fine—that would give them confidence to
handle it. Bringas brought out a slender copper tube resembling a pen. "Here is an M1 delay type firing device—the
detonator for Miss Plastic. I'll show you how to activate it
in a moment." He poked one end into the crack between the
nude's fat thighs. "When she gets goosed by *this* phallus,
she climaxes. Explosively."

They all laughed, but dubiously. Bringas proceeded to
show them how to assemble and set the detonator. This
was a far more delicate operation than the handling of the

plastic itself, for the firing device was far from inert and packed a fair wallop by itself.

They drove to the Talleres Ministerio Obras Publicas—the row of yellow buildings south of the bay. Bringas remembered passing them the two times he had entered Havana with Adelita—once after escaping from La Cabana prison, once as part of Fidel's motorcade. Behind those buildings were now parked about two hundred Russian trucks, and there was a warehouse full of repair parts. A prime target, as such trucks would be used to transport troops and army supplies.

He had an uneasy thought: did the fact that these buildings still stood in 1962 indicate that his present mission had failed? Would paradox interfere again? Not necessarily; the buildings could be repaired in two years. . . .

Baro parked the car at Via Blanca, a block from the depot. Baro was the only one Bringas had real confidence in, in an emergency; the others had become virtual robots in their fear, merely following orders.

The Luyano River passed here, and Bringas had to wade through it so as to enter at the back, while the others waited in concealment. There might be a sentry.

As he came out of the water, stealthily, ears alert for the slightest sound, the Canoñazo de Nueve sounded, startling him unpleasantly: the nine o'clock cannon blast at Cabana. But in that pause he spied the lone guard. Too bad; he was going to have to break a promise to Adelita.

He jumped the fence silently and stalked the man, who was about 45. The guard carried a Russian submachine gun, but faced away and paused to light a cigarette. Bringas came at him rapidly, passed an arm from behind around the throat, put pressure against that throat with the edge of his wrist, joined his hands, and started pulling back while leaning his shoulders against the back of the man's neck. At the same time Bringas dropped to the ground. There was a crack! and the guard's neck was broken.

How far he had come, since hesitating even to carry a gun during his first mission into Cuba in 1962! Now he had killed a man he didn't know, as a minor part of another mission. He did not enjoy it, but he would lose no sleep about it either. It was necessary—better to be a murderer than a fool. This was the fastest way to take out a guard silently, with no chance for the man to wake and give the alarm. And it would show the others, whose courage needed bolstering, that they were playing for keeps. There would be no pardon for anyone caught, and they all had to understand that. He had once tried to spare lives, and had ended up killing many more men far more painfully, and in the process abolished his own wife. . . .

Yet a muffled voice in his head muttered that it might be better to be a fool, even a dead one, than a murderer. Perhaps it was his conscience. . . .

He opened the gate and signaled. The men raced in, each carrying four or five half-blocks of yellow C3, the blocks linked together with detonating cord, or primacord. Melchor, Luis, Macho and finally Baro herding them in. Good enough.

Bringas took Luis inside the building to place charges, while Baro supervised the outside crew. They would place the plastic against several of the parked trucks, so that the gasoline tanks would rupture and spray fluid all over the lot and take out the rest of the vehicles.

Inside Bringas discovered oil drums stacked in a corner, and crates with spare parts. This was a welding shop, with oxygen-acetylene tanks—what a break! Those pressurized tanks would go up with a blast that would ignite the whole building! A couple of charges just so—

Damn! He had forgotten his rubber gloves. He would have to operate barehanded—the last thing he wanted.

"Who's watching for the police?" Luis demanded nervously. Bringas saw he was sweating. Luis was an effeminate, rumored to have a boyfriend named Tino. But that was no concern of this group. Terrorists could hardly be choosy about their company! "I didn't know we were doing it tonight—"

Of course he hadn't known! Bringas had told them this was to be a reconnaissance mission, so no one would get cold feet or give something away to the authorities inadvertently. "No need to watch," he snapped as he set the plastic in place and shaped it to stay. His hands were stinking; it would take forever to get that giveaway shoe polish smell off! "We're inside the complex, the gate is closed, the buildings shield us from the road. No one can see us. And if the police did catch on, they'd come in such force we'd have no chance anyway. So forget it."

Luis hardly seemed reassured. He was a bad choice for this mission, Bringas reflected; he was trembling so that it was unsafe to have him touch any of the makings.

He crushed the tube and set the detonator in one of the lumps of C3. Sweat dripped from his face. God, it was hot in here!

The primacord linked the inside charges with those against the trucks. One explosion would set off the rest. But to be sure, he inserted a second detonator farther along the chain. Then he went out and set a third in a truck charge. It was a triple-safety system: even if a detonator failed, or there was a break in the primacord, the entire thing would blow from one of the other points. He wanted no failure here!

"We have fifteen minutes," he said. "So take your time. Cover your traces carefully, close the gate, don't drop anything. We can't afford any evidence of our presence— except the explosion itself!" And he set the example, walking slowly.

But he would be glad to get out of here. His shirt was soaking with sweat, and the others were no better off. It wasn't just the tension; this was the hottest night he could remember, and no breeze at all! He felt a kind of desperation himself, an urge to run—but he made them take a full five minutes to wrap it up.

At last they walked—slowly—to their car. Luis was white-faced, but it was Baro who fiddled with the lock and dropped the keys in his anxiety. This was the first real sign Baro had given of the pressure on him.

"Take it easy," Bringas said as the man scrambled for the keys in the dark gutter. "We have a good six or seven minutes—"

Then it went off.

Bringas happened to be facing the blast. A tremendous flame illuminated the building and pushed on out, unfolding like a red flower. Then the blast wave picked him up and threw him against the car. The sound smote him as he fell to his knees, ears ringing.

Deafened, half-blinded, Bringas felt a peculiar satisfaction, a release throughout his body. It was akin to a sexual orgasm. Yet his mind was appalled at his body's response. How could a civilized man react with such pure joy to such raw destruction? Was this his true nature under the veneer of rationality? In what way, then, was he superior to Che Guevara or Raul Castro—or even Almejeiras?

They piled into the car, all of them awed and dazed, and Baro drove, wildly and far out of the way. This was not mere confusion; they had to foil any possible pursuit.

"Are we going to ditch the car?" Luis asked.

"No," Bringas said, fed up with the man. "It is registered in the name of an exile; they can't trace us through the car. In a couple of days we'll fill it with explosives and use it to blow up another target, car and all."

They drove on to the shores of the Almendares, crossed through the tunnel and went down along the river. Now their guns were a liability, for they were not hunted men; they would leave them at their supply apartment, then clean up and disperse to their individual apartments. They all stank of shoe polish, Bringas especially, and he was itching to scrub his hands and get rid of that incriminating odor.

Their apartment was in a fifteen story building, so that their entries and departures were usually concealed in the numbers of other people coming and going. Rural guerrillas might find security in isolation; urban guerrillas found it in crowds.

"Drive past first and park a block beyond," Bringas said. "We have to make sure——"

"Do you think I'm a fool?" Baro snapped. "We *always* go past first." He was correct; they always did, and Bringas' reminder had only betrayed his own jumpiness.

They studied the area carefully. There were no police cars. One pedestrian stood near the main entrance; that was all.

"All clear!" Luis exclaimed, vastly relieved.

"*Not* all clear," Bringas said, irritated. "I've never seen a man outside there at ten at night. He was watching us." He knew it was more likely that the man was merely waiting for a friend to pick him up; but this was not the night to risk anything. "Baro and I will walk past and check; the rest of you wait in the car."

There were two somber-looking men in the lobby, a light showing at their floor—and a parked G-2 car in back.

"One of us is an informer," Bringas said grimly as the two of them ambled with pretended nonchalance back to the car. "There was no way for G-2 to know our identity this soon after the blast. No legitimate way."

"What about the timing?" Baro demanded angrily. "That blast could have killed us all—just the way the last one got two of us. *You* set the detonators, *you* made us stay within lethal range unnecessarily. You skipped out entirely on the last one. Were you trying to get the rest of us this time?"

Brother! Bringas held his temper, knowing that there was some justice in the man's suspicion. Baro was quick-tempered and outspoken, but there was no question about his competence or loyalty to the cause. His aging father had been jailed for speaking against Fidel's policies, and had died of a ruptured appendix because of inadequate medical attention while awaiting trial. "I was right there with you,"

Bringas pointed out. "I was the last to leave the building. If I had known—"

They were at the car. Tersely Bringas explained the situation.

"We were all together," Luis said, white-faced. "An informer would have . . . brought the police before we set . . . set the blast. And stayed well clear himself. He never would have let you . . . let us destroy the trucks."

Bringas had to agree. "You're right. Something or someone else must have tipped them off. All of us here have to be exonerated. Any one of us could have screamed warning to the authorities long ago."

"Someone *did*," Baro said. "Someone who didn't know exactly what or when . . . maybe our explosives contact."

"Or someone who knows about us," Macho said from the rear seat of the car. "My family knows nothing. They would never betray me, but if they knew they might by accident—"

"I have no family," Melchor said.

"What about that woman you live with?" Baro demanded of Bringas, standing beside him outside the car.

Bringas started to make an angry rebuttal, but had to pause. Adelita *did* know, and she had tried to get him to stop. Could she have acted more deviously?

"There's the leak!" Baro cried. "You can see it on his face!"

"No!" Bringas shouted, sweating, heedless of who might overhear. "She put me in touch in the first place. She would never—"

"Perhaps she figured you'd be better off in a cell than blown up!" Baro insisted with merciless plausibility. "Cha-cha-cha—"

Bringas slapped him, open hand on the mouth. "Shut up!"

Baro responded with a quick punch to the stomach, but it lacked force. They were friends; suspicion had made their nerves ragged, but they did not really want to hurt each other.

"Stop it!" Luis screamed, almost tumbling out of the car in his effort to get between them. "The G-2 in the apartment—they'll hear us! We have to get out of here, not quarrel!"

Of course he was right. They were doing the worst possible thing, fighting almost in sight of the enemy. They all piled back into the car and Baro drove again.

"She wouldn't do it!" Bringas said. She might, he thought.

"If you believe that, you can test her yourself," Baro said. "We'll go to the alternate hideout. Or did you tell her about that, too?"

"I DIDN'T TELL HER ABOUT EITHER HIDEOUT!"

"Well, go there and phone her and tell her where you are. If the G-2 comes—"

Bringas had no choice but to agree, though he felt like a traitor himself. He would be setting a terrible trap for her. If she were guilty—NO! And if she were innocent— she *was* innocent—would she ever forgive him?

He smiled uncomfortably. Here hindsight helped. Adelita obviously *had* forgiven him by 1962.

But if she had been responsible for sending him to prison, without his suspecting her, she might be eager to rejoin him when he got out, so as to betray him again when something really big was afoot. . . .

He felt unclean, making these conjectures. But he was a multiple agent himself, serving as a Captain for Fidel, a cell leader for the underground, a time traveler from a later century, and, of course, he ultimately served his own ends, trying to recover his wife. He had to view such matters realistically. If Adelita had any hint of his covert purposes. . . .

The hideout was in the Vedado section not far from the Focsa building: an apartment building in front of the former Ministry of Agriculture on Calle 23. The first floor was a cafeteria, but the next ten were notorious for their trysting places and expensive call girls and boys. Marta, a mulatto madam, owned the apartment; she had loaned it to them because she was strongly anti-Castro. The rooms were done in Chinese decor with beautiful red draperies.

There were no G-2 men in evidence, so they mounted to the fifth floor and waited. Bringas made the call.

Adelita answered at once, and he felt a warm thrill at her familiar voice despite the circumstances. "I thought you would be home by now. There was some kind of explosion; the windows rattled, and I thought—"

"Yes, we did that. The G-2 is after us. I can't talk now, but I'll tell you where I am." He gave the address. "I'll meet you in a few days, you know where."

"I understand," she said. He could not tell whether her voice was aloof or tightly controlled.

He had baited the trap. He had killed a man this night, but what he was setting up for Adelita hurt him worse.

As he turned away from the phone, he felt a blow on his head. Then blackness.

His head pounded and it felt grossly swollen. He was nauseous. He tried to get up, but his hands were tied together behind his back and linked to his bound ankles. He was gagged by a balled-up handkerchief inside his mouth under his lip, with another handkerchief bound over it.

Bringas was sick and furious. At himself more than the others who had left him here. He should never have let down his guard enough to be caught this way. He understood Baro's position: when a man was under suspicion, you couldn't just let him call in the G-2 and wait for the capture! But because they had not been *sure*, they'd given him the benefit of the doubt and only incapacitated him long enough for them to escape cleanly. If he were innocent, or if Adelita were innocent—same thing, really—he would be able to work his way free and go home with nothing more than a headache. That was certainly better than being killed.

But he should have fathomed Baro's motive. It was his own failure as an agent that had gotten him into this mess, and it was an inexcusable lapse.

First things first. He chewed on the gag and finally managed to spit it out. He worked on the bonds and though his wrists soon became bruised, then bloody, he was able to free his feet for walking.

Now he could get to the kitchen and find a knife to cut the rest.

Adelita would not betray him, he thought as he moved. He was sure of that. Her arguments and reservations had been for his ears alone. He trusted her.

The door burst open.

PART
SIX

H

e knew what they were trying to do. It was the disorientation treatment. The cell was small and dark and usually silent, and he was alone, with no way to ascertain how much time was passing. Even the temperature seemed to vary little, so there was no distinction between day and night even that way. His meals were brought at different times, sometimes within an hour of each other and sometimes a day apart, so that his digestion was no guide either.

"Pig!" a man's voice screamed suddenly. "Talk! Talk, or die!"

That, too. He knew better than to answer.

He fought it, but knew that the treatment was working. He *was* becoming disoriented. Already it was difficult to keep track of the order of events since his arrest by the G-2.

The door had burst open . . . and they had taken him to the G-2 headquarters, where interrogators had told him that they knew everything, confess and receive a lenient sentence, give them other names . . . Raul Castro had appeared, sneering, slapping him a few times, and he had spit a goober of thick yellow phlegm at the man's face—or had he dreamed that? Had he seen Raul at all, or merely imagined

237

Raul's face? At any rate, he had annoyed somebody, for their goons had given him a professional workover whose expertise he could now appreciate at leisure: much pain, little actual damage. And he had not talked. He knew he had not talked, because they had put him in the cold room, air conditioned, too small for effective movement . . . like treading naked across Antarctica in winter, not that he ever had . . . after some hours it seemed warm, and it took them some time to revive him sufficiently to talk and he *didn't* talk, because then it was the no-sleep treatment, bright lights, banging against the cell bars loudly if he tried to sleep, or forcible walking and he still did not talk because then the injection of sodium pentothal or was that before the cold room? But it didn't work because he had been immunized against this sort of thing before the first mission into Cuba and now disorientation they could disorient him as much as they wanted he stillwouldnottalk . . . still-would-not-talk . . . STILLWOULDNOTTALK.

Before him was Santa Barbara, saint and goddess in her flowing red robe, mounted on her steed, which was a large turtle, and wearing her bright sword. Then an old Indian appeared and told him he was going to survive the war. It was his guardian spirit who always told the truth. "Pig, you are going to paredon if you do not talk soon!"

Bringas woke. There was food again, and he ate, for he could not do otherwise.

How to keep track of the time? He had been arrested in May, Fructo on the real calender, or Aymaray: the dance of the young maize. It must be June now, Prio, Inti Raymi, festival of the sun—Nilo had always said he wanted to die in the sun, and where was Nilo now? No, no! The young maize was Crau, April; May was the song of the harvest. Was he forgetting his own calendar? July, Estrada, earthly purification, Cana Warkis—

It was no use. Mindless repetition of months could not help save his mind. Nor could dreams of women riding on turtles.

Women. . . .

233 clasping his face between her large, muscular thighs,
begging for an extra minute. Even that was over too soon.
Adelita had shown him . . . And it was not Perversion, nothing that pleasured man and woman was Perversion . . . and
impossible to conceive through the rectum . . . except the
joke, that's how Batistianos are born, or communistas, or
whatever.

The Spaniards set up estates, with cultivation carried
on by serflike Indians who could neither move from the
land nor be removed from it. The Revolution had changed
all that; now they were called cooperatives, not estates.
So the old semi-feudal society continued under different
guise, with its communist aristocracy and its growing ser-
vile class. In the twenty-first century it would be made
even more scientific and titled Caste . . . Castro. . . .

Spread for me, woman of all time; I am a superman. I
will fill your anus with white phosphorus. . . .

A closed, barred van, two guards in front, a G-2 car
before, another behind . . . Juan Bringas rode in style to a
familiar residence, the Cabana prison.

Behind a barred window with safety glass, he stared out
all the way from the Miramar section of Havana through
Vedado and on. Down 5th Avenida and its date palms,
across the Almendares River, along the Malecon, past the
apartment houses where he and Adelita—was she there
now? Would he ever see her again? *Had she betrayed
him?* 233 would never have done it, but Adelita, unfath-
omable motives . . . down, under the Bay of Havana . . .
long shining hair, full buttocks . . . the grim walls of La
Cabana.

He had not talked, he had not confessed, he had not
been tried or sentenced. But neither had those people Raul
Castro machine gunned . . . and even a commuted sentence
had not saved Captain Castaño.

The prison was much as he remembered it from two

years later: the same cramped cells, bare patio, forbidding walls with guards atop like living warts. "Carne Fresca!" the guards' prisoners shouted as he entered. "Fresh meat!"

Old home! Even the same ridiculous Coca-Cola machine. Bringas smiled as he went for a bottle. Jimenez had been right: the taste had grown on him.

Then he frowned. He should have reached the machine by now, but somehow he hadn't. He was turned around, walking away—without his drink. The continuing disorientation must have . . .

He turned about again and made for the machine. It was shinier than it had been, as though more recently installed, and . . . he was facing the wrong way.

What was the matter? Why couldn't he do a simple thing like fetching a bottle from a vending machine, as he had so many times before? He wasn't *that* confused!

A third time he went for it, counting his steps determinedly. He was going to settle this right now: could he or could he not perform this simple task. One-two-three-four-five-six—

Someone laughed. "Can't make up your mind, friend?"

Another failure!

Then, mercifully, he realized the truth. The paradox shield held him back. He had used this machine as an aid to his prison break in 1962. If he tried the same stunt now, in 1960, he would expose the secret, get the machine removed, and make his subsequent exploit impossible. He *had* done it then, which meant he *couldn't* do it now. Though the episode was two years in this world's future, it was a similar period in his personal past, and he could no more interfere with his past than any other man could. So the secondary paradox shield kept him away from the machine entirely, playing it safe.

The realization reopened an impressive array of possibilities. The shield had affected him several times before that he knew of, and perhaps had guided him many more times that he hadn't suspected. In the Sierra Maestra, of course, when he hadn't been able to shoot the last Batistiano soldier, and his introduction to Adelita; she had remembered him in 1962, so naturally he had to meet her in 1958. The entire romance of 1958 to 1960, predicated by the vagaries of 1962, preset by his own framework just as this cola machine fiasco had been. Had this same force blunted his awareness at the time Baro was making ready to strike him down? Would his escape from that trap have altered things paradoxically? Adelita—had she betrayed him—*and was this part of the natural order of his mission*?

He shook his head, disgruntled. He would have to meditate at greater leisure, for there seemed to be sub-paradoxes within it. Too bad he hadn't thought to think about it when he had all that time at G-2 headquarters!

As though he didn't have plenty of surplus time right now!

"Juan! Juan Bringas!"

He jumped. It couldn't be Jimenez, for they had not met until 1962, and contact now would really foul that up. But who else in this prison would know him?

"Juan! Still looking for that yegua?"

It was Nilo Parera. "Horse lover!" Bringas cried, rushing to hug his old friend in the traditional Cuban greeting. "What are you doing here?"

"Here? Just resting, Juan. But ask me what I was doing out there!"

"What were you doing out there?"

"Did you hear about the Babalao priest? When they came to arrest him he sent his albino vulture against them, pecking at their eyeballs. And he had this pet boa constrictor, maybe eight feet long, and—"

"But what about *you?* How did you—"

"Well, I had no boa constrictor."

Bringas sighed. Nilo would tell his story in his own time, and not one moment before. The damned guajiro mentality! "Where are you staying? I'm in Galera Twelve with the rest of the Fidelistas—"

• • •

All too rapidly Bringas settled into the prison pattern. Boredom was the main enemy here, and to assuage this the prisoners participated in many internally initiated projects. Some were good with their hands, and made furniture from scraps of wood and cloth; one was a fair amateur artist who decorated the walls with portraits of nude women in provocative postures, to the concupiscent delight of many. Some tried weightlifting with homemade weights. There were endless chess and checker tournaments and a great deal of gambling in many forms—dominoes, poker, gin rummy, even Monopoly.

Classes were conducted in a number of other languages, and Bringas took this opportunity to commence his study of English. He might never have a use for it now, but he had been intending to learn it for some time, and time was what he had, now.

Dr. Carbell, Cuba's leading astrology professor, was here in prison too. Nilo teased him about his inability to read his own future in the stars, but Carbell only shrugged and replied: "I can read *your* future, but mine is a dark veil. A man cannot predict his own life."

Bringas talked to a Babalao, too, a priest of Espiritismo, though he was a bit uneasy in the man's presence. About one-fifth of the prisoners kept a glass of water under their bunks, so that the bad spirits would go into the water, and half those who participated in the evening rosary also consulted the Babalaos. Every night there were requests for the cocos to be thrown: dry white pieces of coconut whose cast was purported to illuminate fate. Bringas remembered the Espiritismo cult of his own time, and the cocos' prediction that he was death to them all . . . But they had let him go. He *had* been death to the Caste Brown—but if his present mission were successful, he would restore it to life. Perhaps that was why he had been spared! Every day there was the cocos, and the caracoles, the sea shells, and the chanting of prayers, and the passing of bundles of albaca leaves around a man's body to drive out the evil spirits in him . . . and there was much evil to expunge in a place like this!

"Do you wish me to cast for you?" the Babalao inquired politely, observing Bringas' unwilling fascination. *No!* he wanted to scream, but morbidly compelled, he nodded. The man cast the cocos, and cast again, and cast a third time, and his lips became thin, his face pale, and he left Bringas and refused thereafter ever to talk to him.

"If you have some corn meal," Nilo said helpfully, "you could scatter it from every corner of the house to abate the evil, if you had a house. Then maybe the Babalao would speak to you again."

"Not his fault," Bringas said. "I *am* evil, at least to him." But he wished it had not happened that way.

"If you had an egg," Nilo said, "you could drop it into a moving stream—"

"If I had a moving stream!" Bringas finished, and laughed. But later he saved a tiny piece of his bread, and formed it into an egg-shaped wad, and flushed it down the communal toilet, praying that the evil *would* be borne away.

He thought the spell had some effect, when the next day they were served stew with meat, and the prisoner-server was a friend of Nilo's and managed to dip out extra meat to him and Bringas. But it was bad meat, and that night he woke with urgent diarrhea and dashed for the toilet. There were only two toilet bowls, and five people waiting, and more coming, and the stench was terrible. Bringas was able to hold out, but there were those who could not, and who had to squat in the patio, unable to contain their heaving bowels.

After that some tried a hunger strike, but the gesture was futile. The prison administration simply didn't care; if a prisoner starved himself to death, that was one less to worry about. If anything, the food became even worse. Sometimes small stones were found in the stew, or dead roaches, and once a guard pulled a battered rat from a kettle of rice. Even at the best of times, the diet was deficient in protein and vitamins, and but for the food parcels sent in by relatives there would have been many fatalities from malnutrition and deficiency diseases.

Mainly there was talk to while away the time, and of course much of it was about sex. There was a Batista sailor dubbed Mikoyan, because he was always talking, and Bringas made the mistake once of listening. "Back when I was with the naval police, before the dictator came—" he meant Fidel, not Batista—"I saw a former girlfriend in front of the Barralito bar. We had parted mad at each other, but that was a long time before, and now she was with the most beautiful blonde I ever—" Pause for gesticulatory description. "I had to have that blonde! And do you know, my ex was quite friendly, and even introduced me, and I took them both into the bar and bought drinks. Then my ex left laughing, she was really a good sport, and I had the blonde all to myself. . . ."

The crowd was growing, for this promised to be a good one. Bringas listened with half an ear, trying to imagine 233 and Adelita standing together outside the barrel-shaped bar, and 233 laughing and—no, *Adelita* laughing and departing. . . .

" . . . took her to a motel. Well, she insisted on putting out the lights so it was completely dark, and she started sucking me with her clothes on, but I wanted to lay her. She told me she liked it in the culo. . . ."

How he had changed! Once he would have been utterly shocked at such lascivious narration of Perversion; now he had fond memories of every type of amatory experience, and could not be shocked. This was Cuba, not Fidelia; when in Cuba. . . .

" . . . the very sweetest ass I ever—she turned her head and gave me tongue kisses tasting of honey and that delicious perfume she wore. . . ."

Mikoyan could certainly tell a story! His audience was fully as rapt as the one that had watched Superman.

" . . . about to come, so I reached around to run my finger into her bollo. . . ."

Bollo—ah yes, Bringas thought.

" . . . rampant prick instead. It was a man! Well, I. . . ."

So the sailor had picked up a transvestite, a female impersonator with sexual inclinations! Bringas had to retire a few paces, for despite his previous thoughts, he was shocked.

Homosexuality was an insignificant factor here at La Cabana, for there was virtually no privacy, and so many of the prisoners were political. Political prisoners were of a higher class than common ones, being more educated and with much higher aspirations. Army officers, bureaucrats, professors, university students, doctors, lawyers, accountants—professional people of all types.

" . . . the leather whip. You should have seen that maricon gather his skirts and run, but I got him across the buttocks. He looked like a rabbit!"

For the common criminal there was little real hope. He would be released, and return to his asocial mode of existence, and be arrested again. But the political prisoner could become a government official almost overnight, if the government he opposed were somehow overthrown. Hope sprang eternal!

"Of *course* it's possible!" someone else cried. "How do you think Fidelistas are born?"

There was a burst of laughter from the Batistianos. Followed by a spot of Fidelista/Batistiano warfare. A normal day.

In the evening they played music on makeshift instruments: pans, empty bottles, and a few legitimate woodwinds. They sang nostalgic songs, and sometimes got hold of medicinal alcohol and fruit juice. Tasted terrible, but helped take the mind off prison life.

And the weeks passed. . . .

•   •   •

"Juan Bringas!" someone cried, shaking him awake. "Didn't you hear? They announced your freedom! You are to report to the Commander's office with all your belongings!"

Freedom! The word had a golden ring! Bringas bounced up, casting about him for his things. Where was Nilo? He would have to say good-bye!

Then he caught on. Often men were freed without trial, when there was no evidence against them, even after months or years of imprisonment. He had never confessed, and it was possible that they had not linked him to the sabotage after all. But unlikely. It was a favorite joke in the prison to wake a sleeping man and tell him he was being freed; then when he tried to leave with all his things, the guards would stop him, laughing uproariously, and the prank would be revealed. There could be very ugly fights after such fun.

"Forget it," he snapped. "I've heard that one before." Worse: he had *fallen* for it before: the variation where they pretended to execute a prisoner. . . .

It was the absence of Nilo that had tipped him off. Nilo would have told him the truth right away. So they had diverted his friend.

They argued with him, but when he began to get ugly they let him be.

Then he heard the loudspeakers on the patio: "Juan Bringas, report to the Commander's office with all your belongings!"

Oh, no!

Nilo ran up. "Juan! Juan! Did you hear? Did you hear?"

Suddenly there was too much to say. He felt the tears in his eyes: joy at his release, chagrin at his suspicion of those who had tried to tell him, grief at his parting from his friend Nilo. In a daze he gathered everything he owned, which wasn't much, and stumbled out through the patio and to the office, surrounded by men congratulating him. "Take a message to my brother!" someone cried, and Bringas accepted the wadded paper, a letter. "Send us a package!"

another begged. "And don't forget the cake and chisel!" another added.

Then the abrupt silence of the office. Only one person was there, and not a Cabana official. It was Efigenio Almejeiras, Chief of Police.

Almejeiras stood up, smiling. "Juan, I could not believe it when I heard you were here! Why didn't you call me?"

"There was no telephone in the G-2 isolation booth," Bringas said sarcastically. He did not like the smell of this at all, for Almejeiras was no friend to those fallen from grace.

"Don't be that way, Juan! I am here to help you. It was a mistake, arresting you; you should have told them you knew me!"

"I didn't think of it." That was true enough.

"I didn't know for some time, Juan. The G-2—you know how they are. But as soon as I learned I got in touch with your yegua. She had no idea what had happened to you, but I told her I would have you out in no time. And here I am, to lead you out of this hellhole."

Dare he hope? "Almejeiras, I think we understand each other. I have not confessed to anything, and if I *were* guilty I would certainly never give away the names of my confederates. Where is the catch?"

"Confederates? There were several people we picked up who tried to implicate you under interrogation, but of course I knew they were lying. You would never engage in sabotage, Juan: you lack the fortitude."

"Who tried to implicate me?" Almejeiras had something in mind, and it was better to get it out at once.

"Oh, you know. Macho, Melchor—there was one Baro, Tomas Baro, but he died evading capture. And another escaped."

"I knew those men." Interesting that Almejeiras knew no more than the names Bringas knew, though. *And that Adelita knew.* And he had contacted her. . . .

"As passing friends, of course. You could not have

known that they were part of a terrorist group, with plastic explosives and a special apartment. When I heard them trying to exonerate themselves by implicating you falsely. . . ."

What a game of cat and mouse! *Had Adelita bought his freedom through some deal?*

Almejeiras shook his head sadly. "You should be more careful about your associates, Juan. In the future, when you make new friends, give me their names and I will check them out and make sure they are of good character."

"Like hell I will!"

Almejeiras leaned forward earnestly. "Juan, you were a good man for Fidel once, and Che Guevara likes you too. All you need to do is go through a small amount of training, a mere formality, and you will be released from here and reinstated with your former rank."

"Training?"

"Education. In communist doctrine. So you can join the Party—"

"Oh, God!"

"Juan, they need good men. For special missions. Men who are good shots, who understand demolition, who can organize an undercover cell, perhaps in Mexico—"

"I am no communist!"

"Juan, listen to me. The Party takes care of its own, and those who cooperate. Consider my case: I was a small-time thief, using the name of 'Tomeguin,' the little bird who picks up other people's property. I snatched purses, I mugged women, I stole car batteries, I peddled drugs, I used marijuana myself. I served a month or two in prison for that in 1949. I am no communist, but I am loyal to Fidel—and now I am Chief of Police. If you are loyal in the same way, Fidel will forgive you your mistake. There is a wonderful future for you in the Revolution! Only give me your word, and humor them about this training. You don't have to be a communist in your heart, Juan; just do what you are told, as I do, and they will not care."

Just do what you are told, as I do . . . and who had told Almejeiras to come here and ply him with this offer? Che? Raul?

"I'll wait for my trial," Bringas said.

"But it is freedom I am offering you! You could die in this hole, Juan, before you ever come to trail! And it is all so unnecessary!"

Bringas turned about.

"Juan, I don't understand you!" Almejeiras cried, running after him. "What do you have to gain?"

"You wouldn't understand."

But the truth was Bringas didn't understand himself. His mission seemed to be served by this offer; certainly he could not do what he had to do if he stayed in La Cabana. Self-respect? His staying here could not unkill the men he had murdered. So why had he assumed a moral posture that was, for him, *only* a posture?

Slowly it came to him: if the offer were valid, it had to be because Adelita was involved. She had turned him in, conditionally; she had made a deal. Thus he was out of the anti-Castro business with a whole hide. Simple!

It was foolish, it was ludicrous—but he refused to have it that way. If Adelita had done it, he was through with her. By accepting the deal, he would be accepting her guilt.

A week later Adelita came to see him on visiting day. A number of the women were permitted in the kitchen, where there were long wooden benches, while the men sat facing them and talking. It was hardly private, but it was a great deal better than nothing.

"Oh, Juan," she said. "I didn't know what had become of you, until Almejeiras—"

"I know." Had the two of them agreed on a story to tell him, or could it be the truth? Here in her presence it was difficult to doubt her sincerity. She wore a voluminous skirt and she was so beautiful that it hurt him to sit and only stare at her.

They were silent for a moment, and he became aware of the breathless murmuring of the other couples. A shudder ran through the bench, annoying him. Then he realized what it was: the men were applying pressure with their feet and legs, nudging the entire bench forward, to be closer to the women. So he cooperated.

"Are you all right, Juan?" she inquired, concerned. "This awful place—I was afraid the lesbian guards would search me, but they didn't."

Yes, he had heard stories about that. Female prisoners had an especially nasty time of it, for the "searches" could be degradingly thorough. "I'm all right." He wanted to ask her point blank whether she had turned him in, but the words wouldn't come. To voice the suspicion would be to give it credence. "Are you getting along all right?" This was stupid—but what was there to say, in a situation like this?

"I've been fired."

This didn't sound like a deal! "I thought they needed teachers!"

"They do. But they wanted me to teach a class of children why there is no God. . . ."

She was Catholic; no more needed to be said.

"Juan," she said, "Almejeiras told me he could get you out, but you wouldn't go—"

"He wanted me to become a saboteur for the communists." He gave the bench another nudge. It was very close now, and couples were reaching across them to clasp hands, and more.

"Oh, Juan, I want you so much, but not that way! I'm glad you—glad you—" She had to stop, for she was crying.

To hell with his suspicions! The guard was occupied elsewhere. Bringas leaned over, caught her hand, and tugged her over to him. She landed in his lap, and he got his hand under her spreading skirt, and found her naked beneath.

Yegua! he thought. But he knew it was for him, and he scraped around to gain the intimate contact before the guards discovered what was happening and rushed to break it up.

Adelita kissed him fiercely, her tears mingling with her passion. She was hot all over, and her thighs were moist, but he could not gain entry in this position and dared not stand. "I love you, I love you!" she whispered, flexing her legs, but still it was not right.

The guards were on their way, but there were several other clinches intervening. Bringas thrust desperately, and thought he had it at last, and came—he missed. Her thick skirt covered it all, the guard was near, and he had to break before being exposed.

There was no chance for more, for the guards were angry about the moved bench and hustled the women out then.

Had she betrayed him? That doubt was worse than all the rest.

The Batistianos were fertile sources for anti-Fidel gossip. Commander Mirabal in Galera 14, a former officer under Batista, invited Bringas in for a cup of black coffee and a kind word. The story he told was astonishing, but it clarified some long standing confusions.

"I was sentenced to die," Mirabal said, as though this were routine. "But Lina Ruz, Fidel's mother, interceded for me and so it was commuted to life."

"Fidel's mother? Why would she—"

"My brother was shot, and she knew I would be too, if she didn't stop it. You see, I was her lover once."

"Her lover!"

"I am not sure of this, for she knew many men at the time. It is not impossible that I am the creature's father."

"The creature—Raul Castro? He's a bastard?" Then he made another connection. "I heard Major Cienfuegos call him a double bastard to his face, and Raul was furious! Is that—?"

"Yes. Angel Castro had not married Lina Ruz at the time most of her children by him were born, so they were all technically bastards. But if Raul was mine and not Angel's. . . ."

Raul Castro did look different from his brothers, and this would explain it. "What does Fidel say about this?"

Mirabal shrugged. "What *can* he say? Raul is his brother—certainly his half brother. But for the grace of his mother's wandering fancy, it might have been Fidel himself!"

Nilo had joined them. "I'll tell you one man who doesn't like being cuckolded. Che Guevara! Did you hear about the affair Pepe Luis had with his wife?"

Bringas hadn't. This was developing into another important session.

"He was about 18, handsome, and very strong, and a member of the 26th of July, a college graduate. Che knew about it, but he bided his time. He acted through friends to get the young man to join the Nicaragua mission in 1959, and after they crossed the border from Costa Rica, two of Che's men assassinated Pepe. It wasn't that Che cared about his wife that much. It was the principle of the thing."

"I heard Che was no doctor," a Batistiano said. "He makes people call him Doctor Guevara, but back in Argentina he was only a veterinarian!"

"A vet is still a doctor," Nilo said defensively. The Batistianos were getting too enthusiastic.

"You know how he got installed at the World Bank?" another Batistiano demanded. "Fidel was handing out appointments, and he asked, 'Who is a good economist?' and Che said 'I am!' so Fidel said 'Fine! You take over the bank!' And after the meeting he said to Che: 'I didn't know you were an economist!' and Che said, surprised, 'Economist? I thought you said *communist*!'"

Even Nilo had to laugh, for he, like so many, had been soured on the Revolution after the communists usurped it.

"The original 26th of July movement was good," Bringas said, for he too was technically a Fidelista. "Later there were problems—severe problems—but at the start it was good. Batista needed overthrowing."

Another Batistiano was quick to take him up. "Good? It was *never* good. Fidel was always a gangster and a coward. He killed his best friend, Manolo Castro, when they were still university students. Bola de Churre, they called him—the greaseball, because he never washed. And I hear he has one of the smallest—"

Bringas stopped him. "I fought in the mountains with him, and he didn't look like a coward to me."

"What about the Moncada Barracks attack?" the man cried. "Fidel hid in the mountains while his men did the fighting—and most of the killing they did was among the wounded in the hospital, who could not fight back!"

"What do you know about it!" Nilo retorted. "You Batistianos murdered most of the men after they surrendered, and raped the girls!"

"Rape? You *can't* rape that kind!"

The two squared off, but Bringas got between them and managed to pacify it. "Don't forget that dove of peace!" he said humorously. "Would a dove land on Fidel's shoulder if he were a gangster or a coward?"

"It was a trained dove! I knew the girl who owned it. The whole thing was staged!"

Fidelista reinforcements had arrived. They too had been imprisoned by the Castro government, but they had little truck with the Batistianos even on this matter. "Fidel doesn't work that way," one said. "I know someone who went to school with him. Fidel was sixteen, and he wanted to go climb a mountain. Their professor told my friend, 'Go talk Fidel out of this foolishness.' So he went, and in half an hour Fidel had talked him into joining the expedition. So the two of them rode the train with another student for three or four hours and got off at a village. 'Where is the mountain?' they asked Fidel, and he said, 'Just follow me.'

So they walked and walked and walked, all night, and no mountain. They walked all day, and no mountain, and they were tired. 'How do we sleep here in the jungle?' they asked Fidel, and he said 'We have these tents,' and they struggled with the tents and couldn't put them up. 'How do we make the tents work, Fidel?' And he shrugged and said 'How do I know about tents?' So they lay on the ground with the canvas over them as blankets. In the morning, no food. 'We find food some way, I guess,' Fidel said, but all they found was some fruit along the way, not enough to stop their hunger. They walked all day again, and slept under the canvas again, and finally they found the mountain, and they climbed it. After that they discovered that there was a good road running right from the railroad to the mountain. Fidel, he gets where he is going, but he never knows how. He just goes, goes, and you go with him or too bad."

"That's Fidel!" Nilo exclaimed and there was a murmur of agreement from Fidelista and Batistiano alike.

"But he learned something since he was sixteen!" the more aggressive Batistiano said. "Now he finds the road and greases it with money and propaganda!"

"Propaganda, yes," Bringas said reasonably. "But money?"

"You were with him in the mountains and you did not know how he stopped Cantillo? Well, I was *with* Cantillo—that's why I'm *here*! I'll tell you how! We had you rebels trapped there, completely encircled, and our lead column was about to advance on your main camp and wipe it out— I had my gun shined for that, I can tell you!—and then we got orders to stop. Why? Because our commander— not Cantillo, he was honest, but the one in the field—our commander got a payoff of one million dollars American to let Fidel go. So he waited, until the rains came, and then he said it was too late. *That's* how Fidel just goes, goes!"

Bringas was shocked. He had never suspected such a

thing—but he *had* thought it was a miracle that Fidel escaped Cantillo's siege. Could there really have been a payoff?

"And when Che and Camilo marched through Camaguey—what made the government troops blind to their ragtag progress? Not fear of battle, you may be sure! Love of money! We had our finger on you all the time, but there was a fortune to be made by sitting tight! And that armored train—remember that? Well. . . ."

Time passed. Adelita visited him every month, except when visits were suspended for disciplinary reasons, which was often. Every time he was with her he found it impossible to believe that she could have betrayed him; but when she left the doubts assailed him again.

How was he ever to complete his mission, confined here? There seemed to be no escape for him but Galera 14, the death cell. He was never brought to trial, never sent on to the Isle of Pines prison; he was in limbo, and he suspected they meant to keep him here forever or until he came to terms with the communist movement. He was tempted; as Almejeiras had suggested, he didn't have to be a communist at heart. But somehow he couldn't do it, even if his mission failed. He had murdered enough; his mission no longer justified the violation of personal morality.

His notions of sexual Perversion had changed completely. Now he realized that so had his notions of ethical perversions. He had grown, in both areas—and that kept him in prison.

He had been in La Cabana six or eight months—it really wasn't worth keeping track—when an American CIA agent was brought in. The man had known people in Cuba, and one of his friends, not realizing his business, had greeted him jovially. "I thought you were in America taking CIA training!" Just like that, and here he was in prison. "Lord protect me from my friends!" he exclaimed. "My damned, stupid, motherfucking friends!"

He was a demolitions expert. "You know that plastic explosive?" he said rhetorically to Bringas, who had naturally sought his company. "That smell? I was walking down the street in Miami, and suddenly there it was: this rich, rich shoe-polish odor! I fell flat on my face and covered my head—and there was this shoe-shine stand, Negro boy staring at me. 'Did you have a heatstroke, mister? Shine your shoes?' "

Bringas laughed. "I had a worse experience. I set a major charge to go off in fifteen minutes, and it exploded in half the time. Almost wiped me out, literally! Must have been defective fuses, because I know I set them correctly."

The agent questioned him, curious about the matter. "Maybe so," he said at last. "It does sound as if you did the job properly. Unless—say! Did you allow for the temperature?"

"The temperature? What has that got to do with it?"

"Was it a hot night, by any chance?"

"Sweltering! My hands were so sweaty I was afraid I'd drop a detonator!"

"Then that's it! Heat shortens the time. If you didn't make an allowance, you could have lost several minutes there. In fact, you could have blown your head off!"

Nilo's temper had not been in evidence very much in prison, but when he lost a cache of hundred-proof "medicine" he exploded. "Boca Chula, you pimp!" he shouted, going after a fellow prisoner. "You told them!"

It was generally known that Boca Chula was an informer, and most were careful never to let him have any information of value. Whether he had actually given away so small a secret as Nilo's potables was problematical; Bringas thought it more likely that another prisoner had stolen it. But it was a matter for the two to settle on their own.

Nilo started hitting Boca Chula. But the guards saw it, and came to the aid of the informer. One lifted his rifle butt to smash it against Nilo's head, and Bringas had to step in. He shoved the guard's elbow so that he missed, then brought the man down with a leg sweep.

That meant real trouble, for he and Nilo were now guilty of attacking a guard. Provocation counted for nothing in a case like this. Both of them were hauled roughly into the Commander's office.

Officerial changes were frequent. The current commander was Trieste Manolito, who was no more popular with the prisoners than his predecessors. "You are traitors to the Revolution!" he shouted.

"For stopping your guards from clubbing an unarmed man?" Bringas said scornfully.

"The Revolution!" Nilo said. "The Revolution has become a whore opening her legs to the communists!"

Manolito was so angry he made as if to strike them. But Bringas had had enough. If this man hit him, he was going to retaliate with a karate blow to the windpipe, then grab for a gun and go down fighting. It would at least be a quick end. He saw Nilo tensing himself too. The room was full of guards, but perhaps if they both acted fast enough. . . .

But Manolito made a visible effort to control himself.

"Let warden Medina discipline these two," he said at last. "I can't stand the sight of them."

Bringas and Nilo were hustled out into the corridor between the capillas, their hands manacled in front. They passed among the rebel soldiers and officers who were there for minor infractions like drunkenness and stealing, and who would be released in due course. These men had much better food, and good bunks, and were even permitted female visitors: an elite class of prisoner.

Sergeant Medina knew where promotion lay. He threw a fine fit of righteous indignation. "I will shave off all your hair, so you look like maricones!" he cried.

Bringas was shoved into a barred cell while they set up to cut Nilo's hair. But Nilo protested vigorously. "Medina, you are not man enough to cut my hair! *You* are the maricon!"

Medina fetched a pair of scissors. "Cut his hair," he said to one of the prisoners, pushing the scissors into his hand. "All of it—so he is completely bald. Then do the other one the same way."

These temporary prisoners had no particular feeling for those in the main prison, and were happy enough to oblige. Three of them piled on Nilo and held him still, while the one with the scissors approached.

"Pig!" Nilo screamed. "I am a Sierra veteran! If you had been there you would know me! Touch my hair and you convict yourself as a Batistiano!"

That struck home. The soldier dropped the scissors to the floor. "I am no Batistiano!"

"This is insubordination!" Medina cried, but the men only shrugged. Medina pointed to another prisoner, who picked up the scissors.

"Do you do the dirty work this maricon coward can't do?" Nilo demanded. The three soldiers holding him developed some sympathy for his courage, and let him go. Nilo stood there with his manacled hands ready to strike. This made a formidable weapon.

"I am not Batistiano either!" the second prisoner said. "I do not shave my own kind."

It was apparent that none of the prisoners were going to touch the scissors now. They were all Fidelistas, and so long as Nilo did not make the tactical mistake of insulting Fidel himself, they would stand clear.

"I'll put you all on half rations!" Medina swore, but it was obviously an empty threat, for these men had no shortage of food packages from their relatives, and were a healthy bunch.

Now Medina did take up the scissors himself, for he knew his tenure would not be long if he didn't get the job done. Two of his bodyguards made to grab at Nilo, but he stood with his back to the big window at the end of the corridor and swung his chain menacingly. Nilo was a small man, but he looked very big while that metal moved.

More and more rebel army men crowded around, partly to watch the action and partly in passive support for the gallant Fidelista. Bringas was proud of his friend in that moment, though he knew it was hopeless.

One of the bodyguards made a grab for Nilo, and he wheeled around with the manacles to strike him. Doing so, Nilo lost his balance and fell, and immediately the two guards were on him, hitting him with their fists.

"You are worse than Ventura!" Bringas yelled from his cell. "We fought in the Sierra so that things like this could never happen again in Cuba!"

Now the prisoners murmured angrily. "Leave him alone!" they grumbled to the guards.

But the guards started to kick Nilo in the head while he struggled to get up.

"That's the way the communists do it!" Bringas shouted.

It was like a goad. These were largely combat-level Fidelistas, and they had no truck with the communists, whom they saw as cowardly infiltrators who had never participated in the real fighting. None of them wanted to be stigmatized with the communist label. And most were about ready for a good riot anyway.

"Get back to your bunks!" Medina shouted, but the turmoil was already well advanced. Someone shouldered him aside, pretending it was an accident, and others enclosed the guards. Bottles appeared—glass Coca-Cola bottles—lethal weapons either whole or broken. The few prisoners who actually were communists were tossed aside like rag dolls, and Bringas saw one of these clubbed on the head so ferociously that part of his skull caved in and blood flowed. Medina himself was down and getting kicked.

The riot continued for fifteen minutes. Prison reinforcements arrived, but they did not dare shoot because these were rebel army soldiers, not criminals, and most would be getting out soon. Finally order was restored from within, by the ranking prisoner: a major who was a Sierra veteran. He and a captain calmed the men, promising that no haircuts would be given and pointing out that they had nothing to gain by prolonged mischief.

Nilo was badly beaten, with a cut on his head, but he had saved his hair and earned the respect of the prisoners. After it was over the captain came quietly up to Nilo and Bringas. "I am a Hubert Matos man, and I am with you one hundred percent," he said, and he gave them two ham sandwiches.

Being the inspiration for a riot meant the capillas for them. These were small cells in the bowels of La Cabana with no furnishings and no light, used only for prisoners about to be shot or for special punishment. Nilo and Bringas were thrown into a cell together, with nothing but the clothing they happened to have on. The walls were brick and cold. There was nothing but a hole in the floor in the way of toilet facilities, and no running water: one small pail of fetid water a day was the ration.

Once a day a trap door in the base of the cell door opened and a plate of slop and piece of bread was pushed through. That was all. By straining at the bars they could make out light from the lone bulb at the end of the passage, but it wasn't worth the effort. They had to huddle together for warmth, as they had no blankets. The first night Bringas felt something touching his leg, and it wasn't Nilo. It was a monstrous rat.

They tried to jury-rig a rat-alarm with the water cans, but still they had to be constantly alert. Fungus crept into their bodily crevices, since they could not wash or change clothes or get out of the dank atmosphere. Under arms, in crotch, the itching grew. Nilo complained that his rectum burned after he used the sanitary hole. "Now I know how a maricon feels!" he said.

Sometimes rebel prisoners were able to sneak them better food, but it was not enough; hunger was constant. Bringas thought of trapping a rat and eating it, but the rodents were too crafty, and their vision in the perpetual gloom was superior to that of the men. There was nothing to do but wait and shiver and try to sleep. And talk.

"What happened to you after you left the Sierra?" Bringas asked. "I was afraid you were dead."

"Oh, no señor," Nilo said facetiously. "Campesinos don't die without cause. I decided it was a bad season for revolution, so I went home."

A bad season—yes. General Cantillo had been closing in, and they had not known at the time that the siege was to be bought off. "Then why are you *here*? Farming shouldn't have—"

"Well, there was a bit of trouble . . . but it was an accident, in the end."

Nilo's understatements could be hilarious. "Like your accident with the machete, back before we met the first time?"

Nilo shrugged amicably in the gloom. It was easy to forget that the man still suffered from his head injury, as well as the Capillas' ordinary deprivations. Campesinos were tough, all right!

Only after tantalizing Bringas for a full day did Nilo condescend to deliver his history. He had obviously been saving it for an emergency like this: a lot of entertainment in the clutch. It came with such vigor and color that Bringas forgot his surroundings and seemed to live through it himself.

"I left you when the Batistianos surrounded us. I watched you with the yegua until the—"

"*What?*" Then Bringas laughed, and it was good to laugh, for it drove back the gloom and annoyed the rats. How much a creature of the times he had become, to worry about who might see him performing a natural function!

"Then I hid under the bushes until the rain came. After that I walked down the mountain and out of the trap. I went to Bayamo, shaved my face, and took a little bus to Encrucizada, my home. But of course I couldn't settle down until that minor misunderstanding was forgotten."

The machete killing. Yes.

So Nilo decided, he said, that the season for revolution

had improved again, and he went to the hills of Escambray in central Cuba with William Morgan and Jesus Carrera, the leaders of the local guerrilla bands. In due course the Revolution triumphed, and he received a pardon for the misunderstanding and took up residence on his small farm with his mother and sister. Things looked pretty good.

Then the Agrarian Reform Law was promulgated. Nilo did not concern himself with abstruse political considerations—until the INRRA decided to expropriate his farm for the good of the Revolution. It was only one and a half caballerias—about fifty acres—but the land was rich and the state needed it.

This was not Nilo's idea of a suitable reward for his services to the Revolution, but he concealed his misgivings behind a broad, innocuous campesino grin. "I am happy to do this for Fidel," he told them stupidly. "I was with him in the Sierra, you know."

But the local officials were desk men who had never risked their lives or fortunes in combat, and they did *not* know. They did not realize that a former barbudo was best left alone, both from respect for his prior service and for the health of whoever interfered with him. They set what was to them a reasonable date for the change of ownership so that he could close down his operations, made arrangements for him to move into town and join a construction project with state-determined wages, and then proceeded to other business. It was all very orderly.

On the specified date Nilo sent his mother and sister into town to take up their assigned residence. "I will come later," he said. "I have a few small matters to finish."

"Now don't speak harshly to the interventor," his mother warned him, knowing his temper.

"I shall not speak to the man at all," he reassured her. "No arguments, I promise. I know they will not change their minds no matter what I say. I just need to fetch some mementos I saved from the mountains."

She knew he would not lie to her—not very much, anyway—so she departed with better spirits.

Nilo went to a special spot and dug deep into the ground. Soon he uncovered his mementos: an oiled sack containing an M-3 submachine gun, acquired in the last days of the guerrilla action, and two hundred rounds of ammunition. He cleaned off the heavy protective grease, loaded the gun, and waited patiently in the house.

When the INRRA interventor set foot on the porch accompanied by two militiamen, Nilo killed all three from ambush. He was not a good shot, and had to use several bursts, but at that range it made little difference. The job was done.

He fled to the Escambray Mountains north of Trinidad, where he joined the guerrilla band of El Conga Pacheco. The tactics he had learned fighting for Fidel now stood him in good stead fighting *against* Fidel. When the band split up, he headed a group of thirty men.

They were theoretically a unit of an anti-communist guerrilla army, but they settled for an easy life. It was a mismatched group: Fidelista rebel soldiers, peasants fed up with INRRA interference, idealistic university students, rebel officers left behind when Menoyo fled for his life to the United States, even a couple of Batista soldiers. Plus a few city fugitives from the G-2.

The area had good cover, the peasants were friendly and brought good food, and there were no clashes with the government armed forces. They received an excellent arms shipment with Garand rifles, two cases of fragmentation hand grenades, and even a .30 caliber air-cooled machine gun, belt fed. Pepin, a black giant, claimed this last weapon as his personal property. He was capable of firing it from the hip as if it were a submachine gun, and carried it hour after hour along with its tripod and ammo cases without seeming to tire. Without Pepin, Nilo liked to say, they would be just another band.

But the campesinos eventually became restive, complaining that Nilo and his band only ate and grew fat without fighting. This was an accurate assessment. But it nettled Nilo, who decided to give them a taste of what they thought they wanted. In one hour he rounded up the fifteen area militiamen and pro-Fidel informers—their identity was of course common knowledge—and proceeded to hang them publicly, one at a time.

As this was his first serious mission, his security was not quite tight. The wife of the first subject escaped and warned a nearby branch of the militia—and Nilo didn't realize it until he saw about fifty armed men converging. Fortunately he was supervising the final execution on top of a hill, so he had an early view of the menace. He realized there was no time to hang the chivato—the billy-goat, the bleater, the informer—no time to do it properly, at least. He drew his Colt .45 pistol and shot the old goat in the face.

The guerrillas fled precipitously—but only fifty meters. Where the dirty path forked beyond the hill there was heavy undergrowth, and he quickly planted his men in ambush fifteen to a side, where they could fire down into any pursuers. The militia, fully as green as Nilo's group and not nearly as careful, charged in a bunch down the path.

The crossfire was dense. Nilo did not lose a man—but when the shooting stopped he counted forty-two enemy corpses. Many were boys in their teens, and he didn't like that, for he knew they had been innocents merely following orders.

But it was a Pyrrhic victory, as he had half-feared. While the guerrillas had been inactive, the government had tolerated them; it wasn't worth the trouble to root them out. But the eradication of fifty-seven men in a single day—such a yank at Fidel's beard enraged the dictator.

Fifteen thousand soldiers and militiamen laid siege to the area—against Nilo's thirty. A ratio of five hundred to one. It was the dread peinazo.

The only thing Nilo could do was to lead his tiny group higher and higher into the mountains, for he had no money to buy off such a campaign. Some nights the guerrillas used grenades to burst through the encirclement; losing one man to perhaps three deaths of their pursuers.

With twenty-two men—six of his original band known dead, two presumed escaped—he mounted the heights of the Escambray near Topes de Collantes. It was the coldest and foggiest spot in Cuba. It was rough going, but it hampered the government helicopters and spotter planes.

A wounded member of his shrinking band slipped away. His name was Arroyo, and he was an ex-second lieutenant in Kenoyo's forces, so he was no traitor or coward. But he knew he was slowing down the group dangerously and would die without medical treatment for the bullet in his leg. He was captured, for the few doctors that remained in the area were loyal to Fidel. That was one of the things about the exodus of professional people: it was precious little comfort to those who needed anti-Castro assistance in an emergency.

Arroyo refused to talk, of course. The militiamen were cold and weary and in a hurry to wrap up the hunt, so they were not gentle. They loaded him into a helicopter, ascended, tied a rope to his injured leg and threw him out the open door. The rope broke his fall, and they hauled him up again. He still would not bleat.

But on the fifth pitchout he broke. He identified all the farmers who had helped the guerrilla band. The army rounded up forty of them, and for the crime of giving food to the guerrillas made them dig a mass grave: their own. They had wanted action; now they had it, and would never have more.

The surviving farmers in the region were removed, so that no possible support for the guerrillas remained.

Nilo was down to fifteen men, their situation desperate. He informed them that no stragglers would be tolerated. One man tried to sneak away; Nilo judged him and sentenced him to death. The others intervened, saving the man's life—but that night the man tried again, and Nilo gunned him down.

The relentless peinazo reduced the group to five men. It was hopeless, and finally they agreed to split up. Nilo spent the night alone, sleeping half under a guava bush and half in a puddle, shivering and hugging his rifle and wishing it were a fat yegua. He had only three remaining bullets. Somehow he slipped through the net—it was said to be impossible, but he did it—reached the coastal highway, and found refuge with a disgruntled charcoal maker. Then he made his way up to Havana.

"What's the matter?" Bringas asked as his friend's voice quit.

"Nothing—nothing—just memories," Nilo said. "The Escambray—after Fidel finished with it that beautiful country was like a desert. Brush all cut—" He coughed. "Batista was like a baby sucking at the breast, compared to Fidel. The things they did at Escambray—" He coughed again, harshly.

Bringas put a hand on Nilo. The man was burning with fever, and the scabbing headwound was greasy with half-dried blood or pus. "You're sick! I'll call the guards!"

"No—no!" Nilo protested. "Don't give that maricon the satisfaction. . . ." He went into a spasm of hacking. He must have been holding it back all the time he was talking, but now the coughing could not be denied. "I talk too much, I strain my throat—"

Bringas wasn't fooled. His friend was ill. In normal circumstances it might have been inconsequential—sniffles, coughing, some congestion, take an aspirin, drink plenty of fruit juice and stay in bed a day and draw sick-pay, you faker—but here in the filthy capillas, in the dankness among the rats and roaches, deprived of food and water, wounded and with no remaining natural reserves—here illness was a truly formidable spectre.

Bringas held Nilo, trying to protect him from the cold even as the fever mounted. How much of the man's story was true? Cold-blooded killing, guerrilla leadership—these were not the campesino's style! The events had to be exaggerated, the viciousness enhanced by the developing fever. The skeleton of the narrative was probably valid, and if Nilo had not participated he had probably heard from those who had. No doubt he had had trouble at his farm and had to leave, though he never would have shot men from ambush. (Yet again: Nilo had been fascinated by the theory and strategy of ambush ever since being wounded himself in one, that time on the Sierra Maestra. . . .) He could have participated in anti-Castro guerrilla warfare, as there were many such bands in the Escambray and elsewhere. Perhaps some group *had* been wiped out as he described—but Nilo was right about it being almost impossible to slip through such a net. The best way to escape it was to be absent entirely. Most likely, Nilo would have decided that it was a bad season for counter-revolutionary activity, before any peinazo arrived!

What difference did it make? Nilo was his friend. He didn't have to be a ruthless guerrilla leader, he just had to be himself. If he had need to represent himself as the leader of men and figure of tragedy, it was because he was human.

Nilo slept at last, and Bringas too, and when they woke the fever had abated, though the cough intensified. Bringas ate the daily ration and saved Nilo's, for his friend had no appetite. The narrative resumed, punctuated by coughing.

Nilo returned to Havana, where he went straight to the house of a former girlfriend he had met during the wild-oats days of the flush of Fidel's victory. This was Manelia: short, fat, dumpy, with long black hair and very hairy legs and hairy bollo. That was his kick: hairy legs, like those of a horse.

Manelia took him in, but warned him that the garage was being used by some DRE students for storage and possibly bombs. That made it dangerous for more than one reason—but where else could he go? He needed time and comfort to recover from the ravages of the chase . . . and she did have those phenomenal legs!

One day two of the boys were making their bombs in the garage when the G-2 raided. Nilo had nothing to do with the DRE, but he was swept up too—and by the time they had verified his record, he was headed for La Cabana.

If his record had been half as bad as he claimed, Bringas reflected privately, Nilo would never have reached prison alive!

"Lucky for me they did not tie me in with Escambray," Nilo said, laughing. But the laughter became coughing, and coughing did not stop. His fever was back, too, worse than before: it looked to Bringas like pneumonia.

"Guards! Guards!" Bringas called.

They let him scream for fifteen minutes before they came to threaten him into silence. Bringas pleaded the situation. "This man is sick! He may die! He has to be put in the hospital!" Not that the so-called hospital was much improvement, with a prisoner-doctor hardly better than a vet. Che Guevara would probably do a better job!

The guards just laughed and went away. Bringas hoped they were only trying to scare him, and that someone would come to take Nilo out. They hadn't *denied* him help, actually. . . .

But as the hours passed, and there was nothing, he knew better. They didn't care if a difficult prisoner died, and they had no liking for Nilo, who had provoked an embarrassing scene and riot. The warden would happily let him rot.

Nilo got worse, and there was nothing Bringas could do to ease his friend's torment. Sometimes Nilo slept; sometimes he just lay there shivering. He could not eat.

Bringas tried to save Nilo's food for him, but the rats got it, so he had to eat it himself rather than waste it that way. He would give Nilo his share when the man was able to digest it.

"Jose Marti! Jose Marti!" Nilo cried suddenly, and for a moment Bringas thought someone was coming. Then he remembered, Jose Marti was the hero of Cuba's other revolution, the man who helped her win her freedom from

Spain: a towering figure in the history of the island.

"Jose, I remember what you said!" Nilo whispered.

Don't kill me in the dark
As a traitor dies!
I am good, and like the good
I shall die with the sun in my face!

It saddened Bringas inexplicably. Thus did Nilo's memory serve him in his hour of torment. Invoking Marti. . . .

"The sun! I see the sun!" Nilo cried, standing up, stumbling, standing again, scrambling as though almost within reach of . . . something. Bringas jumped to hold him so he would not fall again. There was of course no sun visible. Nilo was hallucinating.

"So bright, so bright! Everywhere—nothing but light!" Nilo said, reaching into the air with his emaciated arms. Illness had ravaged him; Bringas was almost thankful that he couldn't actually see his friend. "Text C—"

Bringas stiffened. *Text C?*

"A and B are tyranny; I cannot read the words—"

Of course not; Nilo was illiterate.

"One rubbed out, and written again—"

Nilo was looking at the palimpsest! How could this be?

"But C is the light of the sun! The heart of the sun! Oh, glorious! Oh, it blinds me, burns me—"

Nilo collapsed in Bringas' arms. His body shuddered with the force of his revelation. In a moment he was racked again by coughing.

Bringas laid him down on the cold floor, afraid of what those visions might portend. If Nilo could see across the probabilities—Nilo, who was native to this period—

"Mama!" Nilo screamed, clutching at Bringas. "The sun is gone; it is dark and cold—"

He was coming out of it! Nilo knew where he was!

"Mama, hold me! Mamacita, it hurts. . . ."

Bringas held him.

Finally Nilo lapsed into sleep.

Bringas slept too.

When he woke he knew his friend was dead.
Mourn not the dead that in the cool earth lie—

Time was meaningless, but by Bringas' lonely reckoning
it was March, or Maceo, or Paucar Huaray: the garment of
flowers. Nilo was gone, and his mind was numb with that
grief and drifting back to another: the question of Adelita.
Had she betrayed him? His waking nightmares centered
around that notion, weighing it, sifting it, straining it, pulling it about like hot taffy into grotesque configurations. If
not her, *who*? One of the other men in the group? Throwing
suspicions on her to avoid exposure of the real culprit?
But they had all attended the bombing of the warehouse.
If someone else, how could he have had the information
about Bringas' immediate whereabouts, when only the participants knew it? And Adelita.

He saw her breast, her face. Beautiful, both. How could
these betray him? 233 would never have done it—so why
was he unable to conjure her face and body for his consolation in this time of solitary agony? The only vision that
could hold Nilo's anguished dying cries at bay was that of
Adelita—and he could not decide whether to love her or
hate her. Was it that ugly mystery that compelled him?

From time to time men were put in other cells for a
few hours, on their way to paredon. Bringas generally left
them alone. What could he say to them, these wretches
who would be dead a day later?

But now one called out to him, from across the dark
hall.

"Bringas! Juan Bringas! Are you here?"

Was it a joke? He answered. "I am here." His voice was
hoarse; he had been coughing intermittently himself.

"Juan, it is Luis! Of the sabotage group. Remember?
They said you were here, and now I am to die—"

It *was* Luis; Bringas recognized the voice now. The man
who had been so nervous while they set the plastic charges.
"Why should they sentence you, and not me?" Bringas

demanded, not trusting this contact.

"I escaped. I was the only one. They caught me later, when I tried to get to the Spanish embassy and escape Cuba. Baro was shot down; I don't know what happened to the others, after they were arrested."

"Neither do I." More than ever, Bringas was suspicious. Luis was weak; he could be intimidated into prying information from an isolated prisoner.

"Juan, I hoped I would find you, before the end. I had to tell you—" The voice faltered, but Bringas refused to speak again until he could better appraise the man's motives. Luis claimed he was about to die—but it could easily be a pose.

"I had to tell you I was the one who did it, not your woman," Luis said in a burst. "It has been tormenting me all this time, and I had to—I didn't want to—they threatened Tino, threatened to kill him—"

Tino. That was his lover—a matter he had never talked about before. Bringas had only discovered Tino in the course of his private investigations of his men; he had wanted to know whether any were spies. He had not been concerned about sexual mores; once he ascertained that Tino was as ardently anti-communist as Luis, he let the matter be.

Now he cursed himself for a fool. *Of course* such a liaison would make Luis a setup for the G-2, if they should learn about it—and evidently they had.

"They made me do it—I didn't want to—I told them about the plastic explosives but they still wouldn't let Tino go. They wanted to catch the supplier, told me to find out, to report in before any big job was done. But you scheduled it by surprise, so I couldn't—I called as soon as I could, after Baro tied you up, but they were very angry—"

"*You* told them where to find me?"

"Yes. Juan, I did not want to do it, I am loyal to the underground, but they had Tino—"

Bringas hardly cared about that. He blamed himself for not recognizing so obvious a weak spot in his group. What concerned him was the vindication of Adelita: *she had not been the traitor!* "Thank you! Thank you for telling me!" he said with heartfelt gratitude.

"Baro thought it was your woman, and I knew it wasn't, and I wanted to tell you. I know you love her the way I love Tino—*loved* Tino—"

"Did something happen to him?" Put that way, Bringas understood the betrayal. What would he have done if he knew Adelita was about to be killed? What *had* he done, in his long effort to recover 233?

"He was shot. Killed. Trying to escape, they said. I think it was because I didn't stop the sabotage. It's over for me now; tomorrow I die and I rejoin Tino. I just had to let you know, and beg your forgiveness for what I did—"

"I forgive you!" Bringas said instantly. All these months of suspicion—

"Thank you," Luis said pitifully. "I had to make it right with you before I died."

Then Bringas remembered that the G-2 had been at the other apartment *before* that call. "Did you tell them to pick us up before then, at the first apartment?"

"Juan, that was an accident! I did not tell them—I had no time. They were there for someone else, not us. We panicked for nothing!"

Comedy of errors! They had thought they were betrayed when it was mere coincidence, so had accused an innocent woman, and overlooked the real betrayer—who hadn't done it yet! But Adelita had been exonerated, and that made up for all the rest.

Next day the guards took Luis. Shortly thereafter Bringas heard the guns of the firing squad.

The warden came back through the capillas after the execution. He stopped outside Bringas' cell. "I thought your friend was a coward," he said gruffly. "But he died like a man."

• • •

It might have been another week or another month. Bringas was so weak when they took him out that he had difficulty standing, and he was nearly blind in the daylight. But he had survived the punishment of the capillas.

They put him in Galera 14, and it was like freedom. There were about twenty men here, the majority were Batistianos condemned to die. But some were here because they were too sick for the main galeras—like Bringas now.

A man took his arm and helped him to one of the wire frame bunks. He was about fifty years old, of medium height, vaguely oriental eyes, and a friendly grin. Bringas found him familiar from somewhere. Straight black hair—who was he?

"Mirabal," the man murmured. "Sit for a while until your eyes recover. You are fortunate to have come out of the capillas alive."

Commander Mirabal—the reputed father of Raul Castro! Now Bringas placed him. He accepted the cup of coffee Mirabal gave him—and promptly spilled it, for his hands were unsteady. But it was good to be among people he knew, even as vaguely as this! In the capillas it had seemed that the entire world had been blotted out.

Galera 14 prisoners ate here in the cell, rather than with the others, which made it easier for Bringas, who lacked the strength to wait in line. He was a Fidelista, but the condemned Batistianos did not harrass him. In Galera 14, more than in the rest of the prison, everyone was in it together.

The days passed, and slowly Bringas recovered. If he could not do very much physically, he had plenty to occupy him intellectually, for he resumed his study of English language speaking and writing, and renewed acquaintances. There had been a fair turnover during his absence: some friends had been released, others had died, one way or another. Mainly there was news.

Prison gossip was swift and generally accurate, if you

fit everyone's saga into the proper context. Recent news was significant. Possibly the prisoners were better informed about conditions in Cuba generally than were most outsiders. The word here, in late March of 1961, was that the Americans were organizing an invasion of Cuba to overthrow Fidel.

Cuba's urban guerrillas were active increasingly since January, with bombs and fires being set daily, assassination attempts every few days—some successful, though generally only against minor officials—and major sabotage on almost a weekly basis. Men were taking to the hills to join the rural guerrillas in every province, and the ranks of the DRE, the MRDD and others were swelling phenomenally. Sugar fields were burned, saboteurs were active even in the hills around Havana itself, and there was a rising crescendo of insurrection traveling through the island like wildfire. All of it was leading up to the coming climax of the invasion.

The prison authorities muttered that if invasion came, and if it looked as though it were going to be successful, there would be wholesale executions before it reached La Cabana. But some of the guards made private overtures to key prisoners, providing special food for them and whispering, "Remember, when the time comes—I am a good guy!"

As April began, the prison grapevine tingled with word that a remarkable guest was about to be entertained. Commandante Humberto Sori Marin—the author of the Revolutionary Code of Laws and the chief prosecutor at the infamous trials leading off the Castro regime. It was said that he had sent five hundred men to the wall. Now he was coming to La Cabana as a prisoner.

Bringas had a sharp recollection of Marin's antics at the trial of Sosa Blanco, in which he led the witnesses, insulted the defendant personally, and finally forced a verdict of guilty based on perjured and erroneous testimony. That had been the first of the circus trials, and Bringas had been on the panel of judges, so he was well aware of the farce the conviction was. Sosa's correct and manly behavior had made Marin look like a monkey—but Sosa had been executed.

There was more to the story of Sori Marin. He had been made Minister of Agriculture—only to resign a short time later in protest to the Agrarian Reform measures. He had joined the underground about the time Bringas himself had, worked in Cuba for a year, then defected to the United States. At that point he might have retired in safety. But he had gotten training and returned covertly to Cuba to help organize the anti-communist resistance more effectively. In the past month the G-2 had investigated a house where a suspicious number of cars parked, and netted Marin at an underground meeting. In the ensuing shootout, Sori Marin was wounded in the legs so that he had to hobble with a crutch.

Marin had convicted a dozen of the Batistianos in Galera 14. Originally there had been more than twenty, but one by one over the months individuals had been removed and executed. Those remaining had no way of knowing when their ends would come; they only knew their fate was certain. They owed this to Marin.

A man with no protection to be placed in Galera 14.

Bringas stayed clear of the discussions that ensued. Nor did he want to be present when Marin was brought in. He hated Marin, yet he understood the man's position, which was roughly similar to his own. Fidel's decision to place this man directly in the hands of the very men whose deaths were attributed to him was an act of appalling sadism. *How could you, Fidel!* he thought in anguish. Commandante Marin would never live to see his own execution.

Boca Chula, the prison informer whose fight with Nilo had led finally to Nilo's lonely death, was clever enough to make book on the number of hours and minutes Marin would last in that dread galera. He himself took the estimate of one minute; others ranged from one hour all the way up to several days. The Batistianos in the other galeras were especially grim. "Revenge like that is granted to man only once in a century," one said. "It will not be wasted."

"But it shouldn't come too quickly," another said. "He must suffer as long as possible. . . ."

Bringas, though sickened by it all, was present by his bunk when Marin was brought in. Bringas had not talked with any of his immediate cellmates about the matter, but he could tell by their expectant, controlled attitudes that they had come to a decision.

Marin was a small man, about Nilo's size, about forty-five years old. His face was hawkish behind his glasses, and pinched with pain, for he had to walk though wounded in both legs. He looked about nervously, knowing the situation.

The guards departed, locking them in for the night. Bringas had to remain.

One of the condemned Batistianos, Commandante Mireval, approached Marin. "Good evening," he said formally. "I have two sheets for you and a blanket."

Marin just looked at him, waiting for the trap to spring. Bringas wanted to turn away, but could not.

A second man went to Marin. "Here is a pillow and a pillowcase." Marin, of course, had no bedclothing, since such things were not provided by the prison authorities. Bringas well knew the immense comfort such things could bring in the first cold nights on a hard bunk.

A third came. "Make yourself comfortable. We will make you some coffee."

Marin lay on his bunk, amazed. Then the leader of the Batistianos explained. "Commandante, be at ease. Here you are among friends. Nobody has any hard feelings toward you. What has happened is in the past. Now you are one of us."

Marin, unbelieving at first, finally saw that they meant it. He pretended to sleep, trying to hide the tears of emotion dripping from his eyes. So did Bringas.

Sori Marin was treated with the utmost courtesy in Galera 14 throughout his tenure there. The first day the prisoners arranged a hot meal for him, and someone was always at hand to assist him when he woke moaning from the pain of his wounds.

The other prisoners were incredulous. Then, gradually, comprehension dawned. These were men, not animals, in Galera 14. They would not play Castro's cynical game. They would not grant him a doubled victory by proving that they were indeed as savage as he thought them. Marin too was a man—a man who was here only because he had acknowledged the error of his ways and acted to correct the wrong he had done to his country. As Bringas had done. As every Fidelista had done.

The condemned Batistianos had shown the prison—and the world—what honor was. Galera 14 had become the noblest of cells.

On April 17 the invasion began. The grapevine circulated new details constantly. An army of a thousand men had landed at Playa Giron in southern Las Villas Province. There were also reports of landings elsewhere. A major defeat had been inflicted on Castro's militia. The beachhead was expanding.

Bringas listened avidly, for he could not remember this particular event from history. Exactly *who* was invading? he demanded. Cuban exiles with American equipment, he was told. Exactly *where*? At the Bay of Pigs.

Until that moment Bringas had been as excited as the rest. But now he realized the key: pig. As in the novel Adelita had read to him, *Animal Farm*. Some jokester had decided to follow the parallel one ironic step further, and claim the pigs were invading the men. Ha, ha!

If he had that book now, he could read it himself; he was confident of his limited command of English. But he could still tell fiction from fact! No wonder he failed to remember this "invasion" from history; nothing of the kind had occurred! Maybe this was another trick of Fidel's: to make the entire prison pay for its failure to torment Marin by feeding in a carefully contrived but cruelly false hope of release.

Soon the news bulletins turned sour, as Bringas had known they would. Incredible blunders by the Americans were reported: failure to provide the invaders proper air cover, failure to eliminate Castro's own small air force, failure to warn the underground of the precise plans, deliberate withholding by the CIA of arms for the urban and rural guerrillas so that no local uprisings could occur, destruction of the ammunition ship of the invaders, deliberate organization of the invasion itself at such a place that there was no possible mountain cover in case of reverses . . . on and on it went. The script had been most carefully rehearsed, but Bringas knew it was false, and would have known anyway, for no one would believe that the Americans, who were the world's finest tacticians in war, could blunder so consistently. This story had been designed to bring absolute grief to the prisoners!

Incredibly, it was succeeding! Bringas tried to explain that it was a hoax, but few paid attention. A black mood settled over the prison, even among the condemned Batistianos who had no future anyway. If the supposed invasion failed, they would be shot in due course; if it succeeded, they would be shot immediately.

Incredibly, also, there was a massive influx of new prisoners. It was said that some 50,000 people had been rounded up in Havana alone, and crammed into any space available: movie theaters, the famed Sport Palace, stadiums, prisons. . . .

Victory had seemed so close the first day that there were supposed to have been large-scale defections from Fidel's militia and police. Almejeiras, the drug-using Chief of Police, had fought bravely in the front lines. Only Bringas saw the ludicrous exaggeration of such a report, made only to build up a man who was currently in favor with the government. But why was the government actually piling prisoners into La Cabana? That made little sense, for the prison was already crowded.

Yet here they were: workers, priests, even communists! They filed the galeras, even Galera 14 and the kitchen, and overflowed onto the patio. The common rebel soldiers near the capillas were freed and their cells filled to capacity too. New guards came to handle the influx. It was chaos—yet hour by hour more came! All said the same: the invasion was real.

On April 19, in the midst of constant executions, Humberto Sori Marin was taken from the cell. Humbly he went to each man of Galera 14, including Bringas, and shook their hands. "I am sorry for what I did!" he cried as he hobbled along with the crutches. "I thank you for your great courtesy, and I beg you to pardon me!"

"It is not for us to pardon you," the leader of the Batistianos replied gravely. "It is for God."

Adhering to the code they had made, the Batistianos let him face the reality of the code *he* had made, more severely chastened than by any physical torment.

It was said that Fidel himself attended the execution, hungry to watch his erstwhile friend grovel. It was said that when Sori Marin would not oblige, he was knocked to the ground, his crutches flying. It was said that he struggled again to his feet, clutching at the death wall. "Pig!" he shouted at Fidel. "I am a man and I die standing!" Then they shot him in the legs to *make* him fall, and then in the head, and he was dead at last.

"If God does not pardon him, *I* will," Bringas said, and no one took exception.

When they started letting the surplus prisoners go, it was obvious to Bringas that there had indeed been an invasion, and that it had failed.

For a time there was flux, as old prisoners were released merely to make way for the new. The guards changed too, being constantly shifted around, and many were green. An organized prison rebellion might well have succeeded—but that same chaos prevented organization. The sick and the wounded came to Galera 14, many to lie on the floor.

Bringas recognized one man haggard with fever. "Pepin!" he cried. "Pepin Naranjo! What are you doing here?" It was the officer who had had the nightmares about Raul Castro's ditch slaughter.

Naranjo jumped. "No, no! I am Carlos, Carlos Pascual! I do not know you."

Bringas looked again. It was Pepin Naranjo, all right. But he must be using another name, and Bringas could guess why. "My apologies, señor! I mistook you for another man—Naranjo, Captain Cristino Naranjo, Camilo Cienfuegos' bodyguard. But he is dead, of course. I have not been well; I was in the capillas, and I still don't see well, and I get confused. Of course I do not know you, and I beg your forgiveness."

"Certainly," Naranjo said. "Stay and talk a while, señor. What did you say your name was?"

And when any possible suspicion had been allayed, Naranjo whispered the truth. "I emigrated, Juan. But the nightmares wouldn't say in Cuba, and they were driving me crazy!" Bringas knew exactly what that was like, though his own nightmares had faded almost entirely. He had seen so much evil in Cuba that he knew he was only moderately damned himself.

"I had to come back, Juan! With the CIA—I don't like the CIA much either, but at least I am doing what I can, and now the nightmares are gone! But they caught me in this sweep—they're arresting everybody, everybody, no matter how slight the suspicion! They don't know my real name. . . ."

There was no medical attention, of course, and Naranjo got worse, sinking finally into a coma. Then the loud-speakers called his name. "Pascual, Carlos Pascual to the office with your belongings."

Bringas went to wake Naranjo, who hadn't heard. But he paused. In the crowd, with new guards—it was a terrible thing to do to his friend, who might subsequently be recognized and shot, but on the other hand Naranjo might die anyway. He had to try it!

Bringas quickly gathered his own belongings and went to the office. The clerk looked at the list. "Pascual? Carlos Pascual?"

"Yes," Bringas said.

The clerk looked straight at him, and Bringas had a shock. He knew the man from the Sierra! And the man knew him—but lowered his eyes, nodding wearily. "Go, while the going is good!"

That suddenly Juan Bringas was free.

PART
SEVEN

T he motor quit.

Alarmed, he checked it, and was relieved to discover the gas tank empty. Mechanical failure would be serious, for he was almost completely ignorant about such a motor's internal operations; but this he could readily fix! He lifted one of the reserve cans of gas, and found its attachable spout. Next he located a metal funnel with a small rubber hose, and by maneuvering the combination and spilling some fuel he managed to pour a fair portion of the liquid into the tank.

The motor still would not start. With growing anxiety he checked and rechecked. Everything seemed to be in order. Only the fuel had changed.

The fuel. Suspicious, he removed the cap again, dipped his finger into the tank, and brought his hand to his face. The fluid smelled like gasoline and yet not quite the same, perhaps.

He opened the second reserve can and sniffed. Gasoline, surely. Yet the can was heavy. He poured some out into an open bucket and contemplated it, watching the liquid swirl and settle.

He saw the layer under the surface, the division between

fluids of differing density. Only a thin film covered the denser medium. The gasoline had been cut with water. More than cut—probably the fuel was little more than the residue from the can. Just about enough to provide the odor—not enough to run the motor.

The marina operator had gotten the best of him, for he had been too dull to notice. Hysterical strength had overcome physical weakness, but there was only so far this could carry him. He could not remember how he had crossed the bay from La Cabaña to Havana; but he had ambushed a soldier in a lonely park in the Vedado section and taken his uniform, weapon, and papers. Then a quick cleanup and shave in a public washroom, and a bus to the Mariano section where there were several public and private beaches, hotels, and yacht clubs. Masquerading as a guard, he had overcome two guards at the Spanish Club, and forced the marina operator to provide him with this fast fiberglass Boston Whaler. The man had seemed too eager to please him, telling him the boat would not sink even when filled with water, and fetching extra fuel cans from a storage room. Bringas had tied him up at the end, of course—but he remembered the man's faint mocking smile and his "Have a good trip, comrade!"

No wonder! Now he was stranded without power, here in the Atlantic or the Gulf of Mexico, depending on how far the Gulf Stream had carried him. He had been suckered in much the way Camilo Cienfuegos had!

Juan Bringas was not in good condition physically. The prison regimen had sapped his strength, and he had not had sleep or respite since. He was weak and nervous, with a bad stomach for food, subject to recurrent dizziness and attacks of nausea.

Now it was hot, and the boat had no cabin. His skin was very pale, another legacy from the capillas where little light and no sunlight penetrated. Already he had a formidable sunburn, and the very salt of the sea air seemed to inflame it worse.

The boat was small, perhaps double his own length, and had a flat bottom. In the center was a bench, and there were oarlocks on the sides. He unshipped one of the oars, but found its weight and drag appalling. He could no more row this craft in his present condition than he could walk across the water!

He pondered that a while. He was weak, but he was light. The waves looked solid, thicker than mercury. Why couldn't he. . . .

A gust of wind brought blessed respite from the heat, and after that a vapor cut off the harsh sunlight. Wonderful, for he had feared blisters would form on his tortured skin. But his cloud had no silver lining: a storm was coming!

"Virgen de la Caridad help me!" he cried, and his voice was a croak. What use was it to fight? He lacked the strength to oppose any portion of nature's careless power.

"They told me you had drowned a year ago." Adelita's voice, so clear he turned to look at her. It was his memory speaking. She had said it in 1962, over a year hence, not knowing. . . .

The waves increased with alarming rapidity, first rocking, then pitching the boat. Now seasickness was added to his other miseries.

This must have been the way it was for Camilo! No, he would have died more quickly, when the bomb exploded and the plane plunged into the water.

So the Fidelistas had not lied to Adelita! Juan Bringas had died at sea, victim of the joint malevolence of a maritime attendant and the fickle weather. And his own carelessness. This was the termination of his tangled spiel. The thread stretched from 2413 to 1962 to 2414 to 1958 and finally up here to 1961, the hard way. There was not to be a successful second mission, whether by fate or by paradox. Text A was not to be restored.

He leaned over the side and threw up. For a moment that gave him relief, but the boat kept rocking.

Text A, Text B, adumbrations of the palimpsest. Parallel

histories—but neither had meaning for him now, as the elements played with his derelict self. What did it matter whether one future prevailed over the other? Whether 233 lived or never lived? His interest in the matter had been negated by his demise.

If only he could lie down! Soon he would have to find relief for his diarrhea, too—but how, in this boat, in this storm?

A wave broke over the boat, smashing him back and swamping the interior. But it did not capsize. He struggled through the water in it, picking up the useless fuel cans and jettisoning them to make the boat lighter. Then he worked on the outboard motor, and finally managed to free it too. He watched it sink down into the swirling water. He was going to die here anyway, but he meant to hang on as long as he could, and that meant he wanted the boat floating.

He was soaking. He stripped off his clothing, for there was no danger from the sun now! He had had a thorough bath, an authoritative washing of his wretched body—could it be considered the final purification? Extreme Unction, in the view of the Catholic Church . . . or perhaps one of the five ritual baths the santero took for an Espiritismo ceremony? How clean should he be, before considering himself fit material to bequeath to the hungry fishes?

He retched again, bringing up a few spoonfuls of green bile. Ay Dios, this perpetual rocking motion! Now he was cold, shivering with a sudden chill, and his eyes were irritated so that it was hard to see. His feet, when he hauled them out of the bilge, seemed swollen.

A ritual bath . . . why not? This mundane world had little to offer him now, for if the storm stopped the sun would emerge, and that was deadly too. Let Espiritismo save him if it could!

There was a swatch of seaweed in the boat. "Roses," he said, chuckling painfully. "Sea roses! I bathe in you!" And he plumped himself down in the tub-shaped boat, bathing in roses.

What else did the ritual require? He couldn't remember the contents of the several baths. But the sea was the ultimate garbage dump of this self-polluting, nest-befouling world; surely the necessary ingredients were present! Let him purify himself in liquid refuse!

Fasting was necessary. He must have fasted—when had he eaten last? Certainly he had disgorged the contents of his stomach, right down to the bilious liver secretions; that was the same thing! He had abstained from drinking and smoking—how could it be otherwise, in the capillas! He had undergone flagellation from the smashing of the waves upon his body.

Juan Bringas, santero! He was pure now, cleansed of all commerciality. He could work magic. At any moment he expected to see Camilo Cienfuegos' fish-gnawed body rise from the depths to bestow his benediction!

"Oachita, speak to me!" he cried. "I believe!"

His wasted body was too lean to drive an oar, his demented head too foggy to keep his surroundings in focus—but he could see across the texts of the future, A, B, and C.

A—his origin, his world of 233, now scarcely real.

B—the alternate his first mission had made.

C—the brilliance of the sun.

Nilo had glimpsed them all before he died, and so would Juan.

Yet mysteries remained. What point were his struggles in this realm? Why had the ornate scroll he had perceived in his vision across the texts sent him here, to accomplish nothing? Who had written that elegant document and left it for him to read?

Now he could not even go back to look, for his time phaser was buried where he could not reach it. Even if he had wished to do so the moment he escaped from La Cabana, it would have been impossible, because he was a marked man and Cuba was in a time of crisis. No, he had to remain here, finish his mission—which meant getting to the United States, contacting the CIA, establishing his underground bonafides, returning to Cuba as an agent during the missile crisis . . . and then, at last, picking up the phaser and returning to his own world and 233. . . .

Then there would be a score to settle with the Tens of his own time! He would have to stop shy of the moment they had arrested him, snatch his family. . . .

The waves were tossing him about, but it was as though they operated at a distance. They were merely physical; his chain of thought was the reality. He visualized the palimpsest superimposed on the violent ocean, printed in front of the moving water.

The ocean stilled. The waves frozen in place, the vapors in the air hung motionless, the spume did not fall, the turbulent storm clouds were immobile. No sound came to him, no smell, no sensation of any sort external or internal, except that vision of the waterscape—and the palimpsest.

The elements were fixed—*but the palimpsest was animate!* Text A and Text B rotated for his gaze so that he could scan their overlapping content. And Text C, which was not really a text but a continuing blaze of light.

TEXT A, 1962—The Union of Soviet Socialist Republics emplaces offensive missiles in Cuba. . . .

TEXT B, 1962—The Soviet Union declares the city of Berlin, Germany, to be an integral part of East Germany. . . .

TEXT A, 1967—Israel, in Asia Minor . . .

TEXT B, 2400—Population just under 800,000 . . .

TEXT C—Bright at first, it had gradually turned dark, until now there was no sign of it. A transitory text, not part of history proper. Strange.

TEXT A, 2414—Revolt of the Espiritismo cult. Centered in Caste Brown, but extending in lesser measure throughout Fidelia's society, the cultists were in a unique position to challenge the existing order. Browns debouched from service apertures at all key terminals, imbued with the spirit of the gods and possessed of hysterical strength. The anesthesic darts were ineffective against them, as they were able to repress elements of their own circulatory systems until the antidote could be administered. Armed with frightening knives and clubs, they hacked down their opponents and assumed command of essential facilities. The secret cultists in other Castes threw off their sashes and assisted. This was essentially an anti-waste revolution; the cultists did not mean to establish themselves or the Browns at the apex of the Caste hierarchy, but to abolish the Caste system entirely.

Bringas stopped reading. He had become absorbed in the narrative the moment it passed his own time, but there was a disquieting familiarity about this, a—

The Cuban revolution! The revolt of the future paralleled the one he had participated in here! Fidel had come not merely to assume control of the existing order, to fatten his personal fortune before being ousted by another palace turnover. Fidel had come to overthrow the entire capitalist system, and to replace it by a fundamentally alien system at incalculable cost to the nation and its people. The cultists were out to do the same, for similar idealistic motives— and the cost would be the same.

The Tens of Text A were no paragons of virtue, and 197 had severe grievances to settle with them, but perhaps they were historically the lesser of evils. They had foreseen this devastation that would affect the entire society of Fidelia. They had acted—wisely!—to forestall it, by sending an emissary to change the prevailing reality slightly, to eliminate the primary locus of infection without sacrificing the beneficial aspects of the system.

Had there been someone to travel back in Cuban history to rectify the problems that fueled Fidel Castro's initial foothold in American imagination. . . .

197 looked at the palimpsest again. He saw that in one day the Espiritismo takeover was virtually complete. Only Complex Purple remained secure, sheltering a number of

Nines and Tens of other Castes within its demesne. Purple had had forewarning, and had taken minimum precautions. At least it had done so in the subtext following 197's refusal to make the necessary changes in history. But deprived of the resources of the remainder of Fidelia, the Purples' situation seemed hopeless in the long run.

197 could see that the parallel Text B entry had no such development. His operation had been successful; the breeding ground of revolution had been eliminated. And it was the only way, for any attempt to delete Caste Brown within the Text A framework would only have precipitated the revolt. He remembered that he had suggested a convocation of Castes—but he saw now that that would have been no more effective than replacing a Batista with a General Cantillo on the eve of Fidel's victory. It was too late for first aid once the phosphorous grenade exploded. . . .

Yes. Juan Bringas' life had brought new insight to 197—an insight that perhaps only participation in a revolution and repentance in an abysmal prison could provide. He agreed with the Tens' decision, in principle, now. They had really made a better world. Their commitment to him personally had been honored. They had not known that his mishandling of the details would eliminate his own wife.

It was clear, now. Yet there was an element missing.

Who had tried to change it back?

Who had written the Spanish Scroll?

Obviously the war of the texts was not over—and though he might be dying, he had a need to know the truth. He thought he had done right, after allowing for his mistakes, but only full information would make him *sure*.

197 resumed his perusal of Text A, while the waves of the storm remained petrified.

The Espiritismos were in control, except for the Purple enclave. Castes were abolished, citizens discarded their sashes, celebrations continued day by day. The santeros were accorded the best of everything by a grateful populace.

The machinery of Fidelia halted. Real knowledge of administration lay with the Purples; it was impossible for people trained to other employments to step in and organize as efficiently as those born to it. The operations of the society were phenomenally complex, and precise integration of functions was necessary, or everything suffered.

197 understood the situation well. Juan Bringas had seen it in Cuba, whose system would have failed entirely without the massive support of the external Soviet Union. He had read of it in connection with the Inca Indian royalty, whose extermination destroyed Inca civilization and left a vacuum for the Spaniards to fill. No society could function properly when its most capable elements were excluded on a class-wide basis. That was a lesson history had reinforced many times. When a minority was purged, such as the Jews in pre-holocaust Germany, the efforts of their Einsteins could throw the balance of atomic weaponry to Germany's enemies despite their later start, leading to the political overthrow of the nation. But when there was only *one* society on Earth, such purges threatened the very continuation of mankind.

Then came the Purple counterstroke within Text A. A man went back in time—not 197, not to Cuba—and assassinated the key santero of the cult. Before the revolt broke out. The span of time travel was too short to invoke significant paradox, being only a few months. The assassin was caught and killed, but he had done his job.

The cultists were disorganized, and the revolt was necessarily delayed—but only a few months. Actually, killing was new and shocking in Fidelia, but they adjusted quickly to that situation. A new chief carried the revolt through despite the Purple's limited precautions.

Here 197 paused. Why hadn't the Purples made an all-out attack on the problem in the grace-period provided? Surely the first successful revolt had given them ample warning!

But it had not—because reality had been changed. In this

alternate, *no revolt had occurred*! The majority of Purples gave little credence to the notion of a successful rebellion against the system. How could a cult overturn four centuries of government? The time-change had only delayed things, not changed them.

Another assassin went back, not realizing he was not the first. But the Espiritismos of that period had been alerted by the prior loss, perhaps advised by their gods, and were able to foil this attempt. They captured the agent and obtained his confession, and learned precisely what it was they were up against. Local paradox would ordinarily have prevented the transmission of such information; but the Espiritismos had special talents. And the span was too brief for strong paradox.

It was impossible to guard completely against an enemy who could strike, literally, before they learned of his existence. The third assassin was successful, and the revolt was delayed again.

The cult's resources were large, and its leadership diffuse. Each murder created a mesh of potential paradox that restricted the scope of the next. Espiritismo might have been halted in this manner had it been no more than superstition; but in several centuries it had developed considerably beyond that.

197 realized now why he had not been able to see actual people when he peered across the palimpsest from the B text. Text A was no longer a steady stream, but a looping one: it was being continually revised. The date of the revolt kept shifting, the people kept doing different things—yet it was all one text. Or a merging series of subtexts. Only the physical facilities remained firm.

So it continued, this internecine war, with neither side gaining a decisive advantage. The only real victory had been the first, that set up the B Text. The subsequent history of Text A, when that Juan Bringas mission had been negated, showed that his effort had been the only real chance to preserve the Fidelian/Guevarian society intact. And his mission must have *been* negated, because the lingering waters of Text A reality should have run out otherwise.

Yet he hadn't negated it yet. . . .

197 skipped ahead—and was appalled to discover that *it didn't stop*. Ten years, fifty years, a century—war was the essence of Text A existence.

Fidelia's citizens were unable to change the pattern, because its nature concealed the truth from them. It was a costly irony.

Through short-range time travel, the Purples maintained the status-quo—but it was always temporary expedient, causing a continuing attrition in lives and resources. It was a negative policy, dealing with the symptom rather than the cause. Steadily the balance shifted to favor the cultists. More and more citizens turned to Espiritismo to alleviate the subtle wrongness of war conditions.

Meanwhile, Text B was placid. There Espiritismo was not a significant factor. The superior structure of Guevarian society militated against genuine dissent, and the absence of Caste Brown robbed the cult of its heartland.

Text A was withering, its population actually declining as it struggled invisibly with itself. Text B waxed populous and proud, colonizing the surface of the earth. The texts were hardly parallel now; one was a failure, the other a success.

If he were to change it back, somehow, and recover 233, he still would not want to remain in Text A.

Yet someone or something preferred it. *Who?*

The author of the Spanish Scroll, obviously. Friend or foe?

He followed the palimpsest compulsively, seeking the answer. 197 would die, but he would die cognizant.

Two centuries after his time, the tide of history began to turn again. Text A stabilized, though at a perilously low level. Text B stabilized at a high level. A remained at war, B at peace.

Then A began to gain—while B, surprisingly, atrophied.

What had happened to B? It was not obvious. It was as though the people had run out of ambition. They were less healthy, they had fewer children, they accomplished less. Their civilization waned.

Was it the final exhaustion of resources? There had been little enough left after the holocaust, and B had developed a considerable population, inhabiting all available land surface. Was it lingering radiation, perhaps exerting an unmeasurably small but cumulatively significant effect on the human germ plasma? Yet many people remained below the Bolivian mountains, and they too declined.

Could it be inbreeding resulting from the elimination of the Indian blood in Caste Brown? No, for the *blood* had not been eliminated, just the Espiritismos; Text B was more truly integrated than Text A, even after many centuries, and had, if anything, a wider genetic pool. What about the loss of challenge? B had nothing more to drive for, seemingly, no horizons to conquer any more. 197 simply couldn't tell.

Text A, in contrast, had stayed small and never returned to the surface. The attrition among its citizens had been terrible—but by the same token it had not exhausted its environmental resources, and not ventured into the lingering radiation. Challenge remained, certainly—the challenge of sheer survival.

He beheld a significant flash of insight that was not particularly sweet. Was it that survival was in fact impossible in a situation that failed to challenge it? Since man typically overcame his environment, eliminating challenge from that source, was artificial challenge essential? Was war necessarily the natural state of man?

Well, that was not his immediate concern, since his present environment was about to challenge him to death. He resumed his perusal of the palimpsest.

Text A was slowly recovering. But there was more than that. The peculiar war of Caste and cult continued, with its constant drain on life and development. Yet Fidelia was gaining, as though the wind intended to snuff out its flame was instead fanning it. It was as though neither side wanted the war to end. The Purples made time changes just sufficient to maintain the balance, and the cultists countered just enough to make another change necessary.

He jumped ahead another century. Still the impasse, still the limited population. But there was a change, as subtle but as definite as that in Text B. There was a leashed dynamism about the suppressed cult, a power like that of a grenade: ready at any moment to explode with devastating effect, yet quiescent.

He moved along another century—and it happened. The grenade exploded. A streak of light speared down the long text of history, illuminated his own crisis in 2413, and continued into the past. All the way down to the twentieth century—

It touched him, metaphysical phosphorus.

It was the scroll:

Juan Bringas manned the oars, using them to orient the boat. He

"No!" he cried. "I won't read it! I followed that scroll before and it only led *here*!"

But there was no sound, and his own voice was only in his mind. He had been silenced as effectively as the storm.

The illuminated text continued to hang before him.

"Who are you?" he demanded voicelessly. "Show yourself! I will not deal with anonymity!"

The scroll did not move.

Bringas stood up, feeling no pain. He stepped out of the boat and walked across the water toward the scroll. He reached up, caught it by its tubular base, and ripped it from its invisible mooring.

There was a jagged hole where it had been. Reality was a picture; this was a gap in the canvas.

197 caught the edges of the hole and hoisted himself inside. He weighed so little that it was easy. There was just enough room for his shoulders to pass.

As his head emerged on the other side, his senses were inundated by grandeur. Sight, sound, touch—the stillness of the frozen storm outside was complemented by the magnificent chaos of the inside. No, not *in*side—*other*side, for this was a complete universe, too. It was a larger universe—dimensionally larger. It was the future he had experienced momentarily in Text B, when he tried to jump ahead using the phaser and landed in the channel before the stream of reality reached it. But this was not empty; this was full—as full as an infinity of conventional universe!

Full? Perhaps it had been full before, and he had not been able to endure within it and appreciate its magnitude. He must have changed—as obviously he had, after these years in Cuba—and now he was ready for it.

Gradually, he perceived a certain pattern to the confusion. It was not the absence of reality—it was the presence of too much reality! More than the paltry human brain could tolerate. He saw the time-stream flowing . . . flowing in myriad channels, one overlapping the next, so that no clear course was evident. There were currents and ripples comprising events and people, the whole so dazzlingly rich that it was possible for a single perception—his own—to become quickly immersed and lost within any part of it.

He had been looking at Text A and Text B and what there was of blank Text C and thinking he knew history. Here were a billion texts—and they were *not* texts, *not* excerpts printed for mortal comprehension, but living streams! Every alternate probability, every conceivable facet of reality was spread out here—more than he could ever comprehend!

He stood back, mentally, and surveyed the whole. He could grasp aspects of meaning by visualizing the derivatives, by dealing in exponents and the exponents of exponents. Probability was a billion streams, but the streams were clustered in typical patterns, and the patterns honored certain category conventions, and the categories—

Place a twig upon the proper current of the proper portion of the proper substream, and its course would inevitably illuminate a specific reality.

He searched for his stream to eternity, but time was merely direction of flow, a commodity that could only be used, never dissipated. He found a spot, became that twig, he traveled the precise flow, observing the multiple palimpsest from the inside. His brain was dazzled, sunburned, blistered . . . but he shut off most perception and drifted, waiting for the end of the journey.

He waited centuries.

He found them.

Future spirits derived from the Espiritismos of the past. The authors of his scroll.

They were human in form, these Future spirits, but not in mind. They could see across reality's myriad texts, not in special moments but always, and this living super palimpsest was their intellectual home.

Four centuries of subtle but vicious warfare in that channel he knew as Text A had made ruthless selection among the adherents of the Espiritismo cult. Only those aspects of it conducive to survival in a situation of changing realities developed. The nonsurvival aspects—the true superstition, the irrelevant ritual—these perished. And in due course—

Geologically, mammals predated reptiles. But a placid environment had given the simpler reptiles the advantage, and for a hundred million years they had dominated the earth. Tiny, complex mammals had been suppressed for all that time, yet in that fugitive environment they had improved the species. When the landscape and climate finally changed decisively, those insignificant mammals were fittest for survival under the new conditions.

The spirits had preceded the technologists, but had been similarly suppressed. It had seemed impossible that their discredited disciplines could ever achieve dominance—

yet when the climate of reality changed, those spirits had been the fittest. For they preserved their existence by comprehending the flows of history, and influencing those flows as necessary, despite time travelers' crude machinations.

197's first trip to Cuba had changed the time-flow, and threatened to extinguish the spirits. To survive, the spirits had acted to nullify that change.

But they were not time travelers themselves.

The spirits could not send their agent to do the job. Actual travel up the stream was contrary to their entire philosophy, and therefore paradoxical for them. They had to work through the original agent, Juan Bringas. The only leverage they had was information, and its presentation was severely hedged by the shields of the worlds 197/Bringas knew. Their action had to be devious, no more than a vision in the mind of the subject.

Juan Bringas had become a policy instrument. Unless he completed his second mission, the spirits would lose their basis for reality.

He saw now that he had to do it. The spirits were the true long-range hope of mankind. Text B was a dinosaur. . . .

He was not unique, merely one link in a perpetual chain. Threats to the Future were endless, for its evolution was as devious as that of Man himself, and with only one stream had it been brought to a successful culmination. A billion alternates would not produce it again, as they would not produce Man again—this was not guess but fact. The spirits devoted their entire capability to alleviating every threat as it occurred, to reshaping the stream, for failure in any one link meant extinction. Extinction of the spirits—and of Man.

A million disruptions preceded Juan Bringas; a billion followed him. Every single one had to be neutralized, as his was being neutralized, or the entire effort was worthless. The entire population of the Future was engaged in doctoring the stigmata of history.

197 understood now that there *were* other longshot changes of similar scope to his own, resulting in many alphabets of texts, requiring Future spirits for each. Still, the fate of his species depended on him. Every element of the endless palimpsest had to be correct.

"But I am dying at sea!" he protested aloud. "I cannot hope to complete my mission!"

His words were nothing but wraiths in this framework, and the spirits did not answer. They could never answer, for they existed only in potentiality. But he saw that his protest could have no relevance: death at sea was not sufficient justification for the obliteration of the species.

197 returned to the hole in reality and climbed back into the picture of the storm. He picked up the fallen scroll and put it in its place, carefully, so that the edged locked. He walked back across the water to his boat.

"Am I going right, Camilo?" he inquired.

Juan Bringas manned the oars, using them to orient the boat. He tied one oar into position adjacent to the motor-mounting, causing the boat to drift in the storm in such a way that it intercepted the path of an American naval vessel then approaching

"So be it, Camilo!" he said, and the storm resumed.

Juan Bringas landed on the extreme southern coast of Cuba, in Oriente Province west of the American Guantanamo Naval Base, on September 15, 1962. This was the opposite end of the island from the region of his mission—but things were entirely too hot in Pinar del Rio now, with the coasts full of militia. Two CIA teams had been captured there recently. His former self was about to mess up the Sagua la Granda region hopelessly with paradox, so he had to stay well away from there. The only way to do it *now* was to infiltrate from an unexpected direction. Fortunately, the CIA had an operating network here in Oriente that would facilitate things considerably.

Two frogmen helped Bringas and his companion onto the small shelf just feet above the water line. Even so it was tricky, because they were at the base of the cliff. There were very few portions of Cuba's coastline with such cliffs, so that was where an omniscient, omnipotent CIA decreed he would land!

The waves broke over the little ledge, making it slippery, and Bringas was no mountain climber. Without the competent assistance of his guide, whose name he did not know, he would never have made it. Fortunately he traveled light: a small .32 silencer pistol, 5,000 pesos in shiny U.S.-minted 20- and 50-peso bills indistinguishable from the originals, and a small new-model automatic radio.

They scaled the cliff, crossed a jeep-patrolled road parallel to the coast, and trekked unmolested through a wooded area, where they contacted the CIA network. A car came for him, and from then on it was easy. The CIA did, it seemed, know how to infiltrate Cuba with minimum fuss.

He landed just west of the village of Imias. He was chauffeured in easy stages to Guantanamo, Santiago de Cuba, Camaguey, Santa Clara, and on along the Central Highway and lesser roads all the way to San Cristobal in Pina del Rio, only bypassing Havana to the south in the interests of avoiding possible paradox. The CIA wasn't aware of that wrinkle, of course. He was finally deposited with a pharmacist in San Cristobal.

The pharmacist's young son took Bringas to the wood where a cache of special supplies had been buried by a commando team: food, clothing, camera with telephoto lenses, spyglasses, military maps, and so on. He was ready to spy in style, and he had hardly exerted himself! If the CIA ever needed a testimonial for its travel services, they could certainly call on him.

His mission: to ascertain whether the Russians were or were not constructing offensive missile sites in Cuba. He had been trained to do the job authoritatively.

There had been a welter of recent reports from agents in Cuba. Most had been discounted, as they were from untrained or unreliable observers. But some had a disturbing ring of authenticity, and it was important that they be checked and rechecked before being considered substantial enough to pass on to President Kennedy. Senator Keating claimed that six IRBM—Intermediate Range Ballistic Missile—sites were under construction, and Bringas suspected that the American administration was as much interested in refuting gadfly Keating as in defending the nation from atomic devastation. The regular U-2 films showed nothing conclusive or even alarming, and if there *were* offensive missiles in Cuba the evidence had to be substantial enough to convince not just the United States, but also the governments and peoples of the world. International opinion was an extremely sensitive matter to the Kennedy administration, which had been heartily singed by the Bay of Pigs fiasco the prior year. It was not about to rock the boat on the basis of unsubstantiated refugee reports.

So Juan Bringas, who possessed excellent bonafides as a revolutionary-turned-counter-revolutionary, was re-entering Cuba under the code name, "ENRIQUE." He would see what he could see, and make due report.

He was going to see much more than the CIA anticipated!

Thus he faded into the San Cristobal forest region on September 20. The CIA might *suspect* offensive missile sites, but Juan Bringas *knew*. His only concern was to convey the information to the proper authorities in a manner that could not be confused. And to do nothing that could bring a peinazo down on him! Absolutely no phosphorus grenades!

He was making his way tediously through a prickly forest of marabu when something happened.

The marabu shimmered. Blurs appeared, as though his vision were partially obscured—yet it was not. Rather it was doubled. He felt a kind of nausea—and yet did not.

It took him an alarmed moment to comprehend. *This was another vision of the palimpsest*—or at least its contemporary segment. When he had returned to his own time, 2413-14, he had been able to cross the realities, for he was native to both of them. Now—

Now his other self had arrived in Cuba, and the division of the texts was commencing. The marabu itself was unchanged, but the small wildlife—the rats, the birds, the many insects—differed. Because in this text he was *here*, driving them into hiding by his presence. In the other text he was in central Cuba, and these local creatures were going about their normal pursuits. So he saw blurs, and when he concentrated they came clear: phantom animals, alternate-text ghosts.

If the texts had already divided—did that mean that paradox was no longer possible? Rather, did it eliminate the paradox *shield*—for paradox itself was never possible, pretty much by definition. He was *here*, while his other self was *there*, no more real to him physically than these misty animals. If so, was it already too late for him to nullify the change that had caused such mischief almost a thousand years hence?

Probably not, he decided. This division was fresh, and the separation of channels had to be so slight as of yet as to be historically insignificant. His action here would heal the wound before it festered, and reroute the river back where it belonged. So the Future spirits said!

Actually, this visible adumbration was a signal that everything was in order. If the time of his other arrival had come and there had been *no* reaction, wouldn't that mean that he was now powerless to affect the situation at all? Of course he was powerless to affect the specific things he had done before—the recurring paradox shielding demonstrated that—but his intention now was to bypass that action and neutralize it from a distance. He could slink past paradox by sending a message equivalent to the one he had aborted before. If the two realities had instead remained identical—

Then he would have phased into his other self and committed the murders all over again!

No! He was years older now, physically, and he had a tremendous volume of important additional experience. He could not phase into one self until the other self had equivalent age and experience. And since there was no years-long split of texts here—at least, not texts in which he personally existed—such matching was impossible.

Full circle. He *had* not phased in because he *could* not. The spirits of the future were correct, and he was now a free agent. The potential paradoxes that had blocked his return to this time had been circumvented by the circuitous adventures that made him a different person in body and mind. Beautiful! The paradox shield strictures could be used as an aid to performance as well as a preventive, if managed properly. The spirits had guided him, and all was well.

But what a route they had charted for him! He had needed experience, and received it in full measure. Between one and two years in the Sierra Maestra as a Fidelista guerrilla; a similar period in Havana as a government officer and underground agent; a year in prison; another year in America . . .

America: he had read so much about it in the old histories, and heard so much while in Cuba. The Colossus of the North, the most powerful individual nation of all time, supremely arrogant yet peculiarly ineffective—what was the truth about the United States of America?

Unfortunately, he hadn't seen much of it, after all. His body had been wasted by prison and capillas, and the exposure in the ocean had very nearly finished him. Had the future not needed him, he would surely have joined Camilo in the depths. As it was, he had awoken in a military hospital and spent some weeks recuperating in virtual confinement. The Americans had good food and good medicine, but he was a Cuban refugee without friends or money. He could not simply walk out, shrugging off the substantial debts he had incurred to the American government.

Juan Bringas bought his keep with information, though it was never put on such bald footing. It just seemed to happen that no monetary charges were made so long as he provided explicit details on the workings of the Cuban government and the machinations of the key figures within it. It would have been another matter had his information been inaccurate or if he had not been able to document his counter-revolutionary activity by identifying legitimate CIA contacts in Cuba. But that was the beauty of the spirits' formula: his experience had been so arranged that he could be extremely useful to the CIA. His real wealth was his potential activity in Cuba at the time of the coming missile crisis. When they needed a competent agent to check on the Russians in Cuba, he would be there, tailored by the insight of future and Future.

Naturally he joined the CIA. There was a standard lie-detector test, easily circumvented by a person of intelligence. "Have you ever had homosexual experiences?" they asked, when they should have asked "What is your actual position and loyalty within the palimpsest?" In some ways the CIA was marvelously stupid.

And as though to further demonstrate their ludicrous obsession with perversion, there was the physical examination: a greased gloved finger thrust boldly into the rectum, to twist and probe inside like a prehensile phallus. Bringas had long been cured of anatomical squeamishness, but the process was highly offensive to the three Cuban guajiros he was grouped with, and for whom he served as translator.

"I never want to be a doctor in my life," sixty-year-old Tomas the fisherman expostulated. "Now I get buggered! I beg of you, do not tell the others of my disgrace!"

"If Fidel knew the atrocity we suffer in order to fight him," the second man moaned in Spanish when his turn came, "he would go on television and say all exiles are maricones! Please, for me, tell the others this part was suspended!"

The third man had been in prison, like Bringas. He remembered the degrading routines the prisoners had been put through during requisa, forced to pile against each other naked, loin to buttock, while the guards remarked obscenely. He took one look at the doctor's huge thick fingers, greasily poised, spun about, and slugged him. When word got out, support for his protest was so vigorous among other Cuban indoctrinees that the rectal examinations had to be suspended.

Though they received plenty of American food, Bringas' three companions insisted on cooking rice and black beans to accompany each repast. To them a meal was simply not a meal without such guajiro staples.

The four spent three months alone in a farmhouse near Homestead in Florida, learning how to operate the variety of communications equipment. Tomatoes grew all about so they called it "La Tomatera." An American instructor was with them from 9:00 to 4:00, Monday through Friday. They all had their lessons, so Bringas listened to a tape recorder: Morse code groups faster and faster, starting at three per minute and working up to twenty. He also practiced on telegraph keys for sending, and pored over the signal code books. It was lonely work, and extremely boring, so he took time out for secret spy-mission practice at a nearby nudist camp . . . and almost got shot one day!

They were taken to the Miami airport in a sealed delivery van, whisked into a "secure" plane, and flown to a U.S. Army base for intensive map reading and further instruction in weapons, guerrilla tactics, demolition methods, and so on. Bringas flourished. They were not supposed to know where they were, but a professor unwittingly carried a ruler with the name of the base imprinted, so they *did* know. Apart from such gratifying lapses, their trainers were quite competent Green Beret veterans home from campaigns in southeast Asia. Bringas had to remind himself that at this time the U.S.A. was not officially involved in Vietnam or

Laos, any more than it was in Cuba. Ha, ha!

By the time the training ended, Bringas could sort and reassemble a stripped machine gun, BAR 20mm rifle, .45 pistol and several other guns whose pieces had been mixed together in one bag—within five minutes—blindfolded.

Next came a week of survival training in the mangrove swamps of the Florida keys. There they enjoyed crystal clear beaches and lovely weather. During a theoretical 14-day-long slog through the swamp, they holed up instead in a small secluded beach, caught lobster barehanded, and feasted while radioing false reports of their marching miseries.

That was the America he had seen. Not Broadway, not Hollywood, not baseball or apple pie; just weapons, tomatoes, radios, and the greased finger.

He found the San Cristobal missile site. There was no doubt about it: trucks were massed at the fringes of dense forest, heavy construction equipment was present, and a constant parade of supplies and personnel entered the region. Though so far only limited survey and groundwork had been done, everything natural and man-made was being readied for a truly extensive operation. Camouflage insured that hardly anything would be visible from the air. However, so much equipment was in readiness and so many skilled foreign workers were here that even something as devilishly complex as a secret ballistic missile base might be completed within a month. Obviously the intent was to do the job extremely rapidly, so that exposure to the view of United States U-2 planes would be minimal before the missiles became operational.

Ironic, he thought. If this same technology and effort had been donated to facilitate Cuba's own industry or farming program, the nation might rapidly become economically stable. But of course the Russians did not desire such a Cuba, for there would then be little reason for it to follow Moscow's lead.

Juan Bringas got the story. He took pictures of the tents going up, and of massive foundations being set, pre-fabricated building materials moved into place, missile trailers and wheeled launchers organized. Despite the risk, he also pinpointed the locations of a surface-to-air missile site, a MIG-21 airfield, a ground force installation for Soviet troops, and a patrol craft base. He knew exactly what he was looking for, since he had the perspective of history—or, less exotically, hindsight. He had studied photographs and reports of just such things before he ever traveled back the centuries to this period, and could draw from memory where specific documentation was too tedious.

In five days he was ready to make an authoritative report—just about the time the original Sagua report would have been made. But his was more complete, for he had details about such things as the missile-equipped patrol boats at Mariel, and better pictures.

The effort kept him too busy to worry about the growing divergence of the texts of reality as his other self wreaked havoc at Sagua La Grande and went to prison. The change was gradual, for even such a thing as a murder took time to affect a wide number of people, unless an important person were involved. The assassination of John Kennedy would affect hundreds of millions in a matter of hours; but the slaughter of a dozen or more men in the Cuban marabu might not affect the majority for generations. Of course Bringas' particular murders had, by altering the nuclear balance of terror, affected world politics and given Kennedy reason to stay in Washington the day he might have toured Dallas. But that was not inherent in the killing, rather in the situation. Kennedy might have been saved more readily had the CIA *not* made half a dozen attempts to kill Fidel, arousing his understandable ire and encouraging retaliation in kind.

Yes. And now he would change it back. Was he thus to assume responsibility for Kennedy's murder too?

It was time to use the automatic radio. The transmitter was a marvelous example of American technology manufactured, he suspected, in Japan. It would send his message so rapidly—at the rate of three hundred 5-letter groups in less than a minute—and the frequency and call sign changed as often—every hour—that it was virtually impossible to intercept or monitor. It was necessary to record the message in advance, of course. He had already spent his hours turning the little dial and tediously punching each letter of his message, but now the cartridge was ready. The actual transmission would be merely a push of another button.

He strung the antenna, checked the batteries, and inserted the cartridge. Now he had to send his call-sign, which would be monitored on an emergency basis at the Miami station . . . .

He took down the antenna. And halted. He hadn't sent the message yet! What was he thinking of?

He opened a food package. Time to—*what about that message?*

Oh, no! It was the too-familiar paradox shield. Every time he tried to transmit, he found himself doing something else. *He could not send the message. . . .*

He was not really surprised once he thought about it. His other self was here to stop the message, and had succeeded. If he sent his version now, it would be a direct negation of that other mission, and paradox protected the prior effort. The texts still interacted to that extent—which was just as well.

Soon, the other Bringas would depart for his own framework, or reasonable facsimile thereof, and there would be no further direct conflict.

He put the extra time to good use. He ranged more widely, knowing that an Intermediate Range Ballistic Missile site was under construction at Guanajay, just east of San Cristobal. These missiles required hardened launch pads, for they had a range of 2,500 miles. They would be able to reach Washington, New York, Chicago—and virtually all Latin America north of the Equator.

Yes, there was more at Guanajay than the gray women's prison with its inmates toiling in the fields. Some Latins who were flirting with communism might discover themselves the victims of a shotgun wedding. Or worse: they might be poised between the missiles of the Soviet Union and those of America, and subject to either—or both—on a straight friend/enemy basis impossible to accommodate jointly.

Meanwhile his vision of the texts grew stronger. The two realities were diverging farther. Soon, he was aware, it would be too late to change it back. Once the missiles were established and operative in Cuba no message he could send could eliminate their threat. It was also possible that he would send his message in time to stop the missiles in this text, but find that the other texts were not affected. That would mean the formation of yet another long-range variation, and possibly a worse one for him. Text C?

Through September the charade continued. Bringas could not speak to America, but he could listen, and he was aware of the living passage of history. President Kennedy issued a warning on September fourth to Russia that the introduction of surface-to-surface missiles into Cuba would not be tolerated. On the eleventh, Moscow publicly disclaimed any intention of taking any such action. It was a disclaimer the Russians were to maintain with every evidence of sincerity right up until the moment the missiles were operative.

The atomic warhead potential being established in Cuba was equivalent to half the ICBM—Inter Continental Ballistic Missile—capacity of the entire Soviet Union. As planned, a few minutes after those missiles were fired, eighty million Americans would be dead. And that was only the beginning, for the effect of an atomic weapon did not end cleanly at the moment of detonation. Radiation poisoning would persist, even longer than it had after Japan was bombed twenty or so years previously. And once the cataclysm of an American second-strike capacity was loosed upon the world—the end would be the beginning.

On October first Bringas felt the change. The vision of the palimpsest was gone! His other self had departed, returning to his frustration of Text B, and so there remained no figure for him to connect with. That did not mean the alternate *text* was gone; merely that it was now closed to his perception. There were intriguing vagaries of the palimpsest effect he would have to explore some day, such as why his prior self hadn't had the adumbrative vision while in Cuba, and why his Text A self had *never* had it. It seemed to be strictly a downriver effect, and there must be a logic to explain it.

But right now he had to switch the river back.

Juan Bringas set up the radio, strung his antenna, and sent his call sign: QBX FROM ARI, QBX FROM ARI. When he got the go-ahead he pressed his send-button, and "ffitt!" There went as concentrated a message of specific alarm as this framework was to experience. He had established the full range of Russian interests in Cuba, including everything he had assembled in the extra time forced on him by the paradox shield. He had more than replaced the message his other self had aborted!

Two days later he rendezvoused with a submarine along the north coast near Guanajay, per radioed arrangement. He stood in a moderately exposed position near some trees at the mouth of a small river and signaled the dark ocean with a black light flashlight. The sub surfaced silently and sent a rubber boat with frogmen to pick up his photographic materials.

"You'd better evacuate with us," one frog told him. "It's going to get downright hazardous hereabouts once *this* hits the fan!"

But Bringas demurred. "I am Cuban," he replied in English. "I'll stay."

"Got a gal in Havana?" the man asked, winking.

"Got a gal."

"Can't blame you. What I hear about Cuban women . . ." The man made an unfroglike gesture and rejoined his companions.

Watching them go, Bringas was tempted to join them after all. There was so much of fabulous America he wanted to see, before the holocaust of one text or another obliterated it. And it *was* dangerous in Cuba now, especially for him. But he knew that though the coming missile confrontation would be tense, it would be defused without actual bloodshed. (Blood*shed*? If those missiles ever fired, it would be blood *vaporized*!) He had redeemed himself; *he had delivered the information*. Now the U.S. of A. had the proof; now the primacord would unwind without deterioration. There would not even be the interdepartmental bickering that had delayed the October U-2 survey; not even the four-day interference of Hurricane Ella at such a critical time. The facts were in hand. He had seen to that.

A blockade would be established, Kennedy and Khrushchev would exchange anguished messages, philosopher Bertrand Russell would send a message praising Khrushchev for his conciliatory position and another castigating Kennedy for his warlike attitude. Kennedy would reply: "I think your attention might well be directed to the burglar rather than to those who caught the burglar." Adlai Stevenson, at a meeting of the United Nations Security Council, would publicly confront Ambassador Zorin of the Soviet Union: "All right, sir, let me ask you one simple question. Do you, Ambassador Zorin, deny that the U.S.S.R. has placed and is placing medium- and intermediate-range missiles and sites in Cuba? Yes or no? Don't wait for the translation, yes or no?" And Zorin would demur, "You will have your answer in due course." And Stevenson: "I am prepared to wait for my answer until hell freezes over. . . ."

Yes, Bringas saw it all . . . and meanwhile he did have a girl.

But not in Havana. As soon as he recovered the time phaser, he would sail down the timestream of Text A to

233 in about 2412, so as to intercept her before the cataract developed. Then—perhaps they would travel into the future, the Future; no paradox that way. . . .

Juan Bringas donned civilian clothing and took a bus to La Esperanza, where he had left the time phaser in 1958. His job was done at last; he was free to go home!

He found the place—but the ground had been disturbed. Anxiously, he dug.

The phaser was gone. In its place was a box, and in the box was an unsigned note: "I WILL KEEP THIS. COME TO TANIA'S AND WE WILL CONTINUE OUR CONVERSATION."

Only one person could have done it: Che Guevara. Only he had been realistically suspicious. Now it was apparent why the man had let him be. Guevara had wanted to ferret out the mystery surrounding Bringas, without destroying whatever aspect of it he might potentially use. No doubt he had had Bringas watched during his entire underground involvement. That might have been the reason the screws had been put to Luis, making him a G-2 bleater. But Guevara had never interfered directly, knowing that would alert Bringas.

As it happened, for other reasons Bringas had not gone near the phaser in all the time he had been in Cuba. Still, Guevara had found it. He must have conducted a thorough and meticulous search for Bringas' origin, and finally traced it to this point. It was a monument to the man's intelligence, determination and patience. Che Guevara had Juan Bringas where he wanted him.

Che could not use the phaser himself. There would be too many paradoxes buttressing his departure from this framework. But he could certainly prevent Bringas from using it.

Tania was Che's Argentinian mistress. Bringas seemed to remember a historical note on her to the effect that she was actually a Russian NKVD agent assigned to watch him.

She had died a month before him, pregnant, in Text A. In Text B she bore him a child and outlived him. Her most basic loyalty was undoubtedly to Guevara—but Bringas just might be able to exert a bit of leverage against her past. It would not be a pretty tactic, but this was a rough league.

Was Guevara planning to bargain for Guevara's best future? He had considerable leverage himself, so long as he held the phaser. But the paradox shield would hem them both in so tightly that not as much could be changed as thought.

No matter. Of necessity, Juan Bringas was bound for Havana, and not for entertainment. He had to get that phaser.

Havana. It was good to ride along the Halecon again, to see the splendid parks and monuments and buildings. There was not the glow and bustle of pre-Castro times, but he had many memories tied up with this city. Even the forbidding La Cabana fortress—after a year's absence and more from Cuba, that too had its macabre fondness.

He would need a place to stay, for his negotiations with Guevara would not be simple. The phaser might be at Tania's or elsewhere; in any event, it would be proof against Bringas' possession without Che's consent. It could be booby-trapped. He would have to settle with Guevara first—and that was going to be difficult.

The authorities would be on watch for him doubly. He had escaped from prison here twice! The paradox shield must have erased the records, so that they had not recognized him the second time—*his* first time—but there would be people who knew him now, aside from Guevara himself. Nightmare: "Hey, Juan Bringas! What are you doing here in Cuba?" spoken by an innocent friend in the hearing of an enemy . . . disaster!

There was of course one place where he would be welcome—but he had blocked that from his mind for more than one reason. He had never actually accused Adelita of betraying him, but she must have known she was under suspicion. By the time he had learned the truth in the capillas, it had been too late; he had not seen her again.

Adelita.

No, his first priority was to recover the phaser. Then he would be leaving this time forever. It would not be fair to tantalize her with so brief a visit. His other self had already done that once, unwittingly.

Adelita. . . .

Juan Bringas had never deceived himself about his priorities. 233 had been his object. Adelita had been a dalliance along the way. That Cuban phase was virtually over now. Yet he had known both girls three years, and while the memory of 233 was now five years old, that of Adelita was two years. They were both fine women, and he had married both. . . .

Adelita had a right to know the truth. It would not be a truth she liked—but it would be far better than a lifetime of doubt. After he left, she would be free to make her own life. There would be no record of their marriage; she could forget that.

And she would help him, once he located her.

He went to Luisa's.

This time Luisa dealt with him personally. She was almost openly hostile. "I thought you understood. I cannot keep you another night. It is too dangerous."

"I only want to see Adelita," he said, reminding himself that though it had been almost five years for him since he had been here, it had been only two or three days for her. Five days, perhaps; so much had happened that it was hard to keep track. Odd that she recognized him so readily, for he had surely changed.

"It is better that you not see her." Luisa's voice was cold.

"I don't understand."

Abruptly she turned and walked briskly away from him. "Here," she said, gesturing.

He followed her into a plush downstairs room. She closed the door, leaned against it, and contemplated him, cynical lines showing around her eyes. "You look older."

"I *am* older." More literally than she could suspect.

"Do you know what you did to her?"

He shook his head negatively.

"You left her dead in life—muerta envida."

"What? I don't—"

"You pimp of filth! Degenerate without heart!" she screamed explosively. "Other men come here for bollo. Why didn't you?"

Was that all? She resented his taking up space in her bordello without availing himself of the facilities? "I'll gladly pay the fee," he said. He had plenty of the American-minted pesos left. "I'll pay ten fees. I only want to see—"

"*Fee!*" she hissed. "Are you the devil?"

Bringas lost patience. "Lady, I've been through more hell than you can know, but I'm not the devil. Tell me where my wife is!"

Luisa's mouth dropped open. "You *married* her? When? Where?"

"In the Jesus de Miramar Church," he said heatedly, as though making a point in a bitter debate. "In 1960. You were there. I told her to go to you if ever—"

Her eyes widened in surprise. "Why so you did. I remember now. I saw you, but only for a moment. I knew you had to be underground, though I did not know you then. I never made the connection!"

"Where is she now?" he asked firmly.

Wordlessly she led him to an upstairs room.

Adelita was there, sitting in a chair. Her eyes stared out the window. She wore a light bathrobe, and was lovely.

"Adelita—are you ill?" he cried, crossing to her. God! He had forgotten her impact on him!

She did not move. Her eyes blinked; her bosom heaved gently with her breathing. That was all.

He put his hand to her arm, squeezing for attention. "Adelita!"

There was no response. Her flesh was soft and warm, but without animation.

"This is—catalepsy," he said, awed.

"She put you in the taxi," Luisa said. "She came back here and sat down. She said to me 'No volvera. He will not return.' That was all."

Bringas shook his head, feeling a lump in his throat. "I meant her to be rid of me."

"She loved you!" Luisa flared. "Have you any notion what that means?"

"I thought I did." For a moment, strangely, he pictured Nilo, dying in the capillas. Mamacita, it hurts!

"She waited for you two years. They told her you had escaped from prison, but you did not come. They told her you had gone to sea—alone in the storm. But she had faith you were not dead, that you would have come to her first. So she knew they lied, that you were still in prison. And then—"

"I did not even know her," he said, speaking for his ignorant other self that had now skipped out. "I told her she should be a stranger to me—"

Luisa was silent, looking at the still figure. She had always retreated when hurt. And he had hurt her terribly.

It had broken Adelita. This vibrant girl, who had waited with such patience for so long, thinking she had only to survive until he returned. Not believing what he told her, at first, not daring to—until he really did leave her. As though he still believed her to be a traitor, but lacked proof.

It would have been better if he had never come. Better to let her think he was dead.

Yet he was here again, knowing her, knowing her loyalty, loving her for it. Surely he could bring her out of it!

Why? he demanded of himself abruptly. *I am only going to leave her again!*

He almost wanted to stay. He did love Adelita. More
than he had thought. But this was weakness; he had always
known it was a temporary liaison. Paradox would prevent
too long a stay. It would restrict him more and more in
Cuba, for the critical nexus had been passed and he knew
he could not change history again. It would be no life for
her, bound to a man who for mysterious reasons could not
go to certain places, could not do certain things—and could
not explain. No, his time in this period was done.

"You were right," he said dully to Luisa. "I must leave
her alone, now."

As he left, he thought of Adelita's warm thighs, her
amazing lessons in loveplay. She had transformed his life,
sexually—but there was no sexual motive now. He had
killed her, horribly. He had put her in the capillas of her
own mind. He was phosphorus burning out her heart and
mind.

Tania lived near the Camp Columbia airfield, in the
Miramar section of Havana. Bringas approached her house
several times in the course of the next two days, but Che
Guevara's car was always there, and Che's armed escort.
That was no good. Bringas wanted to check the house
over before confronting Che himself, and he wanted to
talk privately with Tania. If he could get to her on NKVD
business, convince her that Che would dispose of her if he
knew, perhaps she would reveal where the phaser was. It
was a small hope; probably she would not be subject to
intimidation even if she knew about the phaser. Che would
hardly leave himself vulnerable that way. Put in the neg-
ligible chance the man had been careless or overconfident
just this once. . . .

Time was short. Bringas' message and photographs
would precipitate prompt American action. At this moment
the U-2's were no doubt verifying his information, and specialists were studying his pictures. Very soon the Russians
and the Castro government would realize that their secret

had been discovered, and would begin clamping down in preparation for trouble. Bringas had better recover the phaser before then, for his chances would surely diminish sharply as the missile crisis intensified. Every day he remained in Havana increased his likelihood of getting caught, especially in the general roundup Fidel would order at the first sign of real trouble. Che might flee Havana or even Cuba—taking the phaser with him.

But the quest had lost much of its urgency. He kept seeing Adelita, sitting alone. He kept hearing Luisa saying "She loved you. Have you any notion what that means?" Past tense, as though Adelita were dead.

He *had* a notion what it meant! What he felt for 233— that was love!

Yet he could no longer imagine 233's face.

Adelita sat there. . . .

On the third day, as he watched the house from a distance and fought his own conscience about Adelita, he became aware of a growing noise. A noise in the sky. It had been swelling for some time before intruding itself on his awareness.

With a shock of recognition he looked skyward to see a formation of American Phantom jet fighter-bombers coming in low. *What were they doing here?*

Then the rockets began to fire and the bombs fell. They were blasting Camp Columbia, catching Castro's planes on the ground, destroying the airfield's hangers and the runways.

He understood. His message had been too specific! Instead of providing enough information to make the Americans properly suspicious, he had delivered the proof. He had destroyed the delicate balance of decision. They must have reasoned that if one agent could come up with the amount he did, Cuba must be an arsenal of unprecedented proportion. There would be no time for United Nations confrontations; the missile site had to be neutralized, *now*.

The United States Air Force was making a pre-emptive surgical strike against the military facilities of Cuba and Russia-in-Cuba.

This was worse than he had anticipated. He didn't dare wait longer to go after the phaser!

Bringas charged up the slightly curved street toward Tania's house, having no specific plan, just trusting to the situation and the paradox shield to bring him through successfully.

As he drew near, the door burst open and Che himself ran out. As well he might, with American planes passing directly overhead on their way to bomb the airfields barely two blocks south! And incredible luck—or miracle of paradox shield—*Che was carrying the phaser*! There was no mistaking its particular configuration.

A giant SAC heavy bomber, a B-52, was passing high above. Its massive bombs were already falling, destroying residential buildings in a line from the ocean to the airfield. That was one way to be certain of scoring—but it meant *Tania's house was directly on that line of destruction.*

Bringas threw himself flat, barely in time.

The concussion knocked him dizzy. For an instant he fancied he was still on the sabotage mission, with Luis and Baro and the rest, when the plastics had gone off prematurely. Then he saw the crater in the street and knew better.

One dazed glance sufficed. Guevara's car had been struck, and Guevara himself had been dismembered. Beside him was a small wreckage that must have been the time phaser.

Juan Bringas could never return to his own world. A single clumsily-aimed American bomb had destroyed two futures.

Yet as Bringas stood bemused, hardly aware of Tania's emergence and screams, or of the awed crowd gathering, he realized that the bomb itself made no difference. In neither Text A nor Text B had Cuba been touched directly.

The moment those planes appeared over Havana, 197's framework ended. It would be paradox to return to a world where no 197 existed. So, perhaps the direct strike on the phaser was merely an aspect of the paradox shield.

If the holocaust came now, Cuba would not pick up the pieces, for she would be destroyed herself. And even if by some miracle Cuba escaped, Che Guevara, essential to at least one of the texts of the palimpsest, would not participate.

Juan Bringas had violated paradox. He had done his job too well, and thus blundered even more blatantly than before, sundering his own reality. Unless somehow his own family line survived this drastically altered situation.

His own—perhaps. Because that would mean no paradox, just massive change. But it was hardly possible that any other family lines he knew would make it unscathed. 233 was really gone this time.

He looked south, watching the bombs still bursting without being personally moved. If he could not return to 233—

Amazingly he felt relief. *He could stay with Adelita!*

233 had been his steady vision—but now he realized that the sub-structure of the pedestal had gradually leeched away, leaving only a framework without actual strength. In the interim a real woman had filled in the adumbration.

To hell with paradox! He was going to wake Adelita!

But she was gone from Luisa's. "I thought you might return," Luisa said frankly. "So I moved her. You are nothing but grief to her."

"But I can wake her!" he protested. "Are you trying to keep her a zombie?"

"Better zombie than damned," she said grimly. "You are not a Christian man. I feel it, I know it—she is best away from you. I'm sorry I ever helped you."

The statement stung him. He was *not* Christian, for there was no formal religion in Fidelia and little in Guevaria.

And his impact on the flow of history was certainly damning, for now he had abolished both of the texts he knew. Bombs over Cuba, Che dead—where would it end? But he loved her!

He tried again. "I am her husband. It is not for you to interfere in whatever may pass between us. What have I ever done to hurt *you*?"

Luisa was stung in turn, being branded a meddler. "You hurt my friends, you hurt *me*!" she cried. "You brought the G-2 down on my house, and now my friend Jimenez is back in prison! I would betray you to the G-2 myself, if I did not know already that you are one of them. Get out of my sight, traitor!"

Stunned, Bringas found himself out of the house. So the G-2 had been that close behind him! Jimenez, who had purported to help him make that first escape, must have called them in the moment he realized Bringas was gone—and Luisa blamed the wrong man!

It would take time to move Luisa, to convince her of the truth, and he was ill equipped to move her. Why should she believe that her friend had actually been rearrested with great show, so that he could shill for some other suspected CIA contact?

Bringas loved Adelita—but it was more than likely that his love would destroy her. He could no longer anticipate what the paradox shield would do or prevent, for he had no knowledge of this text. Certainly he could not have children by her, for that would introduce excruciating paradoxes of ancestry—unless he and his children were entirely unable to interact with any historical lines. And that would be an increasingly literal prison.

Or was this very action of Luisa's another function of the paradox shield? To keep him from Adelita . . .

Numb to right and wrong, he walked the streets of Havana alone. He risked discovery and capture this way, but he hardly cared. There was sniping and bombing going on, and here and there actual pitched battles between Fidelistas and pro-Americans. At one point he saw two women approach a militiaman on guard near a government building, distracting him with visible cleavage and suggestive manner—and knife the man by surprise, taking his weapon. Bringas didn't care; there was no organized rebellion, and in a few hours the government would have things under control. Again the prisons would be bulging.

Time became irrelevant. He must have eaten and slept and avoided capture, but he was not aware of such mundane details. If Adelita were a zombie, so was he, in his fashion.

Where had Luisa hidden her? He had no notion, but he had to keep looking. Days passed.

On the way back from Guanabacoa, east of Havana, Bringas' thoughts were morose. Guanabacoa had been another blank. He had thought Adelita might be at the place he had first seen her, when she had come to pick him up with Jimenez. But that had been a far-fetched notion, for it had not been the first time for *her*. And *she* wasn't hiding from him; she was in catatonia, subject to Luisa's will. Luisa, who thought she was doing Adelita a favor— rightly, perhaps.

Juan Bringas was committed to Cuba now, and that meant Adelita. 197 was dead, 233 had never existed. He had tried once more to convince Luisa, but she had remained immovable. "If you love her, you'll find her," was all she had said. Infuriatingly.

The taxi moved south, retracing the route he remembered so fondly now, for he had seen it first with Adelita. Into his brain sifted the events of October, 1962.

The United States had made its "surgical" strike, more like butchery in practice. The objective had been to eliminate the Russian missile sites under construction. To do this effectively it had been necessary first to knock out the defensive capability of the island, lest losses be prohibitive. Hence the airport raid in Havana.

The strike had not caught Fidel or the Russians by surprise, whatever the intent. Secrets were very hard to keep in Cuba, especially American military secrets. The missile sites were well defended by the SAM bases completed earlier, and though a number were destroyed, a number were not. Further, the United States could not be *sure* the missiles were inoperative without sending in observers—and that meant troops. Whereupon it must subdue Fidel's forces. In short, full scale invasion.

Everyone knew this was building. No one was certain how soon it would happen. There would be no surprise in Cuba.

The *Americans* were caught by surprise, however! The Cuban reaction to the initial bombings was swift. The great majority of the population rallied to Fidel. Guantanamo Naval Base was overrun by human-wave attacks directed personally by Raul Castro. Most of the defenders were machine gunned to death after surrender. Three surviving MIG 21's flew low over the ocean and raided Homestead Air Force Base in Florida, destroying several B-52 super bombers before being shot down. Americans on the island were arrested and then butchered. Fidel talked to the nation on television for nine consecutive hours, and there were few who did not listen.

Oh yes, the American invasion was coming. *Where was Adelita?*

He heard something. This time he was instantly alert, rolling down the cab window and cocking his ear. Airplanes—not one or two, but a massive formation! And he knew exactly what that meant. The Americans had acted with remarkable dispatch.

"Driver!" he cried. "Bombers are coming! Get off the road!"

The cabbie's eyes stared back at him in the rear-view mirror. "Mister, I have kids at home. I'm not getting stranded out *here* while they get bombed *there*!" And he accelerated.

"You're crazy!" Bringas shouted. "We're coming up on

the oil refinery—a sure target. At least detour around it!"

But the cabbie, intent on his own mission, paid no heed. He had been expecting the invasion for days, and now conditioned reflex had taken over. He sped on down the highway—right toward the refinery.

Bringas couldn't really blame him. Half of him felt the same. Adelita might be under those bombs too. He would go back and choke the truth out of Luisa!

The planes were overhead now—swift phantom jets diving low. One peeled off and strafed the road, coming right at the taxi.

The windshield shattered. The car slewed. Bringas dived over the seat and grabbed the wheel around the slumping driver. He managed to get the motor out of gear and bring the taxi to a halt beside the road.

Almost directly in front of the refinery.

A fragment of glass had slit the cabbie's arm—and his throat. Or perhaps one of the bullets had struck him. At any rate, the man would not return to his children.

Bringas, hunched in the back seat, had been spared. But he couldn't count himself lucky while he was stalled in sight of the refinery! All he could do now was take over and get out. And pray he made it.

He dumped the cabbie's body into the back, brushed out some of the glass, and took over the driver's seat. The windshield was just a jagged outline, but the motor still ran and the tires were sound. Warning lights indicated that the battery was discharging and the hydraulic brakes were out, but he could drive the car. He did.

He hated to continue right beside the smoking refinery, but the road had been torn up behind, and he feared it would take too much maneuvering to turn about and detour south around the Virgen del Camino, fond as its memory was to him. He was feeling unreasonably urgent about what lay ahead. He decided to save time by chancing it—exactly as he had urged the cabbie *not* to do. At least the planes were absent for the moment.

He couldn't help looking at the refinery as he passed it. It was spectacular. Several of the huge oil tanks had been scored on, and black smoke roiled up, revolving into itself as though it hurt inside. This was the southern fringe of Havana Bay, and he saw a Russian tanker trying desperately to steam out. But it had taken several good hits, and flames danced along its deck. Tiny figures, like flies from this distance, jumped from it, only to be engulfed in the burning oil extending over the water.

There was a series of great explosions as one oil tank after another went up. The fire was spreading everywhere. Thick strands of oil crossed the road, black pseudopods seeking to escape the heat. Bringas splashed through them recklessly, not daring to hesitate now. Even shielded by the taxi and the breeze of the open windshield, he could feel the ambient temperature rising, rising. He held a handkerchief to his face, driving one-handed, to facilitate breathing. If the car failed here . . .

Then a tremendous blast shoved the entire car forward as though it were goosed by a giant hand. The fire had reached the huge gas depot tank of the Cuban Gas Company and ignited it just after he passed! Bringas clung to the wheel, aiming the vehicle forward though the wheels seemed to be skidding on a continuous oil slick. On, on, away from the inferno, into the Rio Luyano—

When Bringas woke, he thought a long time had passed. But it hadn't; the refinery still burned behind him, the planes were still absent. The taxi had plowed into the river Luyano. The front end was full of water, and that rising wetness had brought him out of it in a hurry. Good place to be, for it was cool; bad place to be if the oil reached the water. . . .

He climbed carefully out through the windshield and staggered up the bank to the road. He would need another vehicle; he couldn't make it to Luisa's on foot. Not today.

He looked about—and there was the row of workshops he had once sabotaged with plastic explosive. Talleres del Ministerio de Obras Publicas. Men were swarming there, starting the trucks, moving out.

Bringas smiled. He hurried down to the compound. No one challenged him. He walked up to one of the trucks that was just beginning to move and climbed into the seat next to the driver.

"Havana!" he snapped. "I'll tell you where."

The driver never looked at him. The truck eased out, turned left onto the highway, and accelerated. Now the rivulets of oil were burning, and both men flinched as they crashed through.

Blessed distraction and confusion! In a crisis like this, the mere tone of command was sufficient. Nobody had the time to ask questions.

They drove north along the familiar route. Castillo de Atores had not been bombed, surprisingly. But the railroad yard had. The elevated tracks were broken and twisted, some of them falling across the road, blocking it. Coolly, Bringas gave directions for detouring around the tangle and continuing on up the Malecon.

As they drove, the shelling began. American battleships were standing offshore, their big guns zeroing in on secondary targets. The individual explosions were smaller than the bombs at the refinery, but in another way the experience was worse because there was no warning before a blast.

"Keep going," Bringas snapped, affecting nonchalance. "They aren't firing at *us*."

The driver kept going, obviously relieved to have someone else making the decisions.

The main nuclei of Havana's resistance were being leveled. Atores took hits behind them; Fuersa, Morro, and La Cabana were being blasted methodically ahead. Bringas could see the stones flying as shell after shell demolished the prison he had stayed in for so long. They were driving right toward it now, but the neck of the Havana Bay separated them from the great prison. He hoped the inmates would escape; he knew that most would die.

One did not die. He was in the capillas, punishment for attempted escape. As the prison crumbled, as the walls and ceilings of the galeras crashed on the prisoners locked within and men killed each other merely for a place to hide, he scrambled out through a sudden gap in the wall. The light of the sun seared his face, but he ran past the paredon and escaped unnoticed. He did not cast up prayers of thanksgiving. He was not happy, only determined. One thing obsessed him: vengeance against the man who had betrayed him after using him. Somehow he would find that man and kill him. Kill Juan Bringas, Juan Bringas, Juan Bringas.

A shell had dropped on the crew of an anti-aircraft installation along the Malecon. Bringas had the driver stop. All the men were dead. Men? *Boys,* fifteen or sixteen years old. Bringas picked up a Czech submachine gun and ammunition and carried it back to the truck. "On," he said.

Shells seemed to be falling indiscriminately in the heart of Havana. Cars were stalled, buildings were collapsing, bodies littered the streets. The driver grew increasingly nervous, but Bringas kept him going by sharp commands, around the craters, over the corpses, cross-country through Central Park when the road became impassable. Rubble clogged the entrance to the tunnel under Havana Bay. The beautiful statue of Jose Marti was headless.

The barrage continued. The Americans were indulging in a destructive orgy from the safety of their ships. The magnificent edifices that lined the waterfront were spouting flames. The Malecon was a road through hell.

The way became impossible, and they had to cut away from the water. They were forced around and back, squeezing through narrow defiles between ruins, splashing through flooding caused by caved-in sewers. They passed the National Capitol, whose white dome had been bombed out. A pall of ugly smoke hung about Havana, hiding some of the worst of the destruction.

But the way got worse, not better. Finally their path was closed off entirely by debris from the shelling. As they backed out of this dead end, a shell struck just behind. The truck was unscathed, but the explosion undercut a tall apartment building and tumbled one glassy face of it into the street. The vehicle was trapped.

Ah, well. He could walk it from here, if a shell didn't get him. "Can you make it to your home on your own?" he asked the driver.

"Yes, sir."

"We're out of business. Get your family to the country somewhere, where at least you can live off the land. Do you have a gun?"

"Yes, sir."

"Good luck. Dismissed."

The driver dismounted with alacrity. "Thanks, Captain," he said, saluting.

Bringas nodded acknowledgement automatically. Only after the man was gone did he realize that the man had called him "Captain"—when he was in civilian clothes, incognito. The driver must have recognized him . . . and not realized that Bringas was no longer an officer in the Rebel Army. Had his arrest been hushed up . . . or was this another fringe benefit of the paradox shield?

He got out, cradling the submachine gun, and walked to the back of the truck. He pulled aside the tarpolin and peered in.

It was a quartermaster shipment. Boots. Uniforms. Boxes of Rebel Army insignia. Bedding. Mess kits. Shelter halves. Entrenching tools. No weapons, no food.

At first he was disappointed. Then he realized that he would make some use of this. Many Cubans had become disenchanted with Castro, but a bombardment like this would make the Americans an anathema in Havana. His best bet was to resume the role of a Rebel Army officer. If anyone found him out—well, he did have the gun. Quite possibly such a uniform would preserve his life more effectively than any other measure he might take, apart from being where the shells were not. And he certainly knew how to act the part.

Very shortly he was Captain Bringas again. He resumed his march toward Luisa's.

Havana was in ruins. Now that he was on foot, every detail was clear. Fires burned uncontrollably, as the water mains had been blasted and the fire trucks could not get through. There was no electricity, no food delivery, no medicine. Most survivors were in shock now—but soon they would grow hungry and thirsty. Looters were already in business.

Luisa's house had been gutted. If she lived, she was far away by now.

Juan Bringas wandered. His motive in life had gone, yet he fought to survive, reflexively. The news of the day filtered in.

A task force of 50,000 well-armed American troops had parachuted in during the bombardment. The military planners' optimism proved unfounded. Considerable resistance to the invasion developed, and few of its immediate objectives were met. The threat of atomic missiles still hung over the cities of the United States.

The size of the task force tripled, tanks were landed, and there was saturation bombing of Havana that made the prior raids and shelling seem mild. The civilian casualties were staggering—yet many would have died anyway, from disease and starvation. Fidel, who had evacuated just before the initial raid by no accident, withdrew to the mountains again with the bulk of his forces. Guerrilla warfare was what he knew best—and the Americans knew worst, despite their frequent experience with it.

Fidel Castro had to be eliminated quickly, for he was a prime rallying figure and the Russians were maneuvering diplomatically and militarily to neutralize the American effort. They applied heavy counter-pressure on Berlin: if the implications behind the censorship were accurate, Berlin very much resembled Havana at this moment. A leftist reaction swept Latin America, toppling half a dozen governments in the massive anti-American reaction to the invasion of Cuba. Bolivia, Chile, Guatemala, Peru, Ecuador, and the Dominican Republic were openly antagonistic to the Colossus of the North, and there were bloody border clashes between Mexican and American troops along the Rio Grande. Warnings and counter-warnings were flying, but the strife continued. Meanwhile China had acted more boldly yet, aware that the American reserves had been committed to Cuba. Quemoy and Matsu islands were overwhelmed, and both South Korea and South Vietnam were openly invaded. America itself was torn by savage protest riots.

No half measure was feasible in Cuba now. The conquest had to be complete, for American prestige as well as American security was on the line. It was doubtful whether a million men could rout Castro out of his Sierra fortress before the situation in Latin America deteriorated to the point where, hydralike, seven or more aggressive communist governments would sprout to replace the Cuban one cut *off*.

Amazingly, the American forces began a hasty evacuation. There was no visible military pressure on them now, for Fidel's militia had taken up purely defensive positions and the cities were already no-man's-land. What had happened?

Then Bringas saw the final shape of the final piece to this puzzle. *They were going to use nuclear weapons on Cuba.*

Text C—a bright light, fading in time to nothing.

Cuban holocaust.

• • •

Juan Bringas snapped out of it. *He knew where Adelita was!* The one place he would look if he really loved her.

He stood near the Havana Cemetery. He planned his route: cut across the southern portion of the cemetery, cross the Almendares River at Calle 23, trek north to Avenida 5 . . . maybe he could find an operative car. Or better, a bicycle—he could portage over rubble with that. But he'd have to keep alert against snipers, for riding would necessarily be in the open.

The cemetery had been bombed. Maybe a mistake, or perhaps American Intelligence could explain. The stench was horrendous. Craters gaped amid the memorial parks and headstones were scattered indiscriminately. Mausoleums had been ripped open and sundered crypts released their vapors into the atmosphere. Bones showed amid the tumbled stone. Not all the disinterments were ancient; vultures were feeding avidly on grave-carrion.

Half outraged, half laughing with the sheer sickness of it, Bringas fired a burst at one of the ghoulish birds. Then he rebuked himself. Why begrudge the scavenger his due? The buzzards had not bombed Havana; they only pecked up the pieces. Well, maybe he could turn this to his advantage.

The stone bridge where Calle 23 crossed the river had been bombed out. He should have realized that it would be. The Americans had tonnage everywhere. He would have either to wade the river upstream, or hope the tunnel at its mouth remained, or find a boat or raft.

He moved downriver, through the parklike ground bordering the water. Here for the moment the destruction did not show; the bushes and trees remained green, and exotic wild animals ranged contentedly. A couple of lions were feeding on a carcass—

Lions?

Bringas gripped his gun. He had seen so much horror in the past few days he had become inured, but this was different. They *were* lions! And their dinner was human.

The zoo, of course! He had to laugh with relief at the simple explanation, startling the giant cats. Everything else had been bombed; why not that too? Maybe a cobra had hissed at a passing jet, so the pilot had retaliated in the usual fashion. Now the surviving animals were loose, roaming the city. . . .

He saw the remains of sunken fishing boats in the river. The bridge at Calle 11 was down, the tunnel at Calle 9 flooded. But, by the kind of blind luck he had gambled on for no good reason, the Calle 7 tunnel was intact. He hurried through it gratefully.

As he emerged he saw that the fountain with the colored lights was neither fountain nor lighted now. Its mermaids and mermen lay broken in the street. Beyond it a few blocks, smoke was still rising from the Blanquita Theater, once the world's largest. A few blocks down his own route, once the lovely parkway of Avenida 5, was a steaming hole a full block long: what remained of G-2 headquarters. Bringas felt little compassion for it.

Some churches had been hit, others not. St. Anthony Church at 60th Street was rubble—but, miraculously, the Jesus de Miramar Church stood unscathed.

Bringas entered, alert for ambush. But the interior was quiet.

"There is no food here," the priest said, eying his uniform and weapon. "Go your way in peace."

So that was why it was quiet. Hunger was a stronger scourge than exposure, and the savages had left the church alone because there was nothing here to eat. The priest himself was gaunt but familiar.

"You married me here two years ago."

The priest studied him more closely for a moment. "A Captain . . . active in the underground. I am surprised you survived. Yes. A special dispensation. . . ."

"I thank you now for your service and your discretion. Politics are immaterial now. I bring you food," Bringas said. He drew from his jacket the eviscerated carcass of the vulture. "Can you cook this without making a smell? There should be enough for your present congregation. The white meat should taste like turkey breast, if you do not advertise its source."

The priest nodded. The odor of cooking meat would attract the scavengers, animal and human, and the church would then be no sanctuary. "I thank *you*."

"My wife," Bringas said. "She is here."

The priest gestured as he concealed the vulture under his robes. Bringas went where indicated.

A few people prayed silently in the pews, seeking the peace and comfort of the church in this apocalypse. Perhaps they also prayed for food. That prayer would be answered shortly.

Adelita was lying near the front, hidden unless a person peered along that particular aisle just as Bringas was doing. Her religious medallion lay neatly on her bosom. She was still in trance, but did not seem to have suffered much physically. Obviously Luisa had been taking care of her, feeding her somehow, and probably her nutritional needs were slight, in this state. She was absolutely lovely.

He kneeled beside her. "Adelita, I have come for you," he murmured in her ear, bared by her richly falling hair. "Juan Bringas, your husband. I will take you to America."

She did not respond.

"I knew you were innocent. I learned the truth in the capillas. But I could not come to you while they were after me—"

She remained still, except for her regular breathing.

"Adelita, I love you. I say it to you, I say it in this church where we were married, I say it before God. I love you, I shall not leave you again."

A tiny tremor went through her.

He shifted position between the pews, getting as close to her as he could. "Adelita, wake up. We have to get out of here."

She did not wake.

"Sleeping beauty, I kiss you," he said. "Wake!"

Almost her lips responded. But it was not enough.

He was tempted to pick her up and carry her with him as she was. But he had to have both hands and all his body to defend against the savage outside, or they both would quickly perish. It was no longer a matter of mere robbery or rape, for money was worthless and sex pointless here in this devastated city. It was fresh meat the beasts were after.

Adelita had to be mobile and alert, able to watch behind him and to fire a pistol herself. They had about six hours, as he judged it, to get to the final evacuation point of the American rearguard. He had good bonafides; he could leave with them, and bring her too. They could make a life in America, where the forces of paradox would be less, since America had little part in his ancestry. But if they missed that boat (actually it was a giant helicopter), they would have to remain for the blaze of light.

Why did she refuse to wake? He had come back to her, he had told her he loved her, that there was no suspicion against her. Wasn't this what she had wanted?

It had to be! Did she not believe him?

She must have dreamed of this constantly, and always been disappointed. Even when he found her in this state at Luisa's he had left her—and she must have been aware of that. She was afraid to wake, for then she might have nothing, not even the dreams.

If only he could make her understand! Adelita was not a jealous woman. She knew there had been other women in his life before her, just as he knew there had been other men in hers, right up to the fat playboy from whom he had snatched her in Santiago. It was their life together that mattered, not their lives apart.

Yet he had returned to her and called her stranger . . . and left without explanation. What a colossal violation of their understanding that had been! She had known then that he was returning to the other woman, that he no longer trusted Adelita, and that there would be no future together.

She had been right. . . .

Nothing in her framework could change the reality she understood. There was no way for her to comprehend the truth—unless he told her. All of it.

Paradox prevented him from telling her.

Bringas knelt beside her, shivering with longing and frustration. His tears fell on her blouse, soaking in. And a great rage built in him.

He would not be balked this way! If he had to tell her the truth, he would *tell* her, and to hell with paradox! It wasn't as though there were any world to save, here; he had already destroyed his two futures.

In fact, he had probably abolished his own family line, and his present existence was no more than the ebbing water remaining in the streambed. That was his penalty for circumventing paradox the first time!

Why, then, should there be any barriers to his speech? The damage had been done. There could be no further paradox.

"Adelita, listen carefully. I am not—"

He ran out of words. But he knew what he wanted to say!

"Adelita, I am not from—"

Damnation! The shield *was* operating! But he would not be denied, for now he was sure this was the way to save her. If it really made no difference, there would be no paradox of any kind involved. Since there *was* paradox—

Could it be that if he made it to the Americans in time he would somehow be able to stop them from the nuclear bombing? That would save the majority of Cuban lives, and preserve his own family line, that could have been protected from the bombardment so far by the shield. This version of reality had more substance than he had supposed! But if he told the truth to anyone of this time—

But he *had* to tell Adelita! All the universe could flash into nonexistence as far as he was concerned, if he didn't have her! "I-am-not-from-this—"

"I have prepared the fowl," the priest said, startling him. "Do you wish a portion?"

"Get out of here!" Bringas shouted at him. Fowl: euphemism for vulture! Then: "Sorry, Padre—I am overwrought. I brought that bird for you alone. And your congregation. I only wish to wake my wife."

"I know that," the priest said. "Something brought me here—"

The shield, of course. It acted in diverse ways, taking the most natural courses. Block one channel, it used another. "I appreciate your solicitude. But if I may talk to my wife alone—"

"Certainly," the priest said, disgruntled. But he lingered a moment longer impelled by what he may have thought was a godly prompting, then slowly departed.

Bringas knew he would have to ignore or override other interruptions. First the paradox shield had stopped him from talking. Now it was bringing other people in. If it succeeded in delaying him too long. . . .

But the shield had to act in a natural or coincidental fashion, lest it create paradox itself by overt manifestations. That was funny: a secondary shield to prevent the primary shield from transgressing the rules! The system worked pretty well. Che Guevara was the only person of this world who had spotted the effect—and Guevara had died without ever using the information or passing it along, significantly. Probably the bomb that killed Guevara had been aimed by the shield, since nothing short of death would have stopped such a man from making use of what he knew.

Guevara had not been aware of the danger in wrestling with potential paradox. Bringas *was*. He could fight the shield by forcing it to be obvious. There was no American bomber it could call within the next five minutes. It was not going to stop him again!

"Adelita, I am not—from this—not from this—TIME!" he cried at last, and it felt as though great chains were snapping. "I came from your—from your future—several centuries." He was breathing rapidly and his pulse was racing, but it was easier now that he had broken through. "I came —twice. The first time to the—to the missile crisis in 1962. Russian missiles in Cuba—you don't know about that yet. So I did not know you. The second time I came to 1958—remember how I knew you then. I called you by name—"

Her eyes opened: como el azabache—black as sin.

"I love you!" he cried. "Come with me—we'll never part again—"

She looked at him, dazed. "Juan—the future?"

"*From* the future. To change history. And I met you, and now the future is ours!"

"Yes!" she said. "Last time you were younger, strange—"

A harsh voice broke in. "Look at me, tratiro, before you die!"

Both Bringas and Adelita jumped, startled.

For a moment he thought it was Nilo, raised from the dead. But it was Manuel Jimenez—the man who had helped him escape from La Cabana the first time, then returned to prison. That was only a few days ago, in this framework.

"Juan Bringas —I thought you were CIA, so I helped you. I thought you would get me into America. Then you disappeared, and your woman went into shock, and the G-2 came for me. Che Guevara himself interrogated me, before they threw me in the capillas with the rats. He said I was a fool, that you had been Fidel's bodyguard in the Sierra, and that you were about to visit Che himself to discuss important mutual concerns—"

Che Guevara! The man must have acted the moment the palimpsest effect abated, when Bringas of A departed for the future. Guevara, who had known of his presence in La Cabana in 1962—*and thought it was the same Bringas, just returned from America*!

"I swore to kill you if I ever saw you again—and here by incredible fortune I find you, in your old uniform, serving Fidel even while Fidel's folly has completely destroyed our country!" Jimenez raised his rifle.

The shield again! While Bringas had been breaking down his speech inhibition, oblivious to all else, Jimenez had been urged in here by "incredible fortune."

"I was freed from the capillas for this!" Jimenez cried, his eyes burning as he sighted down the rifle.

There was absolutely no point in trying to reason with the man, for it was not his own finger on the trigger, but a nebulous force acting to stop Bringas from interfering with fate—any way at all. The irony was that he respected Jimenez's motives entirely. The man was a real Cuban! So many had taken the easy path, following the leader no matter what he did; Jimenez had resisted, and was still resisting.

But Bringas too refused to be part of the apathetic throng, cowed or meek! He too saw the world's great anguish and its wrong, and dared to speak! Once he talked to Jimenez, convinced him of the truth, then the three of them could go to America and make it right.

But Jimenez's finger was tightened around the trigger. Bringas leaped up, hoping to surprise the man and disarm him without injury. The gun went off.

He felt no pain. In a moment the firing squad would laugh, calling him the orinaste, and later he would escape, tour Havana, see Superman, and Adelita.

Yegua.

The light of the sun.

Text C—

"Am I going right, Camilo?"

Mourn not the dead.

Mamacita, it hurts!

EXTRAORDINARY ADVENTURES
by *New York Times* bestselling author

PIERS ANTHONY

__KILLOBYTE   0-441-44425-3/$5.50

Walter Tobin and Baal Curran lose themselves in the adventure of the virtual reality computer game Killobyte. The rule is simple: if you lose, you die. The game grows frighteningly real when a deranged hacker infects Killobyte with a virus, physically trapping Walter and Baal in the system and leaving them at the hacker's sinister mercy.
"If you enjoyed the movie *Total Recall*, you'll love *Killobyte*."
                                                    –Chicago Tribune

__HARD SELL   0-441-31748-0/$4.99

The Mars Ltd. salesman offers retired millionaire Fisk Centers a real estate deal that sounds too good to be true. It is. Now, penniless and unemployed, Centers will do anything to make a buck. And that's where the trouble–and the fun–really begin.

__BIO OF AN OGRE   0-441-06225-3/$4.50

Piers Anthony's remarkable autobiography! A rich, compelling journey into the mind of a brilliant storyteller. "Fascinating!"*–Locus*